THE

Book 1

PHOENIX ANGEL

THE SHARDWELL SERIES

Book 1

PHOENIX ANGEL

A. Gerry
C. Hall

Synergy Books Publishing
St. George, Utah

Copyright 2011, 2013 Amanda Gerry and Christy Hall
Cover Art by Jennifer Reid
All rights reserved
Published by Synergy-Books Publishing.

No part of this publication may be reproduced, or stored in a retrieval system, or transmitted in any form by any means, electronic, mechanical, photocopying, recording, or otherwise, without written permission of the publisher.

ISBN: 978-0-9896529-0-2 (Hard cover edition)
ISBN: 978-0-9896529-1-9 (Soft cover edition)

Prologue

Fate is a curious concept. I cannot recall when I first recognized mine: the knowledge that no matter how far I run, how much I learn, or how much power I attain, inevitably my destiny is realized. The magic will always consume me in the end. Flight seems my only option, the only way to slow my future's progress. I have escaped fate's snare through battle, agony, and—oddly—time. But only temporarily. I can almost feel it stalking me.

Before this bitter epiphany, I had such hopes for my life. I remember vaguely that at one time my head swam with dreams of a happy, uncomplicated life. That one day my knight in shining armor would whisk me away to a fairy tale ending. Maybe that is why I trusted so effortlessly. When I began, my nature was oblivious to malevolence—an unfortunate failing, I must admit. It led to so much anguish. Today I stand with palms stained crimson.

Blood that cannot be cleansed from the soul.

Time dulls everything, and I have been running for so long that I cannot quantify its passage. Memories of loved ones blur: I can no longer remember my mother. I might have had a sibling once. I can never be sure. Certainly someone, somewhere recalls my birth or reminisces about the events of my childhood. Emotions alone remain constant in my mind, and dread is dominant. The anticipation of unavoidable suffering when death invades my life. And then the forgetting. I can feel memories slide away from my sense of self: moments of contentment, people I loved. Sometimes forgetting is the worst part.

One memory, however, is burned so deeply that even death cannot remove it. A face. His face. How is it that he is always stronger? Fire smites my enemies from the heavens and flames leave me unscathed. Wounds of battle do not hinder me. Nevertheless, it is not enough. He displays such power, such calculating ruthlessness—such control. And he always comes. I am forced to flee each time he discovers me.

How do I explain my existence? It ended—and began—with my death.

PART 1

1: Beware Geeks Bearing Gifts

The second hand on the wall clock crawled. Tick, tick, tick. Maggie Brooks stared at its black and white surface, agonized boredom seeping between her fingers as she gripped her desk. She drowned in the monotony.

Twelve more minutes. I just have to survive 12 more minutes!

Tick, tick, tick. How long could the teacher chatter about infrared spectroscopy? Maggie's eyes slid from the clock, searching for something to relieve the tedium. A group of cheerleaders passed notes in the back of the classroom, a self-assured athlete—Maggie didn't know his name, but recognized the football jersey—flexed his muscles in their general direction, hoping to attract attention, and was it her imagination, or was there an actual drool puddle forming on Nathan Hinton's desk? She slipped her eyes back to the clock.

Eleven more minutes. I just have to survive 11 more minutes.

"And as you can see from the infrared portion of the electromagnetic spectrum," Mr. Warner droned in his nasal voice, "the specimen is illustrating a distinct form of asymmetrical stretching, indicative of—"

Maggie covered her face with her hands, stifling a groan. How could he not notice how freaking much the class didn't care? She dropped her head to the cold exterior of the desk, allowing its cool surface to temper the frustration oozing from her pores. Nothing was worse than boredom—especially when it involved jocks, cheerleaders, and Mr. Warner.

She rubbed her sapphire-tinted eyes with the tips of her fingers. There had to be something to distract herself from the last dreary minutes of chemistry. She lifted her head and extracted the hair tie binding her sloppy ponytail, allowing strands of long, dark hair to tumble about her shoulders. Just as she twisted it back into position, Nathan's head jerked suddenly off his desk. He rubbed the back of his head with his palm and looked toward the rear of the classroom. Maggie watched the football player chuckle amicably to himself as the cheerleaders giggled. Nathan grumbled and lifted the offending rubber band from the floor, obviously contemplating return fire. The huge athlete smiled maliciously, displaying his teeth in a terrifying grin. *Bring it on*, his dull eyes taunted. Nathan hesitated, then pocketed the band and turned crossly to his notebook.

Maggie glanced forward. It was unsurprising to see Mr. Warner buzz onward through his lecture, his attention fully engrossed by the scientific paraphernalia littering his display table. The football player's assault on his fellow student passed without consequence.

Maggie hated high school.

She skimmed the clock again. Its thin hands mocked her, seemingly frozen. How could there still be eight more minutes of class? An inward sigh was interrupted by something prodding her right arm.

"Psst. Maggie! We have a test on this next class. Take notes!"

Maggie turned, meeting the expectant eyes of her best friend. Sweeping blond curls framed Lily Ivers' insistent expression. She poked Maggie again with a pencil. Maggie feigned disinterest, but knew ignoring her friend of almost 18 years would prove impossible. No one could breach the walls of apathy like Lily.

"Maggie," she whispered urgently, "if you don't pass it, you won't graduate!"

Maggie lifted her pencil with dramatic exaggeration as Lily slid a blank sheet of paper onto Maggie's desk, thwarting Maggie's usual attempt to squander class time by uselessly rummaging through her bag for a notebook. Lily's ice-green eyes sparkled with expectation; she lifted one eyebrow in challenge. Maggie, resigned, pulled the paper closer and scribbled some notes.

Of course, Lily didn't have to know Maggie was merely writing the lyrics to her favorite rock song. Lily seemed satisfied, however, and returned to her own note-taking endeavors.

Halfway through penning the chorus, Maggie felt a prickle against her neck and instinctively scanned the room. The jock stared at her. Naturally, as the most strikingly beautiful girl at Bonneville High, she received attention from all the shallow-minded guys she encountered. But she hated that "look." Maggie turned back to her paper, pretending she hadn't noticed. Lily often argued that Maggie's exotic beauty was a gift, but Maggie felt it was some kind of curse.

The athlete in the corner was part of that rationale. Ever since freshman year, Maggie had been dodging the advances of the guys in her school. In her mind, they only wanted one thing, and it wasn't to get to know her better.

That was Matt Larson's fault. Maggie could hardly believe that just over two years ago she had been duped into dating him. At the time, he was everything she thought she wanted: a popular senior who told her everything she wanted to hear. It had taken less than a day after she spent the night with him—her first time—for him to latch his face onto some other girl. He dumped her right there in the commons, in front of everyone, making sure to publicly announce that he had been the usurper of her virginity.

The weeks that followed were a torment of embarrassment, prolonged by the daily harassment she received from her classmates. She almost didn't go back to school.

But Lily had been determined to save her. Lily held Maggie close on the nights that were too terrible to bear alone. Even as a ninth-grader, Lily possessed a gravity beyond her years, and her cheerful influence soon drove the ridicule away. Only a handful of students—like Katie Maxwell and her gaggle of followers—remained immune to Lily's sway. Though Maggie came back to school, Matt had forever destroyed her faith in dating. Since that return, she had developed a blade of anger and a sheath of sarcasm that effectively distanced her from everyone.

Mr. Warner lit a burner for an experiment that wasn't near as interesting as his anticipation promised. Maggie released a silent snarl and wished momentarily that the flame would catch the chemistry teacher's sleeve. Class would be much more entertaining that way.

Mercifully the bell rang and Maggie jumped from her seat, eager to leave. She had a feeling that the football jersey was on the hunt, and she wasn't in the mood to deal with him. Lily quickly grabbed her backpack, struggling to catch Maggie's flight from the room.

"What are we doing after school?" Maggie asked as Lily caught up to her in the hallway.

"Spirit Club," Lily answered cheerfully. "We're making a card for Jeremy Rodgers. He's been really depressed ever since the accident."

Maggie turned to Lily with a blank expression.
"Who?"

"Really, Maggie," Lily persisted, "I know you're not into school spirit or anything, but you have to have heard. It's been all over school since Monday."

Maggie blinked twice.

"Jeremy Rodgers? Captain of the football team? Quarterback?" Lily paused, but Maggie made no sign of acknowledgement. With a sigh she continued. "He broke his leg in a car accident last week. He's pretty much out for the rest of the season. The whole team is bummed about it."

"Well, good for him," Maggie stated with perverse merriment, turning down the stairs to the hexagonal commons room. "Maybe now we can actually start winning."

"He's a nice guy, Maggie," Lily protested, "and we did come really close to winning some games."

"Close doesn't mean anything at the whistle. Losing is losing."

Lily bit her lip, her usual indication that, though she wanted to argue, her pacifist nature squelched the desire. Instead, she changed the subject.

"Well, rumor has it that Coach Graff is replacing him with a new student from California."

"Great," Maggie said as they reached the bottom of the stairs, "another prime example of undisciplined testosterone to parade the halls. Do we really have to go to Spirit Club today?"

"Well, I do, but I guess you could skip."

The timbre of disappointment in Lily's voice plucked at Maggie's heartstrings. Her friend would never pressure Maggie to stay, but Maggie felt guilty anyway.

"Yeah, but I'm your ride," Maggie admitted, "so it's either hide in a classroom with you, or deal with jocks and cheerleaders messing around in the hallway."

"They aren't so bad, you know," Lily disputed as she twisted the dial on her yellow locker.

"Yes they are," Maggie replied. "I don't see how you can stand to be friends with them."

"They used to be your friends too," Lily replied a little sadly.

Maggie snorted, remembering the dark month of persecution she had endured simply for their entertainment.

"I have since seen the error of my ways," Maggie announced, leaning against the line of lockers. "I've learned that you don't need to be fake to be happy."

Lily's lips pursed into a familiar expression of patience. This was an old argument—one that always ended in a stalemate and a quick change of topic. Lily accepted everyone as they were, often discounting unkind actions as misunderstandings or misplaced immaturity. Maggie's passionate character, however, refused to be so forgiving. Sometimes Lily's conscience could prove suffocating, but her opinion carried the only significance in Maggie's universe of cynicism.

Maggie was impatient for graduation. She vehemently avoided social gatherings, refused the affliction of dating, and chose to maintain only an average level of academic achievement. Her sloppy wardrobe and disregard for trends was just another indication of her dissent with high school mentality.

Lily, in contrast, delighted to throw herself into all available activities, flourishing in the companionship of others. Her friendly enthusiasm earned her a prominent place in the school, and everyone from the leader of the chess club to the student body president considered her a friend.

Maggie and Lily's unswerving relationship was therefore a popular enigma at the school. The other students were baffled that an affable girl like Lily chose the most quick-tempered, disliked person at Bonneville High as her best friend. Maggie sometimes wondered that herself.

"Hey, Lily."

Both girls turned toward the intruding voice. Maggie swore irritably in her head. The chemistry jock had followed them.

"Oh, hi, Trent," Lily responded politely with a smile. "How are you?"

"Great," he said, "that is, if you'd be willing to do me a favor?"

"I'll try my best," Lily said.

Trent's gaze slithered boldly across Maggie's figure then turned back to Lily.

"Could you ask Maggie Brooks if she would go out with me tomorrow night after the game?"

Trent smiled proudly at Maggie, as if flirting through her best friend was somehow clever. Lily brightened, but Maggie rolled her eyes in disgust.

"No thanks," Maggie answered, curtly cutting Lily off before she could speak. Lily's shoulders dropped, but Maggie chose to ignore it.

"Would you like me to ask you myself?" Trent asked in a voice reeking of misplaced confidence. He didn't seem to realize that, to Maggie, the conversation was over. Evidently his intelligence was as average as his looks.

"What I would like," Maggie said, taking a step toward him, "is for you to stick your over-large head into the nearest trash can."

Lily shifted nervously. Trent eyed the small crowd of students who watched his humiliation. He shifted his attention back to Maggie, puffing like a wounded peacock.

"You'd be lucky to go out with me, Brooks," he seethed. "Right now you're nothing."

"I have no intention of being just another notch on your belt, 'jock boy'," she said condescendingly. "There's no chance in hell that I would go out with a loser like you."

Trent's face blotched with ugly spots of red. He stepped forward so that his body loomed over her. "What makes you think you can say 'no' to me, Brooks?"

Maggie refused to flinch or back away. "What made you think you could ask me out? Besides," Maggie said, lifting both eyebrows contemptuously, "I'd never date a guy who walks around with his fly open."

Trent's eyes shot to his pants only to find them properly fastened. The audience laughed without reserve. As Trent's face flushed darker, Lily slammed her locker shut, drawing both of their attention.

"Look, Trent, she's not interested," Lily apologized, looping her arm through Maggie's and dragging her away from the locker pods. "I'm sorry."

Trent stared angrily at the retreating girls, but Maggie only laughed. Lily remained silent until they reached the stairs.

"You could have just said no," she chided as they descended toward the history classrooms. "You didn't have to make such a scene."

"What's the fun in that?" Maggie returned without remorse. "You really think he would have left me alone if I had been nice?"

"Maybe," Lily said, "but now he'll likely do something to retaliate."

"He doesn't scare me," Maggie said and shrugged.

Lily pulled Maggie to a halt on the side of the stairs.

"Would it be so bad to trust someone again?" Lily heaved in exasperation.

"I already trust you," Maggie stated with narrowed eyes. "I don't need anyone else."

"It's been over two years, Maggie," Lily continued, undeterred. "Not everyone is like Matt."

Hot fire sizzled into Maggie's head, as if Lily had physically stabbed her.

"Trent is," Maggie said, nodding back toward the commons.

"How will you ever know if you don't give anyone a chance?" Lily argued.

"I don't want to."

Maggie wrapped the words in resentment. Lily sighed and looked at the tiled linoleum.

"I might not be around forever, you know."

"Of course you will," Maggie said without hesitation.

Lily raised her head. "Maggie—"

"Can we just talk about something else?" she asked.

Maggie knew she had lost the disagreement even before Lily responded. Lily's arguments were always well grounded, but on rare occasions such as this, they also radiated a quality of overwhelming wisdom. The soft volume of her voice delivered the killing blow.

"Is it so bad for me to want to see you happy?"

"I'm fine," Maggie asserted with furrowed eyebrows.

"You pretend you are, but you can't fool me, Maggie. You're still upset about what Matt did to you. Just because he was a jerk doesn't mean that every other guy is the same." Lily's green eyes glistened. "Just don't keep denying yourself the chance to meet someone great."

Maggie looked away, unwilling to relent. Lily placed a hand on her shoulder.

"Promise me you'll think about it, okay?"

"Okay," Maggie compromised, "but only if you agree not to bring up Matt again."

Lily nodded, lightening swiftly with a smile. She led Maggie down the remainder of the stairs, prattling about the current gossip involving the people at school. Maggie shook her head in amazement as she followed her friend. No one knew the realm of forgiveness like Lily. Already she had dismissed the quarrel. Lily skipped to the bottom of the stairs, turning to wait as Maggie sauntered down after her. When Maggie reached her, Lily spun forward too quickly, colliding with a tall, lanky boy. Lily rebounded off his body and nearly fell.

"Lily, I'm so sorry. Are you okay?" the pesky boy asked as he helped to stabilize her.

Lily giggled shyly to mask her embarrassment.

"I'm just fine, Mark," she answered, looking up. Mark Weston towered over her by almost a foot.

Irritation rumbled under Maggie's skin. She didn't like Mark. He pestered her regularly, misguidedly believing that his friendship with Lily equated to Maggie's. Maggie wondered momentarily how to get rid of him, but Mark acted faster.

"Can I walk you to your next class?" he asked Lily.

"Sure," Lily responded with a squeak, glancing away with bright eyes. "That would be great." She peeked at his face as he snatched the books from her hands with a silly smile.

Lily rarely suffered from the typical crush, a fact that Maggie accepted gratefully. But when Lily did fall for a guy, she practically drowned in him. Though Maggie often overlooked the details of Lily's discussion topics, she hadn't missed her best friend's sudden obsession with Mark. Last year he hadn't even ranked an appointment in Lily's calendar, but over the summer he had somewhat grown a personality. At least one that Lily liked. Maggie huffed. She already felt sandwiched between Lily's leadership responsibilities and family. To see her at all this year, Maggie had resorted to grudgingly joining half a dozen clubs in which Lily involved herself. There was no way Maggie was going to share that with some guy, least of all Mark.

Lily and Mark conversed through the corridor as they approached Lily's next class. Mark just wouldn't go away, no matter how many "get lost" glares Maggie shot candidly in his direction. He had just managed to invite himself to the Spirit Club meeting after school, and, Maggie realized with annoyance, had positioned himself to ask Lily out. That was when Maggie decided it was time to take action.

"So Mark, have you given up on your truck yet?" Maggie plunged into the banter, endeavoring to divert his attention.

"Well actually, I just installed a new stereo and some speakers. It's pretty awesome. I finally took care of that problem with—"

Maggie blocked out the rest of his explanation and smiled to herself. In her mind, she was one-to-nothing. Mark was bound to discuss the improvements until the tardy bell rang. With any luck, whatever he really had to say had been postponed until later.

Lily rounded on Maggie with a pleading glance, biting her lip. *Please don't mess this up*, her eyes seemed to beg. Maggie almost heard the words spoken aloud. One of her personal goals was to never lose a confrontation with anyone except Lily—but in this case, Maggie conceded. Mark was lucky Lily was so smitten.

When the interest in his truck waned, Mark strode in front of Lily and twirled to face her. Maggie knew she couldn't resist interrupting Mark, so she took a step back and waited alongside the hallway, letting students pass between her and the couple.

"So—uh—Lily," Mark stuttered, running his hand through his mopish hair. He fidgeted. Maggie wondered if she had disrupted his cheerful confidence.

"I was wondering—"

To Maggie's infinite distress—and revulsion—Mark dropped to one knee, took Lily's hand with his left and produced a budding pink rose in the other.

"Would you please be my date for homecoming?"

Maggie wondered how he had managed the rose. Probably spent an hour practicing it at home. *So lame,* she thought acidly to herself. Maggie would have stuffed the ridiculous thing in his mouth.

Of course the flower won Lily over completely. She flushed scarlet from the tips of her toes to the top of her head. Maggie rolled her eyes. Her best friend suffered from an obsession with fantasy, and here was prince charming offering to escort a blushing Cinderella to the ball. Mark's performance did not go unnoticed by the other passing students. They actually paused and leaned toward the romantic pair in anticipation of Lily's answer. It was the realization of a high school fairy tale.

Until the school fire sprinklers sputtered to life.

If Lily managed to answer, it was lost in the sudden blaring of the fire alarm. Students scrambled everywhere toward exits, slipping on wet linoleum and carpet. Bags were abandoned, soggy books littered the floor.

"Oh that's too bad. Of all the unfortunate times to have a drill," Maggie exclaimed as she and Lily joined the throng of students milling outside in the main parking lot.

Somehow they had lost Mark. Both girls shivered in their wet clothes, their hair hanging limply against their cheeks. Sirens began wailing in the distance.

"Come on Lily," Maggie said, weaving through the other Bonneville students in the direction of her car. "Let's get out of here."

"But I didn't give Mark an answer!" Lily exclaimed breathlessly, scanning the parking lot for her lost crush.

"And I have a paper due next hour. Do you think Mrs. Anderson will dock me points?"

"What does it matter?" Maggie threw over her shoulder. Leave it to Lily to worry about classes when they were standing outside, sopping wet in the frigid September air. "There's no way they're going to have fourth period. The school is doused in water."

Lily stared longingly back at the building, her teeth clattering in the cold, worry plain in her face. Maggie stopped to wait. The parking lot was emptying quickly, though a group of students had stopped to watch Principal West herd stragglers out of the front entrance. Soon teachers clustered around him. Lily, who was starting to look pale, scoured the group of adults for her English teacher.

"Honestly, Lil," Maggie said, "you'll be able to turn in your work tomorrow. And Mark will be around, I'm sure," she added reluctantly.

Lily didn't answer, but started to tremble.

"Lil, are you listening to me?" Maggie asked, taking her best friend's hand. Lily's fingers were unusually warm, considering the low air temperature. "Lily? Are you okay?"

"I'm feeling dizzy all of a sudden," she replied, teetering.

Maggie put one arm around Lily to stabilize her and placed a hand against her cheek. Lily's skin was hot and flushed, her eyes exhibiting the tell-tale glaze of a fever.

"Let's get you home," Maggie said urgently.

Lily looked like she might object, until the teachers began formally excusing everyone for the day. Without further resistance, Maggie grabbed her best friend solidly by the arm and pulled her to the car.

2: Jocks of a Feather

Friday the entire school building dripped damply from the explosion of fire sprinklers. Students were drafted from their first-hour classes, equipped with a battery of towels and mops, and directed to swab the wet classrooms. Open windows helped circulate the dry autumn air, while teachers attempted to salvage sodden school supplies.

The administration kept the cause of the alarm confidential, which of course allowed wild suppositions to breed throughout the halls—everything from cigarettes in the girls locker room to reports of Brandon Jones blowing butane fireballs from his mouth on a dare in shop class. Whatever the truth, Maggie rushed to her car the moment her trigonometry teacher's back turned, ditching the rest of the school day. She stopped to visit Lily, who had stayed home due to the fever, but Lily's mother vehemently refused to allow anyone into the sick room.

After two attempts at television, one magazine, and a load of dishes, Maggie wondered just how much longer the weekend could last. Had it really only been three hours since she had abandoned school? She flipped absently through her favorite video games, uninspired to play. She hadn't bought a new one in months.

Up until a few weeks ago, her mother's paychecks had barely covered the grocery bill. Bankruptcy had loomed precariously close on the horizon until Tara Brooks decided to take on a new job, one that paid well and offered good benefits. Being a flight attendant suited Tara well, and Maggie enjoyed the newfound freedom she gained through her mother's frequent absences.

Though Tara Brooks worked hard as a single parent, she had never intended on such early motherhood. Tara would have ended her pregnancy altogether if it hadn't been for the support of her closest friend, Linda Ivers. Maggie was proud that her mother had been strong enough to leave Miami and attempt the single-mom scene. Linda and Tara shared a bond of friendship that was only surpassed by their daughter's. In a way, Maggie felt that her relationship with Lily had been destined at birth. Even as children, the two girls were inseparable.

Maggie couldn't remember the last time Lily was sick enough for house arrest, and with Tara somewhere above the American Midwest, Maggie became desperate for entertainment.

At least that was what she told herself as she stared unenthusiastically into the stands overlooking the football field. What cheerleader-happy, athletics-supporting demon had suddenly possessed her?

She climbed the bleachers, scanning for a seat removed from the host of people. As she searched, the expressions of the audience surprised her. Everyone seemed excessively excited. Halfway up the stairs, the crowd exhaled a sudden uproar of sound. Spectators jumped to their feet. Bonneville's team had obviously scored. Maggie didn't know anything about football, but as she checked the score board she could tell that not only were the Bonneville Bees winning, they were slaughtering the other team. Maggie had to admit, it marked a notable moment in the high school's history.

"Hey, Maggie!"

Mark Weston grabbed her arm. Maggie growled a sigh. He was seated along the aisle. She yanked her arm from his grasp and continued climbing. Unfortunately, Mark followed.

"Is Lily okay? I haven't seen her all day," Mark asked.

His voice was swiftly becoming one of her least favorite sounds.

"She's fine, Mark," Maggie answered irritably, plopping onto an isolated bench near the top of the bleachers.

"So then, where is she?" Mark inquired, inviting himself into an empty spot next to her. His voice quavered nervously.

"She didn't want to come to school today."

Maggie's answer was second nature, she'd said it without thinking. If she could convince Mark that Lily was avoiding him, he might abandon the chase. Playing with people's minds was the only way to really alleviate the blandness that saturated high school. It was especially rewarding when it tormented Mark.

"How come?" he asked, panic evident in his tone. "I mean, I asked her to the dance and—"

"I'm sure she'll be back next week," Maggie offered nonchalantly.

"Oh." Mark slumped in his seat. "I guess that's good then."

Maggie felt something weird in the bowels of her stomach. It tasted somewhat like guilt. But Mark was making it so easy! Freedom was only one sentence away. All she had to do was confirm Mark's worst fears.

A looming image of Lily's tear-streaked face invaded Maggie's mind. She could see the disbelief and betrayal carved into her best friend's expression. Her compassion for Lily prevailed.

"Honestly Mark, you're so gullible," Maggie said gracelessly. "Lily's really sick and her mom wouldn't let her come to school."

"Really?" Mark perked so quickly Maggie was surprised he didn't leap out of his seat. "I guess I'll have to call her and see if she's all right," he added happily.

Mark was pleased, but Maggie creased her forehead angrily. She'd been so close to permanently vanquishing him. He would have avoided her for the rest of the school year. Lily owed her, big time.

"I met the new quarterback of the football team today in weights," Mark said. "He can bench 290 pounds without breaking a sweat."

"I really don't care," she spat.

"You don't get it." Maggie knew Mark emphasized his words with dramatic hand gestures, even though she hadn't looked in his direction. "This guy created cool factor."

Maggie's eyes gleamed as she turned toward him.

"Mark, I'm going to give you one last chance to stop talking. I told you already. I don't care."

Maggie accented the last three words with such finality that Mark shrank away from her.

"Sorry, I was just—"

Maggie scowled and Mark fell silent. She turned to the game, hoping it would distract her. The football players ran about the field, neither side gaining any advantage during the next two plays. Kyle Spencer was easy to spot. He towered over the others. Maggie projected at least six foot four inches without his football pads and helmet. His prowess certainly explained why the boys at school idolized him. Less than a week had passed since Kyle's enrollment, and he had already turned around the team's abysmal game record. And unless she was mistaken, all 200 pounds of him was unadulterated muscle.

Ugh. The girls around school are going to be disgusting. They'll be even worse if he turns out to be hot.

"Spencer is the best thing that ever happened to this school," Mark inserted awkwardly after a few minutes. "We haven't won a game in like, 10 years!"

Maggie ignored him, wondering why he was trying so hard to win her attention. He bit his lip uncomfortably as she glared at him.

Suddenly she realized why. *He must understand the cardinal rule of dating,* she surmised. *The best friend must approve all boyfriends.* For Lily's sake, Maggie was willing to at least feign interest, though she didn't have to like it.

"So that's the new student from California," Maggie stated, trying to curb the disdain in her tone.

"Yep, the way he plays is gonna make him a star over night!" Mark replied exuberantly.

"Hmm," Maggie returned, scrutinizing a spider crawling next to her bleacher. Being nice to Mark was a harder task than she thought. As Maggie offered another flippant comment concerning the new athlete, she chanced to turn in the direction of the football field. The center snapped the ball and the players scrambled forward. Bonneville's new quarterback danced left and right, looking to find an open teammate for a pass. As he turned toward the stands, Kyle Spencer locked eyes with Maggie Brooks.

The next thing Maggie felt was inexplicable. Reality slid away in a wash of color. The sound of the crowd's collective voice pounded around her body, yet she heard only silence. A soft breath of air slid across her lips, gliding longingly across her cheek. It lingered around her ear, whispering. Maggie knew it had delivered a message, but she could not discern its words. Something inside her screamed in agony, and Maggie felt as if a part of her soul had suddenly died.

Her sorrow dissolved in a swell of nausea. Pain seared through the base of her spine, spiraling up to the back of her head. The torturous wave convulsed across her every nerve, as if it was too severe for her brain to process. Air was suddenly too hot to breathe and she gasped for relief.

Then someone tackled Kyle Spencer, breaking his gaze. Maggie regained a sense of herself instantly, though her vision spun in sickening circles. For a few minutes, she concentrated simply on breathing. Next to her, Mark was saying something, but the words seemed to slide through her head like water. Everything around her seemed to buzz strangely, and she had to focus on not being sick.

What the hell was going on?

"Are you okay?" Mark's repeated concern finally penetrated her spongy brain.

"Fine," she heard herself snap. She felt a sudden need to compose herself. The girls restroom looked to be her best option, but she wanted to make sure Mark's sense of gallantry stayed on the bleachers with him. "It's girl stuff. I have to go. See you at school."

Mark spared her a glance as she stumbled her way down the stands. Her fear of falling belied her apprehension of Mark's following. Sheer will brought her to the bottom of the bleachers without mishap. As the crowd screamed with energy, Maggie rushed for the bathroom, where, for the first time since raiding her mother's liquor cabinet at the age of nine, she was violently ill.

*

Maggie waited until the game had ended before finally vacating her bathroom stall. Her hands shook under the sink faucet, spattering the large mirror with water droplets. Its surface reflected a face she hardly recognized. Pale, slightly green splotches marred her features and dark halos garlanded her sapphire eyes. A pulsing throb assaulted her temples and pricks dripped across her skin. Maggie tried to turn off the water, but her shivering hands failed to function; her efforts nearly caused her to fall. Finally succeeding at the task caused a queasy tremble to invade her insides, and forced her to pause before she tried moving again.

Purposefully, Maggie had not left the bathroom until she knew the football crowd outside had left for home. That way she evaded any awkward questions. The bathroom door slammed behind her as she left. She stepped into a pool of light staining the sidewalk. Her timing hadn't been exactly accurate. A group of students still lingered on the green between the outside of the restrooms and the school. The distance to her car was far too long for Maggie's liking.

Several football players, mixed with snickering teenage girls, were shouting excitedly and celebrating the outcome of the game. The boys were enacting some of the more exciting aspects of the night, while others seemed engrossed in flirtatious advances. Though her vision was obscured by pain, Maggie was sure the cans being distributed weren't a variety of sodas.

Steadying herself, Maggie tried not to let their proximity worry her. They had gathered on the outer edges of the green, so if she took a straight path she would be able to avoid them. She moved forward slowly, struggling not to aggravate her condition. She concentrated on reaching her car, sorely aware that it was parked around the other side of the building.

Whatever had happened tonight while she was watching the game, was buried beneath dizziness and vomit. She needed to sleep before she could digest the bizarre events that had destroyed her evening.

A change in tone from the rambunctious group of students across the green spurred a quickening of her pace. A murmur of collective anticipation emanated from their direction. Maggie didn't glance toward them, hoping that her lack of acknowledgement would keep her unnoticed. She had just reached the corner of the building when she heard an assortment of footsteps approaching from behind. A hand thrust against the wall to block her escape.

"Hey Brooks, what are you doing here?"

The voice sounded somehow familiar. Maggie stepped back from the arm, fighting the nausea-induced weakness that sent her head spinning. She was too weak to run. Instead, she equipped her verbal blade and turned to face her aggressor.

"Who the hell are you?" she spat icily.

"Trent Smith. You know, the guy you embarrassed in the hallway yesterday?" He flashed an assertive smile. "I'm thinking I might show you what you're missing."

He leaned closer and brushed a finger through her hair. His breath exuded a pungent and bitter odor. Undisguised mirth painted the faces of his companions who surrounded her. Maggie rearranged her features in an appropriate mask of disgust and slapped his hand away.

"Wow, really? Because you look too drunk to even walk."

Laughter rent the air. Trent grabbed her arm, pushing her back against the coarse brick of the school's outer wall. Clearly he was angry she had managed to disgrace him again.

"You should be more careful who you mess with," Trent warned, squeezing her arm uncomfortably. "You might get hurt."

Maggie tried to wriggle loose, but his grip was too tight.

"Let me go," Maggie commanded, raising her fist, but Trent was quicker.

As she swung her arm forward, he hooked his leg around her ankle, knocking her off balance. Maggie's blow missed entirely, and the back of her head slammed against the wall. His friends were laughing again, this time at her. She could feel terror sliding up her body. Mob mentality urged Trent forward.

"Why would I do that? I'm just getting started," he said, pushing his weight against her.

Maggie tried to kick, claw, and knee whatever part of Trent was available, but he seized her wrists. In her state, his strength overwhelmed her. She started to panic. Just as she figured screaming was the best plan, Trent stuck his tongue in her mouth, nearly choking her.

Maggie had never been physically attacked before, but she had imagined all manner of horrible things she would do to an assailant if the situation arose. She had visualized herself empowered with righteous anger. Now, however, she discovered just how helpless a victim could feel, especially with about 20 of her peers standing nearby laughing at her degradation. Trent's lips refused to relent and soon she couldn't breathe. The need to scream, spit, and cry all at the same time overwhelmed her.

And then Trent was gone, soaring away through the air at a startling speed. The shocked look on his face as he smashed into two of his friends was almost comical. All three of them fell backward onto the lawn, gasping. For a moment, they were a mass of tangled arms and legs struggling to right itself. A wave of whispers swept over the horde. With Trent's weight lifted off her body, Maggie slumped to the ground. She blinked quickly, unable to process her sudden freedom.

"I don't believe the lady here gave you permission to be an ass, Trent."

A muscular figure stepped between her and Trent, blocking him and his friends from view.

"There was no reason to be so rough, Spencer. I wasn't hurting her," Trent whined peevishly.

Maggie used the wall to push herself up. By leaning sideways, she could see past her rescuer.

"That's not what it looked like to me." Kyle Spencer's voice was strong and deep.

"She deserved it," Trent snarled as he picked himself up. "She can't keep a lid on her snotty mouth. Besides, everyone knows Brooks is willing to put out."

A sudden hush fell over the group. Maggie wasn't sure, but Kyle's expression must have turned menacing, because Trent's face drained of color. Others in the circle were taking tentative steps in retreat.

"You've got no right to treat a girl like a piece of meat," Kyle almost growled. "So I'll say this only once. If you ever come near her again—" as he leaned forward, his fingers curled into a fist at his side "—I'll tear you in two."

"Whatever you say," Trent replied, trying not to appear intimidated. He failed miserably.

For a moment, no one moved, until Kyle spoke again.

"That wasn't a cue for you to stand there lookin' stupid. Get lost before I decide to help you do it."

Never before had Maggie seen a group withdraw so fast. Several of the spectators were muttering apologies to both Maggie and Kyle. They obviously wanted to retain his good opinion. Trent had taken the quarterback's threat seriously. He kept his back to Maggie and Kyle as he hurried across the green. Kyle didn't turn until he was sure Trent and his gang had disappeared.

For the first time, Maggie saw Kyle Spencer's face. *Yep, the girls are going to be disgusting,* was all she could think.

His wide shoulders defined a muscular frame. A tan sheen emphasized his strong jawline and his hazel eyes gleamed mischievously. Russet short-cropped hair shielded his head like a Marine. Adding in his noticeable skills of chivalry and the halls at school would swoon with fan girls.

"Are you all right?" His voice had become gentle.

"If I say yes, will you go away?"

Maggie couldn't help but reply sharply. She knew she should be grateful, but she was scared and confused—two feelings that she wasn't used to confessing.

Kyle's eyebrows arched in mild surprise and his lips turned up with humor. *Yet another reason for the girl's to go nuts,* Maggie thought. She deliberately turned away from his face. The warm feeling she felt in the pit of her stomach when she looked at him annoyed her. In an instant, she had rounded the corner. She could hear Kyle following behind.

"Guess Trent was right about the snotty mouth thing," Kyle chuckled to himself. He didn't sound offended in the slightest.

Maggie stopped and turned to glare at him. She already hated him. He looked at her with an expression she had never seen in a guy before. There was no sign of any lust in his eyes. Just interest. Worst of all: now she owed him a favor. There was no doubt that he had just rescued her.

"I don't believe we've met?"

He stretched his hand toward her, expecting the usual pleasantries. Maggie scowled at his hand.

"And we never will," she replied.

Kyle remained still as she raced to her car. She left him standing alone in the school's shadow without an answer or a thank you.

3: Out Of The Football Field

Fifty different things had already gone wrong and Maggie didn't care. She merely accepted her doom, admitting that the night wasn't likely to improve. Working at the movie theater was not a complex job, but yesterday's events plagued her attention. Distraction met her every encounter. No matter how hard she tried to concentrate, she still managed to start two movies early, three movies late, and spilled an entire large soda on a customer. Frustrated beyond endurance, Maggie barricaded herself in the manager's office. Here she intended to rest before she was forced to endure the last five hours of her shift.

A migraine had harassed her all day. At times, pain still exploded in her skull and numbness would possess her fingers. She pressed her forehead to the cool metal of the desk hoping to lessen the pain throbbing behind her eyes. Reaching blindly for her purse, not bothering to disconnect her forehead from the desktop, she rummaged through the bag until her fingers brushed against the most important object it housed: a bottle of pain reliever.

Last night she had crashed in her room, but not before flipping on every light in the house and turning her stereo volume as high as possible. The blaring noise had effectively pounded her thoughts into submission. Around four in the morning, she had escaped into oblivion. She slept through the morning and the afternoon, purposely avoiding any moment of solitude that might lead to reflection over her recent abnormal experience. When Maggie finally dragged her body out of bed, she was forced to scramble for work. She had managed to call Lily twice. Lily's voicemail had answered both times.

Now she found herself completely alone with her unwelcome thoughts. Questions bombarded her brain in a tangled fury. Why was her body still so weak? Had it been her shared gaze with Kyle Spencer that caused the painful vision, or was it coincidence? Why had she felt such sudden sadness? The last question bothered Maggie the most. She knew she hadn't felt that close to tears since her freshman year, since Matt. The thought that she was capable of such weakness produced a fume of anger directed toward herself.

And yet—when she remembered the wistful feeling before the pain, a sorrow and regret so deep it drank into her very soul, she wondered if her body might again fracture with anguish. She forced her mind away from the subject.

Any other girl would have been shaken into dismay by the attack after the game, but the greater mystery of the phenomenon at the football field overshadowed all other fears. She kept imagining those warm, hazel eyes every time she tried to puzzle it out. As soon as Maggie banished the image, Kyle's magnetic smile crept into its place. Somewhere, deep inside a dark corner of her psyche, those eyes devoured her.

She hated him. Completely. She hated the way she couldn't get his face out of her mind. She hated that he had rescued her when she had been entirely helpless. She hated that someone, anyone, had seen her in such a humiliating situation.

Maggie decided she was going to avoid him at all costs.

This of course lightened her mood somewhat. Immersed in her ruminations, she was startled when a faltering rap came from the door.

"Maggie?" One of the employees poked his head into the office hesitantly. "Are you okay?"

"I'm fine, Drew," she lied as she stood. Mentally she prepared to do battle with the rest of the evening. "What do you need?"

The flashing neon lights of the lobby did nothing to improve the aching in her head. Drew seemed to have forgotten what he was going to say, or just didn't dare. Almost everyone in the movie theater had suffered her temper at least once tonight. She glared at him.

"Just tell me already."

"Someone says the sound is too loud in theater four." His voice was practically a whisper.

Maggie rolled her eyes. It was probably just some old guy who only came into public to annoy the hell out of everyone else. Without answering Drew, she started up the stairs to the projection booth. As Maggie reached the projection platter, she briefly entertained the idea of turning the sound a little louder. The thought made her almost smile.

Almost.

At least the medicine is starting to kick in.

Her eyes adjusted to the dim light. The familiar purr of the outdated projectors emanated a calming aura, allowing her mind to relax. She double checked the settings on theater four. Everything seemed to be in order. Just to be sure, she turned the volume down a notch. Stupid old guy. Maggie raised her eyes for a fraction of a second as she turned the sound dial.

Something moved in the darkness.

She caught her breath. The movie theater workers often jested about the creepy atmosphere of the projection booth.

The dim lights and flickering of the projection bulbs caused crazy shadows to trick the eye. The muffled sounds from multiple movies confused the ears. Usually she just called the others cowards and enjoyed the looks on their faces when she ordered them upstairs.

But tonight her imagination had escaped its leash.

Nothing seemed amiss as she scanned the room. Cautiously she made her way down the long rows full of machinery, peering around the metallic bodies. She nearly tripped when her watch alarm sounded.

Damn!

The movie in theater six was supposed to start; she hadn't even prepped its projector. More profanities escaped her lips as she shook herself free of creepy notions and returned to work. Pulling the film into place, she threaded it through the many rollers and brackets. Just as she checked the framing to make sure the movie would appear properly on the screen…

…Something hissed.

Maggie's heart pulsated frantically in her chest. She was at the end of the long corridor and the stairs were on the opposite side of the room. A tool table was directly at her side. She slid a heavy flashlight from its surface and flipped the switch on the silver handle. The light revealed only the normal projection booth equipment, but she could sense…something. Like the shadows themselves were suffused with energy. Like the darkness had eyes.

Dead black eyes.

The shadow reared in front of her so suddenly that Maggie almost dropped the flashlight. Every inch of its body was swathed in dark cloth, adeptly masking its features, except the eyes. She couldn't be sure if the figure was male or female. The only clue was its height; at least several inches taller then herself, she guessed most likely male.

His eyes were mesmerizing. Irises and pupils bled together, completely black, like a night devoid of stars. And there was something—barren—about them. Lifeless. The strange hissing began anew. Maggie couldn't place the sound. It was the voice of a campfire when doused with water, yet it reverberated through the air with an unmistakable echo. It penetrated the air in her lungs.

On the surface, Maggie knew this ridiculous stunt was meant to scare her—some kind of stupid jock retaliation for Trent's lost honor the night before. Probably jerks from school who felt she needed to be taught a lesson. She denied herself any other explanation. Entrenched in her subconscious, however, those flat black eyes stirred terror.

Maggie's perception of time became distorted; every breath seemed to stretch across minutes. The invader didn't move, almost as if he'd lost sight of her. His eyes stared not at her, but at a point somewhat above her head. It was unnerving. Maggie watched him carefully. His entire body seemed rigid, muscles taut, poised snakelike to spring, yet he never once blinked. The only movement came from his left hand. It mechanically grasped the air, closing into a fist then opening again. Open, close, open, close.

Maggie decided to be direct and authoritative. Especially if this was some brainless prank. *I have watched way too many zombie movies,* she chided herself.

"What are you doing up here?" Her hand constricted around the heavy metal flashlight, sweat bleeding from the edges of her fingers.

No answer. He took a step forward. She slid back. The hiss permeated the air once again.

"What do you want?" she repeated, hefting the flashlight into an attack position.

He lunged forward so fast his actions blurred, catching Maggie by the throat with his left hand. Though she hadn't been able to dodge his initial attack, she was determined to execute some damage. She would not become a victim twice in the same weekend. As she slammed the flashlight into his jaw, she felt the satisfying crack of bone. The blow knocked him off balance. Amazingly, he refused to loosen his grip on her neck. They both fell, bodies colliding into the tool table with a crash. Maggie lost her hold on the flashlight, and it clattered on the painted concrete floor.

She was trapped on the ground, side by side with her attacker. A sharp ache shot through her ribs where her body had rammed into the table. Her lungs were burning for air. His hold would not relent, yet he made no move to right their position on the floor. He was statuesque, completely stiff. And still, the black eyes never blinked, never looked directly at her. She pried frantically at his fingers with her nails, but she couldn't penetrate the leather gloves covering his hands. Her vision exploded in red. She could feel herself suffocating.

Desperate for escape, she grabbed the hand at her throat. Using it as leverage to swing her weight forward, she smashed her heel into the terrible black eyes. Maggie felt a sickening crunch. Though the attacker's fingers never loosened, the force of Maggie's blow released her body from his grasp. A wailing hiss careened through the room. As she gasped for breath, she clutched her neck instinctively. Her hand came back sticky and warm. She scrambled to her feet, slipping once from blood on her hands and a second time in the black ooze that coated the bottom of her shoe.

She ran for the door, seemingly forever at the end of the corridor. Just as Maggie reached for the knob, something closed around her right arm and jerked it down painfully. Her head slammed into the floor.

She looked up into dead black eyes.

For a second she was confused. She knew she had smashed the intruder's face. She didn't move. The empty eyes weren't looking at her, they were gazing slightly to the left, away from the door. Maggie hardly breathed. When the hand came down, reaching again for her windpipe, she was ready. Using her wrist to deflect the blow, she pushed her body into a roll with her legs and free arm. As she spun to her stomach, Maggie glimpsed a heap of black cloth draped over the smashed table in the back of the room.

Hell! There's two of them! she thought to herself in disgust as she scrambled to her feet. Her only chance was the door and the stairs behind it. The second one pounced in her direction but Maggie twisted out of his reach. She bolted for the exit, but a strong grip entwined itself in her shirt, halting her progress.

"Let me go, you bastard!" she commanded.

The dead eyes looked directly at her.

Without explanation, he released his hold. Maggie didn't wait to figure out why. She crashed down the stairs, taking two at a time, bursting through the lobby door. The normalcy that met her was eerie. Patrons stood in line at the counter, played the video game machines, and generally milled about the popcorn-strewn floor. No one had noticed her frantic arrival. Her heart continued to beat furiously and her brain refused to contain its panic. An unexpected voice called from somewhere around her.

"Hey, our movie hasn't started yet, do you—"

Kyle's comment stopped short as she accidentally collided with him. She lost her balance and almost fell. Kyle caught her deftly in his arms.

"Whoa, whoa, whoa," he soothed, "you should be more careful, Sparky."

Maggie grasped his arms instinctively. He was flesh and blood, something real in a hazy nightmare of black cloth and movie projectors. Kyle greeted her with his charismatic half smile. Maggie felt the anxiety leak out of her body as he held her, as if his touch calmed her. She was acutely aware of his skin, so close, yet not quite touching hers. His hands slid up her spine as he pulled her upright, but he didn't release his hold. She stared into his eyes, her nerves tingling. Her blood still pounded loudly in her ears—but no longer from fear.

Kyle's flippant demeanor vanished, obvious concern straining his features as he noticed the blood on her clothes. He raised a hand to her injured throat, touching it softly. Maggie winced. He slid his fingertips up to her ear and across the line of her jaw, lingering delicately around her lips. Unaccountably his eyes revealed pain, as if he carried the wound himself. She couldn't speak for astonishment.

"Who did this to you?" he whispered.

"I don't know," she almost choked. "I—uh—"

Maggie caught her breath. It was really hard to think when his face was so close to hers. She mentally swore at herself. How could some guy confuse her this much? It was annoying. She sharpened her glance and her tongue. "I was up starting movies and these two jerks attacked me."

As she watched, his expression transformed from tenderness to unrestrained wrath. Even in her own reflection she had never met such raw fury. He turned to Drew, who had rushed over when he noticed Maggie's state.

"Call 911," Kyle said.

Kyle removed his arm from Maggie's body and headed for the stairs.

"What are you doing?" she demanded.

"I'm gonna check it out," he replied heatedly.

There was no fear in his face, simply the guarantee of retribution. Maggie grabbed his arm.

"You can't do that."

"Why not, Sparky?" Turning back to her, he grinned slyly. "Worried about me?"

"Of course I am," she answered instantly, not thinking about the implications of her statement. When Kyle's smile widened, she quickly amended her reply. "I'm in charge here. What would happen if you got hurt? I could lose my job!"

He chuckled at her clumsy attempt to mask what could have been affection, or at least bodily concern for another human being.

"Don't worry, I'll be fine." He shook off her arm easily and began mounting stairs.

Maggie took a deep breath. Then she followed.

When they reached the threshold of the projection room Maggie started inside, but Kyle adroitly slid in front of her, using his body to hide her from sight. She tried to push past him, but it was like trying to move a parked semi-truck.

"There's nothin' here," he said after a few seconds.

"That's impossible," Maggie answered angrily, storming past him. "The only way out of this room is down the stairs."

Kyle raised his eyebrows, humor crackling across his jaw. "It doesn't change the fact that there's nothin' here, Blue Eyes. They must've found another way out."

"There's not another way out," she snapped stubbornly, ignoring his flirtatious remark.

"What about the roof, Sparky?" Kyle reasoned, inspecting the ceiling tiles to see if any were disturbed.

"Why do you keep calling me that?" Maggie asked, viciously righting the fallen table and replacing its spilled contents: an odd assortment of tools, empty film canisters, and the flashlight. There wasn't a mark on it, she noticed with disgust, and no evidence of black gore on the floor.

"Since you won't tell me your name, I came up with one on my own. Thought it might fit your personality." He smiled at his own cleverness.

Maggie's heart practically stopped.

"Well, don't call me that."

She arranged her face into an unmistakable glare, one she used to intimidate her fiercest opponents. Kyle simply grinned.

Grumbling, she grabbed a tissue off the table and dabbed at the cuts on her neck. The bleeding had stopped, but her endeavor to clean the wounds only broke them open again. Kyle had obviously finished his search because he was leaning against a nearby wall, looking directly at her.

"Why don't you tell me your name so I won't have to make one up?"

His question was so logical that Maggie instantly felt irritated. She had walked right into his trap. His nickname disarmed her scorn. She wanted him to stop using it, but relinquishing her name would be rewarding him with exactly what he wanted. No matter how the exchange ended, she had already lost.

Maggie's thoughts must have been playing across her face, because Kyle let out a little chuckle. Striding forward, he snatched the tissues from her hands and ministered to her injuries. It made her uncomfortable when he was so close, so she slid her gaze to the nearest projector reel.

"Maggie Brooks, satisfied?" she spat ungraciously.

" 'Course I am," he retorted, twisting his lips into that galling nonchalant smirk of his; she could see it reflected in the projector window. "We should probably go back down. Bet the cops are here. C'mon, Mags."

Somehow he had managed to get his arm around her waist and was pulling her toward the stairs.

"Maggie. My. Name. Is. Maggie." She tried unsuccessfully to remove his arm. Her glower at this new development only made him laugh.

"I know."

"Then use it properly." Maggie smacked him in the shoulder, but the impact made her knuckles crack. Just what was this guy made of?

"What makes you so angry all the time?" he inquired.

Her eyes flashed.

"You don't know anything about me."

"I know that you have a knack for gettin' into trouble, and you never say thank you."

Maggie told him to do something with himself that would have made Lily gasp in horror. Maggie hated it when he laughed; his mirth replaced what should have been angry indignation.

"Does that usually work, sayin' things like that to people to get them to leave you alone?"

"Do you think I would still be doing it if it didn't?"

"Wouldn't surprise me."

Kyle released her when they reached the lobby.

"Are you sure you're gonna be okay?"

His voice had reverted to gentle tones. She turned to reply but, strangely, he wasn't looking at her. Maggie swallowed. His concern absorbed her anger and enticed her to voice thoughts she hadn't intended on revealing.

"I'm not sure. The odds aren't looking good, considering I've been attacked two days in a row."

Kyle's face was earnest when he finally turned toward her.

"Look I didn't mean to make you mad, Mags."

Unaccustomed warmth spread through her. She could feel her body tremble. What strange ability allowed him to pierce her so completely? Its simplicity terrified her.

"Thank you. For yesterday," she whispered quietly, hoping he wouldn't hear.

A small look of shock flitted across Kyle's face before it resumed its original grin. As he opened his mouth to reply, she interrupted.

"But stop calling me Mags!"

And she walked through the front door toward the flashing red and blue lights.

4: Minds Over Matters

Monday came as usual and the world seemed blithely unaware that Maggie's life was suddenly an episode of some late-night horror show. She stood in the doorway of the school for 10 minutes, observing her peers. Girls giggled in the hallways, whispering anecdotes concerning their latest romantic interest and boys discussed the newest improvements to their cars. Apparently, the horrible events of Maggie's weekend had evaded the popular gossip circles of Bonneville High.

It was a relief. Maggie regularly dodged attention and questions regarding her personal life, and the happenings of the weekend were sure to provoke both.

It was difficult for Maggie to enter the school assuming life would continue as normal. The attack in the projection booth haunted her thoughts. At random moments, the memory of empty, dead eyes would loom before her. She found herself jumping nervously at small disturbances and checking over her shoulder frequently in paranoia. The more she tried to banish it, the more her weekend experience felt like a dream, especially here at school where everything was ordinary. Was there a possibility that she had imagined those eyes? Too many details surrounding the event didn't make enough sense to be real. She almost believed it was all an outrageous hallucination to dispel the Lily-less Saturday. But Maggie couldn't deny the presence of black blood that still coated the heel of her shoe, or the blue turtleneck she wore to hide the abrasions on her neck.

Lily. Maggie had never before found herself dreading her best friend's return. She doubted she could hide the two attacks from the blonde's uncanny perception. Maggie couldn't care less if the entire school thought she was crazy—but she worried that Lily might find the story a little too far out. Lily had never doubted Maggie, ever. And Maggie had never lied to Lily—teased, maybe, but honesty was an important part of their friendship. What if Lily didn't believe her?

Tears pricked Maggie's eyes while she delved through her locker to find the items she would need for her next two classes. She stuffed them into her bag a little more vigorously then was necessary. She had to compose herself quickly. Kyle was likely to ambush her at any moment; he had an aptitude for showing up at the most inconvenient times. She needed to be in control of herself if she was going to get rid of him.

The thought of Kyle inflamed her with frustration. The universe must be mocking her. What was the probability that someone she had just met would share her most terrifying experiences? Maggie didn't need anyone's protection, and she intended to keep it that way. Kyle's personality continually itched her temper—especially his fondness for nicknames. To make matters worse, Maggie was positive Kyle intended to start a relationship. That would be impossible to keep from Lily, who, no doubt, would try to persuade Maggie to date him. But this time Maggie's excuses would prove inadequate. Even Maggie couldn't deny it. There was something different about Kyle Spencer.

Maggie trudged into English and assumed her usual seat in the back just as the final bell rang. Coach Thomas swaggered into the room, teasing and joking with everyone he saw. Maggie liked the coach; he was a strict teacher, but understood she wanted to be left alone. That was probably because the one day he had called on her, she had chosen to explain in great detail how he ranked as a substandard teacher. But, every so often, the coach surprised her by producing an abnormally good lesson. Unfortunately, today was not one of those days, so Maggie rested her head against the wall and let Coach Thomas' lesson be unconsciously absorbed. He called out for a group unison answer.

"Homer," Maggie answered.

No one had recited with her. Startled, Maggie looked up at her teacher. He stopped lecturing and stared at her oddly. The rest of the class looked confused.

"I wasn't quite there yet, but you're right Maggie, *The Odyssey* was written by Homer." Coach Thomas continued to look at her suspiciously.

Maggie broke eye contact. This wasn't her idea of a successful class. The coach was supposed to be ignoring her. Her peers should be overlooking her existence. The instruction continued and Maggie refrained from further participation. She was the first to exit the room when the bell rang and she sped through the halls quickly, so as to avoid any potential encounter with Kyle. She was, therefore, the first to arrive in computer technology.

Mrs. Collean never actually taught class. Instead, she would put instructions on the board, return to her desk, and proceed to lose herself in a book. Once in a while, she would poke her head up from behind the pages and discipline someone for whispering too loud, then disappear behind the novel once again. This provided Maggie with a perfect opportunity to spend quality time with the Internet. She had just entered her login and password when she was interrupted by an unpleasant event.

"Hey Mags, how's the weather?"

Maggie swore under her breath. Kyle had managed to enroll in one of her classes. Most of the students had already chosen seats—as far away from Maggie as possible. Only one remained unoccupied—the seat on her left—and Kyle slid casually into it. He smiled at her, slinging his coat around the back of her chair. Annoying butterflies formed in her stomach.

Is it too much to ask for a break? she complained to herself.

"Can you believe how lucky I am? I was hopin' I'd get to see you today."

Maggie grimaced and turned from his dazzling eyes to her computer screen. Her reply was curt.

"Well, that makes one of us."

Her statement seemed to amuse him. The challenge had commenced. "Do you ever smile, or are you worried you might wrinkle that perfect face of yours?"

"I don't think that's any of your business."

Maggie refused to look at him. Opening a window into cyberspace, she promptly entered the address to her favorite movie database. The bell rang, signaling the start of class and Kyle lowered his voice to circumvent Mrs. Collean's notice.

"Maybe so, but when someone's tryin' to be nice, usually you return the favor."

"What are you, my conscience?" Maggie returned.

She snarled when her computer screen indicated that her beloved site had been blocked.

"Maybe I should be, since you don't seem to have one."

Kyle reached over and turned her keyboard in his direction.

"Just leave me alone."

She tried to take the keyboard back, but he held it firm. His fingers zoomed across it skillfully.

"Why's it so hard for you to let people help?" His captivating gaze successfully deflected her glare.

"I don't need anyone's help," she retorted.

She tried the glare again.

"Didn't look like that at the football game or the movie theater. It seems like you need more help than you think."

The glare thawed into something else—shame.

"I can take care of myself," Maggie admonished as she returned to the monitor.

Kyle replaced her keyboard and leaned back in his chair.

"Of course you can."

Maggie slowly inhaled, trying to suppress her temper's flame. Her fingers were shaking with restrained emotion. She wasn't trying to spare Kyle from her heated retorts—he totally deserved it—but she wasn't entirely confident that she could control the volume of her voice. Mrs. Collean would definitely react to that.

Concentrating on the computer in an attempt to distract herself from Kyle, she entered the title of a new movie into her web browser. Abruptly she stopped. Kyle had liberated her movie site. She unwillingly snapped in his direction. Kyle grinned.

"Do you find something humorous?" Maggie's voice was ice.

"Yeah. You."

It couldn't be possible. Kyle's smile nearly doubled in size. Maggie detested how attractive it was—a normal girl would have swooned. Luckily, Maggie wasn't normal. She replied carefully, keeping her voice low and her eyes away from his face.

"Sorry, not interested. Try one of the cheerleaders. They're always looking for a new boy toy."

Kyle let his chair fall forward.

"You don't get it. You try so hard to get rid of people, but you don't realize some of us like a challenge." He leaned toward her, halting his lips just a breath away from her ear and whispered, " 'Specially one with eyes like yours, Sparky. Personally, I like it when you glare at me. Your eyes have this kind of glint—"

Maggie's heart throbbed. Half of her wanted to blush, but the other desired violence. No one had ever flustered and enraged her all at once. It was impossible to discourage him; it looked as though he would never leave her alone. She couldn't manage to generate an adequate response. For the second time, Maggie lost an exchange of words with Kyle.

A female voice interrupted Maggie's musings, hostility etched into every syllable.

"How can he smile when sitting next to that bitch?"

Maggie turned to see Samantha Hodges, sitting one row closer to the board, peering haughtily over her shoulder. The bleach-blond snatched glimpses of Kyle repeatedly, hoping to merit his notice. Maggie's temperament finally burst. Kyle's infuriating flirtation combined with Samantha's comment opened the floodgates of rage.

"Why don't you keep that kind of crap to yourself?" Maggie returned caustically.

Samantha recoiled under Maggie's fury, curling her lip in response.

"Why are you talking to me? I didn't do anything."

"You know exactly what I mean. Turn around and mind your own business."

Mrs. Collean sent a loud "shush" in their direction. Maggie's eyes narrowed until Samantha followed instructions, then Maggie faced Kyle, fully prepared to defend her actions. Surprisingly, his expression wasn't the expected glower of disapproval. It reflected contemplation instead. He slipped quick glances between Maggie and her prey, as if he was accumulating information. Maggie was tired of his unpredictable responses.

"What?" she gasped, exasperated.

"Nothing." He shook his head faintly but his expression remained unchanged.

Maggie opened her mouth to counter his non-descriptive clarification but was suddenly interrupted by multiple student comments.

"I hope Jonathan asks me to go to homecoming with him."

"Kyle just looked at me! I wonder if I should say something to him? But what if it sounds stupid?"

"Three hours of football practice today, Coach must be crazy."

Maggie scanned the room in shock. Mrs. Collean never tolerated any talking in her class. Maggie glanced in the teacher's direction. Mrs. Collean's face was completely hidden inside the book. She hadn't reprimanded any of the speakers. Students continued their chatter.

"I know I put those pictures on my flash drive."

"My mom's gonna kill me when she finds out I'm failing science."

"Will this class ever end?"

An abrupt pain erupted sharply in Maggie's forehead. Reflexively, she shut her eyes as bright spots burst inside her head. The comments were getting louder, as if each person was vying to drown out the others. The noise was unbearable.

"Mags? You okay?"

Maggie glanced in Kyle's direction. His hand lay gently on her shoulder and his eyes were heavy with worry. Maggie didn't know what she disliked more, the pain in her head or the burning sensation his touch generated throughout her body.

"I'm fine," she lied, brushing his hand away. "I have a headache, that's all."

Kyle obviously didn't believe her. She could only imagine her appearance. Her eyebrows were creased in pain and the color had most likely fled her face. Her hands had also begun to shake and she couldn't hide them fast enough to escape Kyle's notice.

"Really, I'm just fine," she persisted.

Maggie wished her head would clear so she could think.

"Maggie Brooks, stop talking!"

Mrs. Collean glowered over her book, aggravated that Maggie had interrupted the flow of her reading. A second stabbing penetrated her skull, a searing flame that throbbed where her neck met the base of her head. Maggie dropped her face in her hands.

"I love it when teachers yell at her."

"Wonder what she and Spencer were talking about? He looks upset."

"I bet Kyle was teaching her a lesson in manners. She's such a jerk all the time."

Maggie shoved her chair back. This was completely unacceptable. Today was supposed to be normal. Everything in her life suddenly defied reality. And Maggie had no doubt that, somehow, it was entirely Kyle Spencer's fault. Seizing her bag, she threw it over her shoulder and sprang for the door.

"Maggie, where are you going?" Mrs. Collean cried in outrage.

Maggie didn't respond, but escaped into the hallway as fast as possible. She pushed her way through a group of students en route to the library and turned at the nearest hallway junction. She could see the exit to the parking lot. So close.

Not close enough.

"Gotta catch Mags before she disappears," Kyle's voice broke into her thoughts.

Maggie was tired of his conversation. She was determined to halt his pursuit.

"What do you want, Kyle? Just get lost!" she yelled ungraciously.

All traffic in the hallway stopped. Apparently, her peers felt inspired to intercede into her business.

"What is her problem?"

"I can't believe she yelled at Kyle Spencer. He didn't even say anything to her."

Maggie tried to ignore their voices. Why couldn't they leave her alone? It was then that she realized Kyle stood 50 feet away. How had he managed to talk to her without shouting? He looked at her, thoughtfully puzzled. She pushed open the glass doors, desperate for any kind of relief. Kyle caught up to her halfway to her car.

"Are you sure you're feelin' okay, Mags? You don't look so good."

The concern in his voice sounded genuine. Maggie ignored it.

"Don't call me that."

"You didn't answer my question."

Maggie spun around angrily, angling her pain-inspired fury fully in his direction.

"Kyle, just leave me alone!"

"Nice try, but you can't scare me off, Sparky."

Her eyes flashed.

"My name is Maggie, Kyle, not Mags, and definitely not Sparky!"

"There's no need to get angry," Kyle returned quizzically. "I didn't call you Sparky today."

Kyle's expression was sincere, but his response made no sense. She had definitely heard him use the nickname. What was he trying to do, cover an awkward moment? Confuse the hell out of her so she'd jump passionately into his arms? The last option lingered seductively in her imagination. She cursed herself. Since Kyle's arrival, nothing but disastrous events had infused her life. Why couldn't he just move back to California? Maggie ventured a bolt to her car.

"Hold it, Mags."

Kyle stepped in Maggie's path before she had time to escape. "I didn't mean to upset you. I was just worried, that's all."

"Well, I don't need your concern. Back off."

Maggie made to dodge around him, but he was quicker than she anticipated.

"So what time should I pick you up tonight?" he prodded as she unlocked her car.

"Keep dreaming, Spencer," she retorted as she climbed in the driver's seat.

"It's all that keeps me going, Princess." He grinned as she slammed the door.

*

Monday nights were Maggie's least favorite of the week. It meant a night of dullness without Lily. Her best friend's family spent the evening together on a regular basis. Lily never missed one. A few times Maggie had joined them. Those had been ruinous evenings.

As a result, Monday had become homework night. Maggie wasn't interested enough in school to pressure herself with achievement, but she was cautious enough to accomplish the work required to maintain average grades. With a trigonometry assignment in front of her and a cup of coffee to recharge her frying brain cells, she discovered the ability to offset her lonely state. A few hours later her concentration was so engrossed in homework that she almost missed a knock on her door.

The loud rap startled her, and she was uncertain if she should answer. The only person with an open invitation to visit was Lily. The fact that it was Monday night ruled out that possibility, plus Tara Brooks' friends knew Maggie's mom was out of town for work. It was the third probability that prompted Maggie to reach for the closest available weapon. The last few days had been unreal, punctuated by outlandish attacks and weird events. After the fiasco at school today, Maggie doubted things were likely to change.

The knock was louder the second time. Snatching a knife from a kitchen drawer and hiding it behind her back, she cautiously approached front door. It was unfortunate that her small home lacked windows anywhere near the entryway. She made a mental note to ask her mother to install a peephole.

Third knock. Maggie decided that surprise would be her best defense. She yanked open the door and launched her weapon at the same time.

Kyle Spencer caught her wrist easily. The knife dangled limply in her hand. His dark blue shirt was only buttoned halfway, allowing a white undershirt to effectively hug the contours of his muscled chest. A black leather jacket loosely framed his body and he carried a red backpack over his shoulder. The color combination enhanced the warm hue of his hazel eyes. They flickered with delight as Maggie gaped at him in open-mouthed astonishment.

"What are you doing here?" Maggie finally sputtered, ripping her arm from his grasp.

"You didn't tell me what time to pick you up, so I figured 6:30 would be safe."

"I vividly remember rejecting your offer," Maggie rebuffed.

Kyle shrugged, and a brazen smile crept across his face.

"You said keep dreamin'. I figured that meant to keep tryin'."

"Well you figured wrong. How did you know where I live?"

"Magic," he said charismatically. "You mind if I come in?"

Maggie battled inside herself. Her choices were simple: face the evening alone or risk encouraging his interest. She toyed with the idea of slamming the door in his face. It probably wouldn't deter him in the least. Maggie chose the less dramatic route and moved aside to let him pass.

"Thanks," he said, brushing past her in the entryway.

He must have done it on purpose. His alluring cologne virtually froze her into a stupor. The scent lasted only a second as he passed. If she wanted to experience it again, she'd have to sit near him, almost touching…

Angrily she threw the door closed. Stomping into the kitchen, she tossed the paring knife into the sink.

"Were you expectin' trouble?" he asked.

Maggie turned toward him but refused to look up. Her eyes remained locked on the dirty linoleum floor.

"After the last few days, it wouldn't surprise me."

His feet moved closer. Kyle's hand swept aside a stray strand of hair clinging to her face. Gently, he slid his fingers down her skin to the top of her turtleneck sweater and pulled aside the collar, examining the hidden bandages protecting her wounds. Maggie could feel the pulse of her blood. Her fingertips tingled.

"You were pretty upset today." He had moved so close that his lips were almost touching her hair. "You doin' any better?"

Maggie hated how his concern melted into her, like he was a part of herself that she had lost long ago. Cold chills scrambled up her spine and she swept his hand away in response. He was uncomfortably close. She felt her cheeks burn with a blush. There was no way she would let Kyle see that! The living room looked to be her most effectual escape option.

"I'm fine," she exaggerated, walking into the next room and plopping down on the couch. "Look, I have homework—"

Kyle chuckled. Maggie hated it when he chuckled. It meant he was one step ahead of her.

"I figured you'd say that, so I brought our date with me."

He invited himself to sit next to her and removed his backpack. He began to pull cords and equipment from its cavity.

"This isn't a date." Maggie was frustrated that he wasn't intimidated.

"Okay, have it your way." Kyle produced a video game console from his bag. "Not a date. I just brought entertainment with me."

She grimaced.

"How do I get rid of you?" she asked rhetorically.

"For tonight?" His amusement impelled her antagonism.

"How about forever?"

Kyle laughed quietly as he spoke. "Well I don't know about forever, but for tonight you just have to hang with me."

"And then you'll leave me alone?" Maggie intended on getting something out of this disaster.

"I'll even promise to behave myself," he said, sidestepping the question and feigning innocence.

"And tomorrow?" she persisted stubbornly.

"Can't make any guarantees." Kyle stopped arranging the cords and looked at her.

"Two hours, and then you're gone," Maggie conceded.

"Three," he bargained.

She sighed angrily, knowing she would never win the argument.

"Fine."

Kyle hooked up the machine with little effort. She watched him, almost as if she couldn't help herself. She wondered if that blue shirt was long or short sleeved. He inserted a game and tossed her a controller. He peeled the jacket off. She forgot to breathe.

Short sleeves. Maggie looked at the television. She didn't need another reason to blush.

It only took her a few minutes to get the hang of Kyle's game. She'd never played it before, but was mildly surprised to discover that she enjoyed it. Maybe too much. She perversely wanted to hate everything Kyle liked. After hours of playing, however, she glanced at the clock.

"Turn it off," she said suddenly, throwing her controller to the floor.

"Why? There's only one level left."

"It's two in the morning. I've filled my quota for at least two days of your company."

"Alright, alright," Kyle agreed. Maggie was surprised he didn't argue further. He switched the game off and turned to look at her. "Next time we'll have to invite that friend of yours."

He slid closer to her. Maggie reacted by shifting away.

"Who? Lily?"

"Yeah, I hear she's quite the girl. People only say good things about her."

Did he think talking about Lily would somehow make her jealous? And how did he know about Lily anyway? Maggie was determined to win this conversation. In her mind she flitted through the possible strategies he might take.

"Doesn't surprise me. She's nice to everyone," she countered guardedly.

"So you guys are opposites." He leaned in nonchalantly. "Explains why you're friends."

Maggie tilted away but met the arm of the couch.

"So what if it does?" Kyle had edged her into a corner. "What does it matter to you?"

"I want to know everythin' about you. Isn't that obvious?"

"Don't get your hopes up. If I have my way, you'll never know anything about me," Maggie snapped.

She wondered how it would look if she moved to the floor. Probably like she was losing. She decided to stay where she was.

"I know that you blush whenever I'm near you."

Kyle's blunt statement infuriated her, mostly because it was true and she had convinced herself that he hadn't noticed.

"Are all football players this dense? You mistake blushing for disgust."

Kyle didn't even miss a beat.

"I bet you want to kiss me, don't you?" he said.

Maggie couldn't answer. His question alarmed her. What if he actually did kiss her? Maggie was sure her anxiety was reflected in her expression.

"You're such a jerk," Maggie stated, faking indifference.

Kyle laughed and stood to retrieve his equipment. For a few seconds he was mute as he stuffed all his accessories into his backpack.

Did you forget? I promised to behave myself.

"I wish you'd promise to leave," Maggie returned impatiently.

Can't do that, Sparky.

Maggie jumped to her feet.

"My name is not Sparky."

Kyle slung his bag over his shoulder and turned to face her.

"I knew it."

"Knew what?!" she yelled.

His smile grew ominously wide. *You've been reading my thoughts.*

"What? That's crazy." Maggie was distinctly aware that his lips had not moved.

Clearly, he thought, *not as crazy as you think*.

He walked to the door and opened it. Turning back from the threshold, he paused to say goodbye.

Sleep well, Blue Eyes.

She sat unmoving on the edge of the couch for a few moments after Kyle had left. He was right. The ability to read minds wasn't crazy. It was insane.

5: Lips Unsealed

"My mom was ruthless! She was so worried that one of my little brothers might catch whatever I had that I couldn't even leave my room. Did Mark ask about me? I can't wait to see him!"

Maggie found herself surrounded with sunshine and butterflies. As soon as she had crossed the school's threshold, she heard a squeak of delight off to the right. Lily nearly suffocated Maggie with the fervor of her greeting. Silver-gold curls bounced cheerfully around Lily's shoulders, ribbon bedecked to reflect her eagerness to rejoin her best friend. Lily's smile practically sparkled around her; its natural brightness effectively pushed the shadows of Maggie's weekend into retreat. With Lily present, Maggie could face anything.

Including a certain hazel-eyed aggravation.

Maggie pried herself from Lily's grasp, and her best friend's musical voice launched into a lengthy tirade detailing her four-day confinement. Maggie's heart lurched with joy. The longest she and Lily had ever been separated was a couple of days, and though she had accepted the inspirational effect Lily instigated in her life, Maggie had never before felt its presence with such poignancy.

"She even confiscated my cell phone!" Lily continued. "I had to sit in bed and read the same books over and over."

Everything suddenly seemed so normal that Maggie loathed to dispel it. She knew there was no way to keep her evening with Kyle a secret. Lily's romance radar would ferret that one out in a heartbeat, but Maggie felt apprehensive about discussing the two attacks she had suffered. Lily was bound to overreact to Trent's attack and the incident at the movie theater. And then there was the whole reading minds phenomenon. Would Lily think she was crazy? Maggie decided to let Lily dominate the conversation as they walked to trigonometry. Unfortunately, Kyle's face kept resurfacing in Maggie's mind. Consequently, she missed Lily's next question twice.

"Maggie? Maggie? Are you even listening? I was asking if you went to the game on Friday," Lily said as they entered the classroom.

"Uh-huh," Maggie retuned distractedly.

Lily set her books on the desk and scrutinized Maggie from sloppy ponytail to pleather booted toe.

"Something happened." It wasn't a question. Lily paused speculatively. "Spill it."

"Spill what?" Maggie rebuffed, hoping to forestall the conversation.

"Whatever's bothering you," Lily insisted.

"Nothing's bothering me," Maggie shrugged, but knew she wasn't likely to deter Lily.

Her best friend had a knack for extracting information with those innocent ice-green eyes.

"Nice try, Maggie, but I know you better than you know yourself. Something is definitely up." Lily pursed her lips and raised an eyebrow.

There was no alternative. Maggie surrendered, at least partially—to buy some time to think.

"Look, I promise to tell you everything, but not until lunch. It's really nothing big, but it could take a while."

Lily looked puzzled. Usually Maggie told her everything, regardless of its interruption of class. Lily obviously thought it was unusual, but didn't seem concerned over the delay and agreed to the condition. Maggie might have avoided the issue for a few more hours if it hadn't been for Mark.

When he drifted into class, his face plastered in a goofy grin, Maggie actually breathed an internal sigh of relief. Lily would be entirely distracted; no unfair prodding for information in-between math problems. Mark, of course, screwed everything up when he opened his mouth.

"Hey look, it's my favorite flower!" he greeted Lily as he plopped on the table. Lily giggled. Maggie rolled her eyes. "Maggie, are you feeling better? I thought you were going to pass out at the game. I think you actually turned green."

Lily's head snapped toward Maggie with an almost panicked expression. Maggie gleefully entertained the thought of slapping him. Though Maggie had been ignoring most of the alien thoughts buzzing around her head this morning, she was unprepared for the force of Lily's sudden distress.

Oh my gosh, this is more serious than I thought. I can't believe my mom took my cell phone!

Lily's thought caused Maggie to wince with pain.

"Are you okay?" Lily prompted, touching Maggie's arm lightly.

"Fine. At lunch okay?"

They took their seats as Mrs. James entered the classroom. Lily peeked concernedly toward Maggie throughout the hour and a half of math, but Maggie pretended not to notice. Mark, however, was the recipient of some intense glances of distaste. Her mind sifted through possible approaches to her dilemma. All the while one question loomed savagely at the forefront of her mind: Just what should she tell Lily?

*

"What?!" Lily's eager reaction was hardly unexpected.

"It's nothing to get excited over." Maggie tried, unsuccessfully, to skim over the subject of Kyle Spencer. Lily of course couldn't hear enough of him.

"Are you kidding? I've never heard you even mention a guy who wasn't covered in zombie gore! This is the best news ever. We can go on double dates! Mark just loves Kyle. Tell me everything again. And, this time, don't leave out the details."

"I said it's no big deal." Maggie had known Lily would be fixated on the almost date with the football hunk portion of the story, but the mention of double-dating incited a moment of unease. The movie theater zombies would be easier to face! "I only hung out with him because you were unavailable. If I had known he was going to make me play that stupid super soldier game all night I would have kicked him out."

"But you love video games," Lily protested, shock evident in her expression.

"I like RPGs and zombie shooters," Maggie argued, biting into her sandwich.

Lily sighed in frustration. One video game looked the same as another to her. There was a moment of vexed silence as the two friends pondered the next verbal parry. Lily finally quashed the stillness.

"You just don't like to play anything you can't win."

"Exactly. Hence my evening was miserable."

"Maggie, would it kill you to give him a chance?"

"It might."

"I don't understand why you hate him so much. He's obviously completely in to you," Lily observed as she munched on a carrot stick. Her expression turned shrewd. "In fact, you seem to hate him more than you hate most boys."

"Because he's more annoying than most boys," Maggie countered, too quickly. "He doesn't know when to quit."

The look of comprehension on Lily's face was like a death sentence to Maggie.

"You like him don't you?"

"Absolutely not!" Maggie said as she opened her soda more forcefully then she intended. She cursed as it detonated all over her lunch and clothes. "Every bad thing that happened this weekend was his fault."

Lily produced some napkins and cleaned the mess off the lunch table while Maggie attempted to salvage her jacket.

"Was your weekend really that bad?"

"Yes. Kyle wouldn't leave me alone," Maggie answered, so engrossed in cleaning duty that she neglected her own comments. "He practically stalked me."

"Maggie, I'm sure he just likes you. I bet he's really cute. What does he look like?" Lily's tone was enchanted with delight.

"He's 200 pounds of pure sarcasm," Maggie snorted irritably.

Lily didn't notice.

"I bet he's tall," she fancied. "You wouldn't like him if he wasn't tall. And strong! He'd have to be, since he's the new quarterback."

"Lily it doesn't—"

"What color are his eyes?"

"I don't remember," Maggie lied.

"They're probably warm and romantic," Lily supposed with a dreamy sigh. "He's perfect for you."

"It doesn't matter what he looks like," Maggie spat stubbornly. "I hate him."

She slammed her soggy sandwich onto her soda-soaked plate and kicked her bag vehemently under the table. Lily immediately turned anxious. Desperate to calm her temper, Maggie sucked in a loud breath and exhaled slowly.

"Okay, there's no way any guy could have worked you up this much, no matter how much you pretend not to like him. What else happened?"

Maggie felt uneasy about relating this part of the anecdote. She knew that the confrontation after the football game was not her fault, but that knowledge did little to prevent the debasement she felt. She evaded eye contact with Lily.

"Do you remember when I embarrassed Trent the other day?" Maggie started, almost timidly.

Lily nodded and Maggie recited the episode with Trent. Her life had plunged into such a chaotic discord of unbelievable events since that first attack that the initial fear surrounding Trent's assault had been smothered. Dredging up the memory produced a storm of concealed emotions that caused her voice to shake and her hands to tremble. When Maggie finally looked up, hushed tears streaked the porcelain surface of Lily's skin. Maggie's new ability failed to reveal Lily's exact thoughts, but the deep unconditional force of love issuing from Lily's mind washed the remembered horror and mortification of the event from Maggie's consciousness.

"We have to tell someone," Lily demanded, wiping her face. "Trent had no right to treat you that way."

"No," Maggie stated firmly, "I've had my fair share of attention the last few days. I don't need any more."

"Maggie, this is serious. You have to tell someone."

"It doesn't matter, there's more to the story, Lil."

Lily looked incredulous as Maggie related the weirder parts of her weekend: the black shrouded men in the projection booth with the flat, dead eyes; Kyle's timely appearance whenever she seemed to be in danger; and the wave of sickness she had felt at the football game. Still, Maggie withheld disclosing her mind reading ability. Maybe she wouldn't be forced to tell Lily about that at all.

"All I know is," Maggie continued when Lily's shock seemed to subside somewhat, "my life is suddenly full of idiotic men."

A moment passed in silence.

"I don't think Trent could have been behind the attack at the movie theater," Lily said. A swell of relief enveloped Maggie. Her best friend hadn't asked intrusive questions; she hadn't doubted Maggie's sincerity. Lily accepted Maggie's interpretation of events, despite their implausibility. "Even if his ego was hurt, it all sounds too strange."

"What else could it be? Someone obviously has a grudge against me."

"I don't know. But I doubt it could have been Trent. It all started with you getting sick. And then Kyle showing up every time you needed him. It's too coincidental." *He's like your knight in shining armor.*

"More like a shining pain in the ass," Maggie snarled.

Lily had been staring at her hands, perplexed, but Maggie's statement caused her to look up in astonishment. Maggie cursed herself, realizing that Lily's last comment must have come from the mind. Lily leaned forward across the table, staring pointedly into Maggie's eyes. Maggie feigned confusion.

"Lil, what are you doing?"

Lily moved closer, barely an inch from Maggie's face.

"What aren't you telling me?" Lily persisted.

"What do you mean?"

"How did you do that?"

"Do what?"

"You read my mind."

"What are you talking about?"

"You responded to something I thought but didn't say."

"That's ridiculous, Lily."

You're in love with Kyle.

"What?"

You like him and you know it!

"Stop it. I don't like him."

"Oh my gosh, you can read my mind!" Lily squeaked with excitement as she moved back to her chair. She rearranged her features into a mock expression of mystical sobriety and wiggled her fingers in a mesmerizing manner. She dropped her voice into a low pitch. "What am I thinking right now?"

Maggie sighed. "You're hoping that Mark is a prince in disguise and at homecoming he'll whisk you off to his secret fairy tale castle."

Lily giggled for a few minutes, apparently expanding her prince charming fantasy until Maggie interrupted with a clearing of her throat.

"Wow, Maggie, this is a fantastic gift! Think of all the good you could do."

"Or think of how annoyed I will be. I'm hearing things that aren't meant to be heard. You don't think that's a little weird, or terrifying?"

"Maybe," Lily admitted, "but you were clearly meant to have it. There are so many people you could help."

"I don't want to help people. I just want things to return to normal."

"Normal's boring, Sparky," Kyle said, sliding into the seat next to Maggie and putting his arm around the back of her chair. "Why don't you introduce me to Sunshine here?"

Maggie grimaced at Kyle's arrival and prepared a retort. She expected a maidenly giggle from Lily's direction—Kyle was incredibly attractive after all—but was mildly surprised at its absence. She looked toward Lily quizzically, only to discover that her best friend's face had completely drained of color. Staring torpidly ahead, Lily swayed dangerously in her chair, and Maggie was suddenly concerned that her best friend might faint. Leaping from her chair, Maggie snapped around in Kyle's direction to see if he could help. To her dismay, Kyle gawked numbly at Lily, his pallor the same shade of unnatural white. Sweat trickled down his temple.

"What are you guys—"

Maggie didn't finish her statement. An overwhelming onslaught of emotions and impressions bombarded her mind, so entirely jumbled that Maggie couldn't tell which were Lily's and which came from Kyle. Still supporting Lily, Maggie groaned as agitated images burst through her vision. A torrent of metallic resonance crashed inside the back of her head. Darkness exploded into sound as a consciousness—neither Kyle's nor Lily's—danced with chaotic excitement.

It stopped suddenly. Maggie, Kyle, and Lily drew a collective breath, as if something had released them simultaneously. Lily's body trembled. Kyle used his sleeve to wipe the sweat from his face. Maggie felt bile at the edge of her throat.

"Just what," Maggie gasped, "the hell was that?"

*

Tara Brooks spoke excitedly into her cell phone, relating details—his perfect hair, broad shoulders, and likable character—to Linda Ivers concerning her new favorite passenger, some rich businessman from New York. Maggie only heard one side of the conversation as she maneuvered the car through highway traffic. She tuned out most of the details, as usual when her mother discussed a latest love interest. He would be lucky to keep Tara's interest for more than a week.

"You should have seen how incredible he was. He promised to call, but I'm determined not to get my hopes up."

Then Tara paused. Slowly, shock seized her face. Her mother's reaction caused a sliver of panic to curl in Maggie's stomach. Whatever Lily had told her mother, Linda was sure to pass on.

"You're joking—what?! Are you serious? Let me call you back. Bye." Tara snapped her phone shut and turned on Maggie. "You went on a date and didn't call to tell me about it?"

Maggie groaned inwardly. Dodging her mother's questions wasn't going to be easy.

"I didn't go on a date, mom. I just hung out."

"All by yourself, just you and him?"

"Yes."

"Then it was a date. Is he cute? What's he like?"

"He's infuriating. I don't even like him. Lily was sick, and I didn't want to be home alone."

Tara didn't waver. "But is he cute?"

"It doesn't matter, mom. I'm never going to hang out with him again."

"Maggie you're almost 18. It's about time you had a boyfriend."

"Mom, can we please talk about something else?" Maggie's patience had expired.

"Not until you answer me. Is he cute?"

"I guess—if you like the all-star jock type."

"Hmm, sounds like a winner. Did you kiss him?"

Now Maggie's temper lashed outward. Of all the terrible things happening to her, discussing Kyle with her mom was the most embarrassing.

"Different subject mom. And no, I would never kiss him. Ever."

"Okay, I don't need you to tell me. I bet you already told Lily all about it. I'll get the juicy details from Linda later."

Maggie sighed. She usually looked forward to the infrequent conversations with her mother. Now, however, Tara's next flight duty seemed too far away.

"What did Lily have? You said she was sick?"

"A fever of some kind. I think she caught a cold when the fire sprinklers went off at the school. Rumor is some idiot turned their burner on too high in the chemistry lab. It got me out of half a day of school though."

"That's why I could never be a teacher. I couldn't handle all the teenage drama."

Tara's thoughts slid unbidden into Maggie's mind. *I can barely handle my own.* Maggie flinched. She was trying hard not to answer unspoken material, but it was difficult to tell which remarks her mother had actually voiced.

"I missed you mom. It's been quiet around the house."

Something's wrong. "Are you okay Maggie? You seem skittish."

"I'm fine. It's just been boring this weekend without you. Especially since Linda put Lily under quarantine."

"That's Linda for you. She's always been a little overprotective. She used to be that way about me before she got married and had kids. Used to drive me crazy."

"Yeah, it drives me crazy now."

Of course, I should be grateful. If Linda hadn't passed that trait down to Lily, Maggie would probably be wild like I was. "I'm sorry your weekend was so boring. We can watch a movie or something—have a mother-daughter night."

Maggie didn't know whether to be thankful or hurt by her mother's thoughts. Tara's undisciplined past had only resulted in strength, something Maggie regarded with respect. But it seemed as if her mother disapproved of Maggie's frequent misbehavior—which was nearly impossible for Tara to curb. Maggie knew herself to be impulsive and stubborn, but she didn't realize it would be so hard to hear her mother mention it.

"Mom, I'm sorry."

"What for Maggie?" *Oh, no, what has she done now?* Tara seemed worried at her daughter's sudden revelation.

"Everything. Mostly my temper."

"You're a teenager Maggie. I don't expect you to be perfect." Maggie could feel her mother's relief pouring outward. "But I would like to know what's wrong."

"Nothing's wrong."

"You're acting pretty strange." *Maybe I should try finding a job that doesn't travel as much.*

"No, I'm fine mom. Don't worry. I'm just glad you're home."

Tara was silent a few moments after this hasty explanation. "It's good to be home," Tara said, finally smiling. "Even if my daughter went on a date and didn't tell me."

"Mom! I told you it wasn't a date!"

6: Between A Friend And A Hard Place

Lily drummed her fingers absently on her desk. The sharp scent of dry-erase marker permeated the room. As usual, fervent science equations sprawled across the four whiteboards that dominated Mr. Warner's classroom. The scritch, scritch, scritch of 20 frantic pencils resounded throughout the otherwise hushed room as a score of students tried, with varying success, to survive their chemistry final.

Student 21, however, suffered from unreserved distraction. Usually Lily attacked her academic assessments with ardor, but today marked the end of an especially savage week. She forced her brain to interpret question five—something involving covalent bonds—but her rebellious eyes kept sliding off her paper and across the desk to assess the figure sitting in the adjacent seat.

Maggie, resplendent in a tight sweater and black fitted jacket, stared with abnormal strain in the direction of Mr. Warner's desk. Every few seconds, Maggie would detach her gaze and scribble something on her test, almost lazily. Then her supernatural concentration would refocus on the teacher. Whenever Mr. Warner lifted his head to scan the behavior of his students, Maggie shifted her attention dutifully to the paper, mere seconds ahead of him. Everyone knew Mr. Warner rewrote his tests every year to prevent cheating. It was also well known that he devised his answer key at the same time his students took the test. Lily had little doubt that Maggie was plucking the answers directly from the science teacher's mind.

Lily's grip on her pencil tightened. She swallowed hard, though her mouth was relatively dry. Blinking rapidly several times, she struggled to decide whether the threat of tears would overwhelm her self-control. Maggie's blatant disregard for honesty was only the latest incident in a stream of selfish behaviors that had troubled Lily's ordinarily optimistic demeanor for the past week.

At first, Maggie had feared her ability, but as soon as she had discovered how to reasonably manage her mind reading powers, she employed the gift for inappropriate matters: revenge, harassment, and now, cheating. Wednesday, Maggie rapturously announced to everyone in the hallways that Elisha Gowers, a member of Katie Maxwell's pack, had orchestrated a secret rendezvous with her best friend's boyfriend after the most recent football game. Maggie harbored a personal vendetta against Elisha that stretched all the way back to the Matt episode. Lily expressed disapproval of Maggie's conduct that day at lunch, but Maggie only laughed satisfactorily. The next morning, Maggie discovered an embarrassing story in Sarah Perkin's mind. Lily acknowledged that Sarah's bearing toward Maggie was less than polite—sometimes it was downright hostile. Still, to Lily's sensibilities, Maggie had no right to disclose the story to half the school. By noon, Sarah's personal humiliation was painfully public.

Lily jumped when the bell rang, nearly dropping her pencil. Sighing, she tossed the half-finished test into the homework basket and hurried out the door. For the first time in her life, she had failed a test.

"That was the easiest 'A' I have ever pulled," Maggie boasted with gleaming bravado, catching Lily in the hallway.

Lily felt the muscles in her back throb with strain. Her answer was decidedly cross.

"Maggie, I can't believe you would—"

Maggie interrupted her smoothly, as if anticipating Lily's reprimand, which, considering Maggie's supernatural abilities, was most likely probable.

"Lil, give me a break. We can't all be superhuman geniuses like you. Cut me some slack. It was only one test!"

Lily pursed her lips in an effort to stifle an angry reply. Her jaw began to ache. Maggie was simply ignoring the possible negative consequences that could result from her newfound moral ambiguity. Maggie changed the subject abruptly.

"Don't forget that I'm leaving school early today because I have to drive to the airport to pick up my mom. Are you sure you have a ride home?'

Lily considered not answering, but knew Maggie wouldn't leave without some assurance. A quiet nod illustrated Lily's acquiescence.

"C'mon Lil, you know I love you to death."

Maggie embraced Lily in a friendly hug that smelled concurrently of hair products and fake leather. Such obvious warmth from her best friend gnawed away the edges of Lily's consternation. As Maggie waved farewell and exited the building, a troubling question sprang into Lily's mind.

Just how many dangers surrounded Maggie's new talent?

*

It was unusually warm for October, and the sun's rays glistened on the football field in the late afternoon. Lily wrapped her arms around her legs and rested her chin on the top of her knees as she perched on the bleachers. The coaches' whistles reached her ears as echoes, distorted by the chanting of the cheerleaders rehearsing in center field. Several of the girls waved cheerily in her direction, so she politely returned the gesture. Lily didn't feel like socializing, however, so she replaced her arm and surveyed the field from the stands.

The football team trained in scattered groups of five or six. Kyle Spencer was easily the most skilled player on the field. As Lily watched, she noticed how he managed to complete every pass, finished first at ladders, and dodged every tackle during the practice plays. He appeared to be a good leader as well; his teammates followed his orders obediently. When he laughed several cheerleaders actually paused mid-routine, huddling together in a mass and pointing in his direction.

Lily smiled to herself. If they wanted to catch Kyle's attention, they were wasting their time. Rarely did Lily believe in destiny, but Kyle's dedication to Maggie was no less than a design of fate. Lily had grown fond of his nonchalant charisma over the past week, and his ardent connection with Maggie only endeared him further. For over two years, Lily had attempted to push Maggie into social associations—ever since that catastrophic business with Matt. Thus far, her efforts were rewarded frugally at best. Kyle's new friendship was sure to help foster the humanity that lurked somewhere inside Maggie's prickly personality.

Oddly though, Lily felt that she had known Kyle all her life. He was like an older brother who had been missing from her family, but she hadn't noticed his absence until he arrived.

"You keep mopin' like that Sunshine, and I'll have to call you Frowns instead of Smiles."

Lily looked up into Kyle's chiseled features, his cheerful smirk lighting his eyes. Practice was over.

"Ready to hit the pavement?" he asked.

"Oh, hey, Kyle," Lily answered, his intrusion scattering her thoughts. She gathered her things absently. "I was just thinking."

Kyle shouldered her bag in a gentlemanly manner.

"About?" he asked as they left the bleachers.

"Maggie."

"Ah, she gives us all a lot to think about," Kyle agreed with a solemn expression. "Go ahead, lay it on me."

"Thanks for the offer, but I don't want to ruin your day with my complaints."

"You're always takin' care of everyone else. How 'bout you let someone else take care 'a you for a change?"

"Well—"

Kyle opened the passenger door of his flamboyant red jeep. Lily slid inside as he tossed their belongings in the back. The sun warmed her skin and a gentle breeze stirred her hair through the open window. Kyle revved the engine and peeled out of the parking lot. Lily remained quiet, wondering if her concerns might damage Kyle's opinion of Maggie. The need to express her anxiety over Maggie's decisions finally overwhelmed Lily's sense of decorum.

"I'm frustrated, furious, and disheartened all at the same time," Lily exuded, hands gesticulating zealously with every word.

"Wow, it's a wonder you don't explode," Kyle interjected.

"Maggie's been given these fantastic powers, but she's using them to hurt people. And to cheat!" Lily's forehead wrinkled, signifying the weight of her accusation.

"Don't be so surprised," Kyle added lightly, but Lily remained undeterred.

"Usually Maggie at least listens to me, but she's completely ignoring my advice. These abilities could be dangerous! What if someone knows and is after her? She's been attacked twice! Who knows if she's giving herself brain damage every time she uses it!" Lily's cacophony of emotions tore through her painfully. Every spoken thought raised her level of distress. "And what if she can't resist the temptation of, say, stealing someone's credit card number or bank account PIN? What if cheating is just the beginning—there are so many terrible things she might choose to do, just because suddenly she can!" Lily's voice broke. Her last statement was barely above a whisper. "And maybe I'm discouraged the most because she just doesn't seem to care."

"She will in time, Smiles. Give Mags some space. My guess is she keeps playin' around with these powers to avoid the truth."

"And what's that?" Lily sniffled and wiped several rogue tears from her cheeks with the back of her hand.

"She knows she's been given a large amount of responsibility, and now she can't keep ignorin' the rest of the world. That scares her. And if there's one thing I've learned about Mags," he grinned, "she hates bein' scared."

Lily managed a timid smile. Kyle's infectious charisma eased a portion of her emotional turmoil. She suddenly felt better for having confided in him.

"She does hate that."

"That," Kyle said conspiratorially, "and me."

Lighthearted laughter escaped Lily's lips. Distracted by her conflicting feelings, she answered without thinking.

"Kyle, she doesn't hate you. I've known her long enough to know when she's—" Lily stopped abruptly, appalled at what she had almost revealed.

"What?"

"I can't tell you," Lily apologized sheepishly. "I probably shouldn't have brought it into the conversation. Let's talk about you instead—you really like her, don't you?"

"Yep," Kyle stated shortly.

Lily waited for him to elaborate. When he didn't, she changed the subject back to her friend.

"I wish I could convince her that she doesn't need to hate everyone."

"That's like tryin' to budge a train from its tracks, Sunshine. But you'll still love her, no matter how much she claims to hate everythin'."

"She wasn't always like this, you know. Angry a lot, for sure, but not so unapproachable. Since high school started, she's pretty much driven away most of her friends. New people don't even try to get to know her. You're the exception of course."

"What can I say? The first time I saw her, I couldn't take my eyes off her. Like those gorgeous blue eyes had me under some spell. She took my breath away before the guy tacklin' me could."

His justification could have been explained as simple physical attraction, but Lily believed something extraordinary had passed between Kyle and Maggie. Her best friend had described her first meeting with Kyle to Lily in detail. Lily recalled it had been so physically painful that Maggie's body had become ill. Was it more than coincidence that her own introduction to Kyle had resulted in an almost faint? She watched the buildings pass in a blur as she mused.

"So this—" Lily was unsure of how to phrase her thoughts without sounding ridiculous, "connection you had with Maggie—what did you feel when it happened?"

Kyle answered instantly, as if he had already pondered the question and determined the answer.

"I just knew I loved her, even before I met her, and meetin' her just let it all out." Kyle flashed his teeth at Lily in a comical exaggeration of a grin. "Why, did she say she felt somethin' back for me?"

"Actually you made her sick."

"Always nice to hear when you make a girl feel that way!" Kyle laughed, though Lily noted a concealed bit of disappointment in the line straining his chin.

Fear that Kyle's determination of pursuing Maggie might diminish caused Lily to explain quickly.

"Maggie told me it was agonizing, like a part of her had died or something, and that's what caused her to be sick. Do you think your connection and her powers are related? She said that you weren't even surprised that she could read people's minds."

"I wasn't. At least not by her havin' powers. Maybe the mind readin' thing did—I wasn't quite expectin' that."

Kyle's confession surprised Lily considerably.

"Then what were you expecting?"

"Honestly, super strength and speed."

Lily looked quizzically at Kyle's profile as the car sped along the highway. His brow furrowed thoughtfully, and his answer was uncharacteristically solemn.

"I've always been really strong, but that doesn't explain why I was able to throw Trent 20 feet with only one hand. The day before I met Mags, I could only bench press 290 pounds. The day after, 290 felt like nothin', so I thought I'd try pushin' myself. I benched 600, probably could have done more but I didn't have enough weights to test it. Suddenly I'm the fastest guy on the team and can dodge every tackle. I figured it must have somethin' to do with what happened between me and Mags." He shrugged. "That made me wonder if she had powers too. I was watchin' to see if anythin' weird happened."

"So both of you have abilities?" Lily blurted in astonishment. "That's fantastic!"

"Are you kiddin', Smiles? Gettin' super powers is cool and all, but bein' different isn't always the best. I've become what most people would call a freak. And I look terrible in yellow spandex!" Kyle chuckled heartily as Lily wrinkled her nose in confusion.

"Yellow spandex?"

"You know, from—never mind. I was just happy that I wasn't alone."

"Kyle, I don't believe anyone would ever think of you as a freak."

Kyle forced the brakes, ejecting a scream from the jeep's tires as they pulled in front of Lily's house. The Ivers' family home settled comfortably on a well-manicured lawn between two gigantic lodgepole pine trees. Needles littered the walk.

"Keep thinkin' that if you want, Smiles." Kyle turned the key and the engine quieted. He turned to face her. "It's always nice to have someone like you around. You only see the best in people."

Lily smiled as she gathered her schoolwork from the back seat.

"You know, it's possible that meeting each other triggered your powers, but on the other hand, you might have always had them locked up somehow. Maggie has always had a knack for guessing what other people were feeling or going to do. Maybe meeting you just brought them out."

"It's possible," Kyle considered as Lily exited the vehicle, "but then shouldn't you have powers too?"

Lily poked her head back in through the open window.

"Me? Why? I'm not like you and Maggie. I mean, you guys developed powers barely hours after you met."

Kyle shook his head. "I felt somethin' odd when I met you too, Sunshine. All I remember is a darkness fulla pain—then all of a sudden, it was gone. What about you?"

Lily pressed her lips in thought. The wind whispered musically through the trees during the few minutes of calm, bringing the sweet smell of pine into the jeep. Lily wondered how to explain to Kyle what she had felt; words seemed inadequate to describe the chaos that had ripped through her during his introduction. A presence had leapt outward from his body and bored painfully into her consciousness. The invading force danced throughout her mind, touching parts of her personality with a wild sense of recognition. Its hectic investigations had almost caused her to black out. Lily had felt a part of Kyle, yet this new entity had been somehow disconnected, a force of life energy. Its nature was comprised of such complexity that Lily almost lost her sense of self when she had tried to analyze it.

"Um, I'm not sure I want to tell you," Lily finally admitted.

"Why not?"

"It's sort of strange. It felt, like, almost another side of your personality, something that seems to be a part of you, yet isn't. It was really confusing. And, kind of—well—girly. With giggling."

Kyle blinked quickly, scratching his head. His eyes emitted a spark of amusement and curiosity.

"Gigglin' huh? That doesn't sound like me."

"Sorry, I warned you."

"Don't worry about it." Kyle dismissed the feminine side of himself away with a wave of his hand. "I haven't lost my manly ego just 'cause I giggle like a girl."

"I could have sworn it recognized me," Lily continued, "and it was almost, welcoming me. Like—like, the way someone would react if they saw an old friend from years past."

"Weird."

"Yeah. Strange how all this supernatural stuff started happening as soon as you moved here. I wonder why both me and Maggie had such crazy reactions to you and never to each other?"

"That's an interestin' thought," Kyle reflected. "Wait. You two have known each other since you were little, right?"

"Since we were babies."

"Maybe you did have one and you were just too young to remember it."

Lily gasped in astonishment. "Holy Moses, you may be right."

"Moses?" Kyle wrinkled his forehead.

"Oh sorry, it's just something my dad says whenever someone in our family has an epiphany."

Kyle laughed. "Holy Moses it is then."

7: Empty Dance Card

Nearly two weeks passed without incident—Maggie's fear wilted as days piled in front of her horrifying episodes. Black clothed figures with dead flat eyes became phantasms sprung from too many sleepless hours in front of video game consoles and horror films.

Testing the limits of her new ability now consumed Maggie's interest. She shamelessly cheated on tests, produced correct answers in class discussions, and destroyed the happiness of several members of Katie Maxwell's pack. Curiosity became her excuse. It justified her weakness—the realization of an innate piece of her personality impossible to ignore. After all, she reasoned, why should she resist her own nature? In her place, anyone would have exploited such circumstances.

Unfortunately, one complication arose that marred her eager expeditions into the consciousness of others. The ability to tell the difference between thoughts and spoken statements eluded Maggie. Although she had a temporary solution—a process involving serious consideration and review of every comment angled in her direction—it was difficult to maintain. She found herself exhausted by the end of the day. Unmoving lips and blunt, tactless inflection were sure signs of a remark's status, but noticing these details required seconds of concentration that delayed her responses, sometimes causing her to appear ludicrous.

Still, her progress had been enough to retain her sanity. Pandemonium bombarded her brain the first few days as the hundreds of separate minds infusing her head amalgamated into one gargantuan migraine. Deliberation had finally separated the tousled filaments of thought. Maggie found she could filter the disarray of human emotions permeating her surroundings, allowing distinguishable streams of voiceless words to enter. Her migraine subsided exponentially, though a part of the pain deviously lurked somewhere in the back of her skull, waiting to pounce if she wavered in focus. Unscrambling different mind voices required nonstop concentration. Blocking all of the voices simultaneously seemed impossible. She might never be alone with her thoughts again.

Maggie rubbed her eyes. The odor of stale food and spilled ketchup wafted through the cafeteria. She nibbled at her breakfast without appetite as she practiced her mind reading skills, skimming the thoughts of the other students chatting vigorously in the vicinity. The topics of shoes and dresses, tests and homework, football and girls filled Maggie's mind. Homecoming loomed dreadfully near and a deadly virus of excitement spread through the student body, possessing its every move and thought. Gratefully, Maggie retained immunity to its effects. Social events equaled angst, and she scorned the giddy enthusiasm infecting her peers.

She despised homecoming week. Its arrival meant ridiculously early mornings and monotonous alone time as Lily helped to decorate the school and oversee activities. Usually this time of year, Lily's conversational topics betrayed a deluge of homecoming blather. But this morning, only one topic had dominated Lily's attention on the short drive they shared to school: Kyle Spencer.

Unconsciously, Maggie picked her muffin into crumbs. Yesterday, Lily had related the information about Kyle's abilities over the phone minutes after he had divulged them. Maggie had feigned disinterest, but Lily—accustomed to this tactic—continued discussing the subject for the next half hour. The harder Maggie tried to ignore her best friend's enthusiasm, the more she noted an increase in the tempo of her heart whenever Kyle was mentioned. The struggle between the will of her head and the desires of her heart provoked continual confusion. Consequently, it was impossible for Maggie to interpret her feelings for Kyle. At times she knew she detested him more than any other creature. At others, she lost herself in the memory of warm, hazel eyes. They calmed and angered her simultaneously. Her life had become an emotional paradox.

At least her phone call had not been a complete catastrophe. As Lily's voice sailed through the earpiece, Maggie noticed a lack of what she had come to term "thought static," the echo or elaboration of spoken statements through thought that people seemed to generate as they conversed. Armed with this new detail, an essential truth revealed itself: mind reading did not transverse technology.

Voices, both verbal and unspoken, hummed a little louder throughout the cafeteria. Maggie checked her watch: only a half hour until class started. She swept the crumby mass that used to be her meal into her hand. Already the strain of keeping others' thoughts on the periphery of her mind had generated an ache behind her eyeballs. As she stood, a deep voice whispered in her ear.

"Hey Blue Eyes, whatcha doin' here so early?"

Muffin crumbs launched themselves all over the table.

"Lily had to come early for exec council stuff," she answered grumpily, brushing the muffin bits back into a pile.

Her fingers trembled as rage crackled up her neck. Or was it from the tickling sensation of Kyle's lips as they brushed her hair, passing only a breath from her skin as they delivered his greeting?

"Ah," he returned, plopping himself comfortably in an empty chair. "She's always busy isn't she?"

"She wouldn't be Lily if she wasn't," Maggie replied casually, gathering her things and preparing to escape.

Kyle anticipated her objective and snatched her purse before she could grab it.

"I don't doubt it," he replied easily, setting the purse on the table to the left of him, just out of her reach. "I see her everywhere, and she's always doin' somethin' different."

He smiled pleasantly, stretching his arms behind his head and leaning back in the chair in a silent challenge. *Let's see how fast you are, Sparky,* she heard him think.

Maggie wanted to bolt for the door. An unwelcome warmth quivered along her nerves.

"That's Lily, always thinking of others." Maggie strained her face with a smile. She quickly contemplated her options. She could just turn and leave, but with her keys snugly in the bottom of the purse, she'd be forced to search him out later and demand their return. If she lunged for it, he would just snatch it off the table before she could reach it, making her appear foolish. Sending Lily for it after lunch briefly crossed her mind, but she was sure Kyle would consider that a victory.

Any time now, he goaded.

Nervous tingling crept into her leg muscles. Suddenly she worried they might buckle. Kyle would undoubtedly catch her. Maggie knew she couldn't survive that indignity, so she chose to plunk angrily back into her chair. Awkward silence ensued. After a few minutes both began talking at once.

"Would you just give that back please?"

"So Mags, I was wonderin'—"

Kyle didn't finish his sentence out loud, but Maggie clearly heard its unspoken conclusion. Her eyes widened in horrible alarm.

"No. Absolutely not. I'm not going." Maggie's mouth was suddenly dry. She could feel a blush creeping into her cheeks. "I don't do dances, so you can forget about it."

"C'mon Sparky," his soft expression was agonizingly irresistible, "just this once, say yes. Just you, me, and the dance floor."

"I hate dances."

Kyle's laugh reverberated through the linoleum-lined cafeteria.

"Mags, that's because you've never been to one. Come with me, I promise you'll have fun."

Terror slid its cold fingers into her body; her veins burned with ice and froze with fire. She could feel her muscles trembling. His proposal itself wasn't the source of her fear. Suddenly, some secret longing, kept securely imprisoned outside of conscious thought since she met Kyle, was loosed inside her. She felt the word "yes" singe her lips, begging for release. Her desire for his attention, arriving with such unexpected sharpness, fundamentally overwhelmed her sensibilities. Maggie latched onto the only thing that could conquer her traitorous yearning: scorn.

"How would you even know? It doesn't matter, I don't want to go!"

"I'm beggin' you Sparky, be my *Lady in Red*."

Kyle seemed undaunted, sliding his hand over hers with such speed that she didn't notice until she felt the warmth of his fingers pressing firmly against her skin.

"No. I've already told you, so lay off!" Maggie pulled, trying to free her hand but Kyle's grip was hard as concrete.

"Why do you always have to fight everythin'? What will it take to get you there?"

"No force on this planet could make me go." Maggie's voice dripped venom. "Especially not you."

"So you're gonna sit there and tell me that you don't like me?"

His voice retained its playful timber, but for the first time ever, she saw doubt tarnish Kyle's eyes. Emotional dichotomies, crowded psyches, and sheer exhaustion drove her response. The words discharged from her mouth before she fully appreciated their possible consequence.

"I don't like you. Hell, I can hardly stand you! You're so high on yourself that you don't ever listen to what I'm actually saying, otherwise you would finally realize that I hate you!"

Kyle's expression reflected a mosaic of disbelief and injury. Maggie averted her eyes. She hadn't meant to respond with such reckless vehemence, and regret's bittersweet flavor dissolved in her mouth. She could avoid his face, but not his thoughts. The pain of her own rejection coursed through her synapses, ripping agony from each nerve. She suffered his aching disappointment; if damaged hope could weep, Maggie met its mournful song. He released her hand slowly, rose from the chair, and mechanically walked toward the exit. This was not the victory she had anticipated.

"Kyle, wait, I—"

She took a few steps forward, but when Kyle twisted to face her, the savage arrangement of his features made her hesitate. He spoke softly, but somehow his words roared inside Maggie's ears.

"You wanna be left alone Sparky, you've got it."

He stormed away and yanked on the heavy cafeteria door, wrenching it open with such fury that it slammed into the bordering wall, mangling the handle beyond repair and smashing a hole in the cinder block. Students from all over the lunchroom turned his direction, searching for the source of the commotion. He didn't look back, and Maggie dared not follow. She turned to the table, a tear leaking from the corner of each eye. As she lifted her gaze, Lily's agonized expression filled her vision.

"How long have you—?" Maggie trailed off, unsure of her voice.

The severity of her emotional wreckage overshadowed the foreign voices infecting her brain. Lily's next statement entered Maggie's head without superhuman ability.

"Long enough."

Lily hugged her tightly.

"Don't worry," Lily soothed, "we can fix this."

*

Maggie's hands gripped the steering wheel, limbs paralyzed and knuckles white. A surge of panic heaved through her innards. Even with his super strength, Kyle would have been hard pressed to break her hold. Outside the car window, dusk kissed the sky with grey winged lips. An endless expanse of spent green stubble stretched in all directions on the frost-coated ground. Fifteen or so shadows of what Maggie assumed were her classmates busily piled wood and newspaper in the center of the field, well away from the makeshift car lot. They would be lighting the bonfire any second.

Lily had spent most of the morning convincing Maggie that the confrontation with Kyle could be rectified. Maggie left trigonometry feeling hopeful—until the next period when Kyle was suspiciously absent from computer technology. He had never before missed an opportunity to see her. She half expected him to appear at lunch, but his jocular smile and tantalizing biceps remained missing. Maggie tried seeking him in thought, but couldn't sense his presence in the vicinity. She admitted, however, that the range of her abilities still remained questionable.

Lily's hope that Maggie could still repair the situation remained undeterred by Kyle's continued truancy. She asserted that boys with slighted dignity just needed time to compose themselves before reappearing in public. He would most likely attend the homecoming festivities that evening at Jolley's Farm. As the quarterback of the football team, Kyle was required to make an appearance.

This is a really bad idea, Maggie thought to herself, staring wide-eyed at the group of students in the center of the field. The laughter and enjoyment of others piling out of cars filled Maggie's mind with spongy fuzz. A sharp rapping on the car window startled her.

"Maggie? Come on!" Lily yanked open the door from outside. "You have to get out of the car."

"I don't think this is a very good idea, Lil."

"That doesn't change anything. You still have to get out of the car!"

Lily poked her blond curls into the driver's side cavity. Her cherry-balmed lips pursed with determination.

"He hates me now," Maggie's muttered, dropping her head onto the rim of the steering wheel. "I should just go home."

Lily rolled her eyes, obviously prepared for this excuse. Pink polished nails curled around Maggie's knitted sweater and resolutely pulled.

"Oh, don't be so dramatic. Get out of the car."

Maggie braced her free hand and leg against the doorframe, effectively wedging herself in the vehicle. Her social estrangement suddenly overwhelmed her need to apologize to Kyle. Much to her consternation, she realized that any admission of guilt that she made would be performed in front of an audience. The zeal of her argument with Kyle this morning had dissipated somewhat, and Maggie now concluded the fault of the situation lay more with him than herself. After all, not only had he been idiot enough to ask her to an event she despised, but he had pressed the point after she had clearly imparted a refusal. Besides, Kyle wouldn't miss two days of school—maybe she could just track him down in the morning.

"No, I changed my mind, I want to go home."

"Maggie! Don't. Be. So. Difficult!" A ferocious tug emphasized each of Lily's words.

Maggie briefly wondered how Kyle would react if he witnessed this over-exaggerated tug-of-war. No doubt with a highly attractive chuckle. The idea caused Maggie to waver in concentration. Lily's last pull liberated Maggie from the vehicle, albeit in a rather undignified manner. As she picked herself off the ground, Lily snatched the keys from the ignition.

"You're not leaving until you've apologized," Lily affirmed, slipping the keys into the inside pocket of her lavender jacket.

Maggie grimaced, every muscle in her face agreeing with her displeasure. Then she sighed and yielded to Lily's determined will.

"Okay, but I'm leaving as soon as it's done—and I'm still not going to the dance."

"Maggie, this will work better if you'd stop being so stubborn," Lily replied, her breath forming rimy puffs in the October evening. "Going to a dance won't kill you. Especially since you'd be there with Kyle."

Maggie crossed her arms, defiance flashing from a furrowed brow.

"Lily, I'll say I'm sorry. That's what I came here to do. But it's not my fault he asked me out. I have the right to say no. If he can't accept it—that's his problem."

Sudden music wailed across the field. Lily's gaze turned in the direction of the bonfire, which was now flickering into feeble life. Maggie could hear Lily's frustration plainly. As a member of student council, Lily was supposed to be arranging the activity with her fellow elected officers.

Do the right thing for once, Maggie, Lily thought, chewing her lip hopefully. More students had arrived, and several called out greetings to Lily as they headed toward the livening party. She returned their overtures with a friendly wave, then turned back to face her best friend, her thoughts openly inviting Maggie to join the throng.

"It'll work out, Lil, one way or another," Maggie compromised graciously. "You need to go help set up. I'll worry about Kyle."

Lily didn't look convinced, but neither did she argue.

"Okay, but when I'm done helping, I'm coming to find you!"

After a brief embrace, Lily hurried toward the growing group. A quick glance around the parking area revealed Maggie to be alone for the moment. As she watched her friend's form retreat into the darkening twilight, an idea caught her attention. Maggie wasn't exactly sure of the distance between her position and the bonfire, but it was at least the length of the school athletic field, maybe even somewhat further. At school, Maggie had to concentrate on pushing her peers' thoughts into the fringes of her mind, and she was often unsure just whose ideas belonged to whom. Right now, the only "thought static" she could hear came from Lily; apparently those gathered around the bonfire were too far for her abilities to perceive. The clarity of Lily's mind remained relativity constant for about 50 feet or so. Lily's "voice" receded in volume as she wandered farther into the field. Just like sound dulls with distance, so too did Maggie's perception of Lily's mind.

By the time Lily had crossed three quarters of the field, Maggie had to concentrate intently to hear Lily's individual thoughts, and even then, Maggie kept losing distinct idea patterns. It was like listening to a cell phone that kept cutting out every few seconds. A shadow detached itself from the main group of students, trotting toward Lily excitedly. Maggie couldn't tell who the figure was with her mental abilities. Interestingly, even though Maggie couldn't distinguish between Lily's individual thoughts, Lily's presence was acutely palpable. Maggie could sense Lily's identity clearly, but her companion remained anonymous.

Maggie centered herself in her mind, closing her ears to the natural world, losing herself in her abilities. The noiseless tendrils of her mind searched through the field, seeking to recognize the person with Lily. The attempt was even more difficult as the couple drew farther from Maggie's view. She could still feel Lily plainly; even when Maggie could no longer see her blond curls bouncing around the crowd. It took about five minutes of significant focus, but finally she managed to filch a piece of personality she knew. It was Mark.

Maggie snorted at herself. Now that she knew he was there, his character was easier to sense. She noted as she scanned the rest of the crowd that her abilities were unable to perceive anyone else for certain. Some students had a stronger sense of presence than others. Maggie wondered if she would have better luck searching for someone she had "heard" before. Her hypothesis proved correct. After 15 minutes of deliberation, she discovered Nathan Hinton, Elisha Gowers, Sarah Perkins, and even Coach Graff, the advisor for student council.

Though intriguing, her new discovery had not erased the reason for her attendance to this obnoxious social gathering. The sooner she found Kyle, the faster she could leave.

Maggie concentrated on filtering the consciousness of everyone else, probing for him. He wasn't in the group by the bonfire.

He was standing four cars behind her.

Her attention had been completely consumed by her experiment for over 25 minutes, so the arrival of Kyle's jeep had escaped her notice. Milky stars stabbed the night sky, but the absence of the moon allowed night's darkness to swallow Jolley's Farm with its shady jaws. The cold air that Maggie pulled into her lungs burned her throat; her fingers were ice as she turned toward him. Several other cars pulled into the makeshift parking area, their headlights illuminating Kyle's features for a few seconds. The radiance let Maggie glimpse his expression briefly. The spiky tone of his thoughts warned her not to approach.

Don't come over here. This is what you wanted.

She wished that, for once, he could read her thoughts. Saying them out loud seemed an inadequate means of explaining her tumultuous feelings. A stitch plagued her throat, stealing her voice. As other students exited cars, their thoughts buzzed in her brain, clouding it with distraction.

Then Lily's sudden panicked yelp tore through Maggie's mind.

Maggie's feet were moving toward the bonfire before she was aware of her actions. Kyle's sudden start of surprise at her unexpected movement touched the corners of her perception. A quiver of movement flitted through the bonfire crowd as students turned in one direction at some sort of disturbance. Though he obviously couldn't sense Maggie's motivation, Kyle launched himself toward the group of students as well. He outdistanced her incredibly fast.

"Lily!" Maggie yelled as she dashed forward.

As soon as she reached the crowd, she thrust milling people out of her way, trying to reach the center of the group. Lily's thoughts, which had been vibrating in a fluster, calmed somewhat. Maggie assumed Kyle had arrived to stabilize the situation. After a few more agonizingly elongated seconds, Maggie finally managed to push past the last person in the gathering. Lily sat at the edge of the blazing bonfire, bewilderedly scanning her hands. Kyle bent over her, hovering with concern. Mark stood sheepishly to one side, shifting his weight from one foot to the other.

"Lil, are you okay?" Maggie asked as she scurried to her best friend's side, ignoring the flaring heat wafting from the fire. "What happened?"

Lily brushed ash from her fingers and arm. Her lavender jacket was dotted with small blackened holes and the edge of her pleated skirt looked singed.

"We were dancing and I dipped her," Mark answered, red flushing his face, "I—guess—I didn't have a good enough hold on her and—"

"You dropped her in the fire?!" Maggie rounded on him, yanking the information from his brain before he could say it.

Mark cringed.

"Not in the fire, though I thought at first he had!" Lily said.

Kyle looked her over, searching for signs of injury. Lily's face was pale in the firelight, but Maggie noticed her friend's skin was warm with exertion.

"I didn't burn myself, thank goodness. It would look awful on Saturday if I showed up to homecoming with great big bandages all over my hands!" She laughed nervously. "Or if I was bald!"

"She looks okay," Kyle announced, straightening his posture, "just shook up a little is all."

After Kyle's pronouncement, the onlookers suddenly exploded into eager chatter as he helped Lily to her feet. Soon merriment resumed throughout the field. Maggie looked toward Kyle, meeting his warm gaze with gratitude in her own.

"Thanks a bunch, Kyle," Lily said, happily brushing dirt from her outfit. "I hope I didn't scare you!"

Lily's cheery disposition returned quickly, much to the relief of Maggie.

Mark approached Lily timidly, though her friendly expression obviously indicated all was forgiven.

"No problem," Kyle returned, though his stare never left Maggie.

His thoughts were wrapped with cool detachment, and his usual carefree manner seemed stiff. Maggie heaved a calming breath and then launched into her apology.

"Kyle, I—"

Several deep voices called out boisterously, and large bodies surrounded Kyle, cutting her off. Maggie lost sight of him amid the flurry of male shoulder slapping and head tousling. When she glimpsed him again, his easy smile had returned.

"I've gotta go," he said to Lily, completely ignoring Maggie. "I'll see you guys around."

Lily started to protest as Kyle walked away with the group, but Maggie stopped her with a touch of the hand and shake of the head.

"But—" Lily argued, gesturing toward Kyle's retreating form.

"It's not going to work Lily, not tonight anyway. I saw it in his mind."

Maggie watched the darkness long after Kyle had disappeared.

8: If The Dress Fits Wear It

The shops in the mall were drenched in October. Sweaters, coats, and jeans posed in the windows of every clothing store. Gloves and scarves littered tables and displays, the occasional hideous furry earmuff could be spied under ugly hats. Once, a cheap Dracula doll sprung from the depths of his mechanized coffin, startling consumers. Dry mist spewed from strategically located fog machines hidden in stores. Maggie inhaled a lungful of fake smoke as she passed a particularly foul display of counterfeit vomit and coughed raucously.

"Alright, whatever it is you have to do, let's do it quick," Maggie stated impatiently when she had recovered her breathing capacity.

The sticky odor of Halloween enthusiasm reminded her of her own misery. She was eager to return home and expend her frustration on some violent video games.

"Oh, come on Maggie. What's the hurry?" Lily retorted brightly. "You love shopping!"

What's the hurry? Maggie repeated to herself. *Only the need to hide from everyone in the human race.*

Usually Maggie enjoyed the solitude of window shopping. Rarely having the funds to actually purchase anything, the shop employees left Maggie to browse.

But that was before everyone in Idaho Falls could jab their thoughts into her head. For some reason, customer activities were louder in thought than the everyday engagements at school. The volume of "Mommy, Mommy I want this," "this outfit makes me look fat," and "no way, that is too expensive" clogged her mind as soon as she walked through the shopping center doorway. Only a few seconds of exposure had awakened the vicious migraine fairy that resided in the rear of her head. Maggie had to build a mental wall between herself and the thought chatter pervading the area. Even so, a grating murmur, like the static buzz on an amplifier, skulked on the periphery of her mind.

Additionally, the shame of her behavior over the last few days made her feel desolate. Her rash actions had driven Kyle Spencer from her life for almost two entire days. As a result, every chuckle caught her attention. She'd even gladly tolerate the name Sparky, just as long as it came from his deep, resonant voice. Every time he didn't appear, she wanted nothing more than to rush home, crawl into bed, and drown in the blankets.

"I don't have any money," complained Maggie.

"Well, this will be fun anyway," Lily said, sauntering cheerfully down the corridor. "I need your help with something, and we're not leaving till it's done."

"I drove. I can leave when I want."

"You wouldn't leave me here without a ride, and you know it," Lily declared, brushing aside the gravity of Maggie's threat. "Besides, there's something important we have to do."

"What?"

"I can't tell you, it's a surprise!" Lily hooked her arm into the crook of Maggie's, yanking her abruptly in a new direction.

"I don't—"

"—like surprises. I know, I know," Lily interrupted. "But this one is good so no cheating." Lily tapped her own forehead with a finger, indicating Maggie's restrictions.

"Cheating? I can't even hear myself think with all this noise in my head," Maggie returned. In an effort to combat the thoughts blasting into her mind, Maggie had blocked everyone simultaneously, something she had figured out the night before.

"Interesting," Lily contemplated, momentarily distracted from her objective. "So you can't hear my thoughts at all?"

Halting, Lily stared keenly into Maggie's eyes, ascertaining Maggie's sincerity.

"Not unless I want my brains blasted out of my head!" Maggie answered. "If I let you in, everyone gets in."

"All right, but no peeking," Lily wagged her finger at her best friend, "even if you figure out how to sort the voices in your head. Promise?"

"Fine. But I still hate surprises."

"This is going to be exciting, trust me!"

Grudgingly, Maggie allowed Lily to guide their progress through the mall. Eventually, Lily turned into one particular boutique. Lacey skirts, sequined gloves, and high-heeled shoes decorated the front window.

"Oh no," Maggie objected, planting her feet.

"Oh yes," Lily responded with a determined curve on her lips.

Lily pulled Maggie across the threshold.

"This is not my idea of an exciting surprise, Lily," Maggie almost whispered.

Lily may have intended to cheer Maggie, but shopping for formal dresses caused something parallel to heartburn in Maggie's throat. The ribbon bedecked, satiny garments were corporeal reminders of her refusal to Kyle.

"Yes it is," Lily replied with maddening optimism. "Don't be so depressing. You've been that way all day."

"This isn't going to lift my mood, you do realize that?" Maggie inquired rhetorically.

"As my best friend, it is your duty to help me pick out my homecoming dress. And you have to be happy about it," Lily commanded.

Maggie gazed around the boutique with indecision. The selection of Lily's fall formal had become an annual tradition the two shared. Maggie was hesitant to break it.

"All right," she allowed. "I'll help."

Lily released a squeal of delight. "I'm so excited! I was thinking I would find something pastel, and then if I could find some silver shoes, and maybe even a tiara, it would be the perfect ensemble!"

Despite her reservations, Maggie couldn't prevent a smile from entertaining her mouth. Lily's ability to bring excitement to even the most insignificant aspects of life provided Maggie a gleam of happiness. She trailed a bouncing head of gold as Lily perused racks of assorted gowns, turning down the aid of an eager sales associate. Accessories winked from glass cases and Lily browsed the costume jewelry as much as the dresses. More than once, Maggie's lip curled in disgust at some of the hideous designs in hues she believed should have been obliterated from the color spectrum, but she managed to select several dresses, appropriately pink, and passed them over to an elated Lily.

Maggie plopped into a chair as Lily hauled her selection of dresses into a draped changing room. As Maggie drummed her fingers involuntarily on the arm of her chair, she decided Lily had been right. The shopping excursion had effected a positive change in Maggie's disposition, though she figured that had more to do with Lily's affection and candor than the outing itself. But now that Lily's aura of happiness was trapped behind a dark red curtain, Maggie's distressful circumstances threatened to leak back into her forethought. Thankfully, Lily reappeared just as the black wave of regret reared its hideous crest.

"What do you think?" Lily asked, cheeks flushed in eagerness. Hopping onto the pedestal in front of the mirror, she offered herself for visual analysis.

Maggie related the advantages and drawbacks of each dress, providing a definite "no" when appropriate. Three were too short to be flattering, and one looked like a maternity robe. Two seemed plausible, though a little risqué for Lily's conservative nature. But each time Lily disappeared into the changing room, Maggie almost failed to prevent the image of Kyle's pained face from consuming her thoughts.

"I really like this one, Maggie."

Lily paraded the last dress in front of the mirrors. Filmy, pale-rose satin flared around the dress's fitted empire waist. The strapless heart-shaped bodice complimented Lily's figure; its length, just kissing the tops of her knees, made her appear taller. A single mauve ribbon separated bosom from torso, fashioning a bow in the center. Pink and silver rhinestones cascaded from the bodice to the hem, as if a shower of crystalline raindrops had sprinkled the garment.

"Wow! I think that's the best we've seen so far." Maggie admired the play of light as it skittered through the rhinestone crystals.

"This is the one!" Lily exclaimed with a twirl.

When she completed the revolution, she paused and looked toward the cash counter with anticipation. *Odd*, thought Maggie, following the gaze of her best friend. The sales associate, who had been bustling around the dress displays, quickly strode to the counter, removed a long, black garment bag from a tall rack and then stepped out of

Maggie's sight. When Maggie turned back to Lily, she had already stepped off the pedestal.

"Wait," Lily suddenly blurted. "I shouldn't decide so fast. I think we should look a bit more before I choose, just in case there's something better."

Lily's pale green eyes shimmered with mischief.

Maggie waited for Lily to change back into street clothes with some suspicion. The pink dress was a perfect match for Lily, ivory skin to blond tresses. Nevertheless, as soon as Lily flounced out of the dressing room, the girls plunged into the maze of racks a second time. Maggie noticed that the pink dress had wandered onto the check-out counter. Just as she was considering lifting the barrier between her mind reading powers and Lily's thoughts, her best friend suddenly began shouting exuberantly.

"Oh my gosh, Maggie! Maggie come and look at this dress!"

Lily cradled a brilliant blue gown in her arms. Floor length and sleek, its only adornment was a hint of elegant lace around the neckline. Maggie felt her eyebrows wrinkle with confusion. The jewel tone color and chic, modern style were completely at odds with Lily's usual taste.

"I think it's perfect," Lily purred, fingering the silky fabric.

Maggie couldn't even visualize the dress on Lily's body.

"I don't think it's really you, Lily."

"No, not for me, silly," Lily said, holding the dress up to Maggie, "it's perfect for you!"

Maggie's eyes contracted with realization.

"You set me up."

"You should try it on," Lily continued, ignoring Maggie's allegation. Lily forced the glossy blue material into Maggie's hands and pulled her into one of the changing rooms. "There's no reason you can't try on a pretty dress."

"I'm not going to the dance. That's a really good reason."

"Well I can think of a million other reasons why you should try it on," Lily said, sliding the velvet curtain closed.

Maggie's resistance proved futile. She resigned herself to modeling the dress. As the zipper tightened the supple fabric around her ribs, a new sensation sizzled under her skin. She didn't dare look down at her new raiment. Quietly, Maggie exited the dressing closet, keeping her gaze determinedly away from the dress.

"Maggie, you look absolutely gorgeous," Lily exclaimed, clapping her hands together with awe.

The azure fabric hugged Maggie's form, highlighting the full curves of her shape. The dress was cut in a mermaid design but for the sensual slit exposing her legs to mid-thigh. The V-neck plunged low across her chest, emphasizing her full breasts. Two straps of blue wandered around her shoulders, crossing at high center back, meeting the torso of the gown at the waist. The gap below the straps accentuated the arch of Maggie's lower back. A touch of lace connected a separate swath of fabric, cascading into a graceful train.

Even at her best, Maggie had never been so beautiful. As she finally inspected herself in the mirrors, she realized that Lily's earlier assumption had been wrong. There were a million and one reasons why she shouldn't have tried on this dress, and all of them involved the magnificence of her appearance. For the first time in two years, Maggie felt a part of her old self spark to life in a dusty, forgotten corner of her being. The portion that wanted to be respected and cherished by others yearned for release.

"You should wear it to the dance," Lily said offhandedly.

Lily's intrusion snapped Maggie from her dangerous reverie. Sternly she reminded herself why she had locked her soul away in the first place.

"We've been over this, I'm not going to the dance. Besides, I don't have," Maggie paused to assess the price tag, "$300 to spend on a dress."

"Yeah, but your mom does."

"No she doesn't. We're barely making ends meet."

"Not according to her," Lily argued playfully. "Apparently, her new job pays better than she thought."

"I'm not going to ask my mother for money," Maggie concluded, yanking on the zipper and backing into the dressing room with a rustle, "especially since I don't have a date. You sabotaged me!"

"I have no idea what you're talking about," Lily feigned innocently, placing a hand on her chest in mock surprise.

"You came and picked out a dress you knew I'd love!"

"Of course I did," Lily answered with a laugh. "How else was I going to get you to that dance?"

"I'm not buying it."

"You won't have to. Your mom already did."

So both her mother and best friend had conspired against her. Lily took advantage of Maggie's stupor. Leading her back to the mirror, Lily quickly replaced the zipper.

"Look how beautiful you are," she persisted, her voice soft. "Can't you imagine the look on Kyle's face when he sees you in this dress?"

"Lily, he's not going to go with me."

Lily rolled her eyes, patience limit exceeded.

"He's totally in to you, Maggie. I'm sure once he understands the whole story and you apologize, he'll forgive you."

Maggie stared at the floor, afraid to face her own reflection. Casual forgiveness was so embedded in the core of Lily's character that she often overlooked the resentment regular people harbored when offended. When Maggie spoke, her voice was almost lost in the thick carpet.

"He was really mad, Lily."

After a few seconds, Maggie felt the pressure of Lily's fingers cupping her chin. Lily forced Maggie's face level with her own.

"Maggie," Lily offered, "I don't think he's mad."

"Really?" Maggie wondered.

Lily nodded. "I think he's embarrassed."

Maggie emitted a nervous laugh, sodden with disbelief. "Kyle Spencer? Embarrassed? I'd sooner believe he'd started ballet."

Lily shook her head again, this time side to side. "I'm serious, Maggie."

"Okay, assuming it's possible," Maggie tried unsuccessfully to stifle her skepticism, "why would he be embarrassed?"

"He usually knows what to say when he's around you, Maggie. But even he gets nervous sometimes. And you're not always the most predictable person."

Maggie stared fixedly into Lily's eyes. Though the remark simply indicated a facet of Maggie's personality, it stung regardless. Lily continued before Maggie could reply.

"But I think he had himself convinced that you'd say yes. So, when you said no, he didn't know what to do. The disappointment must have been too much. He's passionate about you, you know. He's told me."

Maggie began smoothing imaginary wrinkles from the extraordinary gown, allowing a small bubble of hope to form around her heart.

"Do you really think he'll still take me?" she asked.

Lily's cheerful reply nourished the bubble.

"Yes. He'll still take you, and when he sees you in this dress he's going to drool all over the floor. Let's pick out accessories!" Lily skipped gaily to the jewelry counter, Maggie tagging behind.

9: A Pencil For Your Thoughts

Lily recited her carefully concocted strategy for the hundredth time. Maggie's role was simple: find Kyle and beg forgiveness. An easy enough task—except fate seemed to garner sadistic pleasure in thwarting Lily's objectives: first at the bonfire and once again this morning. Kyle had missed his second period class with Maggie, courtesy of the annual football photo shoot. Maggie's disappointment challenged her fortitude, and Lily's incessant reiteration of their apology scheme only increased Maggie's tension.

"Lil, I've heard this plan a hundred times already," Maggie moaned, but Lily refused to relent.

"Well, it doesn't hurt to be prepared. So when you see him, start by saying you're sorry. Then you can tell him you thought about it, and you would love to go to the dance with him. Be nice, and please, please, please don't lose your temper."

"Geez, do you trust me at all, or do you think I can't even tie my shoes by myself?" Maggie grunted.

"Of course I trust to you tie your own shoes, just not to make rational decisions when you're angry."

Maggie arranged her features in an artificial expression of indignation. "Thanks, that makes me feel good inside."

Maggie slouched against the cinder block wall, anxiety harassing her resolve. At least she had her mind powers activated; it might give her insight to Kyle's reception of her plea for exoneration. This morning she had discovered a significant growth in her ability to control her telepathy, like an athlete who, training for months, suddenly discovers himself to be the most skilled player on the team. Random thoughts swirled in eddies within her head, but no longer in a discordant snarl. Rather, it was like an off-key middle school band; each set of thoughts carried a distinct volume and tone. Maggie found she was able to ignore the brain chatter of those she wasn't interested in pursuing, like white-noise, and center on just one person in particular to read.

All of which would have been extremely interesting—except that she was about to face Kyle.

"You can be mad at me but you know it's true," Lily pointed out, "otherwise we wouldn't be in this mess. We can't make things better if you don't stay calm. Don't worry, everything will work out for the best!"

"It would be over already if the yearbook hadn't been taking football pictures during computer tech," Maggie protested bitterly as the two loitered in the hallway.

"Yes, well you can't let that affect you," Lily pronounced with a single nod of her head.

"It's not affecting me," Maggie lied.

"Maggie, you were so upset Kyle didn't show up that you slammed the computer lab door."

"That was an accident," Maggie insisted.

"It may have been an accident," Lily disputed, "but it happened when you let your disappointment get the better of you."

"How do you know I wasn't relieved?" Maggie countered.

Lily lifted dubious eyebrows.

"Because we all know that you like Kyle, whether you want to admit it or not. Anyway, sooner or later you'll end up running into him. There is no logical reason for him to miss history. This is unavoidable."

"How do you do that?"

"Do what?" Lily asked.

"Read my mind," Maggie clarified.

"Well, I wish it was as easy for me as it is for you. As your best friend, it's my job to know what you're thinking," Lily confided, leaning toward Maggie conspiratorially. "Then I can keep you out of trouble."

"You say that like it's a common occurrence."

"It is," Lily affirmed. "Now let's get going. You're going to be late for class."

Lily prodded Maggie down the corridor. As they turned a corner Lily's eyes brightened enthusiastically. "Look, there's Kyle! See, things are looking up already."

Lily pointed to the history door. Kyle held its abused surface open for several girls as they walked into the classroom. His back faced them, but the sinister eyes of multiple U.S. presidents, whose portraits adorned the entry, glared in Maggie's direction, as if daring her to approach. Were they anticipating catastrophe? Kyle disappeared into the portal just as the tardy bell rang through the hall.

"Oh no, I'm late! Now—"

"I know, I know, keep my temper and say I'm sorry. Don't worry, you made me memorize the plan, I won't let you down," Maggie promised.

Lily clasped Maggie's hand and squeezed it reassuringly.

"Good luck."

Maggie indicated the path that would lead Lily to choir class with a flick of the head.

"Hurry up or you'll be in real trouble with Mrs. Tanner. You know how she gets when people aren't on time."

Lily smiled encouragingly and then sprinted down the hallway. Maggie felt her confidence fade as Lily's figure disappeared. Her last thoughts centered on hope for Maggie's success. Maggie confronted the ominous stares of her country's former leaders.

"You can do this," Maggie whispered to herself, eyes closed to blot out the foreboding pictures, "you can do this."

Her efforts to buoy her bravery helped, but her fingers still trembled when she grasped the knob. An unexpected dilemma sprang into her mind. Should she sit next to Kyle as if nothing were amiss? That might be awkward. But it would seem ridiculous if she ignored him completely until the end of the period. And what if he vanished after class before she could corner him? Maggie deliberated for only a few seconds, deciding that the issue would not resolve itself in the hallway. Her best option was to plunge into the situation and react naturally. She took a deep breath and turned the door handle.

The desks in Mr. Cowley's classroom faced the entry. Most of the students looked up inquisitively when the door squeaked open, except the one that mattered. Kyle had chosen a seat on the end of the second row instead of his customary place next to Maggie in the rear of the room. His eyes focused firmly on his notebook as his pen rigidly scratched Mr. Cowley's instructions. A smug pair of eyes regarded Maggie triumphantly from the only chair beside the muscular quarterback. Twirling a strand of her trendy mane with a manicured finger, Katie Maxwell offered Maggie a haughty sneer.

"Maggie Brooks, you're late."

Maggie's attention snapped to the instructor. Her first impulse was, of course, to sardonically comment on Mr. Cowley's ability to state the obvious, but that would contradict Lily's directives. Maggie managed the reins on her temper.

"Sorry," she answered quickly.

Mr. Cowley smiled benignly and pointed to her usual chair.

"Just hurry and grab a seat."

Maggie passed Mr. Cowley's large wooden desk, following an aisle in the row of student chairs. Though the path didn't take her directly toward Kyle, she hoped to make eye contact with him anyway. Maybe she could somehow give him a white flag with her eyes. His gaze, however, remained stubbornly fixed on his assignment.

As she reached her seat, she slid the strap of her shoulder bag over her head and rummaged through it for a notebook and writing utensil. Her attention had been wholly engaged by Kyle's behavior, and she didn't notice the new occupant of his former chair—Lauren Elson—until Lauren produced a small cough. Maggie heard the crude insult her neighbor had deliberately concealed behind the noise. A heart-shaped face, framed by hundreds of black stringy braids turned to face Maggie's surprised glance. Poised unnaturally straight, Lauren contrived a look of innocence in her chocolate features, simultaneously identifying her as the insulter, yet blatantly refusing responsibility for the affront.

Lauren rarely missed an opportunity to shadow Katie; following the head cheerleader's lead was Lauren's only personality trait. If Katie detested something or excluded someone, so did Lauren. Lauren would never purposely arrange to sit near Maggie, so removed from her idol; the entire situation suggested some ulterior motive. No doubt Lauren had transferred to make room for Kyle, who was occupying her regular position next to Katie.

Maggie rolled her eyes at her classmate's immaturity, turning her gaze to the front of the classroom. Another prompt for an in-class essay sprawled across the board. She absently copied the question, not bothering to actually discern the content.

She's stupid if she thinks she can compete with Katie. It was only a matter of time.

Maggie's pencil dug deeply into the notebook paper, almost snapping the lead as Lauren's thoughts seeped unintentionally into her head. Katie was easily Maggie's least favorite person in the entire school; the self-centered cheerleader was the lead harasser over the Matt crisis. Maggie avoided Katie most of the time, and when they did chance on each other, colorful insults enlivened the school corridors. Why would Maggie even want to compete with Katie? Katie didn't have anything that Maggie wanted.

Maggie decided reading Lauren would be a waste of time and could potentially end explosively, endangering her prospects with Kyle. Maggie thrust Lauren's venomous thoughts aside. Three seats ahead, Katie had maneuvered a folded piece of paper onto Kyle's desk, eyeing the teacher warily. Kyle continued writing his assignment as if he hadn't noticed.

Maggie absently tapped her pencil on the desk as she considered. Was he ignoring the missive by design or lack of awareness? A few seconds later her question was answered as he skillfully reached for it, seemingly engrossed in his work. Maggie recalibrated her abilities and converged on him, resolute on reading the note through his thoughts.

Her mind stumbled backward, rebounding off a solid wall. At least that's what it felt like. Involuntarily, she lifted a hand to her forehead. Something bit the inside of her eyeballs. Apparently, Kyle was more aware of Maggie's actions than he had revealed. She could envision his amused smirk, even though his back faced her. Knowing she would be curious about his penciled conversation with Katie, he had intentionally managed a defense to hinder her efforts at reading his thoughts. His surprise resistance had completely stunned her. Her face felt bruised, like someone had slapped it.

Maggie had been mildly curious about Kyle's exchange with Katie before, but now—divulging his secrets was a matter of principle. She pushed into his head, jamming her abilities into his mental barrier like a spiked mace, wrenching the shell apart with her mind's fingers. The makeshift shield crumbled into scattered remnants of thought just as Kyle pulled the piece of paper to the center of his desk. Maggie was anticipating reading its contents through his eyes, an absolute victory, when a caped figure loomed into her vision, startling her into a little yelp. She blinked for a few seconds and met Mr. Cowley's irritated gaze before realizing she had encountered a random memory of some kind. Maggie tried again.

Kyle's mind had become something similar to a minefield. She cursed him under her breath. Tossing useless facts onto her path was distraction enough to prevent her from reading his letter. She collided with old memories from his life in California, stories about his grandfather, and meaningless facts about his favorite TV shows. Maggie kept losing direction—one minute she was visiting his third birthday party, the next she found herself shivering with exertion in the history classroom. Maggie figured Kyle couldn't measure how effective his tactics actually were. Centering on concentration, she pierced through the last of his obstacles just in time to seize the last line of the note, written in a bubbly neat hand.

...excited. My dress is a pale green.

Kyle lifted his pen to respond. When he slid the paper back to Katie, Maggie no longer required a connection to his mind to discover its contents. Maggie wondered if he realized any further attempts to block her would be useless. Katie's psyche was easily penetrated.

Good then, I ordered the right color vest, Katie's ecstatic voice read. She scribbled a line with her pen.

Are you going to pick up your tux after school?

Maggie's lungs refused to operate. Spots clouded her vision with blackened edges. Katie's mind schemed wildly, planning multiple day-dates, hairstyles, and wardrobes. To Maggie's absolute horror, every scenario vomiting from Katie's head included Kyle as her homecoming date.

Yeah, after practice. It shouldn't take too long.

Lack of oxygen made the thought streams bleary, but Maggie didn't dare breathe, ludicrously supposing that inhaling would cause her to miss a part of the unspoken conversation.

Perfect. I was wondering if you could give me a ride home. I have cheer practice today.

Nervousness coated her throat. Maggie couldn't differentiate whether it was her own or Katie's.

That shouldn't be a problem.

Katie's heart must have been beating frantically because blood suddenly roared inside Maggie's head—that, or an abrupt inhalation of oxygen surged into Maggie's arteries. When she had regained control of herself, taking a few seconds to regulate her breathing—remembering to do so at all was stretching Maggie's capabilities at this point—Katie's thoughts were fixated on contriving opportunities to meet Kyle alone.

I thought you might want to hang around for a bit. My parents are going to be out of town tonight.

Kyle shifted perceptibly. Maggie guessed—and hoped—it was uncomfortably, but she didn't dare examine his thoughts. Katie's implied offer was obvious, her superficial fancies swamped Maggie's mind with quixotic pictures:

bodies embracing, lips gently converging, fingers teasing skin—

Who else is coming?

Maggie's nails bruised her palms as she gripped her pencil tightly.

It would just be me and you.

The pencil flew through the air and slammed into the back of Katie's skull.

"Ouch!" Katie shrieked as her hand reached for the injury.

Her face snapped around, seeking the culprit.

Lauren looked slightly astonished by Maggie's attack, but didn't hesitate to point Maggie out as the perpetrator with a finger. The grating of pencil on paper ceased, smothering the room with an abnormal hush. Ventilation system vibrations clearly rang through the absence of sound until Katie's voice split the air like a whip. All eyes, including Mr. Cowley's, shifted between the fuming cheerleader and her pencil-wielding foe.

"What did you do that for?!"

"Sorry. Did it hurt?" Maggie apologized, waves of angry sarcasm spattering unrestrained from her mouth. "I don't know what happened. The pencil has a mind of its own."

"Ladies—" warned Mr. Cowley.

Lightning flashed from Katie's perfectly mascaraed eyelashes as she vaulted from her chair, ignoring the teacher's caution.

"You threw it on purpose," Katie accused, massaging the sore spot on her head, careful not to displace any hair and damage her appearance.

Maggie's riposte laugh reeked with bitter envy.

"Well spotted, Einstein. What are you going to do about it?"

Mr. Cowley stepped forward, intending to intervene. Unfortunately, his passive nature did little to forestall the elevating hostility.

"Maggie, stop disrupting class. Katie, sit back down in your chair."

"What's your problem?" Katie continued sharply, utterly disregarding the teacher's instructions.

Maggie's body rose from her chair to meet the challenge of her opponent.

"You," she spat, "you and your slutty cheerleader uniform—not that you can ever keep it on."

"Mags," Kyle advised, standing from his chair calmly, "stop it."

"Stay out of it, Kyle," Maggie shouted in his direction, not sparing him a glance. This was, after all, his fault.

"At least I'm good at it. Matt said he'd never had worse than you," Katie interjected, arrogantly advancing toward Maggie as if she were in control of the argument.

"I heard he knocked you up just a few weeks later and that's why you told everyone you had to 'move in with your dad' the rest of freshman year," Maggie said, relishing in a piece of information she had gleaned from Lauren just a few days earlier.

Katie of course hadn't actually been pregnant, but according to her friend's thoughts, there was a span of time where it was questionable. Katie's eyes shifted in betrayal to Lauren.

"Both of you girls, in the hallway now!" Mr. Cowley commanded, but Katie wasn't willing to end the altercation.

"You're just an uptight bitch."

"I will not tolerate language like this in my classroom!"

"Call me a bitch one more time." Maggie's eyes narrowed to snake slits, she was close enough to rip the sneer off Katie's foundation plastered face. "I dare you."

"You're just jealous because Kyle likes me more than you and asked me to the dance. How does it feel to lose your boyfriend to me for the second time, B-I-T-C-H?" Katie emphasized the word by elongating each sound.

Kyle must have suddenly comprehended the peril reflected in Maggie's features because he leapt over the bar connecting the chair to his desk, anxious to rescue his homecoming date. But, even as the fastest human being on the planet, he hadn't registered Maggie's intent early enough.

Maggie's fist connected with Katie's nose.

The cheerleader fell to floor, screaming hysterically and shielding her face with her hands as Maggie prepared another swing. A strong arm intercepted Maggie's next attack before the classroom audience had concluded its collective gasp. She struggled halfheartedly to escape, but knew Kyle's grip well enough to recognize the pointlessness of the endeavor.

"That was out of line, Mags," he indicted in a low voice, reprimanding quietly in effort to keep the conversation private.

Maggie tried to push him away, but his hold was relentless.

"She called me a bitch."

"You get called that all time. She didn't do anythin' to you."

"You're right. *She* didn't."

Kyle's knowing grin was devoid of mirth or warmth. The chill of his conduct sliced coldly into Maggie's heart.

"You had your chance Mags. You passed."

Maggie swallowed a rock lodged in the back of her throat.

"I—I dink—she broke—my node," interjected Katie pitifully.

Blood stained the front of Katie's cheer vest. Kyle begrudgingly released Maggie and knelt to assist Katie. Mr. Cowley bellowed orders, belatedly asserting his authority.

"Maggie Brooks, go to the office. Max bring me those tissues, I need to stop this bleeding."

Stuffing notebooks and pencils into her bag, not bothering to make sure they were even hers, Maggie stormed into the hallway, forcing her eyes away from Kyle's gentle ministrations to Katie. Her jaw ached with the strain of composure. Two days. It had only been two days since Kyle's invitation to homecoming. Already he had replaced her with a fawning flunky, someone more willing to grovel for his attention. Kyle's betrayal engraved a new fissure in an old scar.

You're a fool, Maggie Brooks. You were wrong, just like the first time. Just like with Matt.

Maggie paused in front of the main office to calm herself. Brawling emotions devoured fragments of her strength. Adding to the fiendish jumble of sentiment was the dread of Lily's reaction. Her overachieving friend's stratagem hadn't exactly proceeded as planned. News of the confrontation would surely spread to everyone faster than a zombie virus infection. By morning, Maggie would be the VIP of the gossip pool. Not that she would actually swim in it—her actions would definitely warrant suspension from school.

She needed to relax before facing the administration. When her breathing had stabilized, and the coals of rage pacified, Maggie opened the office door. A large counter cut the room in half, the north side lined with chairs. The secretaries briefly scanned her as she chose a seat. Maggie trained her eyes on the azure flecked carpet in hopes of diminishing her presence. She engrossed herself in discerning the garish patterns pervading the carpet's weave while she waited, keeping her mind blissfully vacant. Soon she heard the office door thump ominously, followed by the muffled steps of Mr. Cowley's loafers crossing the floor. There was the click of a rotating handle, then another thump. The carpet swam in Maggie's vision. A few minutes later a stern voice proclaimed her name.

"Maggie Brooks."

The beefy principal stood in the threshold of his office, an austere frown deepening the rectangular lines of his features. He gestured to the interior of his office with a jerk of his thumb.

"Now."

Maggie obeyed unenthusiastically, stepping into the small cluttered room. Files coated every available surface. Rings of coffee stained the desk. A stuffy odor of dust and cologne offended her nostrils. The slam of the door behind her echoed like the stroke of an execution.

"Obviously you know why you are here, Ms. Brooks," Principal West indicated while crossing to his desk.

Maggie nodded but didn't speak. His low, raspy voice demanded respect.

"Mr. Cowley gave me his side of the events," the principal continued, arranging himself comfortably in his chair and signaling toward the history teacher seated next to her, "but maybe you could enlighten me as to your rationale of the altercation."

He flipped absently through her file. Knowing that her explanation would never justify absolution, Maggie chose rebellion as a tactic.

"I don't see why you'd care."

Principal West's age-pocked face manifested condescension, as if immune to this maneuver.

"Because I would hate to suspend you for 10 days just because you decided to punch your classmate in the nose."

His frown sagged lower, emphasized by a pronounced jutting in the lower lip.

"Does it really matter? I'm going to be suspended anyway."

"There's a difference between a day suspension and a week and half suspension. Give me a reasonable explanation, and I'll go easy on you. You and Katie have a history. What set things off?"

Maggie curled her lip angrily. From her perspective, Katie had received retributive justice, but Mr. West would never agree. She could see that undoubtedly in the neatly ordered, black-and-white perspective discharging from his mind. Her replies were short and uninformative.

"She's interfering with personal matters."

"I see."

Maggie remained silent.

"Have it your way. Ten days suspension."

Maggie swallowed hard. Mr. West turned back to her file. Obviously she had been dismissed.

"Will Katie be suspended as well?"

Principal West looked up with a measure of surprise.

"No."

Resentment heaved upward from Maggie's throat, spawning remarks that only served to hasten the arrival of her aforementioned execution.

"What? But Katie provoked me. When Mr. Cowley asked us to stop, she kept the fight going and—"

"She was the victim in all of this. I'm sure you can appreciate how that feels."

His response caught her flat-footed.

"Wait, what?"

"You were a victim yourself, to Trent Smith. When I suspended him, I didn't suspend you too, did I?"

"You suspended Trent?"

Frank astonishment arranged her expression.

"Of course, sexual harassment is inexcusable on this campus."

"But—how? Who told you about that?"

"The only witness willing to testify against Mr. Smith," he said, tossing the folder to one side of his desk. "Kyle Spencer. I suspended Trent immediately and removed him from the football team for inappropriate conduct. His assault on you wasn't his first transgression."

Internal conflict paralyzed Maggie's capability to respond. First, astonishment regarding Kyle's valor caused her posture to straighten. Then an uninvited surge of warmth stemmed from his unsolicited protection. Finally, a puncture of bitterness—realized of treachery—turned her fingers numb. When she had recovered enough to speak, she returned to the previous subject, hoping to solve her emotional anarchy later.

"These are two very different situations, Mr. West," Maggie argued, attempting to redirect his line of reasoning in her favor.

"How so?"

"Trent attacked me without cause or reason. He was showing off in front of his friends."

"You attacked Katie without cause or reason," he retorted, pitching Maggie's words back at her. "You haven't given me any basis for why you both deserve punishment."

"I did have a reason. She called me a bitch. I even warned her not to do it again."

"Name calling doesn't warrant a fist to the face. Anything else?"

Defeat coiled its scaly green tail triumphantly around Maggie's feeble validation. Maggie acknowledged the principal's condemnation. Controlling her antagonism suddenly seemed worthless. Words frothed from her tongue, interlaced with the weight of resentment and unrequited justice.

"You can't suspend me and let her off with nothing. If you suspend me, you have to suspend her too, at least for one day."

"You're right," Mr. West agreed incongruously, "you'll both receive a one-day suspension."

Mr. Cowley, who hadn't moved throughout the whole conversation, raised his face with shock. Maggie blinked in confusion. The principal stared straight at Maggie, a vacant gleam in his eye.

"So I'm only suspended for one day?" she probed, trying to clarify the principal's statement.

"I will make sure to contact your mother about this matter. You may return to school on Friday. Good-bye Ms. Brooks. Be sure to get off campus as quickly as possible."

Maggie didn't need further persuasion. She fled the office before the history teacher could fully form his objections.

*

Apparently, Maggie's predictions regarding the efficiency of the school-wide gossip network was 17 hours off. As the drone of the last bell sang through the hallways, a tirade of text messaging clogged cellphone cyberspace, lathering popular conversation with details of Katie's broken nose and opinions on the two girls' suspension from school. The expected pounding resounded on Maggie's front door at exactly 11 minutes past fourth period. Maggie could hear Lily's distress before the door was even opened.

Maggie swallowed a scoop of rice and meat before answering it. As soon as she lifted the latch, Lily burst through the threshold and into the tiny living room, a reluctant Mark in tow. She said nothing as she plopped on the couch, but looked at Maggie with eyes demanding an explanation. Mark hovered nervously by the TV in effort to avoid any verbal shrapnel.

Maggie returned to the living room floor and took another bite of her dinner.

"Well?" Lily finally voiced with impatience.

"Well what?" Maggie answered.

"Tell me what happened."

Maggie decided it would be best to provide Lily with the events in non-chronological order and—due to Mark's intrusion—edited of supernatural abilities. Starting with Kyle's date duplicity, she related events backward from suspension to pencil launch, dotting the conversation with appropriate defamation of Katie's character. Halfway through the narration, Lily began to absently poke at Maggie's unfinished meal with the chopsticks.

I can't believe it, Lily thought numbly. *This has to be a mistake or something.* Lily stabbed the utensil into the rice with a last despondent stroke. Her hands clutched her face in defeat.

"I realize I overdid it a bit," Maggie admitted, leaning her back on the sofa. "I don't know what came over me—"

"I know." Lily's voice slid through her fingers. "You finally allowed yourself to let him in, and it was too late." Lily lifted her head and looked directly at Maggie. Her unusual insight bored solidly into Maggie's heart. "I'm so sorry he hurt you."

Lily leaned forward and gave Maggie's shoulder an affectionate squeeze. Maggie's chest seemed to implode.

"Not only that," Maggie replied sharply, spewing blame to cover her weakness, "but Kyle really did his homework. He asked Katie to homecoming, knowing that I despise her more than any other person."

"C'mon Maggie," Mark offered, "he didn't do that on purpose. Kyle just asked her because you said no."

Realizing she was about to lose a boyfriend, or at least some vital part of his anatomy, Lily interposed before Maggie could retort.

"Mark sweetie, why don't you run down to the corner market and get us some sodas?"

"This has to be a misunderstanding, Maggie," Lily rationalized when the screech of Mark's tires wafted through the front room windows. "I know Kyle likes you. Is there any way you could have read it wrong?"

"There's no way, Lil. Not only did I see it in Katie's mind, but Kyle didn't deny anything even though he knew I'd read her."

"Why would he do something like that?" Lily asked rhetorically.

"Because he's a guy, and in the end—they're all the same. They only want you for one thing."

"Kyle's not like that at all," Lily argued. "He's not like Matt, Maggie."

"Whatever. If it looks like a duck and quacks like a duck—"

Maggie left the statement unfinished, and Lily stopped arguing. Though the room remained quiet, Lily's mind reeled through possible motives behind Kyle's choices. Her analysis hurtled from one deduction to another, leaving some inferences without conclusion and blending others into inconsistent masses of suppositions. The effect left Maggie breathless and dizzy.

"He's probably trying to make you jealous," Lily proposed at last. "That's the only thing that makes any sense."

"I'm not jealous," Maggie asserted, lifting herself out of Lily's mind.

"Maggie, you punched Katie in the middle of class just for thinking about him. Don't try to tell me you're not jealous."

Maggie brushed aside Lily's explanation as inconsequential. "So what if I am? I can't trust him now."

"No, I think you can trust him," Lily defended. "But you made him desperate, that's all. I think he's trying to prove a point."

"That what, he can piss me off?" Maggie asked in annoyance.

"No, that out of all the girls in school, he could have any that he chooses. But he chose you."

"So I should feel flattered?" Maggie snarled angrily, kicking over the rice bowl and scattering the remains of her dinner all over the floor.

"That's not what I meant, Maggie. He fought so hard for you, but then you rejected him. He's not invincible you know. Maybe he just needed a break—to look at things from a different perspective." Lily sat introspective for a moment, pondering. "There's only one thing we can do. I think we should stick to the plan."

"A little late for that, don't you think?"

"Well it's too late to go to the dance with him, that much is true, but you can still apologize."

Lily hopped off the couch and disappeared into the kitchen. When she walked back into the room she was waving the phone at Maggie.

"It's time to finally fix this," she said. "After the dance, I'm sure everything will return to normal."

Maggie reached out and took the cordless device from Lily.

"In my life, normal is relative."

"Call him," Lily pleaded.

"I don't have his phone number."

"I do."

Lily extricated her cell phone from the depths of her handbag and scanned through the numbers in her contact list. Maggie clicked on the phone, preparing to dial. As she waited, an impious voice ambushed her mind. She was only mildly surprised when she recognized it as her own.

Not really fair, is it.

What? she asked herself.

His behavior was just as inexcusable as yours, yet you're the one who has to patch things up.

Maggie tried to bury the voice, to push its insidious poison into oblivion.

No. Lily's right. I need to fix this. I made the mistake.

The voice refused to be quashed.

It's not your responsibility. He hurt you on purpose. You need to even the score.

The voice whispered a magnificent idea into the folds of her brain, a tempting proposal that burned shivers of triumph through her nerves.

"I found it! Ready?" Lily asked hopefully.

In answer, Maggie tossed the phone away. "I'm not going to apologize, Lil. He doesn't deserve it. Besides, I have a better idea."

"What's that?" Lily asked slowly, apprehension encircling her body like a halo.

"I'm going to beat him at his own game."

10: Scheme On The Table

Lily should have been in Mark-wallowing heaven. She could have been gazing longingly into his eyes or admiring the goofy curve of his smile as he sipped a soda. She wanted to be innocently arranging a coincidental swipe of her fingers against his as she reached across the table to snatch a french fry from the food basket, or contriving a way to suggest ordering a two-spoon-sundae without appearing too forward. Sitting across the booth from her boyfriend-to-be, she ought to be overjoyed with bliss.

But she wasn't.

After winning the homecoming game, a group of Bonneville students gathered at Lou's, a popular, '50s-themed diner in town, to celebrate the victory. Lily's shoulders deflated with a sigh. She struggled to spotlight her attention solely on Mark, because throbbing worry imprinted Lily's temples. Maggie hadn't exactly divulged the details of her revenge method, but Lily predicted the outcome, regardless. *It doesn't matter who wins tomorrow*, Lily thought disheartened. *Someone is going to get hurt and I care about them both.* Across the mustard-yellow plastic seats, Mark recounted the finer points of the game with such excitement that he failed to notice Lily's distracted behavior as she absently drowned a fry in her pool of ketchup.

"—and then when Spencer threw that 40 yard pass!" Mark continued with adulation. "He could be a pro someday! I swear he's like a superhero or something. What do you think?"

"Hmm?" Lily managed to respond, the word "superhero" capturing her awareness and burying the possible consequences of Maggie's retribution for a moment.

"Kyle Spencer? Don't you think he's awesome?" Mark repeated.

"No."

Startled, Lily raised her head just in time to notice Maggie before she snatched a handful of fries. Mark sank his teeth into a gargantuan hamburger and muttered something unintelligible through bun and meat. Maggie sociably slid into Lily, infringing on her personal space until Lily surrendered and moved over.

"So what are we doing tomorrow?" Maggie asked.

"What do you mean, 'we'?" Lily probed cautiously.

Maggie's confident posture sported success, causing an icy unease to coat the inside of Lily's stomach.

"For our homecoming date. You know, me and Nathan are going together."

Mark sputtered soda in surprise. Lily looked accusingly at her best friend, lips pursed in distress.

"Not Nathan Hinton from chemistry, Maggie."

"Yep," Maggie stated with a single nod of her head, happily pilfering more of the food.

Rarely did Lily allow events to dislodge her calm, but Maggie's persistent manipulations threatened to destroy any hope of repairing the situation, and Nathan didn't deserve such malicious exploitation. Lily offered Mark a hasty apology and escorted Maggie into the ladies room for a more private conversation.

"So this is your great plan?" Lily charged curtly as soon as the door slammed and a quick inspection revealed the stalls were unoccupied. "Make things even worse?"

Lily crossed her arms, pressing them tightly against her chest. "Nathan's only a sophomore and I'm sure he has no idea that you're just using him. He could really get hurt in all this, Maggie. Besides, you can't really think Nathan could make Kyle jealous."

"He'll have to do," Maggie answered with a little disappointment. "Everyone else I talked to already has a date to the dance. It doesn't matter anyway," she continued, arranging her hair in the mirror. "The whole point is to let Kyle see me in that dress and make him drool all over the floor, remember? He'll be sorry he dumped me so fast."

"You may look amazing in that dress, but Kyle's not stupid," Lily argued, more than a little desperate.

She couldn't bear to face Nathan tomorrow knowing he was merely cannon fodder—though lacking in social prowess, Nathan was at least a sincere person. Lily stared hard into Maggie's reflection.

"If you show up with Nathan, Kyle will know that he got to you," Lily said. "Not that you didn't make that completely obvious when you punched Katie."

"So what?" Maggie whirled, condemning Lily's opposition with a displeased expression. "When he sees me all decked out and gorgeous compared to his face-bandaged date, I'll be the one who gets to him."

"This is stupid Maggie. People are going to get hurt. Why can't you just forget about this whole revenge thing?"

"Kyle started it. And I'm going to finish it."

"If you do this, you are going to permanently damage any chances you may still have with Kyle, and I'll be the one that has to pick up the pieces!" Lily looked at the floor, lowering her voice to control its timbre. "Just like with Matt."

"I thought we agreed we weren't going to talk about that anymore!" Maggie snarled.

Lily quickly changed her arguing tactics. Impulsive anger in Maggie usually masked a deeper emotion; Lily easily descried the concealed pain.

"You know that Kyle would never do anything to hurt you," Lily said.

"What about dating the person I loathe more than anyone?"

"You know what I meant. Kyle doesn't deserve this kind of treatment. He's only ever been nice to you."

"So was Matt, at first." Maggie sprayed Lily's former subject back into the dispute, salting her edged words with emotional debris. "And we all know how that turned out. How about you let me decide how I want to deal with this?"

"I can't, Maggie," Lily pleaded, raising her gaze level to Maggie's slowly. "I won't survive another two years of you being torn apart. Please listen—we barely made it the last time."

Lily could see her words move some part of Maggie to pity. Lily hoped her sincerity for Maggie's welfare would pierce through Maggie's powers and pacify her need for retaliation. Indeed, Maggie swallowed indecisively. Lily could see the flash of divergent emotions war deep inside her best friend's sapphire eyes. A few tense moments followed without conversation. When Maggie turned back to Lily, her eyes were hard with resolve.

"Lil, I want to do this. Stop trying to talk me out of it."

"Fine then," Lily acknowledged. "This doesn't just affect you, you know, and the decision isn't just yours. I'm going to talk to Kyle myself."

Lily turned to leave, but Maggie caught her wrist.

"Don't get involved, Lily."

"Why not?" she shouted, finally unable to control her distress. "Why should I listen to you? You don't listen to me. If you take Nathan to the dance, then I'm going to tell Kyle everything." Lily paused, choosing her next words carefully, "And I mean everything."

"Yeah, like what?" Maggie taunted.

"How about you admitting that you like him? Or that the day you punched Katie you were going to accept his offer to the dance?" Lily twisted her arm free.

"You wouldn't dare," Maggie returned, her eyes narrowing with skepticism.

"Oh, I would. I'm desperate. Just look in here." Lily tapped her forehead. "I think he'll also be really interested to know that you only asked Nathan to the dance to get back at him for Katie."

Maggie's expression darkened long enough for a sliver to tickle Lily's hopes—Maggie looked as if she were considering the proposal. When a wicked smirk erupted on Maggie's face, Lily sucked in a hasty breath, hope quashed.

"Sure, tell him what you want," she began silkily, "but just keep in mind, the humiliation might make me slip up on a few things next week, like—oh, I don't know—revealing your middle name to the rest of the student body, maybe."

Shock stabbed Lily's heart.

"That's low, even for you, Maggie."

"If it stops you from talking to Kyle, I'll take what I can get. Just think, by next week everyone could be calling you 'Z.'"

"It's not my fault my parents named me Emily Zarahemla Ivers."

Lily knew her arguments had reached irrelevance.

"That's life. Last warning, 'Z.' Stay out of it."

Maggie wrenched open the door.

"Fine," Lily returned, "but when your heart gets broken again, don't expect any sympathy from me!"

But Lily was talking to air. Maggie had already slammed the door behind her.

11: Saturday the 13th

The pulsating bass of the speakers filled Maggie's ears with cotton and the DJ's station flashed the dance floor with glaring multicolored lights. Her heels slipped continually on the silver and gold, confetti-plastered floor. A sea of balloons impeded free movement. The odor of stale gym socks coated her nostrils, and she wondered crossly why no one seemed to have worn adequate antiperspirant. When Nathan stepped on her toes again—he had done so more times than she could count—she ungraciously pushed him toward a line of tables against the far wall.

"Maggie, I am so sorry. Are you okay? Do you need to sit down? Can I get you something?" Nathan fell over himself with apologies.

Maggie wondered, not for the first time today, if that was the limit of his vocabulary.

"It's okay," she replied with false reassurance, "let's just sit down for a minute."

The flush in Nathan's face drained appreciably. His hands plunged into his tuxedo pockets as the pair waded through the surf of cherry and white balloons. Maggie yanked several metallic streamers that hung in her way. At least the tables offered her some protection from Nathan's unwieldy feet, not to mention relief from the pounding music. She gratefully sank into a chair, removing the pressure from her pinched and uncomfortable toes, which had never previously endured open-toed heels. Nathan fumbled into a position close to her, astutely avoiding eye contact.

Disaster had pestered Maggie from the moment their date began. Nathan's nervousness had expressed itself throughout the day via continuous shaking. During their first activity, an early morning campfire, he successfully spilled scorching hot chocolate all over her jeans. Later, while hiking, he stumbled over his own shoes, accidentally knocking her into a mud patch. When Lily announced that they planned to go bowling in the afternoon, Nathan seemed even more anxious. How such a scrawny sophomore had managed to toss a 16 pound bowling ball 10 feet behind him was beyond Maggie's understanding of physics. Luckily, it had hit her on the left thigh instead of the right, so the painful red bruise lay hidden by her dress.

"I really am sorry, Maggie," Nathan's voice trembled self-consciously.

"It's okay, Nathan," Maggie answered, pity tempering her response. She was directly responsible for his misery after all. "I mean it."

Her remorse didn't last long, however. As her eyes darted around the decorated commons, she patted her dark hair absently. Though the graceful up-do highlighted the curve of her neck, the little interwoven silver flowers tickled her scalp. Nathan kept his gaze focused on the dance floor. Maggie needed him to act somewhat dashing or Kyle would see past her façade.

For the first time since Matt, Maggie had actually expended effort enhancing her beauty. Her radiant blue dress and the cunning color palate of her eye makeup inflamed her striking eyes. A simple silver chain complemented the seductive plunge of the gown's elegant neckline. Maggie's classmates gawked at her splendor in surprise as she glided past them.

"Isn't this a great party?" Lily sang happily from Maggie's right.

Mark stood next to her, unexpectedly stylish in his black tuxedo. He acknowledged both Maggie and Nathan with a nod, then encircled his fingers around Lily's hand. Lily beamed so enthusiastically that Maggie wondered if the tiny jewels adorning Lily's hair sparkled with her delight rather than the DJ's flashing lights.

"You've really outdone yourself, Lil," flattered Maggie. "This is fantastic." *Except for some of the company*, she thought dryly, flicking her glance between the two boys.

"Thanks Maggie," Lily gushed brightly, "and just wait 'til you see the homecoming royalty ceremony!"

"Which I'm sure you'll win," Mark said with a confident hand squeeze.

"Actually I won't," Lily confessed with a shake of the head. "I took my name off the ballot this year."

A wrinkle of surprise formed on Maggie's brow. Mark's mouth gaped wide in astonishment.

"Why?" he asked incredulously. "You deserve a crown for all your hard work!"

Mark pulled Lily closer, seeming to tune out all else in favor of her ice-green eyes. Maggie's eye roll was lost in the dim light. Mark's ridiculous flirting style had bothered her all day. She had to keep reminding herself that this torture would be well worth it once she encountered Kyle.

"That's sweet, Mark," answered Lily, cheeks aglow, "but I figured since I've won homecoming queen the last three years in a row, I should probably let someone else have a chance."

"You still deserve it," Mark argued.

At least Maggie agreed with Mark on that point. No one did more for the school than Lily. She merited some kind of recognition. Once again, Maggie felt uplifted by the selflessness of her best friend.

"Well it's too late now," Lily declared, "the votes are already cast."

"That might be," Mark pronounced, "but you're the only queen in my heart."

He placed his palms majestically over his heart. Maggie moaned louder than she intended because Lily looked over in concern.

"Hey guys," she asked the boys sweetly, "do you think you could go get us some drinks? It's really hot in here."

"Sure thing," Mark replied, gesturing to Nathan.

Nathan and Mark cut through the couples congesting the dance floor, heading toward the refreshment table in the opposite corner. Maggie turned from their retreat, unstrapping the four-inch heels from her aching feet, coolly ignoring Lily's expectant expression. Kneading the knots from her arches with her knuckles, she waited until the boys were thoroughly lost in the throng.

"These heels are killing me," she admitted testily, "and it doesn't help that Nathan keeps stepping on my toes every five seconds."

"The poor guy can't help it," Lily suggested. "You're too gorgeous for your own good. He's so nervous, he keeps embarrassing himself."

"Trust me," Maggie said, pointing to the concealed bruise on her leg, "I noticed."

"Well, it takes a certain type of guy to be confident around you."

Lily offered innocence behind her jewel lined eyes, but her implication was poorly masked. Maggie turned away in a huff.

"You know, he's not here yet," Lily offered calmly. "It's not too late to call this off."

"Lily—"

"—and even you think Nathan is too nervous to handle it," Lily continued, ignoring the warning growl in Maggie's response. "Kyle's going to see right through him."

"Stop trying to talk me out of this. I'm here. It's past time to take anything back."

Lily twirled her fingertips in the candlelit centerpiece water bowl, waiting for Maggie to continue the conversation.

"This is driving me crazy," Maggie spurted suddenly.

"What?"

"I can't seem to read anyone's mind."

Lily's eyes danced with friendly intrigue. "I'm surprised it took you this long to notice."

"Notice what?"

"Really Maggie, haven't you realized that every time you get overemotional your powers don't work?" Lily explained. "You're always one step ahead of everyone, unless you're angry. Then they get the better of you. It happens all the time when Kyle is around."

Maggie's reply stuck stubbornly in her throat. Before she managed to release it, a cup of punch slid in front of her. Trust Nathan and Mark to reappear at the most inconvenient of times.

"Thanks Nathan," she said absently, lifting the glass.

"Not quite, Sparky, he had to run out to his car."

Maggie almost choked on the rosy liquid as Kyle's broad figure appeared next to her.

"I offered to bring over your drink for him." A roguish smile turned the corners of Kyle's lips.

Maggie's limbs felt heavy and awkward. A crystalline white rose shone on his lapel, offsetting the rich sable of his tuxedo jacket. His eyes brushed over Lily.

"Look at you, Sunshine. All dressed up."

Offering his hand gallantly, he lifted Lily from her chair, spinning her in a twirl to fully appraise her appearance.

"You're like the goddess Aphrodite. Mark's one lucky guy."

"Thanks Kyle, you're always so nice," Lily radiated.

"Of course, I expect a dance with the prettiest girl at the party." Imitating a Victorian gentleman, he graced a charmed Lily with a courtly bow. Lily clapped appreciatively.

Fury smoldered against Maggie's teeth. Mark's attempts at chivalry had failed gallingly, but Kyle's execution was flawless. Unfortunately, Kyle had discovered her before Nathan had returned, rendering her temporarily dateless. His casual manner illustrated indifference toward Maggie's choice of escort. Her hand twitched with the desire to smack his conquering grin.

"Is your date going to be all right with that?" Maggie commented with ire-laced sweetness. "Last I checked she was the jealous type."

Maggie raised herself from the chair, posing her body to best flaunt her figure. Kyle started, as if he had forgotten her presence. Her face involuntarily contorted into a grimace at his blatant provocation.

"Oh, you mean Katie?" He grinned, stepping toward Maggie. "Nah, she's mild compared to some of the girls I used to chase."

He winked at her. A kind of strangled sound came from Lily's direction.

"Speakin' of Katie, I better go find her. There's nothin' worse than keepin' a girl waitin'."

Spinning on his heel, he retreated back to the dance floor. Maggie watched, unsure if her trembling stemmed from wrath or disappointment. As soon as Kyle reached the edge of dancers he turned abruptly, fixing his hazel gaze on her. His eyes caressed her shiny hair, slid longingly along her neck and fingered her silky dress down to her bare feet. A callous smile twisted his impossibly captivating face.

"Nice dress."

Then he disappeared into the crowd.

Maggie returned to her chair in bitter defeat, angrily kicking her hateful shoes. She smothered a handful of confetti. Lily had warned her that he might perceive Maggie's intentions and counter her attack. Encumbered by her own sentiments, she had been unable to pluck anything from his head. Kyle's actions, however, conveyed an easy interpretation. Her appearance had not overwhelmed his wits as she had hoped; the piercing claws of envy had refused to mar his composure. Lily slipped a reassuring arm around Maggie's shoulders.

"Please don't say anything," Maggie said.

"I wasn't going to," Lily said, squeezing Maggie with affection. "I was just going to mention that it's time for me start the royalty ceremony."

But Lily didn't bustle away. For a few minutes she simply rested her arm around Maggie in silent support. Maggie barely registered the return of their dates.

"Nathan's back," Lily mentioned quietly, "why don't you ask him to drive you home?"

Maggie nodded numbly as the other two looked at her with concern. She mechanically strapped on her left shoe. Maggie felt Lily's arm withdraw.

"I'll be right back with the coats," Nathan offered belatedly, scampering away quickly.

Maggie waited expectantly for Nathan's return, but his passage to the cloakroom was suddenly obstructed by bodies as they pressed forward toward a makeshift platform, vying for a better vantage of the ceremony. Lily stood center stage, a thick parchment envelope in her hand. A fellow student perched nearby, clutching a glitzy tiara and plastic gold crown. As Lily read the nominations for homecoming king, Maggie spotted Nathan in the assembly. Apparently, he had paused to hear the awards. An uproar of applause followed the announcement of the winner.

Maggie scowled, but remained unsurprised. Kyle was insanely popular after all. Several football buddies clapped him on the back as he ascended the stage. He dropped to one knee as Lily placed the crown atop his spiky crew cut. He smiled graciously and waved. Maggie looked away as the crowd articulated its pleasure. Viciously, she replaced her second shoe, keenly ignoring the nominations for homecoming queen.

Maggie stood just as Lily declared the victor.

"And the winner is—"

Lily hesitated, locking worried eyes with Maggie for an instant. A murmur heaved through the spectators. Quickly straining her visage into compulsory enthusiasm, Lily readdressed the audience.

"Katie Maxwell."

The proclamation struck Maggie as a physical blow, the air leaving her lungs in a painful gasp. She watched as Lily clasped the tiara with reserve. Kyle moved to the stairs and lifted Katie onto the stage. As the tiara glided onto her head, Katie blew kisses to the crowd. Maggie could barely discern the masked bandage on the homecoming queen's nose.

"Dance, dance, dance," chanted the congregation. Kyle offered his arm to his elated date, leading her to the floor. A romantic ballad blared through the speakers. Kyle spun her once, then wrapped his arm around Katie's narrow waist. His head pressed against hers as the couple circled the hexagon shaped commons in a rhythmic embrace.

Maggie's heart fragmented into a thousand shards. Every twirl and dip the couple performed propelled those pieces into her soul, ripping jagged cavities through her being. For a few moments she stood transfixed, staring at the couple in horror as if under some terrible curse.

Then she fled the room.

The closest exit led outside into the cold October evening. The breeze pricked at her bare shoulders with frosty blades, sprouting gooseflesh along her skin. White flurries licked the concrete steps and dusted them with a powder of snow. Maggie managed to brush some of it away before perching on the edge. The ice would most likely damage her satin dress, but she didn't care. The sidewalk continued for a few hundred feet, then ended in a large, snow drenched lawn. The parking lot lay on the opposite side of the school, so Maggie found herself alone.

At first she tried to brush away the stinging droplets leaking from her eyes, but her fingers were soon overwhelmed by her sorrow's ferocity. The bitter-crisp air stung her lungs as sobs heaved from her breast. Tears burned frozen channels into her cheeks. Melting snowflakes sprinkled her, as if her skin wept. The black, cloudy sky reflected her grief: frigid, bleak, and lonely.

When the tears stopped, Maggie's strength was spent. Winter's chill crept under her fingernails and throbbed inside her toes. She pulled her knees up to her chin and wrapped her arms around herself. Emotional havoc had numbed her sense of time. She might have been outside for hours or merely minutes. Her limbs began to shiver, but she felt too exhausted to stir.

Unexpectedly, a smooth mantle of cloth blanketed her shoulders. Residual warmth lingered inside the tuxedo jacket and she pulled it tighter around her body. Familiar cologne drifted from its surface, persuading a new swell of tears to crest under her eyes. She swallowed firmly, allowing only one to escape from beneath her lashes. Quickly she swept it away.

"Come back in Sparky, it's freezin'."

Judging by his voice, he stood right behind her. She didn't trust herself to face him, not with a fresh sob constricting her chest.

"Just come in and get your date so he can drive you home," he said.

Maggie chose to let his words sting offensively. Long ago she had discovered anger to be a more satisfying companion than heartache.

"Shouldn't you be inside celebrating your new title or something?" she returned, still staring into the snow drifted shadows. "I'm sure your new girlfriend is lost without you."

"She isn't my girlfriend. Not yet anyway."

"Too bad. You two seem perfect for each other."

Maggie wished her turbulent emotions would subside. Her need to hear Kyle's thoughts was desperate. She stood quickly and walked forward, still refusing to turn toward him. Kyle's voice trailed after her.

"I finally figured it out y'know. Why you hate men so much. It all has to do with this Matt guy."

Maggie spun, anguish momentarily vaporized in an explosion of rage.

"Don't! You have no idea what he did to me!"

"I'm not stupid, Sparky. I can guess what happened," he said, hopping over the stairs.

"It's none of your business," she hissed vehemently. "Matt was a long time ago. I've moved on."

"Did you?" he taunted, strolling closer. "Or are you still so hurt by it that you can't let me into your life?"

"I never wanted you in my life," she snarled, ripping the jacket off her body with shaky fingers. She threw it at him violently, but he caught it with little effort. The misery of the cold stabbed her exposed skin.

"Is that why you hit Katie in the face? Because you didn't want me?"

"That had nothing to do with you," she lied.

"You were jealous," Kyle chuckled, rewrapping the tuxedo coat around her form faster than Maggie could pull away. Leaving his hands on the lapels, he used the garment to draw her closer. "It melts my heart that you would fight over me," he teased.

"Don't flatter your ego," she sneered, pushing him away. "People can barely fit in the same room with you as it is."

"There's no need to get snippy," he mused, genially enjoying the sight of her escape efforts. " 'Specially since you and I both know it's true."

"Don't presume to think you know anything about me. You'll only embarrass yourself."

He leaned closer. "I don't get embarrassed, Sparky. If you really wanted to come with me that bad, all you had to do was say 'yes.' "

Kyle released her suddenly, and turned to leave. As his footsteps crunched into the snow, panic surged from her stomach. Alone, in the darkening flurry, the anger would sputter, quenched by melancholy regret. She said the first thing that reared in her head.

"I tried to! I even tried to say I was sorry, but you were so busy stalking Katie that you failed to notice!"

"It's not like you were beatin' down my door, Princess," Kyle threw over his shoulder angrily.

"What did you want me to do? There's no way I would beg on hands and knees. Saying sorry should be enough."

"You haven't even done that!" he proclaimed, halting his retreat and turning back. "As for beggin' on your knees," he growled ruthlessly, "you should try it sometime. Might help you keep a friend or two."

"I don't need friends. Especially one who claims to care about me, then moves on to the first opportunity with a short skirt."

"Maggie, there's no such thing as movin' on after you!" Kyle yelled in exasperation. "You're so damn gorgeous that a man will regret fallin' for you for the rest of his life!"

Maggie sucked in a breath of surprise. Kyle had used her name correctly. Tears choked her response.

"Life was easier before you showed up," she roared in livid accusation. "I just want you to leave me alone!"

"I can't!"

"Why not?!"

Kyle's super speed crossed the expanse between them faster than Maggie's eyes could process the blur. Before she fully comprehended his proximity, she felt the warmth of his breath on her cheek and the sanctuary of his body embrace her. His lips savored hers fervently, bleeding hungrily into her. The simultaneous sensations of his fingers on the small of her back and the pressure of his hand kneading her hair pulsated ferociously through her blood, suffocating her with passion. She returned his kiss with the ache of ardor.

Slowly Kyle pulled away, anguish rimming his eyes.

"Because I love you, Maggie. Why can't you let me?"

The icy gust left in Kyle's wake penetrated jacket, skin, and bone, leaving Maggie's heart a flaccid, vacuous shell. He withdrew through the commons door before she could react. A mournful melody escaped through the door as it closed, calling out to her in sorrow.

12: Drowning and Hollow

A grunt escaped Kyle's throat as he rolled restlessly over his mattress, submerging his face in a baggy pillow. His eyelids throbbed from the torture of a sleepless night. Any time the bliss of darkness had promised to free his exhausted body, the image of Maggie's feisty blue eyes, dampened by tears, plunged him into insomnia. Then he would mentally bombard himself with vibrant reprimands, sickened at his own behavior.

His coarse twill blanket chafed his chest, urging wakefulness. Gramps' rooster crowed loudly, relentlessly authenticating dawn. The first fingers of sunlight spilled through the bottom of the window shade, creeping stealthy up the A-frame walls. Throwing the pillow on the floor in defeat, Kyle placed his hands behind his head and stared thoughtfully into the faded panel ceiling. Old wires ran the length of aged wooden walls, stapled at irregular intervals. The cables eventually led to several makeshift outlets and switches, the electrical work having been retrofitted years ago.

Some of Kyle's most contented memories were born in this house. Built nearly 70 years previously, the old structure had housed Kyle's father as he grew into adulthood. Every year as a small child, Kyle had anticipated spending the summer in the warm, cozy cottage, running through the muddy fields and shadowing his tough, home-grown grandfather. Russet photos of the Spencer family tree still decorated the sun-bleached wallpaper. The well-loved furniture invited long conversations around the sooty fire hearth. The kitchen still smelled of ginger and apples—a legacy left by his grandmother. Kyle felt a sense of belonging here, like the house itself had invited him, unlike his brother's condo in California.

Kyle eventually hauled himself into a sitting position and snatched a small battery-operated alarm clock from the scruffy dresser next to his bed. The digital pixels flashed half past six. He dragged his hand over his nose and chin, rousing himself. The ancient floor boards groaned in protest as he stood and stretched to remove the kinks from his muscles. Shuffling to the window, he raised the shade. The faded red barn across the yard floated atop a sea of white, glittering snow. Large drifts of submerged farm machinery formed smooth mounds that rolled lazily about the landscape. He pressed his head against the cool window pane, tapping absently on the wall with his index finger. Maggie. Tap. Maggie. Tap. Maggie. Her face even occupied an imagined reflection in the frosted window.

Yesterday morning had occurred more or less the way he had expected—at first. Katie arrived early, flushed with excitement. Her attentions never wavered as their day activities commenced. She giggled at every joke and flirted ferociously. Her inconsequential discussion topics were limited and dull: cheerleading, dating, and her unwarranted suspension. Kyle tuned out most of her conversation unless she mentioned Maggie—always in regard to the broken nose incident—and Kyle had to avert his face to hide his amusement. Katie's conventional character floundered in comparison to Maggie's fiery personality.

Kyle moved to a rickety table on the far wall. Its scratched surface supported Kyle's most treasured possessions: his TV and game console. Throwing himself into a chair, he flipped on the electronics, which he noticed were in desperate need of a severe dusting. Testily, he buffed the screen with a shirt he snatched from the floor. He stared at his collection of games, unsure which would best distract him from his thoughts.

When he had seen Maggie at the dance, that shiny dress clutching her body like the paint on a fully automatic P-90 rifle—

Kyle tried to banish the vision, but the events of last night refused dismissal. As soon as he and Katie had entered the dance, he jail-break dashed to the refreshment table, leaving Katie's high-pitched giggle to occupy Lauren Elson. In an attempt to prolong his escape from his clingy date, he struck up friendly banter with whoever was already there— Mark Weston and Nathan Hinton. Kyle almost choked on his drink when Nathan pointed out his date. Maggie's appearance had completely disarmed Kyle. He gazed at her exquisite image for two minutes before he could recover his sensibilities. When he finally turned back to his friends, wild jealously raked his body, and he had to suppress a feral desire to pound Nathan into oblivion.

Which, after a few moments of tense restraint, he decided was Maggie's objective.

Rummaging through the video game container, he opted for one of the most violent, blood-spattering, first-person shooters in his collection. Maybe splattering alien guts all over the universe would relieve some anxiety. He skipped the intro and dropped into one of the most ferocious levels of the enemy-laden space station. His super soldier assault rifle decimated the opposing ranks.

Kyle suddenly realized that every alien he blasted sported Nathan Hinton's face.

His miniature space soldier exploded in a shower of red droplets. Kyle swore savagely and restarted the level. Absorbed in completing the stage, he amputated homecoming night from his brain. The distraction worked for about half an hour, until the easy rhythm of the game allowed his mind to wander. Last night resumed its infectious scourge on his concentration.

In order to confront Maggie, Kyle had needed Nathan gone. Using Mark's adulation, Kyle maneuvered a query about a new CD Mark had recently burned, then expressed an interest in borrowing it. Mark was only too happy to retrieve the new album from his truck. Fortuitously, Nathan volunteered to accompany his friend. Kyle collected himself hastily, crafting a pretense of polished debonair to conceal the jelly that wriggled inside his nerves. He intended to call Maggie's bluff and entice her to confess an apology.

He supposed he should have known her better.

Fascinating voltage flashed inside her eyes the angrier she became. Her beauty threatened to paralyze him. The only way to resist her allure was to sham indifference. It had worked, momentarily. Her glossy hair seemed to beg for release, her olive toned thigh hungered to be touched, and her lips—just remembering their electric taste caused his spine to shiver.

The game controller shattered in his grasp, the remains falling onto the wooden floor with a despondent clatter, mimicking everything in his life.

Metaphors, he thought with disgust, glowering at the plastic fragments. *I hate metaphors.*

Kyle pressed his palms against his eyelids until stars erupted behind them. The resulting ache diverted his mind from another, deeper pain lodged in his chest. From the first day he'd been drawn to Maggie on the stadium bleachers, he knew he belonged to her, existed for her. She was everything: bones, heart, blood, and soul. He loved her, unequivocally. Kyle knew that the "love at first sight" cliché only occurred in movies, but the universe had offered no other explanation. On that day, the galaxy had simply reversed its clockwise rotation and altered his fabric of reality.

He released his tortured eyes and catalogued the bits of game controller scattered at his feet. He had taken one apart once, curious to discover is mechanization. Scooping the broken conglomerate of metal, wire, and plastic onto his desk, he absently arranged them according to function. He pulled an assortment of tools from a drawer.

Nathan wasn't really to blame, he admitted to himself, mentally recalling the tiny machine's framework. The poor guy had been caught between two passionate individuals and sadly became emotional collateral damage. The animosity Kyle had initially harbored for Nathan was misplaced. After all, it hadn't been Nathan's actions that instigated Maggie's tear-laden requiem on the school steps.

A sigh heaved his shoulders. Kyle flipped on his desk lamp, fiddling with two halves of a silicone wafer. He was directly responsible for the destruction of Maggie's rebellious spirit. Only once had he ever experienced such an intense desire to turn back time.

I'm such a jerk, Kyle reproached himself, carelessly reassembling the interior electronics. *If only my life was this easy to put back together.*

Kyle assessed his handiwork. The plastic cover was hopelessly cracked. This particular controller would forever boast its battle scars. He restarted the game console for a test run. The left joystick interface was a little slow. With a growl, Kyle tossed the offending piece of technology back on his desk and checked the time: 9:30.

He had disassembled the controller again and was rummaging through another desk drawer, looking for a different set of implements when a soft knock from the door startled him. Twisting the handle, he expected to greet the leathery face of his 85-year-old grandfather. Instead, he found shiny locks of blond, framing breathless arctic-green eyes.

"Hey Sunshine, what're you doin' here?" Kyle hailed with genuine welcome, throwing a crumpled T-shirt over his head.

"Does a girl need a reason to come visit a friend?"

" 'Course not. Come in. I didn't hear the doorbell."

Lily skipped into the room, mindful to maneuver around the piles of clothes and school supplies that littered the floor. She politely ignored the mess and settled into the desk's chair.

"Your grandpa was in the front yard scraping ice off the walk. He let me in and pointed me to your room," she explained as she idly lifted an object from the desktop to inspect it. "What are you building?"

"Fixin' a game controller, I broke it this mornin'."

"What did you do, throw it against the wall?" Lily jested lightly, appraising the collection of small parts.

"Actually, I smashed it while playin' a game," he mentioned with a wry smile. "Guess I don't know my own strength."

Lily giggled blithely at his humor. "I guess super strength is sort of a burden, huh?"

"You have no idea."

Kyle plopped onto his bed. The rusty springs squawked loudly at his rough treatment. Lily seemed not to know quite how to respond, so she offhandedly scanned the room. Her eyes lingered on a portrait of two people resting on his dressing table.

"Who are they?" she asked, pointing at the photo.

"My mom and dad."

"Really?" she questioned dubiously, squinting at the faces.

Kyle removed the picture from the dresser and passed it to Lily, waiting. The slender man in the photo, somewhere in his early 50s, sported thick 1970-style glasses and his greying hairline had receded substantially. He seemed to be of average height. Kyle's mother hugged his father affectionately with a plump, frumpy body. Her mousey brown hair hung in unruly waves around her face, and though her expression was pleasant, her features were plain. Both their eyes were a dippy cobalt blue.

"But you don't look anything like them!"

"I know," he chuckled, taking back the frame and running his fingers over the glass fondly. "It's a big joke in my family that I was accidently switched with some other baby in the hospital. At least, that's what my older brother used to say."

"You have a brother?" Lily asked with astonishment.

"Yeah, he lives in L.A. with his wife and two kids. Looks just like my dad, too, includin' the glasses."

"Oh!" Lily looked at him thoughtfully. "How come you never mentioned him before?"

"Guess I never thought about it. Eric and I aren't the best of friends."

"Why not?" The timbre of Lily's voice revealed an incredulity that siblings could be anything but friends.

"I was the first all-star athlete in a long line of chess club presidents. Eric didn't really have a great time in high school. The girls were pretty brutal to him."

"So he wasn't popular?"

"Nope, and he wasn't good at sports either. Which is why he stopped bein' my friend when I broke six foot at age

15 and became dad's pride and joy. My dad always wanted to play football when he was at school but never made the team. I guess it hurt Eric pretty bad when dad got so focused on me."

"But that wasn't your fault."

"In a way it was. I used to be pretty cocky."

"What changed?"

Kyle looked into Lily's face, preparing to gauge the impact of his answer.

"My parents died."

Lily's face contorted in horror. "Kyle, I'm so sorry."

"You don't need to apologize."

"But I brought it up! I never—"

"You didn't know." He paused, then drew a deep breath. "My parents chartered a private plane to Hawaii to celebrate their anniversary. Something went wrong with one of the engines."

Kyle's voice trailed off. It had been over a year since he had mentioned anything about the accident, but his voice still cracked. Lily's face went pallid. He pushed the conversation forward for her sake.

"After that, a lot of things didn't matter that much to me. I quit sports for a while. They reminded me too much of my dad. We sold my parents' house and I moved in with Eric. That didn't go over so well. Me and Eric fight a lot. So eventually, I called Gramps and asked if I could move in with him."

Lily blinked quickly and sniffled.

"Don't cry, Smiles. I've come to terms with it." Kyle stood and replaced the picture on the dresser. "I even decided it was time to get back into sports. Figured it would make my dad turn over in his grave if he knew I'd given up. I contacted the coach at Bonneville right after I talked to Gramps."

"Why didn't you tell us?"

"I didn't want you feelin' sorry for me. Besides, it didn't really cross my mind much. I've been pretty busy chasin' a certain girl." Kyle fingered the soft curves of his mother's face beneath the glass. "I miss her the most, you know—my mom. She would know how to fix this mess I've made with Maggie. She was good at stuff like that."

"And who's to say you're not?" Lily asked kindly. "You've been perfect for her from day one, even though you fight a little. And you win too, something that doesn't usually happen."

"And I also make her cry."

"Nobody's perfect," Lily teased gently. "You both might have super powers, but you're still human. You guys were bound to make mistakes eventually."

Kyle stared hard out the window without speaking. Lily exhaled guiltily.

"Now that I think about it, this whole mess is probably my fault," she said.

"What are you talkin' about, Smiles? There's no way you could be blamed for any of this."

"You think so? I don't. I knew exactly what Maggie was doing. I could have warned you ahead of time and none of this would have happened. I should have told you how Maggie felt about you."

"I already knew, Sunshine, even before she broke Katie's nose. I knew she cared for me. And still I didn't—couldn't—stop. I hurt her pretty bad."

"Well, you still need to figure out how to fix it," Lily observed pragmatically. "Maggie's just as upset with her own actions as you are with yours. Seems like you're both tired of the whole thing. Why not kiss and make up?"

Lily's merry smile indicated that she had already received full disclosure of the incident outside the dance from Maggie. He chuckled heartily.

"Guess you already know I've got the 'kiss' part down."

Lily's dynamic laughter brightened the entire room. Kyle couldn't help but share in her vitality.

"Well, it was really romantic in its own way," she reflected, "out in the cold, both of you really angry. It's so poetic! The point is, neither of you objected."

Kyle refrained from speaking for a few minutes while he digested the suggestion. He could tell that Lily was holding her breath in anticipation.

"I guess the only thing to do is go see Mags and clear this whole thing up."

Lily clapped her hands together with angelic exhilaration. "I knew you'd be easier to convince than Maggie. I tried that with her all night and she just wouldn't listen. She seems to think you don't want to see her anymore." Lily rolled her eyes prettily. "She's always so dramatic."

"Would you like to come with me? She might not let me in if I go by myself."

"You're going to have to wait until Wednesday, I'm afraid," Lily pronounced regretfully. "Maggie and her mom went to Salt Lake early this morning. They'll be gone for a few days."

Kyle shrugged off a mild swell of disappointment. He supposed he could call, but these kinds of situations required more intimacy. Better to wait. He felt a half smile rend his face.

"I guess there's only one thing left for us to do then."

"What's that?" she asked.

"Figure out how I'm going to explain all this to poor Katie."

13: No Fury Like a Woman Torn

Maggie inspected her appearance in the bathroom mirror. Her brunette hair was groomed neatly into a ponytail with a chunk of chin length bangs framing the right side of her face. A dark sweater overlapped her light blue jeans and a fitted denim jacket completed her ensemble.

I need some new clothes, she complained to herself.

Satisfied that it was at least the most flattering outfit in her closet, she sludged through the piles of excess belongings that crowded her tiny bedroom. Digging at the bottom of her petite wardrobe, Maggie produced her favorite pair of well-worn sneakers. She pushed the heaps of earlier rejected clothing off the bed and slipped on the shoes.

She tightened the laces with tense fingers. School would be awkward at best, most probably excruciating. Though four days had passed since homecoming, she still felt unprepared to handle Kyle. Her excursion with her mother had prevented any opportunity for Maggie to see him in person, and the thought of trying to talk with him over the phone foreboded heartburn. Several times during her trip Maggie considered calling Lily—at least her best friend could satisfy the desperate need to discover if Kyle and Katie had become official—but a deep part of her dreaded the answer.

Instead, Maggie turned off her phone and buried it inside her duffel bag. Denial was easier.

Regrettably, the respite had been brief. In less than an hour she would be at school, confronting—what? Kyle had proclaimed his love Saturday night, but retreated back to Katie. Maggie had spotted them leaving the dance together. So, what did it mean? That he loved her but wanted to date Katie? That he was still waiting for an apology? Or worse—had he finally given up? The thought drove her to dial Lily's phone number frantically.

Of course Lily's voice mail answered. Lily was most likely at school already, dealing with some new extracurricular event. Maggie stood and collected her school gear, then navigated the haphazard terrain of her bedroom floor. The odor of brewing coffee greeted her in the hallway on the way to the kitchen. Once there, she found her tousle-haired mother fiddling with the coffeemaker.

"Mom," Maggie asked in amazement, "what are you doing up this early?"

"I thought I'd make you a cup of coffee before you left," her mother answered unconvincingly.

Tara Brooks was a notoriously late riser. The only time Maggie saw her mother this early in the morning was for some type of emergency.

"And?" Maggie probed, hoping to encourage her mother's thoughts to reveal the underlying motive.

Tara voiced her intentions at almost the same time Maggie read it. The effect was unsettling, like listening to a stereo when one speaker is three seconds slower than the other.

"I just wanted to see if you were willing to admit anything to me before I have lunch with Lily's mom. She's going to give me the info about why you've been acting so strange the last few days."

"I have not been acting strange," Maggie objected.

"Really? Let's see." Tara poured two cups and settled herself at the table. She took a sip before continuing. "You didn't fight with me during the trip, I bought you that new zombie game you've been begging for—you didn't even look at it—and you practically broke down and cried when we walked past that sports store."

"I've just got a lot on my mind," Maggie dodged, fidgeting with the shoulder strap on her bag. "That's all."

"Fine," Tara replied, tapping the lip of her coffee mug. "Try to be sly all you want. Linda will give me the details I need." *Thank goodness Lily tells her mother everything.*

"How could I forget?" Maggie grumbled under her breath, carefully pitching her voice too low for her mother to hear.

She left the kitchen without touching the coffee and hurried to the front door. Plunging her hands into her school bag, she rummaged for her keys as she turned the handle. She allowed muscle memory to guide her down the front step and across the icy pavement toward the driveway, her concentration fully consumed by the search. She was just wondering how her keys could have been swallowed so completely by her textbooks when a stream of thought crept into her unguarded mind.

Hey Sparky.

Maggie halted abruptly, snapping her attention forward. A divergent cocktail of shock, grief, and joy paralyzed her. Kyle's sleek, red jeep snuggled comfortably in the driveway, blocking her shabby sedan. He leaned comfortably against his vehicle and stared at her contentedly.

Need a ride? his thoughts asked tenderly.

A gasp of disbelief escaped her body, hanging visible in the chill air. Gradually, through no conscious direction of her own, Maggie's feet carried her toward him. His magnetic smile drew her onward. Her ears were aware of each crunch of the snow; each breath rasped dryly in her lungs. When she reached him, her eyes traced every line of his face.

"Yes," she whispered, crumpling into the recesses of his muscular shoulder, her tears staining his shirt.

His arms immediately encircled her tightly, holding her against his body.

I'm sorry Maggie, he professed, stroking his lips gently across her hair.

"There's nothing to be sorry about anymore," she replied, sniffles muffled by Kyle's broad collarbone. "Let's just forget about it."

Kyle pulled away, tilting her face toward his with a gentle hand. He brushed his fingers across her cheek.

"I can live with that."

14: INTO THE FIRE

"It's a good thing we were already close to your house when that tire blew," Lily observed, perched on the edge of Kyle's grandfather's favorite armchair, "or we'd be out in the cold changing it by ourselves."

"You guys shoulda called me instead of drivin' the rest of the way here," Kyle chastised, kicking the snow off his soggy sneakers. "I left the tire iron and the jack in the backseat by the way."

Kyle swung the front door closed and crossed the carpet, opening a small cabinet beside the television. Lily noticed an assortment of DVDs neatly lining the interior.

"We were only a mile away, it's not like it was that big a deal," Maggie argued, throwing a knitted couch pillow at the back of his head.

Kyle didn't even bother to turn around. He easily sidestepped and snatched the projectile out of the air.

"On the ice with a flat tire," Kyle continued in reproof, "even at slow speeds you coulda bent the rim or broken an axle." He flicked a DVD out of its case and plunked it into the player, tossing the pillow lightly to Lily for safe keeping. "That's an expensive fix, Sparky."

"I have absolutely no idea what you're talking about," Maggie feigned with disinterest.

Kyle turned to Lily and rolled his eyes, his expression plainly stated, "well, what do you expect from a girl?" Lily smiled sweetly for his benefit.

"Next time, just call me, okay?" Kyle asked, grabbing the remote and pushing Maggie's legs off the couch to make room for himself.

Maggie tried to resist, and protested as he sat down. Kyle simply locked his arms around her. Maggie melted into him.

"Whatever," she said noncommittally.

The few seconds of following silence lagged awkwardly for Lily.

"So, what are we going to do tonight?" Lily asked obtusely.

The three friends had been celebrating Friday "movie night" ever since Kyle and Maggie had officially recognized their relationship nearly five weeks ago. Lily had enjoyed their companionship outside of school at first, but soon "movie night" evolved into "Maggie-and-Kyle-flirt-on-the-couch-while-Lily-pretends-not-to-feel-uncomfortable" night. Lily tried inviting Mark on several occasions, but Maggie complained about his company. Kyle accommodated him politely, but only for Lily's sake. She understood. Mark's presence prohibited super power exploits and limited conversational topics. Maggie and Kyle didn't exclude him purposefully, but Lily understood Mark had become a nuisance to them. His fellowship at school quickly became dangerous. Maggie had to constantly concentrate on distinguishing between Mark's thoughts and comments, and sometimes responded to unspoken remarks accidentally. Kyle's uncanny ability to appear suddenly in their midst had Mark asking wary questions. The effort expended to keep Mark oblivious to the strangeness surrounding her best friends and the pressure of placating Maggie's irritation became exhausting. Soon Lily just stopped hanging around with Mark altogether.

"We've been watchin' those zombie movies Sparky likes so much for the past three weeks now," Kyle announced. "It's time for some good ol' sci-fi."

"What's the fun in science fiction?" Maggie pouted.

"For starters, there's actually a plot," Kyle teased, releasing Maggie from his embrace.

He slid his arm across the lip of the sofa and flipped the television on with the remote.

"But there's not any gore!" Maggie sulked lightheartedly, settling her head into the crook of his shoulder.

She snatched the remote and switched off the DVD player.

"There's plenty of gore, Mags, it's just alien instead of human."

He reclaimed the stolen instrument and the DVD machine clicked back to life.

"Mmm. Sounds boring," Maggie said, sliding her fingers down Kyle's arm and pressing the stop button.

"Trust me Sparky, you'll like it."

A mock battle for the remote ensued and Lily marshaled her arsenal of patience.

Kyle's physical prowess eventually forced Maggie to surrender, and the television roared with sound. Lily tried to focus on the movie—Kyle was right, the plot was surprisingly captivating, something about a group of rebels defying a tyrannical empire in a distant galaxy at some point in the past. But every few minutes, Maggie would giggle because Kyle poked her in the side or Kyle would chuckle as Maggie whispered something in his ear.

Lily's endurance lasted until about an hour into the film—an artificial grey sphere had just blown a planet into space dust—when Maggie slid her fingers into Kyle's hair and kissed him deeply. Kyle returned her affection enthusiastically. Gathering the popcorn bowls and empty soda glasses in her arms as an excuse, Lily fled to the kitchen.

She needed something to distract her hands—and supply justification for avoiding the living room—so she lathered the sink with soap and attacked the pile of soiled dishes around the breakfast nook. Loneliness dripped under her eyelids. She wiped the tears away with a sudsy palm.

She felt squeezed. Like Maggie and Kyle's devotion for each other smothered everything else. She knew it to be unintentional, but she found herself belatedly invited to share their company, or completely overlooked due to her busy schedule. Lily desperately yearned for a girls' night out: just a few hours to stroke a relationship filled with a lifetime of memories. But Kyle rarely left Maggie's side, and Lily's conscientious nature prevented her from asking for fear of bruising his feelings. Concern that Maggie would mistakenly believe she had to choose between new love and longtime friendship gnawed in Lily's stomach.

Besides, Lily had never seen such contentment in Maggie's demeanor—not even before Matt. Kyle was the best thing that had ever happened to Maggie. And it wasn't like Lily and Kyle weren't friends. He slathered her with the affection of a long-lost brother. Maggie deserved a measure of happiness. Considering that, Lily judged her despondency to be petty and selfish.

It's natural to be a little jealous, she told herself sadly. *I just have to make sure it doesn't become a big deal. Otherwise, Maggie will read it in my mind.*

The thought stimulated another quandary. Maggie certainly didn't volunteer for her remarkable power. Distinction from the rest of humanity had to be terrifying. Lily didn't covet the couple's supernatural abilities. It was just difficult to watch the two most important people in her life share something from which she was intrinsically isolated.

More loneliness leaked down her face. Lily brushed her eyes with the dishtowel, sniffling softly. Clean plates filled the dish drainer by the time Maggie wandered into the room.

"Lil, what are you doing? Come back in and watch the movie."

Lily gazed steadily into the sink, holding in her tears by a swallow. She didn't want to spoil the evening.

"I'm just—well—the dishes were dirty," she offered unconvincingly.

A long, quiet pause dangled behind her. Lily had lost control of her thoughts. Maggie most likely encountered an entropic chaos. Lily felt the arms of her long time schoolmate encircle her shoulders in a sympathetic embrace.

"I'm sorry, Lil."

Kyle's casual footsteps rang on the tile.

"The snow's really comin' down out there. Weird, I thought the weather was supposed to be clear all night. What's wrong, Sunshine?"

Maggie removed her arms and Lily turned, fiddling uncomfortably with her jewelry. She felt incapable of conversation. Maggie, however, seemed to have untangled her friend's dismay.

"Grab your purse," Maggie commanded. "I'm taking you home."

"No, it's okay. I can call my mom. I don't want to ruin your night."

"Don't be silly. You're upset. We can talk on the way."

"It looks pretty dangerous out there," Kyle interjected, thumbing toward the window. "Sure you want to leave now?"

"We'll drive slow," Maggie promised, "and text you when we're home."

*

The clouds had already spewed several inches of snow onto the ground by the time the car had crawled three miles toward the city. Maggie carefully navigated the slippery terrain, limiting the vehicle's momentum to snail pace.

"What the hell? You have got to be kidding me!"

Lily stirred languidly inside the depths of her fleecy jacket, Maggie's words just barely decipherable through a fog of drowsiness. The warm cabin air lulled Lily's limbs immobile. As the car slowed, Maggie tapped repeatedly on the brake, avoiding a fishtail on the ice. The abrupt motion propelled Lily forward into her seatbelt, dispersing her lethargy. A final jerk settled the vehicle snugly in the center of the road. Lily looked through the veil of flakes illuminated by the headlight beams.

A lumpy barrier of snow straddled both lanes of the narrow highway.

"What is that?" Lily asked as she peered through the pumping windshield wipers. "It wasn't there earlier."

Maggie launched herself out of the vehicle, muttering irritable curses. The invading cold nipped Lily's exposed fingers sharply.

"What are you doing?" Lily asked.

Her bleated question met the door as Maggie snapped it shut. Lily sheathed her hands in knitted gloves and knotted her scarf against the cold before following out of the car. Lily peered upward into the gloom as she stepped onto the slick road, but the storm's frozen tears obscured moonlight and starlight alike. A southeastern blush reached across the grey clouds, radiating lambent light from the city, but was soon stifled by the callous sky. Maggie's figure paced inside the headlight's glow, her shadow leering maliciously over the obstruction. Ominous chill clutched at Lily's spine. The landscape crushed the resonance of her footsteps in the snow; the swollen ice droplets quelled all sound. Lily hurried to Maggie's side, icy puffs of breath hanging sullenly in the air.

Sharp black needles pricked through the barrier of snow blocking their path. Arms of twigs and branches twisted through the mass like grotesque broken bones. The overflow of multiple road plows lined both shoulders with compacted piles of peppered snow and ice, barring passage around the obstacle. A thin layer of powder tumbled across the mound, entombing it with a satin sheen.

"I think it's a tree," Maggie grumbled with exasperation.

The oppression of the snow swallowed her voice. Though Lily stood only a few steps away, the timbre of her best friend's speech was smothered with heaviness. Lily examined the heap more closely. It was indeed a fallen pine, mangled and maltreated. The edge of the trunk hung in fractured splinters, as if some huge fist had battered it into submission. Bits of shredded bark clung in desperate clumps around the wood, dangling limply like flailed flesh.

Lily surveyed the countryside, pulse quickening uneasily. Tufts of trees stood sentry haphazardly across the farmland—contrived breakers against dry summer winds—but none were close to their position. A natural collapse would have produced a matching stump jutting from the snow near the roadside. The spine-chill spread to her scalp.

"It's too heavy for us to move," Maggie continued pensively. "I wonder what knocked it down. Do you think it was the wind?"

Lily shook her head, observing the vertical curtain of snowflakes shrouding the landscape. A glaze of white sketched Maggie's outline. Flecks of snow gilded her eyelashes. Slivery foreboding pricked Lily's flesh. The absence of sound pressed discordantly against her ears.

"There's no wind," she uttered through stiff lips.

Maggie looked through the flurry quizzically. Lily imagined what her fright must feel like inside Maggie's head.

"There's nothing to worry about, Lil," Maggie soothed. "Let's call Kyle. This tree will be no match for his ego."

"You mean his strength?"

"Same thing!"

The storm gleefully absorbed Maggie's laugh. The silence became suffocating.

"I'll do it, but I left my phone in the car."

Lily scampered as quickly as the slushy footing would allow. She threw the passenger door wide and escaped into the front seat. The hum of the engine and abrasive voice of the heater eased her unexplained panic. She spilled the contents of her purse on the floor. *What is wrong with me?* she wondered insecurely, rummaging through the pile of belongings. Her fingers closed around her cell phone just as an ominous prickle raised the hair on the back of her neck. Lily glanced into the storm through the open door.

The feral form of a huge wolf skulked noiselessly toward the car.

It paused in mid-step, staring with thirsty eyes. Inky violet slaver dripped from bared teeth. Terror assaulted her, and her arms reacted without the aid of her conscious mind. Lily reached for the open door at the same moment the hulking wolf charged. The beast slammed into the metal with a vulgar snarl and a shuddering clash. Lily took one breath.

A low howl reverberated through the air, impregnating the atmosphere with leaden pressure. The resonance collided with Lily's head, ripping a piercing ache through her eardrums. She reeled forward as black mist threatened to engulf her senses.

Maggie screamed.

Lily felt the darkness pushed away with dizzying rapidity by her best friend's screech of sharp, raw-edged pain.

Maggie's cry was deeper than sound, gouging a desperate plea for help wordlessly into Lily's skull. She looked through the windshield. Maggie had fallen to her knees, naked hands clamped over her ears to ward out the attacker's wail. Red welled around her palms. A second wolf crept behind her, shaking its head as if dazed.

"Maggie!"

The white-pelted demon recovered quickly. Bounding onto Maggie, its razor teeth slashed across her neck, knocking her prone. Maggie's face lay buried in the snow.

"NO! Maggie!"

Lily twisted halfway into the backseat, searching for anything that might serve as a weapon. Her fingers closed around the discarded tire iron just as a dull thud cracked from the right. Haughty eyes from the first creature taunted her through the fractured glass of the passenger window, a vicious growl oozing through its jaws. Lily gulped her own fright, submerging fear for herself with that for the life of her best friend. The wolf bashed the glass again with its head. She scrambled across the gearshift and into the driver's seat, glancing in Maggie's direction. Maggie's assailant had ceased its attack. Instead, the second wolf dragged her limp form across the snow and away from the car.

Fragments of shattered glass spewed across the front passenger seat as wicked teeth surged into the vehicle. Lily extended her leg, bashing the flat of her foot into the wolf's nose. The animal emitted a high-pitched yelp and drew back. Reaching frantically behind her, she pulled the door latch and propelled backward out of the car, using her legs as leverage. She clambered off the ground and secured the door just as the wolf rushed through the broken window. Lily knew she had confined it only temporarily—the wolf could escape the same way it had entered—but a more crucial objective loomed urgently in her vision.

She had to save Maggie.

The smaller wolf had almost reached the shoulder of the road, jaws firmly clamped on Maggie's coat collar. As Lily dashed forward, an important question flashed through her panic: Since when did wild wolves roam freely through Idaho Falls?

Maggie's abductor centered its gaze on Lily's approach, but refused to slow its progress. A throaty growl emanated from behind her, warning Lily that the first animal had liberated itself. She whirled, instinctively shielding her face with upraised arms as the monster's momentum knocked her to the snow covered pavement. The tire iron thumped beside her. Blackish teeth slashed through the layers of fabric protecting her forearm, penetrating skin and tissue. Blood rained onto Lily's cheeks.

Without warning the attack withdrew. Lily rolled to her side. Deep gashes leaked dark rivulets of scarlet down her injured arm. The wolf stood between herself and Maggie, waiting. Malicious laughter washed over her.

Lily's muscles suddenly clenched in a taut spasm; rigid needles screamed up her arms and into her shoulders. Black veins snaked under her skin in paralyzing tendrils. The right half of her chest suddenly ceased to function. Numbness slid up her throat. The wolf continued to stare at her, its thick saliva staining the snow.

And then a cooling sensation burned through her blood, a halo of menthol salve blazing forth from her heart. She felt her cells dissolve the poison and feeling flooded back into her body. She snatched the tire iron with her left hand and rose to her feet unsteadily, nursing her wounded arm. The wolf's eyes widened with disbelief, then tapered shrewdly. A gruff voice flipped whip-like across Lily's mind.

I don't know how you resisted my toxin, biped, but you won't survive my fangs.

Lily stared at the wolf in shock. The creature had spoken to her telepathically.

"Leave my friend alone," she commanded unevenly, brandishing the metal tire iron.

It seemed amused by her effort.

Your friend is coming with us. You, however, will meet your death here.

The wolf's muscles tensed, preparatory to strike. Lily swung her weapon as the wolf reared, but the awkward blow only glanced off the animal's thick hide. Its teeth ripped deeply into her side. Lily felt the venom enter her bloodstream again, but her body counteracted it before the paralysis could affect her. The rending of her flesh however, tore a pain-laden gasp from her breath. The wolf buried its jaws into her hip and thigh, twisting its neck and forcing her to the ground. Lily saw the bloody jowls gape wide, intending to crush her face.

A strong hand snapped the beast's muzzle closed only a finger length from Lily's nose. Through a pain choked haze, Lily saw Kyle grapple the fiend, holding the jaws shut while struggling for enough leverage to crack its spine. He grunted with the effort. A furry belly sailed over Lily's head—the other wolf—as it crashed into Kyle and knocked its ally free.

Both wolves latched their jaws onto Kyle as he wrestled against them. Lily watched with amazement as he effortlessly seized the smaller wolf by the fur and hurled its body against Maggie's car. His shirt hung in wilted tatters around his chest, but—incredibly—his skin was completely intact.

Lily didn't wait to witness the conflict's resolution. She revolved onto her stomach, groaning as her wounded muscles contacted the frosty ground. Maggie lay a short distance away, perched halfway up the roadside shoulder breakers. Pushing upward with her unhurt arm, Lily balanced herself precariously on one side and hobbled forward.

Concern for her best friend filled her damaged limbs with determined strength. Maggie's body was still, silver snowflakes clothing her in a delicate shroud. Tears mingled with the blood on Lily's face, a horrifying tension in her chest.

Please let her be okay, she whispered to herself. *Please!*

A sickening pop exploded behind her, accompanied by a shrill yelp. Kyle had dispatched one of the wolves.

Lily reached Maggie seconds later, anxiously kneeling by her motionless form. Wispy black strands spiraled outward from the rupture on Maggie's neck and shoulders, tissue flayed almost to the bone. Lily gently rolled her childhood companion onto her back. The dark poison had wrapped its lethal filaments around Maggie's cheeks and throat. Her cloudy eyes stared wide open into the lifeless sky and Lily's soul shriveled into itself.

Not dead, Lily wept mutely. *Oh please God, not dead!*

Trembling fingers pressed against Maggie's neck, searching for a life pulse. Lily barely noticed the death shriek of the last wolf. She waited, a heave of anguish constricting her ribs. Blood trickled carelessly down Lily's marred skin, showering her friend with crimson tears.

Maggie was dead.

"Kyle!" she sobbed frantically. "Kyle help!"

Kyle's response was lost in a sudden blistering surge of cold that scalded through Lily's veins. Glacial green flame spewed everywhere Lily's blood touched the air, engulfing her injuries in cascades of fire. The delicate blaze prickled queerly, cooling the pain of her injuries. The edges of her wounds flared prismatically then the jagged skin fused together.

Drops of Lily's blood mingled with Maggie's, and Maggie's dull eyes glistened with green radiance. Splatters of blood-fire melted Maggie's flesh together, sealing the gaping neck wound. The venomous black tendrils clawing her face withered in the fire's healing fervor. Color reclaimed the pallid cheeks. As Kyle crumpled anxiously into the snow beside them, Maggie drew a hollow breath.

It was the most beautiful sound Lily could ever remember hearing.

15: A Far Cry From Wolves

The third wolf experienced the battle through the eyes of his hunters. His white mane cloaked a body that spanned twice the dimensions of the younger two. Standing aloft a cylindrical structure, he sang the Mind Howl that stunned the human quarry and signaled the attack. He perceived the elation of the smallest Daughter Seeker as she successfully incapacitated her target, sensed the confusion of the Kin Tracker when the fair-haired prey resisted the paralysis venom. The unexpected interference of the third human caught The Pack Sire by surprise—something that only few creatures of the shards could accomplish. The elder wolf knew then that the mission would fail, but he was too far away to intervene. He felt the Void claim his hunters as they were slain.

By the time he reached the remains of his kindred, the three humans had fled in their hollow metal carriage. He touched his nose to each hunter, disintegrating the broken carcasses and chanted the Death Wail to commemorate their spirits to The Mistress of the Void. The tree snare he left for the humans.

Trudging through the snow, he retraced his steps to the rendezvous clearing. The wolf waited, knowing his partner would reveal himself when ready, that even with his wolf senses The Man Stalker was impossible to track. In the hundredth count of his heartbeat, The Pack Sire detected the bitter scent of death and steel with his sharp olfactory senses. A human, draped in the iron fragrance of old blood, approached the wolf. The Pack Sire bowed its jowls in respect, but did not lower his eyes; the greeting of equal to equal.

Two of the Wolves of Skoh join the Void tonight.

"Yes. I saw."

The man indicated a flat amber crystal, palm width, secured to his leather waistband.

"Your hunters' fangs were unable to penetrate one of the humans' skin."

A low growl vibrated from deep within the wolf's chest.

Only Chano's Champion bears that power.

"Indeed."

The target summoned the male human with a Mind Voice.

"And so our forces were outnumbered. Interesting. It seems the new Corpse Crafter delivered a flawed report." The man chuckled mirthlessly at some secret amusement. "Three with the magic. He described only one."

The man reached into a leather pouch at his hip joint with a gloved hand, retrieving a message gemstone. His teeth flashed with satisfaction.

"The implication is clear of course."

The wolf grunted impatiently. The dealings of humans required a foreign thought process. How could his companion display gratification? Their target had fled. Two kinsmen lay dead, unaccountably slaughtered by the ghost of a nemesis long destroyed.

"Two power spikes," the human prompted.

Sudden understanding shocked the wolf.

You believe the fourth is here as well.

"You do honor to your fallen Sire," the man commended before continuing. "If the fourth is here, the magic will draw him to the others. We should watch and wait."

The wolf reeled under the weight of his companion's proposition. Belatedly he resumed his report.

The fair-haired female possessed regenerative abilities that counteracted our venom.

The Man Stalker seemed unaffected, as one who already possessed the information.

"So she did. We need to contact the general."

He fingered the gemstone, arranging the correct frequency for gate slip. The wolf gazed at the assassin with shrewd anticipation.

"We've been chasing the wrong girl."

PART 2

16: Falls By The Wayside

Carter's black hair swayed gracefully in the chill Friday morning breeze as he tossed two bulging suitcases into the trunk of his rental car. The gentle zephyr merrily teased his sable strands, which he flipped carelessly back into place. After slamming the trunk hood he leaned his lithe body heavily against the vehicle's glossy surface, restlessly kneading his temple with a forefinger.

Of all places to hide, why Idaho Falls?

He scanned the double runway of the airport unenthusiastically. The snow glared ominously bright in the sunshine. Even the moisture in his breath refracted prisms of light painfully into his eyes. The sky gleamed obnoxiously clear for the afternoon hour. He was more accustomed to an early evening haze. He already missed the crisp fragrance offered by the Atlantic.

At least here he hoped to escape his mother's obsession with position and social status. Carter slid his thumb absently across his lower lip, distracted by thought. Seventeen years of constant badgering about the familial contributions of six Bostonian generations of the Drake family was liable to drive anyone to rebellious behavior—and Carter was naturally predisposed to delight in risky mischief anyway.

Unfortunately, his latest escapade had resulted in his expulsion from boarding school. Though his father hadn't spoken to him since a rather public disownment two years previous, the Drake family patron took the necessary measures to ensure Carter's narrow escape from common incarceration. When the uncomfortable event had finally reached its tempestuous conclusion, his mother suggested a change of locale. Neither parent displayed any interest in his destination, so long as his face no longer influenced their standing in the social eye of the American gentry.

Idaho Falls: city of exile.

Carter slid into the leather coated interior of his new transportation. The heady scent of carpet shampoo overwhelmed his sense of smell. The black sedan was definitely beneath his customary choice of vehicle. Regrettably, his parents had been quite specific about his allowance, and the new limitations on his trust account would severely restrict indulgence in his usual luxuries.

He laughed loudly and revved the engine. As if he even cared about any of it. The car peeled recklessly out of the parking lot and flew onto the main highway. His parents were idiots. Likely they thought to pressure him into their perfect ideal of aristocratic behavior through money. Unwittingly, they had rewarded him with the one thing he had ever really wanted: freedom. Liberation from the ridiculous rules of the wealthy. Autonomy from the expectations of high-society. Release from the boredom of the privileged.

Freedom in a town of potato farmers.

He could have chosen any city, so long as it stretched west of the Mississippi. Denver, Seattle, or even Los Angeles would have been logical choices. However, as his mother's assistant prepared his travel arrangements, he had requested this little city without hesitation. Murial had been shocked, but had performed her duty without asking any questions. Carter had been grateful for her lack of inquiry. He wouldn't have been able to explain his choice to her anyway. He barely understood it himself.

Nearly three and a half months had passed since the surprising itch to visit this valley of farmland had suddenly implanted itself in his mind. The bizarre impulse permeated every dream and seeped out of unconscious thought. Curiously, he noticed veiled references to the Idaho Rockies on nearly every city block. More than once, he was surprised to discover his gaze fixated on the western horizon as the sun's rays bent into twilight. He had expected the incessant urge to dissipate as soon as his travel plans were realized, but he quickly learned that the closer his first-class ticket brought him to Idaho Falls, the stronger his unexplained compulsion became.

Carter maneuvered his car onto the City Center exit, fiddling unsuccessfully with the radio. The sedan's speakers boasted only country rock, which made him grimace, so he gave up and switched the radio off. He zipped through wide avenues lined by squat business buildings. The lack of tall constructs and the empty sidewalks unhinged him. Every structure sported considerable personal space and wide parking areas, the tree groves were sparse and unnaturally contrived. Carter wondered briefly if the city's arrangement reflected the nature of its inhabitants.

Preoccupied by his musings, he failed to note a particularly battered blue pickup as it ambled out of a right turn and into his lane. Several long metal poles jutted from its bed and almost clipped Carter's bumper. The scruffy farm implement settled into an unhurried saunter in front of him, lagging profoundly under the speed limit. Carter rolled his eyes impatiently, wondering what other inconveniences would present themselves in this new home. A quick right turn and the old sputtering truck was left well behind.

After an hour of idly perusing the agricultural community, Carter finally guided his car into a freshly plowed hotel parking lot. Snow outlined the asphalt and sidewalk in scraggly piles of dirt-peppered ice. He exited the vehicle and strode gracefully into the foyer, noting the absence of a valet post. Brown armchairs were organized in a design to best conceal several dark stains on the carpet. The tiny fingerprints of small children layered the glass coffee table and black scuffs pockmarked the walls. There were no doormen or bellhops.

A large counter occupied the corner on the far side of the room. A girl close to Carter's age stood behind it, typing methodically into a computer. Her uniform hung limply on her frame, and her fuzzy brown hair hung in damp ringlets around her shoulders. She adjusted a headset almost entirely hidden by her coiled hair and mumbled something incoherent. Carter playfully tapped his credit card on the granite tabletop to attract her attention.

"Yes, I'll be with you in a sec," she apologized impatiently.

With few more clicks on the computer, she turned to greet him. Her eyes widened and color rushed to stain the skin from her throat to the top of her forehead. Carter noticed a whispered intake of breath and the awkward tremble of her fingers on the keyboard.

Always the same reaction.

Carter knew his appearance struck the fancy of practically every woman he had ever met. His dark eyes and smooth features wrapped him in a shroud of charm. When he smiled, even the most faithful of committed females couldn't help but glance longingly in his direction. Love was a game he often won. Even his most skilled targets back home rarely resisted his wayward gallantry for long.

The poor girl accidently input an erroneous function with her nervous fingers, and the computer emitted a load tone. Startled by the noise, she exhaled a loud yelp of surprise and then tried to cover it with a high-pitched, forced giggle.

"Are you okay?" Carter asked, smiling roguishly. He leaned pleasantly against the counter.

"I-I'm fine," she replied, removing her hand from the machine so quickly that she knocked over a container of pens at her work station, scattering the writing implements all over the floor. The red flush deepened as she struggled to replace them. "Thank you," she added belatedly.

"I'm glad to hear it," Carter returned in an amused tone. "It seems," he paused quickly and scanned her name tag, "Ellen, that I have need of a room for a few days. I should have a reservation."

"Of c-course," Ellen answered uneasily, suddenly remembering her occupation. Her fingers zoomed across the keyboard clumsily. "Name please?"

Carter answered all her questions, and he assumed an air of patience for her sake. But she seemed incapable of conquering her embarrassment. For several minutes she refused to speak or even look at him. He tried several versions of friendly banter, but his dynamic compliments only unbalanced what was left of her self-possession. Finally, she ran a plastic card through a little machine, magnetizing it to open his hotel room door.

"It's room 320, on the third floor. I'm going to need a credit card."

Her eyes flicked over Carter's face sheepishly. Capturing her gaze, he twisted his card so it lingered between his index and middle finger. As he slipped it into her outstretched palm, he managed to brush her skin lightly. A visible shiver snaked up her arm, sprouting tiny goose bumps as it went. She completed the transaction in haste, placing a receipt and pen in front of him with quivering hands. Carter effortlessly inscribed his signature. Ellen offered him a packet containing his card key, receipt, and credit card. He reached for it with both hands, one smoothly accepting the packet, the other wrapping gently around her wrist.

"Thank you, Ellen," he teased graciously.

Carter released her arm and headed back out to his car. Ellen's loud sigh of relief at his exit encouraged an enthusiastic grin to sprout across his lips. Maybe he was destined for this town after all.

He flipped the automatic trunk release, intent on visiting his temporary lodgings, when a sudden inclination whispered over his mind. An invisible string tethered itself around his wrist and tugged his body gently toward the sidewalk. He secured the trunk before allowing his body to follow obediently, though unsure of a destination. The pull continued in a distinct direction, despite his passing of several interconnecting side streets.

After several blocks he intersected a bridge that spanned a unique spectacle. The placid Snake River bulged into a wide ice-rimmed lake. A manicured park, mostly empty, chased the banks of the waterway on both sides. At the south end of the lake, adjacent the bridge, white foam frothed over jagged spears of black rock as the river collapsed into a snowy roar of falling water.

The walkway crossed the misty deluge at the base of the falls. Carter paused in the center to admire the view. The sun almost kissed the horizon. Orange and red streaks sizzled along the water's surface. An overwhelming sense of déjà vu trickled into his body, as if he had seen shadows and glimpses of this place all his life.

He spotted several paths along the opposite shore that meandered through the trees, peeking through a thick cloak of evergreen. Carter completed his pass across the bridge, carefully traversing the salt-frosted sidewalk. Once on the other side, thick winter-coated pines obstructed his view of the cascade and muffled its pleasant rumble. A light layer of snow blanketed the ground, effectively concealing the head of the paths he had noticed earlier. Fortunately, two sets of footprints marred the masking shell of powder, revealing a passageway to the riverbank. He followed.

A few minutes later, Carter discovered a little rock-lined cliff overlooking a 20-foot plunge. The footprints encircled a squarish black rock perched near the edge of the precipice, then led back out of the clearing, the same way they had come. Matted snow coated the stone, as if the stone had been recently used for a resting place.

Carter leaned thoughtfully against the boulder. His eyes absorbed the bronzy sheen of the water as he reflected. The liquid spillway pulled at his consciousness strangely. The air felt charged, as if the sighing chill glazed him with intensity. For nearly 10 minutes he merely breathed, basking in the eerie sensation, allowing the roar of the falls to consume him.

Soon, however, the crisp bite of the rock's cold surface forced him to reconsider his posture. As he readjusted his limbs, he noted a bulgy mound of color peeping bashfully from the shadowed side of the stone. Upon investigation, he discovered a lonely, abandoned purse. Curious, he forced the zipper open and rummaged through an assortment of items, searching for clues to its owner. He extracted a slim wallet and flipped it open. An Idaho state driver's license and school identification card stared back at him.

The girl in the pictures enthralled him—the shine in her hair, the depth of her eyes, the curve of her smile. Carter fingered the outline of her face. Her features were profoundly familiar. A name was imprinted next to the photograph, and the title of her school outlined in large golden script: Bonneville High.

Though he made hotel accommodations, Carter had yet to arrange provisions for permanent housing or school. In a town this size, he had assumed public education would be his only option, so he had fully intended to enroll in the local college.

His resolve changed in an instant. Wherever this girl was, he would find her.

Muted voices echoed down the path, startling his thoughts. Crunches of displaced snow followed. An irate female voice slid down the hill.

"Lily, wait for me."

"You really don't have to follow me, I'm just checking to see if I left my purse here," replied a second voice, silky and sweet.

Carter pensively replaced the wallet.

"Yes, but it's icy, and I'd rather not dive into the freezing cold river to rescue you," replied the first impatiently.

"I could always heat up the water around me," Lily returned happily.

"Funny," the first voice interjected with sarcasm.

A third voice entered the conversation, augmented by heavier footfalls.

"I still can't believe you guys came out here without me."

"Honestly, Kyle, I love you, but a girl needs her space," argued the unknown girl. "Besides, Lil and I needed some quality girl time."

"And what if you and Smiles got attacked again, Sparky?" Kyle contended with a growl.

Carter had been contemplating what type of danger might plague a rural place like Idaho Falls when the trio burst noisily into the clearing. A dark-haired beauty emerged next to a tall, impressively muscular companion. Both of them halted with surprise. The third figure, who had been looking at her friends, turned in Carter's direction.

Then several things happened to him at once.

The world around him melted like watercolor. Lines of reality blurred into a bright current that suffocated him from all directions. Vivid pressure curled into a crackling ball at the base of his skull and the ends of his fingers erupted with electricity. The zing of energy raced through his nerves. He felt himself scream. A wall of bright light dissolved his vision, and everything vanished from his sight.

Everything except a pair of ice-green irises.

The eyes captured him, called to him by a name he barely recognized. They spewed unexplained images across his consciousness, visions not quite comprehensible. Devotion, pain, envy, and passion cascaded around him in a dazzling crescendo of power, frothing with massive voltage.

He almost discovered himself.

Then the power exploded in a savage crack. Shadows of glassy shards rained through the clearing. Lily and Kyle were thrown halfway across the open area by the blast, landing on opposite ends in comatose heaps. Carter perched on his knees, gasping painfully for breath. Only the one called Sparky remained standing.

She rushed to her friends, examining them. Satisfied they were at least alive and breathing, she turned, full fury, to Carter.

"Who the hell are you?"

Carter flipped his dark hair out of his eyes before answering.

"I'm Carter—Carter Drake."

17: Needle In A Book Stack

Lily flipped wearily through a largish book of zoology in the reference section of the book store, staring blearily at the caption under yet another picture of an arctic wolf. Its white pelt resembled that of the terrifying predators who had attacked in late November, but lacked the black, salivating fangs that pierced her skin six and a half weeks ago. The behavioral description of the species revealed the same information as the many other books she had recently reviewed: a pack hunter living in isolated areas of the far north, carnivorous canines with rigid social structure. None of the details she uncovered included toxic fangs and telepathic abilities—even by cultural mythologies that wrapped the wolf in religious mystery. Nor did they explain how at least two of these animals could have been displaced over a thousand miles away from their natural habitat.

She replaced the disappointing leather-bound volume and removed a light journal from her bag. As she skipped through the pages of her own tidy writing, she noticed with discouragement that most of the entries still ended in sentences embellished by large question marks. Ignoring some of the other mysteries—dark attackers at the movie theater, friends and self with supernatural abilities, magical connections between strangers—she perused the entry for November 23rd.

A hasty diagram of stick figures illustrated the wolf attack. Little directional arrows attempted to imitate action on the two dimensional surface. Next to the figure, a messy timetable endeavored to organize the events of that night into some kind of order. Lily, Maggie, and Kyle had analyzed the fight repeatedly over the past month, and the diagram was so suffused with tiny additive script that it took Lily a few minutes to skim all the information.

The latest addendum had been recorded only two days ago, when Lily realized that the telepathic howl that had knocked Maggie to her knees couldn't have originated from the two wolves that physically attacked them. The first animal had slammed itself on the car door, and she had clear view of the second as it crept to strike Maggie from behind. She felt convinced that the first wolf had been at least stunned. If the noise had come from the other, she would have seen it pause to howl through the windshield. Maggie pointed out that Lily had been reeling from a mental attack as well, almost passing out. So they couldn't be sure. Lily remained certain that at least one other attacker had been concealed by the dunes of snow.

Furthermore, when they had returned to the scene the next morning—Kyle brandishing his grandfather's favorite shotgun—all trace of the wolves' presence was gone. If it hadn't been for the tree blockade and Maggie's battle-scarred vehicle, they might have believed that the entire incident had been some short of strangely shared dream.

Weirder things had happened. Most of them lately.

Lily reread the last few notes scribbled at the end of the entry. Kyle had removed the tree. Lily buried the bloodstained snow, hoping that if it were discovered, the crimson marks would be attributed to accidental roadkill, a common occurrence on the rural highway.

As Lily slipped the journal back into the folds of her backpack, she scanned the familiar shelves helplessly. The orderly lines of rectangular tomes suddenly seemed a mockery of her former life; neat organized collections of material, all properly shelved and labeled. In contrast, the contents of her life were now scattered wildly all over the floor, pages of her reality torn, shredded, and rearranged in haphazard piles of confusion and fear. Had it only been a month and a half since her life had been completely distorted?

Since then, it seemed she spent all her time engaged in dead-end research or endlessly discussing plausible explanations with her two best friends. She stayed at Maggie's house as much as possible—and at Kyle's, unbeknownst to her parents—for two important reasons: fear for Maggie's safety loomed foremost, but she also worried that her supernatural affiliation might somehow lead her family into harm. What if those wolves had attacked closer to home? Could they have hurt one of her little brothers or her sister?

She hadn't raised a pencil to her homework since before Christmas. She had quit the myriad extracurricular activities crowding her day planner—at least two executive council events had been launched without her. Her teachers objected with concern and had asked if things were amiss at home. Friday she had been pulled out of choir for a special session with the school counselor. He even went so far as to inquire if she had started taking drugs.

Lily suddenly remembered the September afternoon when she had romanticized the appearance of Maggie's powers, thinking the adventure would be fun. How naïve. Her eyes misted over.

High school had become meaningless. Other friends seemed silly and immature, swooning over boys and arguing over fashion. Grades were suddenly inconsequential. They were, after all, only a step for financial aid into college. University plans had slid out of her future options. So had her ideal life as a wife and mother. How could she ever hope to have a family with the peril that surrounded her new reality?

At least, she consoled herself, *I'm not alone. Things could be worse.*

Sadly, she collected her belongings and redirected her thoughts. Maggie wasn't too far away, and Lily didn't want to cause her best friend unnecessary concern by blaring an upset of emotion in Maggie's extrasensory direction. Taking a deep breath, she plunged into her least favorite part of the store: paranormal anomalies. Lily had scorned this section in the past. Her fervent devotion to her own belief system had classified supernatural mysticism as a ridiculous "hocus-pocus."

Telepathic wolves tended to change one's mind.

She examined the numerous volumes tenuously, but titles like *Answers Behind Random Developing Super Powers* or *Wolf Attacks: Was it Chance or Were You Ambushed?* seemed unlikely to appear. Lily laughed lightly, returning a little to her normal cheery self, and removed several books about sixth senses and mental powers that looked intriguing. She settled onto a voluminous couch.

Maggie's powers proved the easiest to research, but despite the magnitude of available data, little actually related to Maggie specifically. Sure there were cases of spontaneous mind reading, and claimants of telepathy—Kyle maintained that he had heard Maggie's scream in his mind nearly three miles away—but all the evidence seemed circumstantial and contradictory. Not one of the books discussed the likelihood of sentient animals with telepathic capabilities.

The intellect behind the wolf attack sent a shiver through Lily every time she analyzed it. The trap's location had been selected to purposefully isolate them from the strongest member of the group—Kyle. The obstacle on the narrow country lane had been devised to lure them from the safety of their vehicle. Lily remembered the wolf's words clearly, "your friend is coming with us." Obviously Maggie's capture was their objective.

Why? she wondered. *Are they simply after Maggie's powers? But then, why were they not interested in kidnapping all three of us?*

"You, however, will meet your death here," it had said. Which meant that Lily's life was expendable. Were the wolves only after the mind abilities? Or did they not realize that there were others with supernatural gifts? Twice now, Maggie had been attacked. Somehow the movie theater zombies and the psychic wolves had to be related.

Don't mention it to Kyle again, please. He already stalks my every move. I'm considering smacking him.

Maggie's sudden entrance caused Lily to start. A sharp stab accompanied her friend's telepathic plea—the newest of Maggie's growing abilities.

"Maggie, don't scare me like that!"

"I scare lots of people," Maggie responded with playful sarcasm, "but no matter how mean I am, Kyle refuses to sleep anywhere but on my couch."

Lily smiled as Maggie plopped next to her on the sofa, but noted a lingering glint of tightness in her best friend's relaxed posture. Since her brush with mortality, Maggie's awareness of her own danger produced a sliver of fear that permanently tarnished her sapphire eyes.

"Speaking of Kyle, where is he?" Lily asked, scanning the forest of bookshelves.

"Over getting some coffee at the café," Maggie replied, snatching the books from Lily's lap and scanning the covers. "He's been really moody since yesterday. Are you really getting anything out of these?" she finished.

"Why would Kyle be moody?" Lily asked.

"Something to do with the new guy. I've noticed the irritation in his mind several times, but Kyle knows I'm reading him and thinks of something else before I can pick out the reason. Personally, I think he's just embarrassed. Whatever happened knocked both of you senseless. He was only out for a few seconds, but I think it hurt his pride. Guys can be so stupid about that crap sometimes."

Lily pursed her lips, trying to recall anything that had happened after she had entered the clearing the previous day. Most of the memories were fuzzy and incomplete—a flash of light and sound, the breath leaving her lungs as she hit the ground, dizziness overwhelming her vision, the jostle of someone carrying her to the car. Only a single event had survived the encounter with any clarity: a low, smooth voice had called out her name, almost reverently.

"Kyle was insistent that Carter didn't lay a hand on you," Maggie broke in, as if Lily had spoken out loud.

Lily felt tiny pinpricks of excitement skitter across her skin as Maggie mentioned Carter's name, which was odd, considering that she couldn't even remember his face.

"Not like it mattered," Maggie continued, "I don't think Carter could have lifted you even if he wanted to. He didn't pass out, but he was in no better shape than you."

"I just wish we could figure out what's going on. It's like we have the important parts of a puzzle, but we're missing the pieces that connect the picture together." Lily pulled out the journal and flipped between two entries: September 21st and 25th, the day each of them met Kyle. "Every time something mystical happens, it's completely different than the thing before. We all have powers, but none of them are the same. You've been attacked twice, by totally different creatures. Yours and Kyle's powers developed right after you met, but for some reason mine showed up weeks later. And now Carter."

Lily's voice refused to continue after she had spoken his name and her lungs felt the need to breathe faster at the same moment. As a result, Lily coughed and nearly choked. Maggie looked at her in concern.

"Are you okay?"

It took several seconds for Lily to regain control of her body.

"Um, yeah, I think." Lily quickly suppressed an embarrassed blush creeping around her ears; the last one had been disastrous enough.

Only two other people in the school knew that Lily had accidentally tripped the fire sprinklers the day Mark had asked her to homecoming, and Lily intended to keep that type of incident from happening again. Maggie looked at her best friend, an odd spark of amusement tickling the corners of her lips.

"Oh. My. Gosh. You like him!" she accused.

The second blush was harder to control. Somehow Lily managed.

"Don't do that! You know what happened last time!" Lily looked away from Maggie, ordering her thoughts. Deflecting the allegation by returning to the previous conversation topic, Lily spoke quieter, emphasizing the seriousness of her remarks. "I don't even remember what he looks like Maggie—and I know I looked right at him. It was so strange and overpowering. It was like I almost found the answer to everything, and then the truth just threw me away."

"Look at me, Lil."

Lily turned and met the keen gaze of her best friend. Lily couldn't actually feel Maggie raking through her thoughts, but just the idea made the sensation seem real. After a few minutes Maggie leaned back, breaking the stare.

"Kyle told me something like that last night, right after we got home and you fell asleep on my bed. We sat up talking for a long time, but he wouldn't tell me what he saw in his connection with Carter, and I couldn't make sense of his thoughts about it either. It's the same with you."

Lily sighed in frustration.

"Another complication. I should add it to our book." Lily turned to the last bit of writing in the green diary and withdrew a pencil. Her attention was consumed with the page as she asked, "What did you see when you met him?"

Lily had written four complete sentences before Maggie answered.

"I didn't see anything."

Lily looked up in surprise. Perplexity marred Maggie's face.

"How is that possible?" Lily asked.

Maggie's brow furrowed, as if unsure of how to communicate her answer.

"Just say it," Lily pressed impatiently.

"I'm not sure how to explain it because I'm not really sure what even happened. It was like I felt wall of energy headed toward my brain, and then, just as it hit, everything shut off and it just—washed around me."

Lily held the pencil to her lips pensively.

"Was it that mind shield you've discovered?" she suggested. "You know, the one that keeps everyone's thoughts out of your head when you can't stand it anymore?"

Maggie shrugged. "Could have been. But I usually have to concentrate to turn it on and off. This time, it was like a reflex. Like when someone throws something at your face and you shut your eyes and raise your arms without thinking about it. That's probably why I was the only one left on my feet. Whatever hit you three didn't even touch me."

"Why would meeting him," Lily purposely avoided using Carter's name, "cause an explosion of power like that? That's never happened before."

"I have no idea."

"So then, after the explosion was over, what did you read from his mind?" Lily inquired.

Maggie frowned. "Nothing."

Lily opened her mouth to reply, but nothing came out.

"I tried more than once to see what Carter was thinking. It's not like he was trying to block me. At least it didn't feel the same as when Kyle does it. And I entered his mind easily enough, but couldn't read anything. It was like, well—" Maggie struggled in her explanation. Lily figured the confused expression on her own face wasn't helping. "It was like his thoughts were surrounded by light, or were made of light, and it was so bright I couldn't see or hear any of them. When I tried to touch them they just slipped through my fingers."

Lily thought she understood, at least a little. "Do you think that might be one of his abilities? Mind influence? Like yours?"

"I don't know. So far all of our abilities have been different. I don't think we'll know his powers until they show themselves. Hell, we're still discovering the full extent of our own."

"What do you think he's like?" Lily asked, trying to form an appropriate set of features to match the captivating voice in her mind.

"Carter?" Maggie replied, rewarding Lily with a sly glance. "Why—"

"I don't like him," interjected a deep baritone.

An ugly scowl discolored Kyle's normally careless expression. He handed Maggie a cup of steaming liquid. Maggie winked at Lily, a sure sign she fully intended to continue this conversation privately. Then she turned to Kyle, who towered dourly over the armrest.

"You're just mad because he made you pass out. Besides, whether you like him or not, he'll be here any minute."

Lily's stomach erupted in nervous swirls. Kyle's frown pulled deeper into his chin.

"I invited him to meet us here today," Maggie obliged, ignoring her boyfriend's displeasure and smiling impishly at Lily. "I figured it would be the best way to find out who he is and what he can do."

Lily nodded helplessly, wondering if she would even recognize him when he arrived. That had potential embarrassment oozing all over it. And what if she choked on his name again? She would look ridiculous. She hadn't been able to say it at all, even in front of Maggie. What if—

"I think we should keep track of him from a distance," Kyle recommended grumpily.

Maggie rolled her eyes in exasperation and turned to Lily. "Did you find anything else?"

Lily shook her head, thankful to redirect her attention. "Whatever's going on with us isn't published anywhere." She indicated the plethora of books strewn all over the coffee table. "As far as we know, we could be the first."

"Great," Kyle inserted unenthusiastically, "and meanwhile another attack could come any day. Who knows what it'll be next time?"

"So far, everything that has come at us has had some kind of intelligent plan, getting to us when we're vulnerable," Lily observed.

"That's a good point," Maggie added. "If these attacks are related, it could be that whoever or whatever is behind them is trying to keep a low profile. That will make future ambushes harder to spot. That's not very promising information."

"It just means we can't let our guard down," Kyle growled. "And we don't do anythin' without each other."

Kyle glared at Maggie meaningfully. Even without psychic abilities, Lily knew Kyle referred to her and Maggie's little excursion yesterday afternoon, before Carter arrived, when the two had slipped away for some girl time. Lily felt a hot stab of shame. Something terrible could have happened to Maggie with Kyle's protective strength absent.

"Did I come at a bad time?"

The rhythmic resonance of the words captivated Lily's will with its satin elegance. The smooth voice called across the chasm of her soul as if from a distance, teasing her consciousness with shadows of familiarity. Enthralled by the sensation, she turned away from her friends, seeking the origin of the beguiling speech.

Carter leaned easily against one of the bookshelves, deep raven locks brushing across his eyes. His high cheek bones and graceful features lent him a veneer of nobility. A light complexion shaded his dark eyes in contrast. His lips curved with a friendly, if guarded, smile. Lily couldn't look away.

"Of course not, we're glad you came," Lily heard Maggie answer, the words sounding tinny and broken. The sound of crunching styrofoam preceded a moody comment from Kyle.

"I'm gonna get more coffee."

He stalked past Carter without a glance. Carter sidestepped agilely and raised his eyebrows quizzically.

"I don't think he likes me very much," he said cautiously, flicking his gaze between Lily and Maggie.

"Don't mind him," Maggie said, rising to follow, "it's a wounded pride thing. I'll go talk to him."

Just act natural, Maggie projected with a sharp pinch into Lily's mind. Maggie disappeared into a labyrinth of fiction novels.

Easy for you to say, Lily thought back. Maggie's silent laugh tickled Lily's synapses.

The sudden realization that she was alone with a boy whose name alone could frazzle her nerves almost induced a nervous panic. Meanwhile, Carter had circumvented the table and settled next to her on the sofa. The combined scent of his russet leather jacket and musky cologne distracted her thoughts entirely.

"So, Lily Ivers," Carter prompted when it was obvious she wasn't going to speak. His fluid voice lingered deliciously on her name. "Why did Maggie ask me to meet you guys here?"

"Well," Lily finally answered, forcing her lips to form words, "it's kind of hard to explain."

"I don't have anywhere else to be but here listening to you."

Carter's tone reflected ease, as if he'd used this particular pickup line before, but his eyes betrayed an innate intensity so complex that Lily felt overwhelmed by its magnitude.

"It's going to sound really strange," she started lamely.

That was the understatement of the century: mind powers, super strength, poisonous wolves. Lily hadn't prepared herself to relate the account without the aid of her companions and Carter's ardent expression kept making her forget what she was supposed to be explaining.

"I've dealt with a lot of 'strange' over the last 24 hours," he said.

"We don't have many answers," Lily said, fidgeting with the spine of her journal. She looked at the happy doodles decorating its cover, and away from Carter's intent stare, which helped to realign her thoughts. "There are only a few things we know for sure. The first time Maggie and I ever made eye contact with Kyle, we shared some kind of supernatural connection."

"Like what happened yesterday?"

"Sort of," Lily tried to clarify. "It's a little more complicated than that."

"What do you mean?"

"It's never the same twice. Each of us feels something different every time we make a connection with someone else. But yesterday was the first time meeting someone knocked us unconscious."

Lily looked up at Carter, curious to see his reaction. She half expected him to reject such an absurd story, label them all crazy, and walk away. But he didn't. His riveting gaze remained fixed on her.

"And what is the significance of this 'connection' you keep talking about?" he asked.

"It's the start of everything. Four days after Maggie and Kyle met, they started developing abilities."

"Abilities?" Carter looked skeptical.

"Maggie began reading thoughts and Kyle gained super strength."

A cool grin spread across Carter's face and he shook his head dubiously. He looked down the aisle where Maggie and Kyle had disappeared.

"I think you guys may have read one too many comic books."

"I can prove it," Lily stated firmly, tossing the journal on the floor and reaching for her purse.

Carter turned his dark eyes back to her. She almost faltered. Tiny wisps of tense energy whipped up her spine, causing her fingers to tremble. She bit her lip in concentration and fumbled through her bag, searching for a specific item. It eluded her for a few frantic moments. Lily felt a blush threatening to creep over her skin.

"Sorry," she apologized, looking up.

Carter's hand had covered an amused smile. A charming glint of pleasure glistened deep in his eyes.

Finally, her fingers emerged triumphant, cradling a slim, shiny pocketknife. Lily surveyed the little reading area, making sure there were no other customers in the vicinity. A quick glance at Carter exposed mild puzzlement. She took a deep breath. Then quickly, she flipped open the instrument and drew it across the skin of her palm.

"What are you doing?" Carter exclaimed.

An edge whipped through his voice. Belatedly, he snatched the weapon from her with one hand and grasped her wrist with the other. A shallow slice marred the cup of her hand. Angrily he tossed the knife onto the table and hastily drew a handkerchief from the inner pocket of his jacket. Lily stopped him from placing the cloth over the wound.

"Watch," she instructed.

Cool warmth spread through her heart, speeding in icy needles to the palm of her hand. Twelve seconds later, small flickers of green flame licked the edges of the gash, sealing the flesh in a sizzling instant.

Carter stared at her skin in disbelief. Not only had the gash disappeared, but most of her blood had vanished as well. She decided it was best to continue.

"I shared a connection with Kyle at the end of September. About four and a half weeks ago, I discovered I had the ability to heal. Plus, I can heal the wounds of others."

Still holding her wrist, Carter brushed the fingers of his free hand lightly across the newly knitted skin covering Lily's palm. An exquisite burst of tingles exploded through her midsection at his touch.

"You said you had a connection with Kyle three and a half months ago? Why did it take you so long to develop powers? You said it was only four or so days for the others."

"I have no idea," Lily's concentration was slipping away again. Carter still hadn't released her hand. "Even before I met Kyle, I accidentally set the sprinkler system off at the school. This guy made me blush and an open flame in the chemistry lab erupted almost three feet in every direction, burning green. That's sort of the signature color of my abilities."

Carter was playing absently with her fingers now, but looking directly into her eyes as she spoke. It was as if he was drawing the story from her lips. Lily continued in a rush.

"And later, after the connection with Kyle, the same guy dropped me in the coals of our homecoming bonfire. I could have sworn that I burned myself, but when I pulled my hands back they were just fine."

"Sounds like you need to dump this guy," Carter said as he freed Lily's hand. "So you heal and are immune to fire?"

"There's not much else I can really tell you," Lily finished. "Like I said, we don't know much about what's going on."

The depth of Carter's eyes flared back to life. "And you think because of what happened yesterday, that I might have powers as well?"

"Yes," Lily said pocketing her knife and recovering the journal.

Carter looked in the direction of the café, almost as if he could see Maggie and Kyle. Lily followed his gaze.

"I wonder if your guy friend thinks I might try to move in on Maggie."

"It's possible. It took quite a bit of work to finally convince her to date him. She doesn't really like guys that much."

"Well he doesn't need to worry. Don't get me wrong," he shrugged lightly, "she's gorgeous. But she's not my type," he turned back to Lily, a pleasant curve twisting his lips. "I've got a thing for blondes."

Heat spilled across her cheeks. Hot slivers flew through her madly pounding blood, pulsing into her fingertips. Carter's fathomless eyes held her captive.

Then the smell of burning paper offended her nostrils.

Lily's attention shot to the journal in her hands. Delicate sage flames licked the surface of its pages. Carter knocked the burning book to the floor and hastily smothered the green flare with his jacket. Then he picked up the singed chronicle and surveyed the damage. The edges of the paper were crispy black, but little real harm had occurred.

"You didn't mention that you could create fire with your bare hands," he flattered, raising both eyebrows.

"That's new," she admitted, sheepishly plucking her property from his grasp.

"I'm starting to think I make you nervous," Carter stated, leaning his body closer to hers.

Lily marshaled all her willpower, forcing a new surge of fiery beating to subside.

"So, I think we should test you and see if any of your powers show up," she said, deflecting the conversation to a new topic.

"I think you should let me take you to dinner," Carter insisted playfully, removing the book from her possession before she could accidentally light it on fire again. "Unless this other guy you mentioned might have a problem?"

"No," Lily managed to answer as Carter flipped through the journal, picking out bits of its contents, "no problem at all."

18: Blood is Quicker Than Water

Exhilaration coursed through Carter's body as crystaled swirls of powder showered across the speeding snowmobile. The roar of the machine tore through the midmorning air, ramming engine vibrations through his gloved hands and booted feet. He skillfully dodged several lodgepole pines, the rails of the snowmobile wedging deep lacerations in the snow banks. Carter sucked the stinging wind into his lungs, reveling in new sensations.

He had to buy one of these.

Slamming on the brakes, the vehicle spun in a reckless half circle, skidding to an abrupt halt in an isolated meadow. Laughing from the exertion, he clicked off the engine and moved to dismount, but was surprised to discover something holding him back. Firmly clutching his waist was a pair of paralyzed arms. Now that the rumble of the motor had ceased, he could hear Lily's shallow breath and feel her body shudder. At first he assumed she was merely shivering with cold, but the longer she refused to release him, the more he wondered if his thrill seeking maneuvering had terrified her. Lily had shouted navigational instructions as they travelled up the remote mountainside, but he had evidently mistaken the panic in her voice for excitement.

Carter reached down and pried her fingers loose, but didn't let them go. He twisted lithely in his seat, touching her forearm with concern. Her eyes were squelched tightly shut.

"Lily, are you okay?"

Lily opened her eyes cautiously and offered a fragile smile. Carter swung his leg over the steering column and dismounted the snowmobile. Tugging on Lily's arm, he helped her slide off the seat. Her legs trembled shakily, and she almost crumpled into the snow. Surprised, Carter caught her, reflexively pulling her closer to his body. She laughed timidly. He inhaled a whiff of her fragrance, something close to vanilla. His pulse thrummed feverishly, the excitement of the snowmobile ride transforming into something else entirely.

"Sorry," she apologized, her smile touching more of her eyes, "I just wasn't ready for such an interesting trip."

Carter supported her weight for a few seconds, fighting the desire to slide his lips across her cheek. He looked at her longingly, watching as a dusting of pink splashed across her gentle features. Of its own accord, his hand lifted itself to gently stroke her face.

"I didn't mean to scare you, I just get carried away sometimes."

Lily's eyes reflected mixed emotions, and Carter presumed that she was still partially dazed from the wild ride. Almost against his will, he released her and slid away.

"It's okay," Lily replied offhandedly, though Carter noticed her rapid breathing hadn't slowed. "Let's just not do that on the way back."

She rounded the back of the vehicle, and after removing her gloves, pulled at the knots securing a stack of wood they had tied to the snowmobile's rack. Carter surveyed the snow laden meadow and wondered what Lily could possible need with firewood in a glade buried under nearly four feet of frozen ice flakes.

He still felt uncertain as to exactly what he had stumbled into two days ago. The inexplicable urge drawing him here had disappeared, in exchange leaving perplexing events in its wake. Lily insisted that the incident at the falls would result in the emergence of his own mysterious powers. Even after witnessing her healing ability, he found the idea hard to believe. He did, however, admit that he was profoundly inquisitive as to what the other two could do.

A few hours ago, part of that curiosity had been satisfied. He'd met the three friends early that morning at Maggie's house. Both of the girls huddled in thickly lined coats and fuzzy scarves for warmth. Kyle had been busily tightening the cords lashing his grandfather's snowmobiles to a small farm trailer. For a few minutes Carter had stared at Kyle, knowing something to be amiss. He failed to precisely identify it at first, but after exchanging greetings with the two girls, it suddenly struck him that Kyle wore nothing more insulating than a pair of sneakers and a sci-fi logo print T-shirt. Thinking that Kyle was simply trying to flaunt his masculinity by underdressing for near freezing temperatures, Carter pointed out Kyle's inappropriate attire to the girls, sure that the guy would develop hypothermia during the outing. Maggie just laughed and hurried into the jeep. Lily obliged an explanation: Kyle was impervious to the elements. Apparently, Kyle's ability correlated only to the environment. Lily had added that Kyle could still burn his skin on a hot stove, for example, because a stove far surpassed the natural temperature of the room. However, he could probably spend two weeks in Death Valley without sunscreen during the height of summer and never suffer so much as a sunburn.

After two hours of careful travel north along the Interstate, Kyle had directed the jeep onto an icy side road for close to a mile. Then he pulled onto the shoulder. After everyone clambered out of the vehicle, Carter politely followed Kyle back to the trailer, offering to aid with the unloading. Kyle roughly rebuffed Carter's assistance with a hearty glare. Carter watched the grumpy quarterback unhook the machines, fully at a loss as to why Kyle harbored such animosity toward his person.

The next event had him staring with unrestrained disbelief. Carter even removed his sunglasses to make sure they weren't the cause of such an incredulous spectacle.

Lily had mentioned Kyle's superior strength the day before, but being told someone could lift an inhuman amount of weight and watching it happen were two completely different experiences. Kyle leapt onto the trailer and placed two hands under the belly of the first snowmobile. His muscles tensed, but Kyle easily hauled the machine five feet into the air. With a smug grin, Kyle hopped onto the ground and set the snowmobile gently on the snow bank. The girls watched Carter carefully, gauging his reaction. Thinking back on it, Carter felt a twinge of envy. Kyle's power was tremendous.

Still thinking when he turned back to Lily, Carter found her still wrestling with the knotted rope. Briefly, he considered physically assisting her, but dismissed the option quickly, given her tendency to light things on fire when he intervened without a proper warning. He cleared his throat meaningfully. Lily looked up from the tussle.

"What?"

"Try your pocket knife," he suggested.

Lily's eyes brightened, and she smiled shyly. "Oh, yeah. Good idea."

A few deft movements and the wood was freed from confinement. In its haste to escape its bonds, the wood scattered all over the snow, despite Lily's attempt to restrain it. Carter laughed benignly.

"Would you like me to carry those?" he offered, indicating the rogue kindling with a flick of his head. "I mean, I'm not capable of lifting a tree or anything, but—"

Lily giggled at his wit, relaxing visibly. Carter figured she wasn't going to provoke anything to spontaneously combust, not anytime soon at least, and trudged to her aid.

"Thanks," she responded, piling the wood pieces into his outstretched arms.

A previous thought reoccurred to him as she was halfway through her task.

"Why did you bring these anyway?"

"Well, like I said yesterday," she answered, piling two more logs into his arms, "I've never created fire like that before. I thought I should practice using it."

"Is that why you guys come out here? To test your powers?"

Lily placed the last log on the stack and brushed small splinters off her hands. Despite the cold, she left her gloves on the seat of the snowmobile.

"Yes, but only for the last few weeks. Right after I got mine."

Lily started into the clearing, sinking to her knees in the snow with every step. Carter followed.

"Before that," she continued, "Kyle and Maggie practiced their powers on their own."

When the two of them had reached the center of the clearing, Lily glanced back at the trees. "Speaking of those two, where are they? They should have been here by now."

"It's only been five minutes since we got here," Carter said moving to stand beside her, "and Kyle probably doesn't drive like a maniac." He winked at her, making her ears turn pink. "I'm sure they're fine."

"So," she said, anxious to fill the silence, "we're going to need some dry ground to start a fire."

Quickly she removed her coat, scarf, and hat, setting them atop the pile of wood cradled in Carter's arms. Then she tromped a few yards away from him.

"Watch this," she instructed.

Lily closed her eyes and relaxed her shoulders. Carter watched closely, anticipation teasing the edges of his nerves. A wave of warmth washed over him, gradually rising in temperature. He could see a thin layer of water coating the snow around her feet. Suddenly, a shroud of mist enveloped Lily's body. Her clothes billowed gracefully as the vapors curled around her limbs, hissing with rosy delight. The snow transformed from crystal flakes to humid steam. Soon the cloud was so thick that only her silhouette was visible.

It took almost three minutes for the filmy haze to dissipate. Lily stood on solid ground, encircled by a six-foot diameter snow-free disk.

"How did you figure out you could do that?" Carter asked, genuinely impressed.

"I dated this guy named Mark," she began, a little awkwardly, as Carter returned her outerwear, "and a couple weeks ago he asked me out for hot chocolate—for old times sake."

Lily paused while she zipped her jacket. Carter hopped lightly into the hole.

"You see, we started dating around the time Maggie and Kyle were developing powers, and it was really hard to keep it a secret from him because he was with us so much."

Carter stared at Lily blankly, urging her to continue with the explanation, though her casual mention of a possible boyfriend caused a seed of envy to appear inside his head.

"Anyway," she resumed, "we thought about telling him, but decided it was too dangerous. So he and I just, sort of, drifted apart. When he asked me to spend the afternoon at the mall, he was so nice about it, that I couldn't refuse. Halfway through he cornered me and demanded to know why I was trying to avoid him. The more excuses I tried to make up, the more embarrassed I got. That's when I lose control of my powers the most. When I went to drink my hot chocolate, nothing would come out. I took off the lid, and all that was left was caked chocolate at the bottom of the cup. I had evaporated all the water."

"So when you turned all that snow into steam, why didn't it burn you?" Carter asked as he dumped the wood on the ground.

When he looked up, Lily had turned back toward the forest, once again looking for signs of Kyle and Maggie. The sunlight played golden rainbows at the edges of her silky hair.

"I think I'm heat resistant," she announced, turning back to him.

Carter smiled back, absently pulling his hand through his hair. He leaned closer to Lily, drinking in her icy green gaze.

"And you're not dating this Mark anymore, right?" he prompted.

Lily looked at him for a few seconds, then turned her attention abruptly to the wood pile, arranging it into a teepee formation. Carter figured his inquiry had affected her ability to control her powers, so he hung back, giving her a chance to compose herself.

"No," she finally answered, accidentally knocking several logs out of place. "He was pretty upset when I told him it wasn't going to work out."

Carter bent to retrieve the offending logs and replaced them on the firewood pile. Turning in Lily's direction, he lifted her chin with his gloved fingers.

"Good," he said, sincerity enchanting his rich, smooth voice, "because I would hate to compete with him for our date on Tuesday night."

Lily's hands rested on the last piece of wood, which immediately erupted into a flare of vibrant green flame. Lily stared at him, frozen and unable to respond. The fire licked her skin, but failed to singe it.

"Is that a yes?" Carter asked when the stillness threatened to become uncomfortable.

Lily seemed to come back to herself, and turned away bashfully.

"That should be okay if we can convince Kyle to let me out of his sight for a night," she answered as she stood. Gathering an armful of snow, she doused the blaze.

"And why should he get a say in that?" Carter asked in a vexed tone. He still didn't understand what had provoked Kyle's unfriendliness.

Lily's beautiful eyes clouded, a sheen of pain almost rinsing away the green hue of her irises. Her response shocked him. A snowy night of fear and fangs. Wolves that spoke and promised death. Maggie's near fatality, averted by the awakening of healing fire. And another attack—zombie-like men with black eyes.

"That's why Kyle's so protective, and the main reason we come out here," she explained when the story was complete. "If another attack comes, we want to be ready. Knowing the full extent of our powers could help us survive another ambush. My creating fire for example," she raised a charred piece of wood with her hands, "if I could train myself to use it and control it, then maybe it would give us some kind of advantage."

Carter watched Lily as she flipped the scorched lump back into the makeshift fire pit, noting the delicate bones of her wrist, the slightness of her build. When he tried to imagine her cheery demeanor drowned by terror and blood, his hands began to tremble. He swallowed hard, startled by the magnitude of his reaction.

"We think that whoever is attacking us wants Maggie," Lily strained to say and Carter looked at her with concern. "But I won't let them hurt her, not ever."

Carter slid his body beside her, offering comfort with mere proximity.

"Is Maggie scared?"

"She doesn't show it," Lily said, wiping ashy fingers under her eyes. "But I can tell she's worried. She works harder than any of us to control her powers. Originally, all she could do was read thoughts, but recently she's developed some offensive attacks as well."

"Like what?"

"She can send telepathic messages to me and Kyle over large distances—about five miles if she concentrates hard enough—and she's only just discovered she can control and manipulate people's thoughts. That's actually how we were able to meet you two days ago. She 'convinced' Kyle to go home for an hour so we could sneak away and hang out at the falls together."

Carter let out a low whistle. "Remind me never to piss her off."

"I'll try," Lily laughed, "but it's pretty easy to make her angry, so no promises."

"I guess I better figure out what my powers are fast then."

"Why?" Lily asked.

"I want to help protect anything you love."

Carter didn't become conscious of the earnestness of his words until he said them. For some reason, this girl filled an empty place inside him, and the need to keep her from harm was consuming.

"It's not easy, being so different," she sighed.

"Yeah, but at least it won't be boring," Carter said, adding a wink that lightened the mood.

"Definitely not boring."

"So what do you think? Do I look like a mind power guy to you, or does super strength suit me better?" Lily laughed as Carter held his arms out, displaying himself for assessment. "How much can Kyle lift anyway?"

"We don't know exactly," she answered. "We started with cars, but that seemed too easy for him. His grandpa's tractor got the best of him though. We've guessed somewhere around 2,000 pounds."

"See, now that would be awesome."

"If you think that's great, you should see how fast he can run."

"You're kidding. He can run fast too?"

"About 85 miles an hour."

"That's just not fair," he jested lightly.

The buzz of an engine interrupted their laughter. Lily hopped out of the snow crater and ran back to the edge of the tree line, waiting with anticipation for the snowmobile to emerge. Carter followed slowly, sliding his feet languorously through the snow. As he reached Lily, the vehicle plunged out of the forest. When Kyle cut the engine, Maggie jumped gleefully off the seat, removing a set of snow goggles from her face.

"Looks like you guys started without us," Maggie said, indicating the hole a few yards into the meadow.

"What took you guys so long?" Lily asked.

"Sorry," Maggie apologized, a mischievous grin turning her lip, "our snowmobile broke down."

"By that," Kyle responded crossly, climbing off the snowmobile, "she means she forced me to stop with that new mind control power she's got. For some reason, she thought you two needed some alone time."

He frowned his disapproval. Maggie whipped back to face her boyfriend.

"Don't make such a big deal about it."

"You promised you wouldn't use it on me anymore, Mags," Kyle accused, pointing at her.

"I was desperate," she shrugged.

Carter wondered how these two had ever formed a relationship. He glanced at Lily, intending to clarify their romantic status, but her pale face caused him to pause. She stared at the couple, worry furrowing her brow. Carter decided to intervene, if only for Lily's sake.

"So it's true you can manipulate people's minds then?" Carter interrupted casually, hoping to dispel the feud.

Kyle's glare only strengthened as his glance flipped to Carter. Maggie turned and nodded.

"And you can communicate telepathically?" he pressed, flatly ignoring Kyle. An abrupt ache shoved into Carter's forehead.

Sure can, Maggie's mind voice asserted.

Kyle turned back to the snowmobile and unfastened a cooler attached to its rack. Yanking on a stubborn cord, he managed to mangle one of the side handles. A few mumbled curse words spewed from his mouth. Carter glanced at the two girls. Maggie pursed her lips in annoyance, and Lily's smile seemed forced. He decided to deflect the bitterness of the situation.

"So how are we going to figure out my powers?" he asked.

Kyle headed into the meadow, the other three trailing behind.

"Easier said than done," Maggie answered.

Carter felt the quizzical expression on his face. "Why?"

"Well," Lily started, "most of the time—"

Her voice trailed off.

"Most of the time," Kyle offered, his voice husky, "our powers showed up when someone was in serious danger." Kyle set the cooler in the snow cleared area. Turning, he leveled his gaze at Carter, arms folded across his chest. "So what'll it be, Drake? I guess I could hold you upside down over a cliff and see if you develop the ability to fly."

Kyle's eyes darkened and his fingers twitched. Carter sensed an uncomfortable amount of truth behind the jest. An appropriate remark sprang to his lips, but before he could return the insult, Lily expelled a concerned whimper. Maggie's response was quicker.

"Stop it, Kyle. Nobody's dropping anyone off a cliff."

"I didn't say I'd drop him."

"You were thinking it," she accused.

Kyle returned a black stare and a tense hush filled the little clearing. Carter looked from Maggie to Kyle. Obviously silent words were being exchanged. This was definitely the eeriest fight he had ever witnessed. Taking a step closer to Lily, he wrapped his arm around her shoulders, and whispered gently.

"Do they always fight like this?"

"They used to," Lily whispered back, "when they first met, but I haven't seen Maggie this mad at Kyle since before they officially got together. Of course, it was a lot louder back then because Maggie couldn't send telepathic messages yet."

Worry tinted her eyes. Carter squeezed her shoulders with reassurance.

"Should we stop them?"

"No," Lily said quickly, "it's usually best to let them cool down on their own. Besides, if I know Maggie, she's getting madder by the second, and her powers don't work when she's angry."

"Really?" Carter asked, mildly surprised.

"Yes. We've been practicing to see if she can conquer it, but we think the emotions must cloud over her mind and prevent her from focusing."

Carter pondered. So Maggie's powers didn't work when she was angry, and Lily lost control of hers when embarrassed or anxious. Interesting. He wondered if Kyle suffered from the same vulnerability to emotional duress. If so, he hadn't shown any sign of it.

No, Carter thought, *both Lily and Maggie's abilities require concentration of the mind. Kyle's are purely physical. That must be the difference.*

"Kyle, you are so impossible!" Maggie screamed, drawing Carter's attention. Maggie fumed mutely for a moment, long enough for an unspoken retaliation from Kyle. "You know I can't hear what you're saying anymore," she spat ungraciously. "Why are you acting like this?"

"Don't bother yourself with it, Sparky," he growled, and plodded fiercely into the trees.

Maggie threw her hands up in frustration, muttering profanities.

"He's starting to drive me crazy!" she yelled at no one in particular. She plopped down in the snow. "I don't understand what's wrong with him."

"It's obvious that he hates me," Carter rationalized, "I just wish I knew why so I could deserve it."

"Maybe we should just leave him be for a while," Lily advised. "I'm sure he'll eventually explain what's bothering him." She glanced quickly at Carter, then back to Maggie. "Let's just finish what we came here to do."

"And what's that?" Maggie asked, staring distractedly at the copse of trees where Kyle had disappeared.

"To figure out what kind of powers Carter has."

"But I thought Kyle said your powers only appeared in times of danger?" Carter asked.

"Not always," Maggie inserted, "Kyle was just being a guy."

"Sometimes they develop during unexpected events," Lily clarified. "Like when I started the book on fire yesterday when you—" Lily halted, then changed the subject quickly. "Or when Maggie almost got suspended for 10 days for punching Katie Maxwell in history class, but got out of it by using her mind influence ability on the principal. Sometimes we use new powers without even realizing it. Most of the time we only recognize them during dangerous situations."

"So I could have some already?"

"It's possible, but it's only been two days."

"Well then," Carter said, taking a mock defensive stance, "how are we going to do this? Just keep in mind that I would never hit a lady."

Lily and Maggie exchanged glances.

"Maggie mentioned something interesting yesterday that I think we should experiment with," Lily declared. "She wasn't able to read your mind. I think we need to figure out if it's an ability you have, or if it was because of the connection."

"Sounds like a safe place to start." Carter straightened his posture.

"Give me a minute," Maggie insisted, hauling her body out of the snow. "I'm not focused, I need to calm myself down."

Carter watched Maggie close her eyes. Her chest heaved with several relaxing intakes of breath. After five minutes had passed, he felt an ache intrude into his mind.

Can you hear me, Carter?

"Yes," Carter said, wondering if her unspoken thoughts stung every head she entered.

Stop answering me out loud. I'm going to manipulate your mind. Are you ready?

Yes, Carter answered, hoping he was thinking loud enough.

Maggie's eyelids flared open with displeasure.

I asked if you were ready.

"And I 'thought' yes at you," Carter defended, "twice."

Maggie exchanged a perplexed look with Lily. She stared hard into Carter's eyes, her smile turning sly.

"Kiss Lily," she commanded.

Carter felt a probing pressure accompanying each word as the phrase tried to sway him into action, but he easily overcame the order's compulsion.

"I would love to," he replied charmingly at a blushing Lily, "but this is hardly the time or place."

Lily looked at Maggie nervously. Maggie's eyes narrowed.

"Did I do something wrong?" he asked her.

"No," Maggie admonished, "it just didn't work. Usually when someone tries to resist my mind command, I can feel them fight it. I can't sense anything from you."

"Then how can you talk to me through telepathy?"

"I don't know," Maggie considered, staring hard at Carter, as if she could peel away the layers of skin on his face to reveal the answer. "But if I had to guess, I would say that reading and controlling your thoughts are based on my ability to find them. Every time I look into your mind I see nothing but white energy, and I get lost. The telepathic messages originate from me, like spoken words. Maybe that's why you can hear them."

"What if he's resistant to other powers, like mine or Kyle's?" Lily inserted thoughtfully.

Carter reflected. "There's only one way to find out. Let me see your knife," he instructed, holding a hand out to Lily. "If I am resistant against other powers, there's an easy way to test it."

Lily dispensed the knife with some reluctance, and Carter guessed she followed his line of reasoning. After removing his coat and rolling the sleeve of his sweater, he skillfully sliced into his forearm, drawing blood in the wake of the blade. Pulling a handkerchief from his jacket pocket, he wiped the crimson stain from the weapon and handed it back to Lily.

"Do your thing," he directed, presenting his wound.

Lily cut into her wrist. Holding her breached skin above his, she squeezed several droplets of blood into his lesion. Carter waited, slowly counting in his head. Around the time he reached the number 12, green flames fused the edges of the healer's gash as a burning sensation spread through his arm. It tingled furiously under his skin, like millions of searing needles sewing his cells together simultaneously. He almost gagged from agony. The jade fire generated more pain than the original injury.

"Carter, are you okay?" Lily cried, using her body to steady him.

He gulped air, wiping sweat from his temple. Carter managed a reassuring smile after a minute, using the soiled handkerchief to clean his arm. The damage was healed.

"Did you practice that on Maggie and Kyle to find out how it worked?" Carter panted.

"Not the first time," Lily replied with a shake of her head. "I accidentally healed Maggie the night of the wolf attack. It took me longer to heal the first time, so I ended up bleeding all over her."

"Hurts like hell though," Maggie inserted. "It doesn't hurt Lily so much, just the people she heals. I didn't notice the first time because I was unconscious, but we tried it again a time or two, just like now."

"But we haven't been able to use it on Kyle," Lily added.

"Despite our best efforts," Maggie laughed.

"Why couldn't you use it on him?" Carter asked.

The needles in his arm had subsided to a dull throb, but he felt drained.

"The last of Kyle's powers," Lily chimed. "We've tried several different knives, but we can't cut through his skin. That's why the wolves couldn't paralyze him. Their teeth were useless."

"Yeah, but even though they couldn't break the skin, their jaws left nasty bruises wherever they tried to bite him," Maggie said.

Carter inspected his unblemished arm before replacing his sleeve. It seemed Lily's physical powers could influence him, but somehow he was blocking Maggie's mental abilities. He supposed Kyle's strength could affect him as well; not that he cared to ever test that hypothesis. When Kyle returned an hour later, somber and taciturn, the group trudged back to the snowmobiles, leaving the experiment—and hope for a quick resolution—behind.

19: Gilding The Lily

"What's his name?" Joseph asked, flicking a hair pin across the room with his gangly fingers. Lily fastened the last lock of her silky blond hair into place before turning to eye her 14-year-old brother.

"Carter Drake," she said pleasantly, "and if you don't stop that I'm telling mom. You know how much she hates cleaning up after you!"

Joseph snorted in defiance, but Lily noted he stopped tossing accessories.

"Is he nice?" a second, younger voice piped.

"Oh yes, David, he's very nice," Lily answered, swinging to face her youngest brother.

After patting his curly brown head fondly, she returned to her reflection in the vanity mirror, double-checking her hair and makeup. Though the night promised to be chilly, she had picked her favorite first-date outfit: a pleated above-the-knee skirt, lacy, form-fitted pink top, and a pair of creamy, white boots.

"Can I try on your bracelet, Lily?" Ester asked hopefully, jumping up and down on the bed.

Lily paused, running her finger along the platinum glittering at her wrist. She held the piece of jewelry closer to her face. Emerald gems sparkled happily from their settings, surrounded by decorative swirls and eddies of the precious metal. The bracelet had accompanied a formal invitation, delivered by the Bonneville High student body president during second period. A formal request for dinner, written in Carter's definitive script, adorned the heavy parchment. When Lily had opened the ribbon bedecked package containing the gift, every girl in the class swooned with excited envy.

Lily smiled at her little sister. Ester's downy pigtails bounced erratically, following the motion of her miniature body. The one aspiration in the 8-year-old's short life was to emulate Lily in every way.

"You've already tried it on twice, Ester," Lily said, "and I'll be leaving any minute."

Ester ceased her activity and bowed her head in disappointment.

"But I'll let you try it on again tomorrow, okay?" Lily promised.

A lovable grin replaced the frown on Ester's face.

"So," Lily asked her siblings, twirling in a circle, "how do I look?"

Her siblings spoke at once. Before Lily was able to decipher their garbled comments, the doorbell chimed.

"Oh he's here," Lily said, clapping her hands together enthusiastically.

She danced to the landing crowning the stairs. The click of the front door handle echoed from the entryway and she heard her father introduce himself. Carter's polished voice returned a warm greeting. Lily waited, calming her bubbling anticipation with a long lungful of air. Paul Ivers' voice carried up the stairs, inviting Carter into the entry and iterating the proper time frame for the return of his daughter. Lily smiled and descended the staircase.

Her date stopped halfway through his conversation as he saw her. A tight cashmere sweater hugged Carter around the chest, casually enveloped by a navy dinner jacket. He carried three burgundy roses, arranged in an elegant bouquet. His dark eyes traced her image, their cool intensity triggering a ripple of tremors up the back of Lily's legs. Blood pulsed heavily under her skin.

"You look incredible," Carter said fluidly, stepping forward and surrendering the scarlet blossoms.

"Thank you," she answered, brushing the exquisite petals against her nose to inhale the rosy perfume.

"Don't worry, Mr. Ivers. I'm a complete gentleman," he promised her father, though his eyes never left Lily's face. "I'll have her home on time."

"See that you do," her father responded, helping Lily with her jacket. "You have a great time, sweetheart."

"Thanks daddy, I will," she assured, giving him an affectionate peck on the cheek.

" 'Bye Lily," Ester called from the balcony.

Lily glanced upward. Her siblings and mother lined the railing. Waving warmly with her free hand, Lily crossed the threshold into the dusky chill. Carter followed, pulling the door shut behind them. Lily laughed nervously as he opened the passenger door for her.

"What?" Carter asked as he helped her into the car.

"My family thinks that every date is a big event."

"I think it's great that they want to be so involved in your life," he added, then rounded the vehicle to slide into the driver's seat.

"Me too," she agreed.

She tried to click her seatbelt into place, but her fingers slipped and the belt zipped back into its casing.

"Nervous?" he asked with a pleasant grin.

"A little," she returned timidly, "but only if you drive your car like you do a snowmobile."

"I think tonight I could make an exception."

"Please do!" she jested.

"For you," Carter laughed, "I think I can manage it. Let's get out of here."

The engine purred to life. Carter turned the wheel, directing the car onto the plowed street. After a few blocks of weaving through traffic, he turned west toward the low ring of hills framing the city.

Lily tried several times to engage Carter in small talk, but between his reluctance to discuss his previous life in Boston and the way his smile confused her ability to form coherent thought, the conversation fizzled into strands of disjointed dialogue. Lily had been on numerous first dates. Most were activities with a friend or an occasional date with a crush, but none had ever left her this nervous. Her usual well of self-confidence had evaporated, leaving her floundering for social grace. Lily bit her lip and peered out the window.

No one had ever looked at her the way Carter did. Every time she met his gaze, those dark eyes pressed passionately inside her. And when they parted company, though he expressed farewell amicably enough, his eyes were lined with a sharpness edging on panic that he was losing sight of her for just a few hours. Like he would shrivel and perish without her.

The black sedan's gentle halt tugged Lily's attention away from her thoughts. Carter handed her from the car and escorted her up the flagstone steps of a building. Lily fiddled with her bracelet absently, astounded by the ambiance. White lights twinkled in the manicured shrubbery, scattering pixie-like shards of light across an icing of snow. The path led to a set of heavy oak doors, propped open for their arrival. Delicate illumination danced across walls draped in cloudy fabric. A single table with two place settings beckoned from the center of the hardwood floor. One wall was completely glass, overlooking the scintillating valley of Idaho Falls. A melodious piano solo whispered in the background. Two white-tie attendants glided across the room, one closing the doors as the couple entered and the other pouring sparkling cider into the tall crystal goblets on the table.

"Do you like it?" Carter intoned in a low voice, handing the coats to one of the servers who then disappeared through a side door.

"Like it?" Lily answered breathlessly. "Carter, this is amazing."

She turned toward him, mesmerized by the splendor. Carter smiled, pleased with her reaction, and ran his thumb gently across her cheek. Blood pounded frantically in her fingertips.

"None of that now," he said, sliding his arm around her waist and constraining her to walk toward the table. "I'm sure the owner of the clubhouse wouldn't be too understanding if half of it suddenly went up in flames."

Lily swallowed hard, forcing the icy tingles under her skin to calm. Carter removed his arm only when they reached the table so he could pull out her chair. An empty china vase adorned the center of the lacy table cloth. The remaining waiter relieved her of the rose bouquet Carter had given her earlier and arranged them inside the empty vessel. As Carter took the vacant chair, the other attendant reentered the room, chauffeuring a serving cart.

"I hope you don't mind," Carter apologized as the waiter maneuvered a covered plate in front of her, "but I took the liberty of ordering our dinner beforehand."

Intrigued as to what he had arranged, Lily exposed the entree.

"Carter, seafood alfredo is my favorite!" she gasped in astonishment. "How did you know?"

"I have my spies," Carter said confidentially, a sly grin teasing his face.

"You mean you asked Maggie."

"I never reveal my secrets."

Halfway through the meal, the anxious edge of Lily's nervousness melted in the wake of Carter's captivating charm, and she felt more like her normal self. She even realized that she knew the two servers—fellow students from school—though Carter had long since dismissed them for privacy. Carter led most of the conversation, focusing on Lily's life and future aspirations. As he took a forkful of pasta, she turned the topic of discussion.

"So, why did you come to Idaho Falls anyway?"

Carter chewed slowly, contemplating his answer.

"Destiny," he answered, picking up his crystal glass and sipping the cider.

"You mean like you had a vision or something?"

"No, not that. I can't really explain it. I just felt like something was drawing me here."

His gaze gleamed playfully from across the table.

"Like what?" Lily asked cautiously.

Carter ran his thumb across his bottom lip, swallowing her with his eyes.

"You."

For several heartbeats Lily concentrated simply on breathing, restraining her abilities. Carter rose from his chair and held out his hand.

"Would you care to dance?"

"Carter, I don't think that's a good idea right—"

Without letting her finish, Carter whisked her onto the dance floor. He spun her around once, then slid his right arm around her waist and pulled her close. The other hand clasped hers tightly as he led her body to the tempo of the music. Lily gasped for control as a freezing burn raced through her veins.

"You really want to know why I came here?"

"Yes," she breathed.

"Last week I had a fight with my parents." He shrugged, indicating its insignificance. "I'm a social embarrassment to them. So they banished me."

"That's terrible!" exclaimed Lily, astounded that any parent could act so callously. Attempting to offer consolation for Carter's plight, she added, "But I'm glad you chose here."

"Me too," he whispered, leaning his face close to her ear, "or I wouldn't be dancing with the most incredible girl I've ever met."

The ornamental candles embellishing the player piano exploded with green flame. Carter laughed and pulled her closer. Lily laid her head on his shoulder, inhaling his intoxicating cologne. He certainly knew how to execute a flawless first date.

*

Carter squeezed Lily's hand affectionately as they walked toward the car.

"I had a wonderful time," Lily announced through a happy smile.

Carter stopped suddenly, twisting Lily's hand so that she was compelled to turn around and face him. His princely appearance enthralled her. She found herself spellbound by the shine of his deep raven hair. He lifted his free hand and brushed his fingers through her hair, tracing her jaw down to her chin.

"Lily Ivers," Carter's satin voice announced, tilting her face upward, "I think I might be falling in love with you."

He kissed her tenderly.

Rather than exciting her blood with passion, the feel of Carter's lips eclipsed Lily's heart with a pang of forlorn longing. It pressed against her lungs painfully, forcing needles of regret into her chest. The impression of discovering something she desperately wanted, yet burdened with the knowledge it would elude her forever, ripped a gasp of sorrow from her body. Carter released her in surprise.

"What is it?" he asked.

She felt tears touching her eyelashes and she blinked quickly. Carter wiped them away softly, but the gentle stroke of his fingers across her skin evoked more salty droplets. Trying to control her ridiculous inclination to weep, she flicked her gaze away from his face and over his shoulder.

A cold fear twisted her bowels instantly, freezing everything else. A tall figure stood sentry on the clubhouse roof, the hem of his white overcoat rippling resolutely in the breeze. The man's blond hair was pulled tightly against the nape of his neck, though the front locks had escaped its binding, veiling his left eye. A sudden gust of wind drew aside his calf-length cloak, revealing a leather breastplate and armor. Metal glinted at his hip.

The figure stared at Lily, his twilight eye glaring with unwavering determination. Death glistened from that silver orb.

"Carter," Lily mouthed urgently, her body stiffing.

The man on the roof grasped the hilt of his sword, the ring of the escaping metal tearing mournfully through the night air. Lily turned her attention back to her date.

"Carter—on the roof!"

Whether Carter heard Lily's whisper, or just responded to the panic wrenching her face, he spun around, shielding her with his body.

The roof was empty.

Impossible, Lily reasoned. She had looked away for less than a second.

"There's nothing up there, Lily," Carter said, his body relaxing visibly.

"I'm telling you, someone was there," Lily scanned the area frantically. "He had a sword."

Carter wrapped his arm around her protectively and stared at her intently. Then, without warning, he yanked her toward the car, unlocking the doors remotely.

"Quick, get in," Carter commanded, thrusting her into the vehicle.

Lily slammed the door and locked it as Carter ran to his own side. Not bothering with the seatbelt as he threw himself into the driver's seat, he rammed the key and throttled out of the parking lot.

"We need to get to Maggie," Lily cried. "Whoever these people are, they're after her."

"You think they sent him after us to keep us separated?"

"It wouldn't be the first time they've tried something like that." Lily scavenged for her cell phone, then quickly dialed Maggie's number. "When the wolves attacked, they waited until Maggie and I were alone."

Maggie's phone deferred to voicemail. Lily tried a text. Still no response. As a last resort, she called Maggie's landline. The phone rang over and over, but no one answered.

"Crap!" Lily spouted, throwing her phone back in her purse with disgust. The car screeched around a corner.

"No answer?" Carter prompted.

"No." Fear for her best friend's safety drove hot splinters of anxiety into her head. "We need to go faster!"

20: Round Peg Complex Hole

Maggie curled stiffly on the far side of the couch, glowering at her boyfriend reclining at the opposite end. Ever since the mind control incident on Sunday, Kyle had been distantly aloof. Initially, she had assumed a night of penance would alleviate the tension between them, and had invited him over for a night of "study." But from the moment he arrived, around nine o'clock, Kyle had revealed a facet of personality that Maggie had never witnessed—even during homecoming weekend. His magnetic smile was absent, the alluring chuckle silent. He answered only direct questions and, even then, only provided monosyllabic answers. Tonight he barely intoned a hello before he plunked down on the couch, pulled out his history book and began an ardent reading session. Maggie could hardly contain her frustration.

"Homework night" was a secret code they used to legitimize their romantic engagements. Maggie invited Kyle over under the guise of completing history assignments, which translated to a night of intertwined flirting, kissing, and cuddling. This was the first time Kyle had ever actually brought his textbook. Worse, Kyle had ejected all thought of her from his mind. As she raked through his brain all she could glean from his thoughts were details that followed the timeline of the Civil War.

Nearly an hour passed before Maggie hissed her displeasure, but Kyle declined to react. She wanted to ask him if he simply hadn't forgiven her for the mind trick she used on him, or if he was still angry that she had supported Lily in accepting Carter's invitation tonight. Maybe it was a bit of both. Kyle's purposeful concealment of his inner thoughts sent a clear message—she wasn't welcome to know.

Red began to swirl behind her eyes. Kyle's soundless recitation of the major political figures supporting secession from the Union kept washing in and out of her mind's ear. Maggie's expanding temper threatened to short out her focus.

Kyle didn't seem to notice. He calmly turned another page. Maggie prepared to unleash verbal wrath.

The doorbell halted the assault. Maggie's eyes thinned lethally. She jerked herself from the couch, stomped to the door, and violently threw it open. A boy decked in blue shrank before her, offering two large cardboard boxes to stay her ire. Maggie had completely forgotten that she ordered the pizza.

"That will be $16.50," he squeaked in a shaky voice, waving the receipt over the food.

Maggie snatched the slip of paper and stormed back into the living room, livid rage encircling her body with a tangible sheen. Kyle feigned disinterest. Yanking a twenty from the depths of her wallet, she stomped back to the door and tossed it in the delivery boy's face.

"Keep the change," she snarled, grabbing the warm containers out of his hands.

"Thanks. You have a nice—"

Maggie slammed the door before he could finish the obligatory farewell. Marching into the front room, she positioned herself directly in front of Kyle. Her proximity had no effect. Kyle still refused to acknowledge her presence. She hovered near him for five minutes, her grip tightening on the pizza boxes. Finally approaching her limit, Maggie dropped the two boxes in Kyle's lap.

His reflexes were a lightning blur. He caught both pizzas and turned another page before Maggie's brain could process the movement. Without a word, he placed the boxes on the coffee table, leaned deeper into the couch and returned to the text.

Veins rose from the tight clench of Maggie's fist. Her cell phone vibrated on the table, but she ignored it.

"Are you seriously going to sit there and ignore me all night?" Maggie finally roared.

Kyle slowly removed his eyes from the history book.

"Mags, you invited me over to do history homework," he said.

"And that usually results in us making out on the couch," Maggie argued.

"Well, maybe it's time we actually got some work done, since we're both failin' history. Are you gonna answer that?" Kyle asked, indicating the cell phone's hum.

Maggie snatched the distracting piece of technology and hurled it into the kitchen.

"You want to spend the first night we have alone together in five weeks studying?"

Kyle simply held up his open book for affirmation.

"Then why the hell did you even come over?" Maggie shouted, moving around to the back of the couch so the temptation to whack him was easier to resist. "You could have done that at home."

"You called and invited me," Kyle returned, planting his volume of *American History* back into his lap.

"Well," Maggie screeched, confidence waning, "then you're uninvited. I'm not going to sit here, bored out of my mind, while you read about Abraham Lincoln invading the South."

"Fine," Kyle acceded, snapping the hardback shut and stuffing it into his bag. "I'll go home then."

"Fine," Maggie agreed passionately.

The house phone chirped. Kyle zipped his backpack and sidled past Maggie, turning the handle of the front door.

"Sounds like someone really wants to talk to you," he seethed.

"Why are you so angry with me?" Maggie asked, her emotions fraying into threads. She ignored the phone. "Why are you being such a jerk?"

"Maggie—" Kyle warned, turning his head to face her.

"Don't do that," she demanded, pointing a trembling finger in his direction.

"Do what?"

"Use my name properly."

"Why not?" Kyle inquired angrily. "You're always pitchin' a fit when I don't."

"Because you only call me Maggie when you're mad at me," she cried, fleeing toward the bathroom.

The wooden portal creaked in protest as she hurled it closed. Weak with emotional upheaval, she leaned heavily against the door, her body slowly sliding down its surface. The hollow echo of the phone's singing permeated the subsequent silence.

A soft knock sounded on the bathroom door.

"Maggie?" Kyle's voice inquired gently. "Open the door."

She hated it when he used that tone. It made her willing to do almost anything for him. She wondered if this was how everyone felt when she used her abilities to force them to her will. But she couldn't yield.

"Sparky, let me in."

"Just go home, Kyle," Maggie begged.

Maggie heard a scuffle of movement and felt the door shift as Kyle leaned against it.

"We both know you don't really want me to go home, Mags."

"So what? What are you going to do while you wait, read your stupid history book?"

"No, I'm gonna let you talk to me."

"Now you want to talk?" Maggie asked doubtfully.

"Yes."

Maggie stood and yanked on the door. Kyle had been fully supported against the opposite side so when it opened he let his back fall against the checkered linoleum with a soft thud. His relaxed half-smile peered up at her for the first time in five days.

"Knew you'd open the door eventually," he said with a chuckle.

Kyle's easy demeanor drained her rage. Eventually, she heaved a sigh and crouched next to him. He took her fingers in his hand.

"I didn't mean upset you, Sparky," he apologized, lifting her hand to his lips and brushing them lightly. "I just haven't been myself since meetin' Drake."

He lowered their clasped hands to his chest, holding them firmly. A wave of calm soothed her synapses, allowing her mind to open once again.

"Why won't you just tell me what's going on?" she pleaded, fondling his close-cropped hair.

Kyle considered.

"I didn't want you to have to choose sides," he finally said. "Smiles likes Drake, and I knew you wanted her to have a shot at what we've got, but anytime he's around—"

Maggie waited, but he seemed hesitant to continue.

"Why do you dislike him so much, Kyle?"

Kyle reached up and pulled his palm through her brunette locks, stroking her cheek with his thumb. His eyes darkened. Maggie heard bits of disordered thought bouncing erratically around his mind.

"It's complicated, Mags."

"Kyle, after what's happened the last few months, I'm pretty sure I can handle complicated."

Kyle pulled her unresisting body down toward him, sliding his arms around her in a firm embrace. He kissed her deeply, the strain of the past several days melting with his lips' caress. As he released her, he heaved a contented sigh.

"I haven't been able to do that five whole days and it's been killin' me."

Maggie's toes tingled pleasantly as her heart worked double time. Though she agreed with his chosen mode of distraction, she wasn't going to be deterred.

"Don't think that kissing me will get you out of answering my question," she warned.

"I wasn't tryin' to get out of anythin'," he bantered, "I just wanted to kiss you before you got mad at me again."

"Why would I be mad at you again?"

"Because of my answer to your question."

Maggie lifted her eyebrows, precluding the foretold adversity.

"The day we met Drake—"

Maggie heard the crack of wood on plaster and felt the icy breath of night invade the house. She jumped to her feet. Kyle instinctively blocked the bathroom doorway with his muscular frame. Pressing into his back, Maggie sent her mind forward, searching for the intruder. Lily's frantic voice spilled into Maggie's head, deluging it with chaotic visions of romantic candlelit dinners, blond strangers bearing swords, and unrequited cell phone calls.

"It's Lily," Maggie announced, just as a clear voice resonated through the hall, calling her name.

Kyle's body relaxed under her fingers. When the couple emerged from the bathroom, they met a wildly harried Lily and a winded Carter. Lily charged Maggie, embracing her in a ferocious hug.

"Lil, what's going on?" Maggie inquired.

She could feel the pounding of Lily's pulse. Lily's overwhelming relief washed over Maggie, but her friend seemed unable to communicate verbally. Carter secured the front door, threw the bolt and barricaded it with a nearby piece of furniture.

"Are there any more ways into this house?" Carter asked.

"A back door," Kyle answered thumbing behind him, "in the kitchen."

"Lock it," he commanded, "and the windows too, if you can."

Lily finally released Maggie, watching as Kyle leapt toward the kitchen and Carter headed into the bedrooms, locking windows as they went.

"Did you get attacked?" Maggie asked, fear squeezing her nerves.

"No," Lily answered, transferring her attention back to Maggie, "but I think someone might have been trying to ambush us."

Maggie listened to Lily's words as well as mind images as Lily described the white-cloaked figure on the clubhouse roof. Both boys reentered the living room as Lily finished the account.

"I tried to call you twice," Lily scolded, "why on Earth didn't you answer? I was terrified that he had gotten here before us!"

Maggie glanced at Kyle, who was conveniently inspecting the catch on the nearest window, then answered Lily with a thought.

Kyle and I were fighting—again. She made sure to include the mental equivalent of a sigh.

About what? Lily wondered, her exasperation bouncing around Maggie's neurons like flies on a zombie corpse. Maggie flicked her eyes meaningfully toward Carter, who had collapsed tiredly onto the couch.

Carter? Lily thought at Maggie. *Why would you fight over Carter?*

"So this guy with the sword," Kyle interrupted testily, looking from Maggie to Lily, "he just disappeared?"

"I don't think he expected me to see him," Lily said, settling on the sofa near Carter, "and when I turned back, he was gone."

Carter comfortably wrapped his arm around Lily and dragged her closer. Kyle scowled.

"He had to have been at least as fast as you, Kyle," Lily continued. "I don't see how else he could have just vanished like that."

"Sounds like you guys were lucky to make it here," Maggie said, laying a restraining hand on Kyle, sensing the inflammation of his displeasure.

Kyle snapped his head to confront Carter.

"Lily's safe now, Drake," he spat ungraciously, "so you can go back to your hotel."

Carter's face started with shock, then deepened into outraged disbelief. Lily's mind surged with wounded incredulity. Maggie felt like smacking her boyfriend upside the head, not because of his rude remark, but for the degree of dislike that Kyle harbored for Lily's date.

No, dislike wasn't the right description, Maggie suddenly realized. Kyle had masked it carefully, vigilantly shielding his thoughts from Maggie's extraordinary ability since Carter's arrival. But now, whether from lack of control or purposeful exploitation, he released his censored emotion. What Maggie felt was beyond dislike. It was cavernous, sordid, and hostile.

It was hate.

"You really think I'm going leave Lily when that sword-wielding manic could barge through the door at any moment?" Carter argued heatedly, standing to challenge Kyle, who had at least three inches on him.

Maggie opened her mouth, intent on dispersing the antagonism, but Kyle cut her off.

"And what'll you do? Get in the way?" Kyle retorted with a snort. "You don't have any powers, Drake. What could you do to protect her?"

Instead of swelling with rage, Carter's face eased into a placid calm. All but his eyes. The dark irises blistered with terrifying fury. Maggie couldn't read Carter's thoughts, but his intentions were clear enough. Intangible tension sizzled madly through the air.

Maggie had heard enough.

"Stop it! Both of you!" she bellowed. "This doesn't help us."

Kyle stared menacingly at Carter, who refused to relent.

"It doesn't matter if Carter doesn't have powers, Kyle," she said, stepping in front of him. "They've seen him with Lily tonight. He could be as much of a target as we are, and since he doesn't have powers yet, he needs our protection."

Lily bestowed a grateful look on Maggie. Carter seemed to struggle with himself, his muscles taut beneath his skin.

Coming to a sudden resolution, he managed an indifferent shrug and returned to Lily, but his eyes still smoldered.

Kyle glowered at each of them in turn, saving Maggie for last, then marched into the kitchen. Maggie's heart drowned in stomach acid. For a brief 10 minutes she had seen the return of the charismatic quarterback she had grown to love, only to be abruptly ripped from her grasp.

"Lily, Carter," she said with a tremulous exhale. She needed to distract them from Kyle's tantrum. "There are some extra pillows and blankets in my mom's closet. Why don't we move the couches and sleep on the floor in here tonight? That way, if anything happens, we're all together."

Carter, Maggie added privately as she moved toward the kitchen, *keep Lily calm. You guys go ahead and sleep. Kyle and I will watch for anything weird. I'll wake you two in a few hours, and we can trade places.*

She heard a rustle of activity behind her as the pair prepared their sleeping arrangements. Taking a deep breath, she entered the kitchen. Kyle was waiting for her.

No more messing around, she sent to him. *I want to know what's bothering you.*

21: FIGHT IRE WITH IRE

Lily's jaw split into a yawn, despite the late noon hour. Her slumber had suffered from hideous flashes of the blond man and his silver sword surrounded by a pack of black-fanged hounds. Interspersed between the nightmarish images, Lily recalled soft murmurs of a silky voice and felt the comfort of Carter's touch as he slid his fingers soothingly through her hair every time she moaned in her sleep. She had lain awake for nearly 10 minutes, curled next to him with her back pressing into his stomach, before finally tottering into the kitchen in search of breakfast.

Lily dropped two slices of bread into the toaster, rubbing her bleary eyes myopically. A sharp bang and mumbled curse from behind caused her to start. Relieved to discover nothing more intimidating than Maggie sucking an injured thumb and the escape of a coffee can as it rolled triumphantly into the sink, Lily relaxed. Her disheveled friend attacked the cylindrical container vengefully, retrieving it and brutally peeling away the lid. Shadows hung tiredly around Maggie's eyes, a result of her night's vigil. She, Kyle, and Carter had taken turns throughout the midnight hours, watching for anything unusual.

The click of rising toast demanded Lily's attention, and she returned to her task, slathering butter across the crispy fare. Taking a mouthful, she turned back to Maggie, who switched on the coffee machine with one hand and rubbed her temple roughly with the other.

"Tired?" Lily asked after a quick swallow.

"Exhausted," she groaned. "Plus, I have a migraine that could kill an ox."

"Probably doesn't help with all of our thoughts invading your brain," Lily observed.

"I've blocked them all. I have no desire to make this headache any worse," Maggie said. She thrust her damaged thumb in the direction of the living room where Kyle still slept. "Besides, it gets annoying to sit and listen to people's mumbled dreams."

The sudden gurgle of household pipes indicated that Carter had stepped into the shower. Lily wanted to ask Maggie about Kyle's behavior the previous evening, but she was unsure of how to initiate the conversation without sounding critical. A mind transfer would have been more convenient, but she didn't want to cause Maggie more discomfort. After considering several possible approaches, she decided that direct and sincere would be most effective.

"Maggie, do you know what's bothering Kyle? Last night he sounded serious about sending Carter back to the hotel by himself."

Maggie's pause lasted the length of the coffeemaker cycle. Its perky aroma did little to ease the afternoon lethargy. Her voice constricted over her answer.

"I think he was, Lil."

Lily looked away, choking resentment down with another morsel of toast. She forced herself to answer calmly.

"Why?" Lily turned back to her best friend, her voice trembling under the yoke of unstable control. "I don't understand why Kyle would want to put someone in danger like that."

"I didn't either," Maggie answered gravely, "until last night."

"What's that supposed to mean?" Lily accused.

"Look, there's no easy way to explain this," Maggie offered, "you're not going to agree with what I have to say, but at least listen, okay?"

Lily didn't trust herself to respond, so she nodded instead.

"Kyle doesn't like Carter—"

"Well he's made that clear," Lily scoffed with a sniff.

Maggie's jaw tightened. "You said you would listen."

"Okay," Lily apologized roughly, folding stiff arms across her chest. "Fine. I'm listening."

Maggie inhaled a composing breath.

"At first I thought Kyle was just jealous—or embarrassed—because of passing out when we first met Carter. But I was wrong."

"Then what is it?" Lily probed waspishly, reflexively interrupting a second time. Her exhaustion was interfering with her patience. "How could Kyle hate someone he barely knows?"

"That's the problem," Maggie pointed out callously. "None of us really know Carter."

Anger sizzled Lily's insides as she realized that somehow during the night, Kyle had persuaded Maggie to his point of view instead of the other way around. Bitterness encrusted her response.

"Well I do," she insisted, "and he's a good person."

"I didn't say he wasn't," Maggie clarified sharply, "but how can you know that after he's only been around for six days?"

Lily's head ached, preventing her from constructing a judicious retort.

"I just know, Maggie. Okay?"

Lily turned back to the toaster and forced more bread into the slots. Maggie seemed undeterred and plodded on with her rationale.

"I can't read his mind, Lily! I have no idea what he's like," she persisted, loudly banging her mug on the counter as emphasis, "and neither do you!"

"So what, just because you can't read his mind that automatically makes him untrustworthy? He doesn't even know why your mind powers don't work on him!"

"Lily, we just want to make sure you're safe!" Maggie countered.

"Really?" Lily persisted, abruptly shrewd. "Or are you just saying this to make Kyle happy?"

"You know I would never say anything like this unless I believed it myself," Maggie yelled hotly, obviously offended. "Kyle just doesn't trust him."

For the first time that Lily could consciously remember, her temper flared unreasonably.

"So, automatically we can't give him a chance?" she shouted, unrestrained indignation wracking her limbs with tremors. "We just decide not to trust him? Because Kyle said so?! That is the stupidest thing I have ever heard! Carter hasn't done anything to harm any of us, Maggie. He's had plenty of chances to hurt me if he wanted to. Why can't you two just be happy for me?" Angry beads of tears spilled over her cheekbones. "I don't want to live my life alone because I've become some kind of freak," she screamed. "Carter understands me."

"So do I, Lily!" Maggie snapped.

"Yeah, like how you threatened to tell the entire student body my middle name, blackmailing me with embarrassment so you could get your own way?" Lily charged. "I can't believe this. We've been friends since before we could even talk, and you're going side with Kyle!"

"Is there a problem here, girls?" Carter interceded, striding into the kitchen.

His dark hair clung wetly to his scalp. Kyle lumbered groggily behind. Lily had been so entrenched by her argument with Maggie that she failed to notice when the shower had turned off. She glanced at Carter, then back to her longtime friend.

"Yes, there is. I think we should leave."

"You can't just leave," Maggie commanded. "Not until this is resolved."

"Sunshine," Kyle's deep voice interjected calmly, "it could still be dangerous out there."

"It's the middle of the day, Kyle," Lily said, an uncharacteristic cynicism contaminating her words. "You don't really think I'll be attacked during school, in front of all those witnesses do you?"

"Smiles—"

Carter interposed himself between Lily and Kyle, shielding her from Kyle's unsolicited counsel. Carter intertwined his fingers with Lily's to illustrate his support.

"I think," Carter suggested firmly, holding up his free hand to ward off Kyle's advance, "that maybe you two should back off. If Lily wants to go, then we'll go."

Numbed by the quarrel, Lily allowed Carter to guide her past a glowering Kyle and into the front room. He scooped together their scattered things and removed the furniture barricade erected the previous night.

The frosty noon air pierced the small entryway as they crossed through the front door.

*

"I can't believe that man," Lily exclaimed, huffing through the school office and into the main hallway. "As if I would shirk all my responsibilities on purpose."

"He's the principal, Lily," Carter said with a noncommittal shrug. "He's just doing his job. Four students don't show up to school and two of them are best friends. You can see why he'd suspect us." Carter steered them into the commons area. "Especially since you and I showed up halfway through third hour together. It's not like you had the option to tell him some crazy guy with a sword is after us, so we all slept over at Maggie's. Think about how that sounds."

Lily sighed, desire for normalcy pinching her chest.

"Five weeks ago, Principal West would have never suspected me of such a thing," she reflected wistfully.

"We didn't do anything wrong, Lily," Carter said, slipping his hand around hers and squeezing it tightly.

When they reached the locker pods, Lily spun the dial fervently, sequencing the combination with a sour shake of her head.

"I know, but it looks bad."

"Who cares," he rationalized softly, sliding a finger across her ear and down the curve of her neck. "We were scared. We did what we had to."

The vacant tone of the school bell echoed through the empty hall, signaling the end of third period. A wave of jumbled voices precluded the students' communal classroom escape as they poured into the commons.

"Yeah, but now when I get home my parents are going to ground me for weeks," she concluded, groping through the locker contents. "He said he was going to call them."

Carter relaxed fluidly against the locker next to Lily's.

"Just tell them I picked you up at Maggie's house. You called your parents last night to say you were staying there anyway, so your story fits."

"That might work. My parents worry when Maggie is home alone because her mom is off at work for days at a time. But even if I tell them that, they'll still be angry that I didn't go to the rest of school."

"True," Carter agreed as Lily slammed door in frustration. He stepped in front of her, a mischievous glint deep in his eyes. "But I bet your punishment will be less than if you told them you slept next to me last night."

Despite her emotional distress, Lily felt blood rushing lustily up her cheeks. Carter touched her chin affectionately. Students congregated around them, pushing to reach their lockers before the next class. Carving a path through the bodies, Carter hastily pulled Lily behind him.

"I hate this," Lily complained quietly to him as they headed for the English classrooms. "I hate having to lie to my parents all the time, I hate fighting with Maggie, and I hate that Kyle is being such a jerk."

Carter paused at the end of the hallway. "So do something about it."

Lily had already stepped forward. She twisted to face him.

"Like what?"

"We'll talk to them, you and me together," Carter replied, sliding next to her. "I know that I can't prove myself to Maggie, since she can't read my mind. But I would never do anything to hurt you. We have to convince them of that."

"I'm not sure they'll listen. They're both really angry."

Her shoulders slumped in defeat.

"Look, Lily, they don't have the right to be," Carter asserted, wrapping his arms protectively around her waist. "Who are they to tell us who we're allowed to love?"

Lily felt a thrill surge through her midsection as Carter leaned closer, his lips brushing the skin of her ear.

"I love you, Lily," he whispered fervently, "and I'm never letting you go."

Lily's head groaned with conflicting sentiment; anxiety over this morning's argument clashed with her devotion for the roguish prince charming who was tilting to fondle her lips. His kiss burned holes of delicious torture through her heart.

"I love you too," she returned, burying her face in his chest.

"So how are we going to do this?" he asked, embracing her tightly.

Lily considered. The way things looked, Maggie and Kyle weren't likely to attend school. Maggie's maltreated cell phone wouldn't function since its unhappy collision with the kitchen floor. Contact through Kyle would only end in disaster. Only one choice seemed to present itself.

"I think the best idea is to corner Maggie at work tonight after she's started all the movies and her employees have gone home. Kyle always goes to work with her, just in case someone tries to attack her again."

Carter smiled into Lily's eyes, kissing her one more time before escorting her to her classroom door.

"Don't worry, we'll convince them."

22: Hit The Mark

    Mark steered his truck into the near-empty parking lot of the movie theater, a sinking gurgle riling his stomach. He had managed to lose his wallet sometime during the seven o'clock movie. Noticing its absence nearly four hours later, he decided to return in order to recover it. The short 15 minutes between home and the entertainment center mushroomed with impending doom. The closer he came to his destination, the more anxious he felt. When he had turned the corner onto 25th Street, the building loomed in front of him like the entrance to a haunted underworld, complete with a monster inclined to eat his soul.

    Her name was Maggie Brooks.

    Earlier in the evening, Mark had noticed she was working the late shift as he purchased a ticket to the newest action flick. She stormed through the lobby, enclosed in a web of sticky ferocity. Mark remembered thinking that if the universe provided hyperboles, a little grey cloud would have been following her around, zapping employees and patrons alike with electric lightning bolts.

    As soon as she huffed through a door labeled "employees only," Mark dashed across the lobby, hugging his ticket furtively to his chest. The usher leisurely reached for the stub, moving altogether too slowly. Mark glanced apprehensively at the threshold where Maggie had disappeared. He chucked the voucher at the usher, sprinting into the appropriate theater.

The first half of the movie eluded his attention. Mark had been avoiding Maggie at school mostly because of her distinctive ability to shrivel his self-esteem into something entirely insignificant. Almost like she could see into his brain and use his thoughts against him. No matter how hard he tried, he proved incapable of outwitting her. But fear of mortification wasn't the only reason he evaded her presence; she was a distinct reminder of his failed relationship with Lily.

Lily Ivers: the girl he had carried a crush for since the second grade. It had taken him four weeks at the beginning of the school year just to work up the nerve to ask her to homecoming. Their sprouting relationship had blossomed for nearly two months, and then, suddenly, his dreams were dashed upon the rocky shoals of high school romance.

Lily's attention slipped away. Mark was unsure of the details, but knew it had something to do with Maggie's new relationship with Kyle Spencer. And then Mark's ultimate nemesis appeared in Idaho Falls: Carter Drake.

It wasn't like when Kyle Spencer enrolled in school. He was admired by both the male and female students, the former aspiring to earn his camaraderie, the latter—though disappointed at his eventual unavailability—content with cordial friendship.

But Carter Drake—his arrival instigated an upheaval of feminine hormones that left every guy in school stranded in a desert of solitude. Packs of girls followed the handsome transfer student through the hallways, hoping for even a miniscule token of acknowledgement. The classroom buzz clustered on his life's story, though there was little real information to tell. And then, scarcely a week later, Carter had the audacity to take Lily as his girlfriend. Mark's Lily!

Mark remembered little of the movie's plot as he exited his seat, sneaking down the hallway, sliding ninja-like along the walls, in order to preclude an engagement with Maggie. Unfortunately, at some point during his gloriously executed escape, Mark's wallet had slipped free of his pocket. In order to retrieve it, he had no choice but to face the intimidating movie theater manager.

He plowed through the back row of the parking lot, spying four free spaces at the front of the line. Always mindful of his truck's spotless paint job, he maneuvered his beloved vehicle diagonally into the area, straddling all four spots. He checked his watch as he removed the key from the ignition—5 to 11.

Mark pushed open the driver's side door, grabbing his soda as his boots contacted the slushy asphalt. A misjudged shift of weight caused the flat of his feet to slide in opposite directions. He dangled on the door frame, grasping it with his free hand, while the other received a dousing of brown soda. After a few seconds of tenacious clinging, Mark righted himself and blotted the sticky liquid staining his hand with a wad of discarded napkins from the cab of his truck. Surreptitiously scanning the parking lot to make sure no one had witnessed the embarrassing incident, he was relieved to discover the area absent of spectators.

The theater's bright neon lights urged him forward. As he swung the truck's door back into place, he noticed four figures through the row of paneled glass at the building's storefront. At first he assumed they were employees, and grateful relief that he wouldn't have to face Maggie alone rinsed the tension out of his nerves. Taking one step away from the transversely parked truck, he noticed that most of the lights in the lobby were dark, as well as those behind the concession stand and box office. It seemed the theater had been shut down for the night. Furthermore, only one of the figures sported the movie theater's uniform. The other three were obviously customers. He paused. The foursome gesticulated riotously at each other, and he had the distinct impression they were engaged in some kind of rampant verbal war. By the time Mark realized the identity of the four contenders, Lily Ivers had thrown open the glass door and stormed onto the sidewalk, Carter Drake close behind. From inside, Maggie Brooks and Kyle Spencer prepared to follow.

Mark briefly considered climbing back into his truck and making a discreet exit. But then he realized he was the only bystander of the spiciest scandal in the history of Bonneville High School—at least this year. No one had ever heard Lily raise her voice in public, least of all to her lifetime best friend. Figuring that he at least owed the student body some juicy tidbits in the name of school spirit, Mark crouched behind the hood of his truck, only the top of his head and eyes visible, waiting to see how the altercation resolved itself.

"Lily, I can't believe you're just walking away," Maggie screamed as soon as she burst through the door. "You're the one who ambushed me here!"

Both she and Kyle had rushed out of the lobby without their coats and Maggie shivered in the cold night air.

"What other choice do I have but to walk away, Maggie?" Lily returned. "It's clear you're never going to accept my choice to stay with Carter."

Mark sided with Maggie on that one.

Lily made a choking sound, and then screeched, "I'm starting to think that you don't care about me at all!"

Mark cared. He cared a lot. He wished that Lily would just ditch Carter.

"Why would we even be having this fight if I didn't care, Lily?" Maggie exclaimed in exasperation. "I'm trying to protect you!"

Protect her from what? Mark wondered. Hopefully from Carter. Then maybe she would be free for a date next weekend…

"A good friend would be happy for her," Carter responded smoothly, wrapping his arm around Lily and pulling her protectively toward him, "not jealous that she's spending time with someone else."

Mark decided he really didn't like the sound of Carter's voice.

"You don't know anything about us, Carter!" Maggie fumed. "I've known Lily all my life, and no one could ever care about her more than I do!"

Yeah, take that! Mark thought.

"From my perspective, it seems she cares more about you than you do her." Carter's eyes gleamed shrewdly. "Are you telling me that if she didn't want you to date Kyle, you wouldn't stand up for him or your decision?"

"That's different," Kyle rumbled.

Mark had forgotten the quarterback was there until he spoke. Mentally he urged Kyle to punch Carter in his girlfriend-stealing face.

"What? How?" Lily sputtered. "You only met Maggie once, and already you were in love with her. You didn't know each other very long before you two got together. I don't remember that being dangerous. Of course, it must be different if it's you two, right? I guess you guys are above the rules!"

"Think about it, Smiles," Kyle said pointing at Carter. "We don't have any reason to trust this guy and my instincts tell me that he's no good."

"But he's one of us!" Lily reasoned.

Now Mark was confused. Instincts? One of us? What did that mean?

"Your instincts also guided you to the bitchiest girlfriend on the planet," Carter added wickedly. "How's that working out for you?"

Mark shuddered at the gritty, hate-infused expression on Kyle's chiseled face. If Kyle had been looking at him that way, Mark would have run for dear life. Still unnoticed, Mark could see the tense bulge twisting the muscles in Kyle's back.

"Apologize, Drake," Kyle commanded ferociously, pushing past Maggie and confronting Carter head to head. The silver-tongued Carter Drake didn't seem worried, even though Kyle towered over him by at least three inches.

"I don't apologize for speaking the truth," Carter taunted.

"Take it back!" Kyle repeated, shoving Carter angrily.

Now, Mark had to admit that Kyle was a big guy, but even taking that into account, it didn't explain how Kyle's shove knocked Carter three feet backward into the pavement. Carter wheezed loudly and massaged his chest where Kyle's palms had made contact, as if it pained him beyond what might be expected from a mere bruise. Lily ran to Carter's side, helping him to stand.

"Kyle, stop," Maggie directed, putting a restraining hand on her boyfriend's shoulder. "He's not worth it."

"Yeah, Kyle," Carter jeered, gasping painfully, "listen to your over-demanding girlfriend. You know, maybe she'd be less crabby if you stuck it to her once in a while."

Kyle took two steps forward and slammed his fist into Carter's left cheekbone.

Lily cried out in distress as Carter crashed into the concrete. Mark blinked in surprise—not that Carter's insult had resulted in a fist to the face, Kyle was well within his boyfriend rights to uphold Maggie's honor and all that—but because Mark could have sworn that he saw a ripple of light undulate across Carter's skin when Kyle's fist hammered into him. Moreover, even though Kyle's strike had forcefully driven Carter to the ground, it appeared that the quarterback had pulled the punch.

Carter rose slowly, a dreadful calm spreading across his features.

"Wow, I really thought that would hurt more, Spencer, considering your abilities and all. Care to try again?'

Kyle swung again in outrage, this time colliding into his opponent's jaw with all his strength, which Mark figured had to be substantial. A wrinkle of white energy pulsed over Carter's face at the point of impact, providing protection from the brunt of the blow. His dark head snapped sideways, but his body yielded no ground.

Carter grinned condescendingly, feeling his undamaged skin. Then he retaliated in kind. White sparks crackled from his knuckles as they rammed into Kyle's gut. Kyle staggered backward, stunned more from shock than actual physical damage from the clout. Howling with resolve, the football hero rushed Carter with superhuman speed, heaving against his rival with the flat of both hands, hurling him 50 feet into the parking lot. As Carter soared through the air, Mark's brain shrieked frantically in his head.

Get out of the way!

Carter's body smashed into the front fender of Mark's red truck, shattering both the passenger window and the right side of the windshield. Mark ducked too slowly. The vehicle groaned in protest as it lurched sideways, knocking Mark to the asphalt and sliding partway over his head. Looking through the narrow view under the truck, he expected to see Carter's mangled body fall on the ground in a broken heap.

But apparently, reality had taken a short lunch break.

Carter lay on his stomach, nearly parallel with the length of the truck, but there wasn't a bruise, scrape or other mark on him. The collision had destroyed his cashmere sweater and woolen jacket. Mark thought he had seen another bright wave of light swell around his fellow student right when Carter hit the street. Carter grunted with exertion and pushed himself into a roll just as a disembodied, clenched hand hurled into the pavement, connecting where Carter's head had rested seconds previous. The asphalt buckled and cracked, fragmenting under the strain.

There was no way Kyle could have covered the distance between the sidewalk and the truck that fast.

But there was no denying the identity of the well-muscled fist cradled in the substantial crater of dirt and crumbled tarmac. Mark scrambled from underneath the truck, terrified of what he saw, yet desperate to see the outcome of the fight. By the time he pulled himself up, Kyle had almost straightened. Carter had already vaulted to his feet and flanked Kyle's left side.

Luminous color burned at Carter's fingertips. A piercing hiss emanated from the flaring radiance. Before Kyle could counter, Carter thrust his hand into Kyle's midsection. Kyle bellowed with pain, and a bright flash launched him across the parking area. He landed on his shoulder with a thud, skidding to a halt in front of the curb. A smoldering hole gaped in his shirt. Mark noticed five, finger-sized burns blistering the athlete's stomach. Kyle heaved for breath.

Carter looked at his hand with curiosity. The tendons in his fingers and wrist snapped rigid and the liquid luminosity gleamed to life. Each finger sizzled with a particular radiant hue: crimson, gold, jade, cobalt, amethyst. Carter stiffened with exertion, forcing the multicolored rays to shine brighter. Rapidly they darted together, intersecting over the center of his palm. As they congealed, the colors blended into a globe of dazzling white so bright that Mark could not look at it directly. Carter glared in Kyle's direction and strode forward.

As he rose, Kyle scanned the immediate area hastily. The girls pleaded for the combatants to stop, dashing into the fray, but neither boy heeded their entreaties. Mark watched with morbid fascination as Carter halted at 30 paces, casting his brilliant weapon. Kyle snatched at the asphalt, ripping a manhole cover free and hurling it at Carter with lethal precision.

Mark yelped an appropriate explicative as both girls ran into the path of the deadly projectiles. He watched helplessly, overcome with horror, as Lily interposed herself between the flying disk of metal and her new boyfriend, intent on receiving the attack in his place. Carter realized her position with only an instant to react. He thrust his palm forward, thumb grazing her ear and ruffling her golden hair. A blast of energy expelled from his hand, forming a rippling barrier of white that protected them both. The manhole plate shattered as it struck the pulsing shield, the remains disintegrating into powder before striking the ground.

At the same moment, Maggie dashed in front of Kyle. He became a blur of movement, whisking her away from Carter's speeding ball of light so quickly that Mark lost sight of them. With nothing to hinder its path, the orb of radiance zoomed through the space previously occupied by Kyle's head and burst on a sleek looking black sedan, which instantly exploded in a terrifying, yet awesome, pillar of fire.

Mark leapt around his truck and trotted down the parking aisle to make sure everyone was okay. Kyle and Maggie perched on the sidewalk, appearing unharmed. Lily stood apart from Carter, facing the blaze, one hand clenched tightly near her forehead and the other stretched out toward the burning vehicle. Her face twisted in concentration.

Unsure of what her posture portended, Mark halted his forward jog and turned back to the spectacular inferno.

The flames momentarily transformed into a sort of jade green color, and receded into a hissing sizzle. Only a husk of used-to-be sedan remained, tendrils of smoke rising sulkily from its surface. Before he had time to turn back to his peers, Mark heard a sharp voice snap through the now quiet parking lot.

"Mark?" he heard Maggie ask. "What are you doing here?"

Wrenching his gaze from the charred wreckage, he turned to see four people staring at him with a mixture of disbelief and apprehension. He swallowed sheepishly.

"Um—I forgot my wallet?"

23: Every Silver Lining Has A Cloud

Carter's glove skimmed the face of his watch as he glanced impatiently at the front doors of the school. He sat casually on the hood of his new vehicle, ignoring the bite of its cold surface as the chill seeped through his jeans. He peered again at the time.

Kyle was late.

Maybe the stubborn quarterback wasn't even coming. Carter had only been able to contact Kyle through voicemail. He had intended to make the request using his ample capability of persuasion. Instead, he had been forced to leave a message asking Kyle to meet him outside during lunch.

Carter tapped his fingers against his cell phone, wondering if he should flush Kyle out. There was still a possibility that Kyle hadn't checked his messages. Deciding that a call would be rash—after all, the lunch bell had only sounded less than 10 minutes ago—Carter waited.

His latest car reflected an ostentatious red shine in the noon sunlight. He ran his palm approvingly across its silky exterior. He had spent the entire morning filling out the paperwork to purchase his previous black sedan rental—a twisted wreck of melted metal and upholstery that now lay somewhere beneath one of Roy Spencer's potato fields. It had taken a measure of calculation to dispose of the evidence created during last night's violent encounter, but Bonneville's quarterback had saved the day. Kyle had smashed the remains into nothing more than four basketball-sized globes and stuffed them into the back of his jeep only seconds before the last movie patrons filtered out of the theater.

Carter slid off the car and kicked lightly at a pile of plowed snow, encouraging his blood to circulate and provide warmth to his freezing extremities. Though his supernatural abilities had awakened the day before, they did nothing to restrict the cold as Kyle's did. Carter pulled his expensive leather glove off his right hand and scanned the school grounds cautiously to ensure no one was around. Apparently his schoolmates lacked the desire to venture into the icy frost of the parking lot.

He stared into his palm, recalling from Lily's description the amount of time it took her, Maggie, and Kyle to develop powers. For them it had happened slowly, and mostly one ability at a time. Carter was sure he had tapped into four distinct capabilities, each sending a burst of exhilaration through his body when he accessed them. The sensation had felt familiar, as though he had used them a thousand times in his lifetime. He summoned the awareness that had stirred the energy locked within him—the discernment of self that had manifested in a prism of liquid light. A spark of multicolored luminance spouted at the tips of Carter's fingers. Clenching his fist hard dispersed the flares. The air's bitter rime numbed his exposed skin.

More than anything, he remembered the way the flow of power had intoxicated his senses as the fight had progressed: blasts of pulsing energy enhancing his punches, the tingling sensation in his fingers as he formed the defensive shield in front of Lily, and the surge of radiant armor that had protected him from Kyle's potent fists. Carter had felt the pressure of his opponent's attacks, but only as a minor physical annoyance. Not a single blemish marked Carter's body.

Rumination of the clash with Kyle ultimately brought Carter back to thoughts of Lily. He had noticed how the contention between all of them distressed her. Her worry and helplessness made him feel regret over something that, several weeks ago, he would have pushed to the emotional limit, regardless of who it hurt. Carter's life in Boston seemed suddenly far away, as if his old life belonged to someone else. His philosophy of existence had transformed in less than a week. In Boston, all of his actions had been driven by the need for parental recognition, negative though it had been, and the gratification of self.

But Lily had changed all that. His love for her extended into every thought; his need for her approval quivered in his cells. She inspired him to treat others with compassion, patience, and respect. For her happiness, he was willing to do anything.

Carter looked up when he heard a steady crunch of snow. Kyle loped across the sidewalk, coatless, nearing the edge of the campus. Carter felt neither animosity nor camaraderie for Maggie's boyfriend. He would rather have let things alone. But for Lily, Carter was keen to initiate some form of amends.

"Make this quick, Drake," Kyle announced when he reached Carter. "Mags thinks I'm in the bathroom. If she knew I was out here, both her and Smiles would come runnin'." His lips curled into something between grimace and grin. "Seems they don't trust us together."

"With good reason. I find it interesting that you managed to lie to Maggie," Carter stated skeptically, referring to Maggie's mind skills.

"She shuts off her power when lots of other people are around. You have two minutes. Don't waste 'em," Kyle declared distastefully.

"I think you and I need to come to an agreement," Carter commanded with diplomatic ease.

Kyle folded his arms across his chest. Carter paused politely until it was clear that Kyle wasn't going to respond. Carter's second entreaty was sharper.

"I've fallen for Lily and you love Maggie."

"And?" Kyle posed.

"And they're best friends," Carter reasoned curtly. "Hating each other is only going to make them miserable or put them in danger."

Kyle scowled, but Carter held up his hands in appeal.

"Now before you start growling at me, remember that we're both to blame for last night. You almost hurt Lily, and I could have killed Maggie. These fights between us need to stop."

"You want me to stop hatin' you?"

"You're never going to like me, Kyle. We both know that," Carter shrugged indifferently, "and the more I learn about you, the less I like you as well. We both have a chance to be happy, but for it to work, we're going to have to get along. Lily and Maggie don't deserve any less."

"Looks like we've got no choice," Kyle conceded after a moment of thought. "But I still don't like you."

"You don't have to. Just pretend."

Carter offered his hand in truce. Kyle, somewhat reluctant, shook it, but continued to glare.

"Don't ever give me a reason to end this agreement, Drake. You'll regret it," Kyle warned before stalking back toward the school.

"I wouldn't dream of it," Carter added softly in satisfaction.

24: Crossed That Bridge Now What?

Maggie's chin rested comfortably in her cupped fingers as she stared across the lunchroom table at Lily and Carter. She watched with pleasant ease as he leaned over and whispered something quietly in her best friend's ear. Maggie released a smile. Lily's thoughts were humming birds and daffodils, true happiness for the first time since the night of the wolf attack. Maggie reveled in the cleansing relief that relaxed muscles and joints. Last week she feared that her oldest and most treasured bond had reached an end. How had the animosity between boyfriends nearly destroyed 18 years of friendship? Maggie vowed that she would never let that happen again.

At least the boys had pounded some of the tension out of their relationship with their fight last Wednesday. Maggie snorted. Men. How predictable. As soon as their reckless hate had placed their girlfriends in danger, they somehow bridged themselves into a truce, precarious though it might be.

Since then, peace had interlaced the group. Carter apologized to Maggie for the horrible things he had said about her so sincerely that, though his mind still remained unreadable, Maggie knew he meant it. Kyle pleaded for Lily's forgiveness for his brash actions. The foursome had even managed a double date last night without incident.

Even so, Maggie could sense that Kyle hadn't exactly been able to expel his dislike for Carter; it lay buried under a mass of willpower and emotional deflection. Despite his emotional struggle, Maggie felt a flicker of pride for Kyle's obvious effort. She had no doubt, that if she could see into Carter's mind, she would discover something similar. Carter's endeavors to mend the rift between himself and Kyle, however, had led Maggie to cultivate a newfound respect for him, which quickly blossomed into trust.

A strong arm wrapped around the back of her chair, dislodging her musing. She turned to Kyle, her expression echoing his smile.

You okay, Sparky? he thought lightheartedly.

Maggie glanced again at her best friend. The shine in Lily's eyes contained such joy that it practically leapt into the air.

Perfect, Maggie returned telepathically.

He pressed his hand gently against her neck, pulling her forehead near enough to be kissed. Maggie closed her eyes, contentedly savoring the tender brush of his lips.

Sparky, I wanted to ask you something, Kyle's silent voice slid into her head. An excited quaver flavored his thoughts.

Yes? Maggie prompted, restraining the temptation to scour his consciousness for details.

I was wondering—

"Hi guys."

Maggie turned halfway around in her chair. Mark's tall, lanky body hopped from one foot to the other. His eyes circled the friends sitting at the table warily, ready to duck should one of the four spontaneously explode. After an awkward moment of silence, he seemed to decide that no imminent danger threatened his wellbeing. He straddled a chair between Maggie and Lily. He smiled at everyone except Maggie, whom he pointedly ignored. She smiled wickedly, knowing the motivation behind both his sudden arrival and his impolite snub.

Mark couldn't be trusted with an important secret—not that he maliciously spread gossip, but his straightforward character simply overlooked the need for subtlety. His unfortunate presence at the theater skirmish last week had forced Maggie to take action. Though no one was likely to believe his story, Maggie wasn't willing to chance it. While Kyle had disposed of Carter's destroyed vehicle, Maggie had cornered Mark, implanting the command that he would not retell the fantastical events that transpired to anyone. Wondering how long her ability would hold him in sway, she entrenched another order in his subconscious. As soon as the first directive faltered, Mark would feel the compulsion to seek her out immediately. So far, it seemed Maggie needed to renew her mind manipulation on him every two days to ensure his obedience.

Her experience with Mark had revealed new insight into her mind control skills. Until now, her command power had been used only for a short-term result: persuading teachers to let her out of class early or convincing them they had misplaced her homework. She was unsure as to how long her ability could dominate any specific individual. Apparently, a person's resolve regarding the situation impacted how long the suggestion could last. Lily's parents, for example, had received a phone call from Principal West reporting the four friends' truancy last week. They immediately curbed Lily's privileges, grounding her for an entire month. Lily, distressed, had called Maggie for advice. The scary blond stranger hadn't reappeared, but all of them felt they were safer together. It had been easy to convince Linda and Paul Ivers that the principal had never called, because neither really wanted to punish their eldest child and Lily had never before acted so irresponsibly.

Mark's situation proved more difficult. Overwhelmed by the strangeness of Kyle and Carter's skirmish, his thoughts were a muddle of restless fear and excitement. He wasn't sure if he wanted to glorify the party of friends or run from them in a terrified frenzy. His determination to expose what he had witnessed continually overthrew Maggie's mental domination.

Thus, Mark unwillingly sat beside her, waiting obediently for her to reset his instructions.

"Mark," she began, forcing her will into his mind, "you—"

"Wait, Maggie," Mark pleaded, "I promise I won't say anything to anyone. Just don't cast your spell on me again."

His brown eyes beseeched mercy.

"Keep your voice down," Kyle said, indicating a group of passing students.

"It's not a spell," Lily added, placing a hand comfortingly on his shoulder. "And it won't hurt you."

"But—" Mark looked at her with the expression of a sad puppy waiting disappointedly by an empty food dish.

"Mark, we can't take the chance you might change your mind about telling everyone," Maggie explained.

"I—"

Carter leaned forward. "Besides, it's not like I didn't compensate you for the loss of your truck. You have to admit, the new one I replaced it with is much nicer than that old pickup."

"Well, yeah—" Mark seemed on the verge of defeat. His shoulders slumped.

"But nothing, Mark," Maggie argued. She filled her voice with power. "You will not discuss what you saw on the night of January 9th, and should you overcome this compulsion you will seek me out immediately."

The weight of her words impregnated the air. Mark blinked languidly, suddenly distracted.

When the first period bell rang, Mark started, looking around in bewilderment. As soon as he saw Maggie, he sighed miserably. Without a word he stood, walking dejectedly toward the mathematics hallway.

"I really wish you didn't have to do that," Lily mentioned sorrowfully.

Her pity for Mark's plight tickled Maggie's mind. Carter put his arm around Lily, offering reassurance.

"I am so glad you can't do that to me," Carter stated.

Maggie delayed her response as hundreds of hurried voices sprang into her mind. She quickly shielded herself, blocking the gurgling worry over late assignments and impending tests as rabbles of students plodded toward classrooms.

"He looks so sad," Lily continued, bringing Maggie's attention back to Mark's demoralized retreat.

Maggie looked pensively at Lily, observing that a few months ago Lily would have been rushing them out of the cafeteria and onward to class, anxious over punctuality.

"I'm just glad you finally promised not to use your power on me anymore," Kyle added, playfully kissing a strand of Maggie's hair.

"You guys aren't any fun at all," Maggie replied in mock disappointment.

"No, we just don't trust you to be responsible with such all-consuming power," Lily teased.

"Thanks," Maggie said sardonically, placing her hand over her chest as if in pain. "I think my self-esteem just dropped six points."

"Don't take it personally, Mags. What if I could get you to do anythin' I wanted without your say?" Kyle nudged her lightly.

"Even without that suggestion power," Carter proposed shrewdly, "you could probably get Kyle to do whatever you wanted."

Maggie opened her mouth to comment, but was interrupted by the late bell. A few straggling students frantically dashed into hallways.

"What do you four think you are doing?" a stern voice demanded.

Maggie looked up into the formidable, lined face of Principal West. His sudden appearance startled a near-silent gasp from Lily. Kyle, though relaxed, stood deferentially. Carter seemed impartial to the principal's authority.

"Well?" Mr. West probed.

"Uh—" Maggie began, wondering if she should reopen her mind to better deal with the situation.

"Sorry, Mr. West," Carter apologized smoothly, "we were just talking and lost track of time."

Carter stood and helped Lily to gather her things. The administrator's eyes tightened, detecting a thread of disrespect underneath Carter's glib assurance.

"We'll get to class right away," Kyle promised, deflecting Mr. West's attention.

The principal continued to glower. Maggie was sure this man had never felt constrained to smile in his whole life.

"Very well," he replied, allowing a warning tone to saturate his response. "Don't let me catch any of you dawdling again, or I'll have to suspend you."

"Of course not," Lily squeaked as they headed across the hexagonal commons area, "we won't let it happen again."

Maggie felt it prudent not to add her own sentiments. Her opinion would, no doubt, result in an escorted trip to the front office. She nonchalantly checked the time on her cell phone. Kyle had tinkered with it on Saturday, and it worked better now than it had before she threw it across the kitchen floor. Principal West watched them warily until they crossed into the math and science stairwell, then he disappeared in the other direction. Maggie, Carter, and Kyle waited until he was out of sight before they burst into a flare of laughter. Lily didn't join them.

"It's not funny, you guys. We could have been in a lot of trouble," she chided as she ascended the first few stairs.

Maggie decided Lily hadn't changed as much as she had previously thought.

"Not much more than last week," Carter pointed out with a wink.

Lily halted with a sigh and turned back to him.

"Carter, my parents are already furious with me," Lily protested.

"Lily, they don't even remember being mad at you," Carter reasoned, leaping up to join her.

"I remember," Lily said, "and that's enough. I don't want to disappoint them again."

Carter cradled her face with both hands. "Lily, you could never disappoint anyone. You are the most beautiful person I have ever met."

He kissed the corners of both her eyes and smiled.

Maggie turned to Kyle, preparatory to part, but was surprised to discover Kyle staring at the floor. Maggie slid her fingers into his palm. He looked up.

"What's wrong?" she asked.

Kyle glanced at Lily and Carter, almost as if to judge whether they were watching. The other couple seemed wholly engaged with each other. Kyle pulled Maggie away from the stairs before he answered. She suppressed a maddening urge to activate her telepathy. She had learned over the last few weeks that Kyle appreciated her respect for his privacy in situations like this.

"I was just thinkin'," he began.

"About what?"

"Well, before Mark interrupted, I was gonna ask you—"

Maggie held his gaze, mutely urging him to continue.

"Nevermind," he decided, shaking his head. "This isn't the time."

Maggie, frustrated, began opening her mind.

"Kyle—"

Kyle put a single finger to her lips.

"I'll tell you about it later, so no readin' my mind. It's a surprise."

Maggie deliberated whether or not to invade his mind anyway—possibly she could extract the information without his knowing—but Lily called loudly from her perch on the stairwell.

"Maggie, we're really late already. Mrs. James is really going to give it to us."

Maggie almost sent Lily ahead to class without her.

"Go on, Sparky," Kyle said, brushing a hand across her cheek. "I promise I'll tell you after school."

Maggie pouted, but the earnestness in Kyle's voice convinced her to be patient. She gave him a quick peck on the lips and sauntered up the stairs. Carter murmured something in Lily's ear that made her cheeks turn dusky, then bent down to kiss her goodbye. Both girls waved farewell as they reached the top landing.

"I take it Carter does pretty well arguing with you," Maggie pointed out as they walked toward their math classroom.

"We weren't really arguing. It was more like playful banter."

"Sounds like flirting to me," Maggie said, poking Lily in the arm.

"A girl is allowed to flirt with her own boyfriend," she huffed good naturedly in return. "You do it with Kyle all the time."

"Touché," Maggie replied, laughing in agreement. "What did Carter say to you anyway?"

Lily brought a finger up to her lips to quiet Maggie as their classroom door loomed into view. "Being yelled at for being late is bad enough. Let's not make it worse by being loud as well. I would like to live to see Carter after class thank-you-very-much."

"Don't try avoiding the subject. You were blushing. What did he say?"

"Come on Maggie, we're really late."

Maggie planted her feet in front of the classroom door, impeding Lily's advance.

"You can tell me, or I can find out for myself," Maggie taunted, crossing her arms stubbornly in front of her chest. "I'll give you the choice."

Lily smiled shyly and her eyes radiated a dreamy glaze.

"He said he loved me, and no matter what happened, he'd always take care of me."

"Smooth," Maggie teased with a mocking roll of her eyes.

"Ha, ha. You can make fun of me, but you and Kyle do the exact same thing every day. Can we go to class now?"

Maggie hid her laughter behind her palm, inhaling an exaggerated breath to calm herself. With a coy smile at her best friend, Maggie turned the handle and threw open the door. Her comfortable mirth twisted into horror as she stepped into the classroom. Lily's whimper echoed through the heavy silence.

Their entire trigonometry class was dead.

25: Deck of Shards

Kyle followed Maggie's egress with his eyes, aggravated by the impending hour and a half separation caused by class. Anxiety plagued him when the girls weren't within his sight. True, nothing dangerous had ever happened during school hours, but that didn't mean that it never would. He felt responsible for both their well-being, despite the recent emergence of Drake's powers. Maggie lifted a hand in farewell as she reached the top of the stairs, a half smile creeping across her gorgeous face. A catch squeezed Kyle's throat, and his heart beat a little faster, the way it always did when she smiled at him. He stared at the empty landing as she disappeared from view.

Kyle pondered over the insane question he had almost asked her. What would her reaction have been? What had he been thinking? Whatever the answer, he had no choice but to continue now. Maggie's interest was piqued. She would glean it from his brain even if he changed his mind about voicing it.

Kyle glanced at Drake's profile. The guy's gaze lingered at the top of the stairs, his features creased with unease.

"C'mon Drake, we have to get through the commons room without the principal catchin' us," Kyle prompted, turning toward the green-carpeted span.

"Kyle, do you ever wonder why we have these abilities?" Carter asked, still looking up into the second-floor hallway.

"Not really," Kyle answered absently, peeking across the stairwell threshold and into the hexagonal lobby area.

He could only see a portion of the room; his peripheral vision was blocked by dented, yellow lockers.

"I mean, why us?" Drake continued. "Why were we drawn to each other? There has to be a logical explanation for it."

Kyle stepped onto the stained green carpet. "Maybe there is. Lily's been tryin' to research it."

He strode soundlessly to the edge of the locker pods, scanning for teachers or administrators. The room was clear.

"Lily told me that the moment you first saw Maggie," Drake said, walking next to him, "you fell for her like you knew you had to love her."

"Yeah, so?" Kyle asked, impatiently crossing the floor.

"When I went to the falls the first day I came here and found Lily's purse, I pulled out her ID. For some reason, when I looked at her picture, I just knew I needed to find her. Just like I needed to come to Idaho Falls. It's interesting that every one of us is full of impulses that we can't explain."

Kyle stopped halfway across the room and turned to face Lily's boyfriend. It seemed they wouldn't be attending weights class until Drake had his say.

"What are you gettin' at, Drake?"

"The puzzle to our lives," he proposed. "I think we're missing the corner piece. If we could figure out what it is, what's driving our perceptions about each other, we might be able to understand what's really happening to us."

Kyle paused, intrigued by Drake's supposition. Kyle had never really considered the origin of his devotion to Maggie, his brother-like affection for Lily, or his obsessive dislike for Drake. He had merely accepted each as part of his being, as

Phoenix Angel

if, deep down, the universe had already explained it to him and he was simply acting on the answer.

"Don't you feel it?" Drake persisted. "There's something missing. Something we can't quite see, but it's there, on the edges of our thoughts. An answer that would explain everything."

"Unfortunately, you will not live long enough to discover it," inserted a heavily accented voice.

Kyle and Carter turned simultaneously, sinew and muscle tightening into defensive postures. The exit doors between the mathematics and athletics hallways gaped wide as a tall figure tread resolutely into the building, his white overcoat billowing around a muscular frame. Tendrils of blond escaped the confines of his ponytail, drifting into his perilous grey eyes. The doors slammed ominously behind him.

This had to be the man Lily described the night of her date with Drake. Adrenaline coursed through Kyle's body. Though the intruder stood at least four inches shorter than himself, the man's posture and self-assurance sent shivers through Kyle. The blond stranger pulled the white cloak away from his hip with his left hand, revealing a gold and silver inlaid hilt. His right, encased in a symbol etched-glove, reached across his torso to grip the sword.

"Who are you?" Carter demanded.

"Who I am is not important," he answered, drawing the weapon.

The scraping of the metal against scabbard set Kyle's teeth on edge. Everything about the stranger sent waves of warning through him. This man was dangerous, deadly formidable.

"What do you want?" Drake probed, attempting to stall.

Kyle noticed his companion's fingertips twitch. Perhaps the two of them could subdue the stranger.

"Want?" the man repeated, his eyes freezing the air with his stoic glare. "Vengeance."

Kyle felt his brow furrow. What the hell did that mean?

"This cycle, you reap the consequences of the pain you have inflicted on those I love," the stranger added with a flourish of the silver sword.

Just as Kyle prepared to spring, the man vanished. The first indication of his enemy's position was a swish of cloth behind his left ear. Before his mind could tell his muscles to super speed out of the way, the silver and gold hilt connected with his temple. Misty vapors of nothingness surrounded the boundaries of his vision. Kyle was unconscious before he hit the floor.

*

A revolting gurgle eddied through Lily's stomach, burning her throat. The bodies of 22 of her classmates, most of whom she had known since kindergarten, lay strewn about the room in various states of mangled carnage. Crimson streaks spattered the walls and desks, trickling into ghastly pools under eviscerated torsos and amputated appendages. A soggy, iron taste coated the inside of her mouth and she forced herself not to gag. Every part of her body shivered with fear and anguish. Her knees wobbled unsteadily and she snatched the back of Maggie's shirt to steady herself.

What had happened here?

Part of that answer came, unsolicited, with a rumbling growl in the outside hallway. She remembered that sound. It was shrouded in cold and pain and terror—and it haunted her nightmares. Leaning on Maggie for support, she suppressed a shuddering sob and turned to survey the corridor. A canine demon with black, salivating jaws, three times the size of the wolves that she and Maggie had faced on that lonely country lane back in November, took a single step in her direction.

Lily's paralyzed lungs inhibited her scream. She felt a hard jerk as Maggie maneuvered protectively in front of her body. Maggie backed away from the gargantuan wolf and into the classroom as it approached, forcing Lily to retreat as well. As soon as the girls crossed completely into the blood-soaked classroom, the creature sat back on its haunches. Lily could have sworn she heard a wolfish cackle in the forefront of her mind.

The door slammed shut with a loud crack.

"Don't worry," an abrasive male voice explained, "he won't attack unless I order him to."

Once the wolf had disappeared from view, Lily felt strength surge back into her body and she rotated, sidling back to stand beside her best friend. A silver-haired man in his mid-twenties—not the blond one she had subconsciously expected—leaned casually against the math teacher's desk. Dark leather armor encased him. A scruffy beard outlined a set of wiry lips, split into a grin of vicious amusement. He rubbed a wickedly long dagger with a cloth, wiping the edge clean of blood. On the floor, bound, bruised, and gagged—but very much alive—was Mark Weston.

"Who are you?" Maggie demanded.

"It wounds me, my lady, that you've forgotten me so easily," he taunted, eyes sparkling maliciously as he slid his polished weapon back into its garishly red sheath.

"How could I forget you?" she growled, anger scarcely masking her deeper fear. "I've never met you before!"

"We've met. In fact, you know me quite intimately," the man laughed cruelly, tapping at his forehead lightly, "as I'm sure you can see."

Lily heard a strangled gasp from her best friend. Maggie's face was a twist of disgusted disbelief.

"That's not possible," Maggie wheezed. "That couldn't have been me."

"Oh it was," he countered slickly. "In fact, I do believe it was that particular night that destroyed your brother's kingdom. I never did ask, did he ever forgive you for your ignorance?"

"What are you talking about?" Maggie snapped. "I don't have a brother."

Lily stabilized herself with a calming mantra of deep breaths, then locked her tumult of emotions into a dark crypt in the back of her heart. Whatever this creep had done to Maggie had her unnerved. Lily knew she had to help her best friend focus. Maggie's mind control abilities were their best chance for survival.

"You really have forgotten, haven't you?" he said, genuine surprise flicking across his brow. "Well, that is interesting, isn't it?" His head fell back in a torrent of black laughter. "Well I guess we're in need of a formal introduction then. My name, my lady, is Feralblade." He bowed mockingly, arms wide open as if in homage to noble visitors. "My furry friend out there," he indicated the corridor on the other side of the closed door, "is The Pack Sire of the Wolves of Skoh. You'll have to excuse him. He's still a little upset with the death of his daughter and nephew. If I let him, he would gladly rip you apart."

"You mean the wolves that attacked us?" Lily asked. "They tried to kill us!"

"One of you, at least," Feralblade answered, turning his attention to Lily. His face grew grim. "That would have seriously hindered our cause."

"And what cause is that?" Maggie asked ferociously, sounding—to Lily at least—more composed and less bewildered.

"There's no need to be angry, Princess Margariete," Feralblade responded evenly. "We were led to believe that you were the one we had been searching for, and as a result we almost let our true target slip through our fingers—yet again. The wolves should have tried to capture Esilwen here," Feralblade indicated Lily with a wave of his hand, "and leave you for dead, not the other way around. But luckily for you, that bothersome lover of yours showed up to rescue you. We had thought we were finally rid of him, but it seems we were mistaken."

Suppositions pounded loudly inside Lily's head, spurred by new names and strangers who mysteriously knew them. Blood dripped around her, adrenaline pumped with fear, and an overwhelming need to flee assailed her. She felt like this had all happened before, like her existence as Lily Ivers, the cheerful 17-year-old straight-A student, had been a dream—happy, but unreal. She had never felt more like herself, her identity stirring achingly deep inside her, than she did at this moment.

And the sensation was heartbreakingly terrifying.

"Enough talk." Feralblade yanked Mark to his knees, who stared in mad fear at the two girls facing him. He had obviously been present for the assassin's first round of brutality. "I could simply kill you, Margariete, and capture my target, but that's hardly entertaining." His face twisted cruelly. "Instead, I'm going to give you two a choice."

Feralblade ripped the gag from Mark's mouth, leaving behind an ugly red weal. Understanding slithered down Lily's neck like ice.

They were after her. Not Maggie. And Mark was the leverage.

"Don't listen to him, Lily!" Mark commanded.

Feralblade cackled and cuffed Mark across the face.

"It would be unwise to ignore me," Feralblade advised, venomous mirth spilling through his teeth. "I've already killed everyone else here, so you know I'm not bluffing," he leveled his soulless eyes even with Lily's, "when I tell you that I will kill your friend if you don't come with me."

Lily swallowed, unsure as to her course of action. Maggie's eyes narrowed, her gaze locked on Feralblade. She slid protectively in front of Lily, shielding her once again.

"Lily is not going anywhere with you."

Feralblade smiled enthusiastically.

"The hard way then," he replied, unsheathing his dagger.

*

Carter watched tensely as Kyle's unconscious form thudded onto the worn commons flooring. The blond intruder stood over the fallen athlete, a stern look of determination—and almost remorse—lining his face. Light crackled angrily at Carter's fingers. He had almost missed the assailant's actions entirely. At first, Carter had thought the man had used something like Kyle's superior speed, whipping around the quarterback's defenses with inhuman velocity.

An instant of deliberation discounted that hypothesis. Kyle would have been able to counter that, or at least anticipate the attack. The stranger hadn't moved. He had phased from one point of the room and rematerialized at another—teleported. Carter felt a nip of fear. This guy had rendered Kyle useless in a single blow, something Carter had previously believed impossible.

He doubted that he could beat this enemy on his own. Carter couldn't reach Kyle, the intruder stood between them. And even if he could drag the insensible football player off to recuperate, that would leave nothing between the blond warrior and the girls.

Carter had no choice but to defeat the man, to keep him from Lily.

The stranger's expression changed instantly to smoldering hatred as he looked up at Carter. Despite the seriousness of the situation, Carter wondered with a margin of self-conscious exasperation what he had ever done to deserve so many people's condemnation.

"I've waited centuries for this," the warrior stated. He bowed politely. "I am Raeylan of House Viridius. And today you will pay for what you did to my sister, my people, and The Warden of the Chalice."

Raeylan twirled his sword in preparation to strike.

"I have no idea what you're talking about," Carter argued, taking several steps backward, trying to keep out of the warrior's sword range.

"Whether or not you understand is irrelevant," Raeylan declared, his grey eyes flashing without sympathy. "You will die here."

Carter barely had time to conjure a shield of white energy as Raeylan lunged suddenly forward. The elliptical shield pulsed with thrumming radiance, its glare so dazzling that Carter lost sight of his opponent. When it dimmed, distress slid its thorny fangs into Carter's abdomen. Raeylan hadn't bothered to evade the bright barrier at all. His blade pierced through its center with staggering ease. With a grunt of satisfaction Raeylan twisted the sword, dragging it horizontally through Carter's protective shell. The barrier of light shattered into glittering shards of brilliance, clattering to the floor like broken splinters of glass.

Carter felt an unexpected swell of déjà vu. The falling shards seemed familiar somehow, like a reoccurring motif in his dreams. Unfortunately, he didn't have time to ponder the origin of the feeling. A scream ripped from Carter's throat as Raeylan's weapon, unhindered by Carter's defensive armor, gored smoothly into his left shoulder. The blade cleaved through muscle and bone, thrusting cleanly out of Carter's back. Had he not instinctively reacted to turn the sword's path with his right arm, the cold steel would have slashed his heart. He heaved a painful breath. The armor that had unfailingly protected him from Kyle's super strengthened attacks was nothing more than silk to Raeylan's sword.

"Surprised that your Light Armor didn't protect you?" the blond warrior alleged, his face close enough for Carter to feel the air stir at the swordsman's words. "You may not remember your transgressions, but I do."

Raeylan wrenched the blade from Carter's body. Carter fell to the floor, clutching his wounded shoulder. Blood pulsed angrily from the torn flesh.

"Your abilities do not protect you from this weapon. How does it feel, to know that you will die upon your own sword?"

The shards, the sword. A vague memory tickled Carter's awareness. They were important. The sword had smashed the shards.

But what did that mean?

Carter experienced a surge of anger. Whatever was happening, he was determined to survive. Raeylan would not kill him. He would save Kyle and Maggie. And above all, he was not going to let the intruder have Lily.

Carter's right hand twitched as he felt white energy gathering into his palm.

26: Falling Apart at the Beams

Mark's scream reverberated through Maggie's bones as Feralblade slashed the gleaming dagger across her classmate's chest, severing layers of cloth and skin. Blood streamed from the wound, soaking the torn halves of Mark's shirt. Agonized sweat beaded around his ears and lips as he gasped for air. He toppled onto his stomach. Lily's emotional reaction was instantaneous. Maggie heard her best friend's intention to dash forward and help before Lily could physically enact the deed. She blocked Lily's path with an upraised arm and projected a warning into Lily's mind.

Don't!

A muffled voice croaked a heartrending entreaty from the carpet. "Lily don't—don't come over here, no matter what he does to me."

Feralblade rewarded Mark with a stiff kick. Maggie heard ribs crack and Mark groaned pathetically. Lily gripped Maggie's sleeve, helpless.

"Leave him alone!" Maggie commanded, pressing her will heavily against the vicious assassin's consciousness.

She hoped her emotional state hadn't encumbered her ability to use her powers. Feralblade smirked, rancor glittering through his eyes, and jerked Mark upright. The dagger tip rested just under Mark's ear, pitting his flesh.

"I'm disappointed," Feralblade cooed. "Once upon a time, my lady, you would have driven me to my knees with the power of that command."

Maggie threw herself at Feralblade's mind wildly, desperate to force his surrender. Her head snapped back suddenly, reeling from the impact of some unseen barrier. It felt as if she had run unheeded into a plate glass window and hadn't realized its existence until she collided with it. She could see into Feralblade's mind, as if from a distance, but was unable to read or access it.

Feralblade laughed maliciously at her obvious strain. One hand held the dagger at Mark's throat, but the other slipped under a thin chain of gold that encircled the man's neck. He pulled on it gently, exposing a sickly stone at the base of the chain. He waved it tauntingly toward Maggie.

"Don't bother trying to control me. I can keep you out of my head, should I choose."

Somehow the necklace hindered the effects of her abilities. Feralblade had let her read his mind earlier, projecting revolting fantasies that couldn't possibly have been real. *But for what reason?* she wondered. Distraction? That only made sense if Feralblade intended to hamper her concentration, something he didn't require as his mind was already shielded. What then? The persona of herself in the visions had been reveling in stolen pleasure. Right now, just the possibility of this killer touching her turned her stomach with disgust. Perhaps it was only a form of sadistic torment, and she was overanalyzing his tactics.

Yet a frail ghost of truth lingered about his sensual images. Once he propelled them into her mind, their reality seemed undeniable. A set of deeply etched emotions emerged from a dusty compartment inside her heart.

Sharp regret. Biting shame.

"Maggie," Lily whispered weakly, "I have to do something, before he kills Mark."

Lily's dread-soaked thoughts were easily read. She intended to surrender herself, hoping the monster before them would keep his word and release Maggie and Mark. Pain stained Mark's cheeks. His eyes were gaunt from Feralblade's abuse. Maggie couldn't fault Lily's logic. In Lily's mind, yielding seemed the only sure way to save two people she loved.

Maggie knew it didn't matter. The assassin was entertaining himself. The carnage around them was proof enough of this silver-haired man's brutal lack of regard for life. Once Lily gave in, the game was over. Mark would be dead.

"I'll come with—" Lily began, shifting to step forward.

"Don't even think about it, Lil!" Maggie interrupted. "YOU WILL NOT SURRENDER YOURSELF TO HIM," she commanded harshly, feeling the suggestion permeate Lily's consciousness.

At first, she felt her friend resist. Lily's resolve to rescue Mark was strong, but abruptly Lily submitted, resigning to Maggie's control. Mark heaved a miserable sigh of approval.

Feralblade's eyes flashed. "You truly don't understand your predicament, do you, my lady?"

"I'm not letting you take her," Maggie stated decisively.

"Your wishes no longer concern me," he spat with a hint of enmity, "nor will they change the outcome. Esilwen is coming with me, and you will die here, along with this pitiful excuse for a person."

Maggie suppressed an angry sob of despair. Mark's thoughts were devoid of hope. He had accepted that, for him, this was the end. He knew his sacrifice might protect Lily. For so many years, Maggie had branded Mark a loser, beneath her time and notice. Danger and death had forced her to reevaluate that judgment. Watching him powerlessly forfeit his life to save Lily's made Maggie profoundly regret every terrible thing she'd ever said or done to him.

Mark was a hero.

"Please don't," Lily begged, "I—"

The statement "I will come with you," repeated cyclically in Lily's mind, but Maggie forbade them to cross Lily's lips. Maggie flooded with wretchedness. Mark's death would be her fault. But she had no choice. What ungodly things would this man do to Lily if Maggie let him kidnap her?

An idea belatedly crossed her mind. She ejected a telepathic scream for help, mentally kicking herself for not thinking of it earlier. Even if Kyle and Carter received the missive, they would never arrive in time to save Mark, but there was a possibility she could distract Feralblade long enough for them to rescue Lily.

The assassin's hand tightened around the hilt of his weapon. It was clear Feralblade had no intention of executing Mark quickly. His sadistic sense of amusement precluded efficiency. The blade bit shallowly into Mark's throat.

Barely a nick into his slice, Feralblade paused. A crystal tinkling, like thousands of glass beads scraping against each other, vibrated airily from one of the pouches at his belt. The killer paused, grinning maliciously at the girls as he whispered loudly into Mark's ear.

"Looks like some god is watching over you, boy."

Throwing Mark ungraciously to the floor with a heavy thud, Feralblade sheathed his dagger and pulled a glowing gem out of the pouch. The chinkling stone was round and smooth, about the size of an ear bud. Feralblade inserted it into one of his ears.

"Feralblade," he announced. "They're here. I was just finishing."

Maggie watched his expression change from annoyed impatience to an eager passion.

"Yes general. I'll be but a moment."

Feralblade plucked the gem from his ear and dropped it back into its leather receptacle. He hovered vulture-like over Mark's prone form.

"Well, it appears I don't have time to kill you myself," he apologized, nudging Mark's chest with his toe.

Mark cried out in pain, his body convulsing in spasms. Then he stopped moving altogether. Feralblade strode toward the girls. Lily grasped Maggie's forearm tightly, and Maggie interposed her body in front of her best friend, shielding her from Feralblade's reach. He halted less than a foot away from Maggie's trembling figure.

"I have to leave for now—something more pressing has come to my attention. But be assured that I will return," he flicked his hand across Maggie's cheek, brushing it lightly, "to collect Esilwen."

Maggie slapped his fingers away, nostrils flaring. Her lips tasted salty.

"Now that temper I remember very well," he sneered. "At least one thing about you hasn't changed. Go ahead, take your best shot."

He offered his chin for a free strike. Maggie obliged.

As she prepped her fist, Feralblade's hand whipped around her neck and she felt his grip on the back of her hair. His movements were lightning quick, yanking her off balance and throwing her across the room before she had managed to swing her arm. Lily's shriek was lost as Maggie slammed into the teacher's desk, pushing it across the carpet with her momentum. She crumpled next to Mark in a heap. A harsh throbbing burned in her lower back where it had impacted the furniture. Ignoring the hurt, she tried to stand, turning her attention back to Feralblade.

His dagger had appeared in his hand. Lily lay comatose on the floor. Before Maggie could push herself into a standing position, Feralblade's form dissolved into dark vines of black smoke. The stench of burned blood reeked in the air.

A disembodied hand, appearing through a haze of black vapor that suddenly surrounded Maggie, grabbed her throat, lifting her off her feet. The rest of Feralblade's body materialized instantly from the shady smog. He threw her face down onto the surface of the desk, scattering pencils, paperclips, and other office paraphernalia. A gurgle of pain choked her throat as the assassin leaned his weight against her and lowered his lips to her ear.

"I could have you spared, if you promise to be mine," he whispered.

Vulgar images flowed through her mind, thick with Feralblade's intentions.

"Never," she spat.

"Suit yourself," he answered, venom burning every syllable.

He lifted her head and slammed it brusquely against the wooden desk. Maggie heard the crunch of her delicate facial bones, muffled by the density of her own skull. Blood surged into her mouth, and she gagged as her hip hit the floor. Footsteps receded toward the exit. The door creaked.

Maggie rolled in torment on the bloody carpet, pushing herself around to see the open portal. A new bubble of fear pricked her as a white furry sentry trotted into the room.

"Kill the boy, paralyze the dark one. I'll take her later," Feralblade commanded.

As you wish, the wolf responded opening its mind. Feralblade shut the door, imprisoning them with the black fanged demon.

*

Pulsing multicolored energy prickled Carter's palm, demanding release. Ignoring the throbbing in his injured shoulder, he swung his legs around in a semi-circle, pushing upward with his feet into an upright crouching position. Bracing his wounded wrist with his left hand he flattened his palm, discharging a globe of sinuous light toward his enemy.

Raeylan phased two feet to the right. The speeding orb of light swept through his previous location and exploded against a set of lockers. The building quaked from concrete to plaster. Jagged scraps of metal impaled the walls and ceiling, scattered remnants of scorched papers fluttered softly to the floor. The intruder seemed undaunted by the detonation. He stared intently at Carter with a silent challenge as the wake of the explosion billowed around him. His sword flickered with reflected light.

Carter instantly reassessed his attack. Organizing light separately from each fingertip, he constructed multiple spheres of searing brilliance, hurling them concurrently at his enemy as he twisted to his feet. As the globes soared outward, Carter smiled triumphantly. The fragmented orbs synchronized an inescapable attack on his opponent. The haughty sword-brandishing warrior wouldn't have time to dodge.

The volatile energy rushed toward Raeylan, who exhibited a distinct lack of tension in his resolute gaze. As the balls of light reached his position, Raeylan sank into a balanced stance, curving the sword with agile grace. Then he spun, sweeping the sword in a wide arc, cross cutting the air around him in rapid succession. Raeylan met each sphere exactly with the edge of the blade. Rather than deflecting the globes, the metal pulsed in a dazzle of shine as the energy melted into the weapon.

Carter swore. The sword was capable of absorbing his attacks.

Raeylan righted himself, slipping nimbly out of his sword dance posture. Locks of blond hair had escaped the leather thong at the nape of his neck and fell across his face. An air of superiority glinted from Raeylan's half veiled stare. The warrior's stormy grey eye promised no mercy.

"Let me remind you how dangerous this sword is," Raeylan pledged.

His body coiled into an erect position, arms crossing at a point in front of his heart. The sword tip pointed away from Carter.

A brilliant opal glow radiated from the tapered point of the metal blade, rolling into a surge of energy. Disbelief surged through Carter's veins. The sword regenerated Carter's previous volley of spheres. Raeylan pivoted the hilt, realigning the weapon's tilt, then slashed upward with the sword as he uncrossed his arms with rapid elegance. A throng of vivid orbs zoomed at Carter. He knew he hadn't the skill to evade them.

Carter gave in to instinct, pooling energy into his Light Armor and poising his weight to receive the impact.

The dynamic spheres collided against him in tandem, shoving him backward across the commons. Pain ruptured through his barrier of energy. New blood spurted from his wounds. The clash of energy fizzed around him like mottled lightning. His shirt disintegrated in a crackle of radiant flare. A pain-engorged bellow spewed from his throat. Carter's protective shell of armor rippled madly across his skin, fracturing against the pressure of Raeylan's energy strike.

Carter's brain insisted that if he didn't redirect the clashing powers, they would consume him completely. He squinted with effort, attempting to concentrate the energy of his protective shield at the points of Raeylan's projectiles. Carter's feet stopped shifting, and the pain evaporated.

Unfortunately, the orbs of light did not.

The spheres began to rotate, swelling with current. Carter could feel them siphoning the power from his body's invisible armor. The orbs merged into each other, clashing in rainbow hue, until a single, giant ball of pearly luminescence swirled before him. Carter focused his will into the energy boil, narrowly controlling its potency.

Suddenly, a scream thwacked his consciousness—Maggie's telepathic voice, calling for help. The sensation stung like a whip, and for a flicker of a moment he diverted his attention away from his gathered energy sphere. Something was critically wrong with the girls. The light swelled intensely, tripling in size in under a second, sucking power from Carter's entire being like a faucet with a broken valve. Desperately he tried to break the connection, but the weapon of light had escaped his influence.

For the first time, Carter saw human emotion slide across Raeylan's face: astonishment. Then the sphere expanded across Carter's vision and he lost sight of his blond rival. Tremors shook the ground. Walls began to sway and tiles shook loose from the ceiling. Weakness weighted his limbs as Carter's supernatural abilities drained from him. Then, the white energy whispered to him, instructing him to walk into its center. He didn't understand, but he obeyed.

*

The wolf soared past Maggie in a great bound, streaking like a slow motion picture. Mark moaned once, his awakening groan melting into a terrified scream as the beast landed by his side. Its jaws snapped expectantly, violet-hued saliva frothed around its gums.

"Stop! Don't bite him!" Maggie screeched, infusing her remaining strength into the order.

The wolf turned in surprise, a low rumble vibrating through its chest. Maggie pushed herself into a sitting position, using the teacher's desk to brace her weight. The wolf surveyed her damaged condition. Maggie could sense the creature's olfactory senses sweep across her, ascertaining her threat level.

You dare impede my actions with mind manipulation? its voice grated harshly, like a dull saw against hardwood. *How foolish.*

The wolf towered over Maggie's head, its shoulders easily clearing the tables by two feet. The beast lowered its head, leveling its unnaturally intelligent eyes with Maggie's. Awkwardly, she tried to wriggle away from its rancid breath, but the desk blocked her retreat.

You cannot run. I will show you true power. The power of the Void.

The massive canine curled its lip around its knife-like fangs in an unmistakable leer. Its eyes gouged into Maggie's brain.

She clutched at her head in new agony. Acidic burns seared through every synapse. She desperately tried to shut her eyes, but the wolf held them open, dominating her vision. A throaty scream hurt her ears, unrecognizable as her own. The most wretched and terrifying moments of her life were relived simultaneously: Trent's humiliating attack on the green, the dead-eyed creatures from the movie theater, the rending of her flesh by the teeth of demonic wolves. She again felt the burning saliva, endured the rattling howl that tore through her sanity. Horror induced her heart to pound at an inhuman rate. She felt tiny razors rip open internal blood vessels that were unable to compensate for the strain. Maggie needed the pain to end, before her heart exploded.

She pushed back, piercing into her attacker's consciousness, hoping to return destruction in kind. Inside the wolf's memories, her mind was assaulted by a different kind of trauma. Through its eyes she experienced the satisfaction of murdering thousands of humans, tearing helpless victims to shreds with black, venom fangs. Maggie recoiled from the carnage inside The Pack Sire's mind, withdrawing into a corner of herself. Her breath straggled in and out of her lungs in ragged gulps.

You haven't the skill to bare my worst nightmares. That is a gift only The Mistress of the Void can give, and you are not her servant. Trying to force such strength only rebounds it on the user. The wolf released several coughs that sounded like a chuckle. *The Man Stalker wants to keep you as a pet, contrary to his orders to destroy you. How pitiful. It seems he has a weakness for you. I, therefore, will carry out the order.*

Maggie felt hot tears spool down her cheeks. She had failed. After killing her, the fanged monster would surely murder Mark, and Feralblade would capture Lily. Not even 10 minutes ago, Kyle had been trying to ask her something important. She would never know what it was, would never again feel the safety of his embrace, or feel the warmth of his hazel eyes. The wolf's panting chafed her face, its sour odor curdling her stomach. Every muscle in her body tensed. The wolf twisted his head, a ripple of a growl undulated its flanks.

Are you ready to die? it asked arrogantly. Maggie glared at it.
Rot in hell!

A sharp yelp pitched from the wolf's throat as its milky fur suddenly swelled with green flame. It stumbled backward, snarling with fury. As the beast danced in a panicked frenzy, Maggie saw Lily remove her hand from its hind leg. The fragrance of sizzling animal hair clogged the air as Lily rose to her feet and rushed to Maggie's side.

"Come on, Maggie," Lily ordered, snatching her hand and pulling Maggie to her feet. "We need to get out of here."

Maggie swayed dangerously, leaning against Lily to keep herself from falling. The wolf's mental invasion had drained her strength. Lily tugged her toward Mark, who had passed out again and lay face down on the floor. The movement set Maggie's head spinning, and she fought to stay conscious.

The wolf's yowls of suffering seemed to come from a distance.

Lily knelt next to Mark and carved a lengthy slice into her arm with her pocketknife. Maggie turned around to monitor their blazing captor, obstinately fighting back the blackness that threatened to overwhelm her. Tremors snaked up and down her limbs. The wolf dropped to the floor and endeavored to smother the flames with ardent rolling.

The ice-green fire seemed impervious to suffocation. Maggie realized that the smokeless inferno didn't adhere to the same rules of combustion as regular flame. Maggie flicked her attention between burning animal and best friend. As Lily redirected her energy into healing Mark, her defensive blaze began to recede from the wolf's pelt. The more concentration she spent on Mark, the less effective her prior attack became.

A concerned breath filled Maggie's lungs. Though badly burned, the wolf was nearly free of flame. She circled Mark, almost toppling in her weakened state, and bent to grapple with the bonds around Mark's wrists. She struggled to unravel the tight knots with shaking fingers. Liquidy emerald crackles licked the edges of Mark's injuries, mending the skin.

"What—how?" Mark babbled as he pushed himself off the floor after Maggie finally loosened his hands. He ran his fingers incredulously across his restored chest.

"We don't have time for this," Maggie said as Lily helped him rise. "We need to get out of here before Feralblade comes back."

Mark seemed incapable of doing anything but stare at his torso, so both girls seized his arms and pulled him toward the door. Maggie stumbled along, leaning against him more than leading. The last of the green flame devouring the wolf died just as the friends crossed into the hallway.

Then the floor began to shudder. Maggie fell, striking her hip a second time against the squeaky linoleum. At first she thought she had slipped and lost her balance, so she was surprised to see Lily on the floor beside her. Mark looked around as if in a daze. As the building swayed, crashes and screams emanated from the surrounding classrooms, followed by the din of teacher voices. Scrabbling noises echoed through the halls as hundreds of students followed disaster protocol.

Earthquake? This is not a coincidence, she heard Lily wonder, as her friend scrambled to her feet and dragged Maggie vertical. Just as they rounded the corner into the stairwell, a sonic howl infiltrated their ears, pounding into their skulls. Collectively they clutched their heads; Lily remained standing, Mark fell onto his face, and Maggie slid to her knees. The panicked shrieks of their peers in other rooms transformed into wails of pain as the wolf's mental attack filled the second floor. The Pack Sire had effectively obstructed any retreat. As the splintering howl ended, Maggie noted that one side of her head felt uncomfortably cold. At some point during the chaos, she had collapsed onto the floor. The wolf limped into view.

The ground heaved more violently, its vibrations cracking the concrete block walls. Stairs lurched away from their footings. A bright white light drowned her vision and the image of the wolf disappeared in a snarl. Blinded by radiance, she felt the floor fall away. For a moment she felt weightless, like she floated on nothing but air.

Then her body crashed into the room below. She lost consciousness as the ceiling stacked on top of her.

27: Without Time or Reason

A firm hand shook Kyle into wakefulness. The base of his skull rang with throbbing stars. A knot ached where the sword hilt had struck him. His eyes fluttered open, and he rolled onto his back, gazing at the heavy mantel of clouds drifting overhead. Metal beams jutted from a ragged cavity in the roof, mimicking broken limbs and twisted bones. Snow from the roof blanketed the disjointed ruins of the commons. With a worried start, Kyle sat up and turned toward the hallway that led to the math and science rooms, the path that led to Maggie. The stairwell led upward into nothing; the second level had collapsed entirely onto the first.

The man with the white coat crouched beside Kyle, a gold and silver blade drawn in his solitary gloved hand. Instinctively Kyle punched in the direction of his foe, leaping to his feet in the process. His wrist met with the sword hilt painfully as his opponent effortlessly knocked it aside. Kyle grimaced, rubbing his bruised limb warily.

"Time is short, Kyleren," the man said as he righted himself, "and I have limits to how long I can slow it."

Slow time? Kyle wondered. He glanced around in confusion. Paper bits, dust particles, and tiny snowflakes hovered gently in the static air, apparently frozen. A distinct shroud of silence hummed in his ears.

"You can freeze time?" Kyle asked doubtfully.

"Time is still moving, only at an incredibly slow rate," the man answered, his words dipped in a strange accent. "To you it may seem to have halted."

Kyle surveyed the damage, arms tense with suspicion. This man had blocked his strike and, Kyle figured, had been responsible for knocking him senseless. Had the intruder also flattened the school?

"I am Raeylan."

"What happened?" Kyle asked, tensing for battle.

"Your friend's abilities did something I did not anticipate," Raeylan continued, nodding behind him.

Kyle glanced in the direction indicated. A smooth, almost melted circle of drab concrete rested in the center of the destruction, empty of debris. Lying unconscious at its focal point was Drake.

"I saved you from the explosion," Raeylan explained.

Kyle's eyes darted back to the blond warrior. The man's expression remained unchanged.

"I don't understand. Why?"

Raeylan looked toward the demolished classrooms, almost wistfully. Then his eyes hardened. He ignored Kyle's question.

"You can save him," Raeylan pointed his sword at Drake, "or the girls. There isn't time to rescue both. You have to choose."

Frosty shock arrested Kyle's brain. Had he heard right?

"What do you mean?" Kyle asked, uncomfortable with implications.

"Your friend or the girls," Raeylan clarified impatiently. "Choose quickly."

"What'll you do to Drake if I go after the girls?"

Raeylan didn't hesitate. "I'm going to kill him."

Kyle glared. Did this man really expect him to abandon Drake for execution?

"I can't let—"

"If you choose him, Kyleren," Raeylan said, "the girls will die in his place."

Kyle swallowed angrily, throat dry. This wasn't a choice. It was some sick mind game. Hand over Drake in exchange for Maggie and Lily? Kyle harbored little love for Drake, but that didn't mean he deserved death. And how could he ever look Lily again in the eye, knowing that he had chosen to let her boyfriend die?

"The timekeeper has broken. Decide now," Raeylan's voice prickled with impatience, "or I will have to incapacitate you again."

Kyle briefly considered attacking Raeylan, then slumped his shoulders in defeat. It wasn't a choice, really.

"The girls."

Raeylan nodded, as if he had known the outcome all along. Reaching into his voluminous overcoat, he extracted a small object and passed it to Kyle.

"Take this. When you find the girls, have them touch you. Then crush it."

"What will happen?" Kyle asked, examining the item. An azure flecked crystal, almost quartz, glittered through the gloom.

"You'll be safe," Raeylan avowed, impatiently turning toward Drake's helpless form.

"Why should I trust you?" Kyle growled, clenching his palm around the crystal. "Why help me and murder Drake?"

Raeylan stopped, turning enough to reveal the profile of his face. A nearby snowflake shifted blurrily. Time would shortly resume her normal flow.

"Your strength has always been that you rely on your instincts," Raeylan stated, "trust in them now."

Kyle inhaled deeply, discontented with the circumstances. *I'm sorry,* he thought remorsefully, glancing temporarily at Drake's fallen form. Then he turned his back and ran for the crumpled stairway, praying that the girls were still alive.

*

Lily awoke, choking as she inhaled. Dust coated her throat and mouth, causing her call for help to croak flatly. Icy fire spread through her body, mending shattered bones and repairing shredded muscles. Never in her life had she sustained such critical injuries. The wringing agony generated by the healing surge was even more painful than the wounds it labored so ardently to mend. Green splotched her vision. Her sense of touch was lost in the burning power of her regeneration.

She held as still as possible, restricting her breathing to shallow gulps, clearing her lungs and enduring spasms of fever as her body restored her damaged tissue. Amongst the concentration, she wondered if the healing hurt her friends this much. As the fiery chill subsided, it left behind a dull ache.

Lily allowed herself to breathe more normally and noticed a significant squeeze with each breath. The air seemed too thin to sustain her. Velvet blackness surrounded her so thickly that it felt substantial. Her body lay horizontal, winched awkwardly between misshapen solids. Lily's fuzzy brain struggled to recall the events that resulted in her current situation.

A brilliant surge of light, the crumbling of the floor beneath her. She remembered a resounding blast, 10 times louder than the sound of thunder. Maggie had slid into dusty darkness, and Mark plunged after. Then nothing.

She reached out experimentally, trying to assess the nature of her surroundings. Her hands met jagged pieces of unknown material. Rough bits of porous matter resembled smashed cinder block. Other fragments were hard and sharp like metal. Crumbly and flimsy substances permeated the rubble, no doubt the remains of drywall and ceiling tiles.

Something, she reasoned, had brought down the building.

Muffled moans and screams vibrated through the splintered mass of wreckage, but nothing distinguishable. Lily had no idea if her friends had survived or how deeply she was buried. She felt a stab of claustrophobia. Could she suffocate or would her healing abilities cure that too, trapping her in a coffin of ruins for eternity?

Her breathing was becoming more frantic as the air became thinner. Maggie and Mark needed healing. They could have been crushed under the school's carcass. She needed to get out, she needed to save them. Lily heaved her lungs uncontrollably, rapidly depleting the small space of air.

Calm down, she said to herself. *Panicking is counterproductive. You can't help Maggie and Mark if you can't help yourself.*

Lily searched the darkness again, seeking something solid and flat that she could use as a lever to shift the rubble above her. Several appropriate objects seemed to have piled around her torso. She pushed against them with her hands and, then as the rubble shifted, her feet. The metal groaned as it showered her face with dust and fragments of concrete. She reflexively shut her eyes to protect them from the falling scraps.

Lil—, came a weak whisper inside her mind. Maggie's voice sounded distant and indistinct. Lily held her breath and remained motionless, afraid that any noise would dislodge her connection with her best friend.

Maggie! Lily projected frantically. *Maggie, are you okay?*

I don't know, Maggie replied, her thoughts flimsy and translucent. *It's hard to breathe. I think I've lost a lot of blood—it's so dark.* Her mind link trailed off. Lily fretted. Maggie's frail response couldn't be good.

Maggie? Lily thought desperately. *Maggie, can you hear me?*

Only stillness.

Lily pushed harder at the wreckage above her, desperate to escape and aid her friends. It moved more readily this time. The third attempt seemed even less difficult. Lily heard clatters and shuffling on the surface of her prison. Someone was digging her out.

She called for help, leading her would-be rescuer closer to her position. More scratchy reverberation followed. Finally, a grey shaft of light pierced her dark tomb; a small opening had appeared over her right side. Lily scrabbled at the edges of the hole, shouting for assistance. A pair of hands, protected by leather gloves, pulled at the debris, expanding the gap so Lily could fit through.

The overcast sky shone clearly through her escape outlet; the school's roof had completely collapsed. An arm offered its support through the opening, and Lily grasped it thankfully. The hand gripped her bicep painfully as it yanked her upward. Its companion reached in and clenched the front of her shirt. Freed of the school's remains, she gasped in the bitter chill of the winter air. She coughed and rubbed the dust out of her eyelashes. Her champion still held her arm, as if hesitant to release her. Expecting to smother Carter or Kyle with much deserved gratitude, Lily looked up appreciatively to meet his eyes.

Dead black eyes.

Orbs that didn't look directly at her, but stared straight forward with no will of their own. Her thanks slid away. It was as tall as a man, completely sheathed in black cloth. Only the expressionless, flat eyes, surrounded by a bit of shriveled grey skin, remained unconcealed. Eyes that saw nothing.

The hand on her shirt shot to her throat. Squeezing fingers deprived her lungs of air as the thing lifted her feet off the ground.

No, she pleaded, *Maggie needs me! I won't let this thing stand in my way.*

She grappled its arm with both hands, firmly burrowing her nails into its clothes. Warmth pulsed with her blood. She commanded it to engulf her assailant. The black fabric ignited with ice-green flame.

But the creature didn't release her. It didn't flinch, twitch, or shout. It simply held her neck firmly, confident that she would eventually asphyxiate. Soon its entire body burned furiously, yet its fingers refused to slacken. And still, it made no move to extinguish the fire.

As the fire devoured the thing's coverings, Lily noticed its revealed tissue was laced together with thick sutures and metal bindings. With the burning she couldn't tell whether its skin was real or not. Was it some sort of construct? How it resisted the pain didn't matter. She needed to find Maggie and Mark. She instructed the emerald blaze to burn hotter, consuming the creature holding her. Its restraining arm incinerated out of existence. When she dropped to her feet, the thing's remains withered into a pile of black ash.

Every precious second she had wasted could have been her friends' last. Lily didn't know where to start searching, but Maggie's thought voice had seemingly come from behind her as Lily had lain in darkness. She turned.

A startled scream fled her tongue. Another construct stood inches before her, staring not at her, but at some point above her head. The thing's hand darted for her windpipe, its movements jerky and unnatural.

I don't have time for this! she thought at it angrily.

Green flared from her palms, disintegrating the dark figure in a wave of melting heat. Its residue floated gently in the breeze. Lily breathed heavily and wiped a drip of sweat from her temple. Her head spun in a dizzy circle.

Finally free to look around, she saw an open fissure in the rubble directly ahead. Piled fragments of material were stacked methodically at its edge. Lily's heart pounded hopefully as she trotted toward it. Maggie's body lay half visible near the surface, Mark's unconscious face rested perpendicular to her. It seemed the second construct had discovered them. Maggie's ragged breath echoed hollowly through the icy afternoon. It was impossible to determine if Mark was breathing at all.

Lily searched her pockets for her knife, but the blade had disappeared during the disaster. She bent forward, scouring the ground for a sharp-edged implement. Lily's finger tips had just brushed something appropriately jagged when a sharp pull jerked her backward. She landed rigidly on her spine, blinking bewilderedly at the stormy clouds. A light shower of snow kissed her upturned face.

Two black-clad figures held her to the ground at the wrists; another pressed its weight against her ankles. Lily floundered helplessly. Her power erupted harmlessly from her palms, scorching sections of fallen floor and chunks of classroom, but leaving her enemies unscathed. She tried to twist, but the construct's grip remained as unyielding as steel bands. They possessed an inordinate amount of strength. Not once did the dead eyes look at her.

Rather than becoming discouraged by her immobility, Lily felt a compelling determination flood outward from the core of her being. These things were preventing her from saving her friends who lay dying mere body lengths away. Fever coiled inside her chest, congealing into a well of undulating heat. The clouds above her began to rotate in a slow spiral, curls of red and green miasma glistening incandescently. A high-pitched squeal of thunder rippled menacingly across the sky. Lily's love for Maggie, the passionate need to heal her, blazed inside Lily's breast like an angel of fire. A fervent yell, stemming from the center of her internal tempest, soared from her lungs, commanding the heavens to obliterate her captors.

A green-kindled vortex of fire slammed into the ground, causing the earth to tremble and quake. The cyclone of emerald and crimson disintegrated everything inside its 10 foot diameter.

She paused for a moment of shock after the firestrike receded, tottering to her feet in a stupefied daze. A blackened crater of devastation surrounded her. As she tried to dispel her disorientation, a familiar voice called to her from behind.

"Are you okay, Smiles?" Kyle asked in concerned surprise as he rushed to her side.

Tears of relief spilled from her eyes and she pointed to the place where Maggie and Mark lay buried.

"I'll dig 'em out, Sunshine," Kyle said, squeezing her shoulder comfortingly, "and you heal 'em."

Lily nodded numbly.

Kyle extricated Maggie first, lifting her battered body gently and placing it at Lily's feet. Worry bent his brow as he took a moment to survey her condition. He turned briskly back to unbury Mark.

Maggie's clothes were grimy and blood soaked. Lily didn't even know where to begin. She gritted her teeth and displaced some of her best friend's torn garments. Selecting the deepest looking wound, Lily slashed into her own arm with a sharp edged fragment of metal.

Usually Lily counted 12 heartbeats before her healing powers sealed her own abrasions and fully restored an injured friend. But by the time her tissue mended itself, the green flame had only repaired a portion of Maggie's damage. Her friend remained unconscious and her breathing faint.

"What's wrong with her?" Kyle asked, now laying Mark next to Lily. "Why isn't she wakin' up?"

Lily deliberated. The cost of her power had already taken its toll. Lily's limbs trembled with weakness, and her vision was blurry. Obviously, Maggie needed more of Lily's bloodflame. And Lily still had Mark to heal. She opened an artery again, this time dragging a sharp instrument the length of her arm. Lily forced as much of her life's liquid from the gash as possible, enveloping Maggie in a radiant flare of green. When it subsided, Lily felt frail and weak.

At last, Maggie's eyes opened. She groaned audibly, and Lily turned to Mark. His injuries were just as severe. It took Lily three tries to restore him to healthy consciousness, but he responded slowly, as if exhausted. Just before she finished, a loud blast resounded from what had been the center of the school.

"That doesn't sound good," Kyle observed.

The loss of blood nearly robbed Lily of awareness. Kyle caught her as she fell forward. He supported her as his hand lifted a starry crystal from his pocket.

"What's that?" Lily inquired, her perception floating away.

"Hopefully, a way outta here. Don't let go of my arm, Sunshine."

Kyle instructed Maggie and Mark to grasp his other arm. Lily looked expectantly behind Kyle, back in the direction of the explosion.

"What about Carter?" she asked.

"I'm sorry, Lily," Kyle apologized. His use of her given name filled her with dread. Kyle's face was remorsefully grim. "Drake isn't comin'."

The last thing Lily remembered before she fainted was the ringing crunch of the crystal as he crushed it in his hand.

28: Phased And Bemused

As Kyle's fist shattered the crystal into granules of dust, a flurry of saline scented wind spiraled about his body, wafting unruly through the girls' hair. It seemed as if the school ruins burst into a thousand stars, slipping away noiselessly into the viscous blackness of space. When the air current subsided, the twinkling bits of light merged into something else, somewhere else.

Kyle stood in the center of a concrete gazebo.

He blinked in confusion, wondering if the image was an illusion. Twelve bronze statues encircled the perimeter of the marquee, each depicting someone famous. A sculptured crest occupied the center of the paved ground. Snow covered lawns stretched gently around him. Several long, brick buildings squatted to the north and west. The structures sported identification plates, but nothing Kyle recognized. A small parking lot, newly plowed and filled with a collection of vehicles, lay a few yards to the south. Past the parking lot, Kyle noticed a two-lane street, another larger parking area, and some kind of sports arena. The surrounding mountains were stubby, short, and almost boxlike. A smattering of trees coated their red-orange surface. Kyle could hear cars in the distance, but no traffic or people anywhere near. The air tasted crispy and thin, like the morning after a snowstorm. He fingered the nearest statue, ascertaining its solidity.

"What just happened?" Mark asked through chattering teeth.

Kyle glanced at him, then down at Maggie who huddled on the concrete. Both shivered with the cold; their torn clothing exposed patches of skin to the elements. Kyle had momentarily forgotten his resistance to the temperature. Maggie's eyelids drooped heavily with exhaustion, an unconscious Lily swooned in his arms.

"I'll tell ya later," Kyle answered, hefting Lily across his shoulder, "we need to get outta here."

"Where is 'here'?" Maggie inquired weakly, pulling herself up when Kyle offered a hand.

She leaned on his free side. Kyle slipped an arm around her.

"I don't know," Kyle answered, hoping his body heat would help to warm her, "but we gotta go, Sparky, in case we were followed."

Neither Maggie nor Mark possessed the energy to argue. Mark at least walked without aid. Maggie stumbled dangerously on the slick turf, even with Kyle's support, as they plowed through the snow toward the rows of cars.

Kyle was a savvy enough sci-fi addict to know teleportation when he saw it. Raeylan's crystal had transported them away from the carnage occurring at Bonneville High School. Though he hadn't been everywhere in his grandfather's hometown, he knew the Idaho Rockies sufficiently well to determine that he wasn't in them anymore. Raeylan could have dropped them anywhere in the world. A quick glance at the parking lot sign revealed English. Kyle hoped they were at least still in the United States.

Once in the parking lot, Kyle crossed to the nearest car. Quickly surveying the area to make sure it was clear of bystanders, he checked the back doors of the clunky white sedan. Thankfully they were unlocked.

"Get in," he instructed.

Mark hesitated.

"Are we stealing this?"

"Yes. Get in!" Kyle barked.

Mark acquiesced guiltily, sliding into the rear passenger seat gingerly, as if his buttocks would alert the police to their thievery as soon as his posterior touched the upholstery. Kyle impatiently settled Lily's comatose form against Mark's shoulder as Maggie tumbled into the front seat. Kyle flew into the driver's side and ripped out the steerage casing before she had finished closing her door.

"What are you doing?" Mark asked as he fastened Lily's seatbelt.

"What's it look like, Weston?" he responded, irritably running his fingers across exposed wires and hardware. "Those people could be right behind us. We need to get outta here as soon as possible."

Kyle's mind wandered as he repositioned the vehicle's wiring, directing the ignition chip to bypass its security protocol. It wouldn't have taken long for the blond warrior to dispatch Drake, and if Raeylan had the capability to send them here, he obviously had means to follow. Kyle had no intention of being here when the crazy swordsman arrived.

"Do you really think they could follow us?" Maggie asked, leaning her head tiredly against her seat.

"Considerin' it was one of them that gave me the crystal that brought us here, I'd say it's a sure thing."

The engine rumbled loudly and Kyle shifted the stolen vehicle into gear. He zoomed out of the parking lot and into the city, determined to search out a highway—or at least discover something identifying their location.

"Are you telling me," Maggie accused weakly, "you accepted help from those people? They tried to kill us!"

"I didn't have a choice," Kyle defended, his attention distracted with a pocket of newfound traffic.

Cars meant information and a possible freeway. He decided to join the mechanical throng.

"Kyle, are you insane? They may have sent us here on purpose!" Maggie splurted from an ashen face.

"I still have no idea how we got here—"Mark said.

"So far, that doesn't seem to be the case, Mags," Kyle responded calmly, ignoring Mark. "Besides, I didn't have a choice."

"What do you mean, 'you didn't have a choice'? Kyle, those people are after Lily!"

"Are you sure? I thought they were after that Esilwen person," came Mark's confused voice from the back.

Kyle squinted in uncertainty as he followed a line of cars onto a larger street. To his knowledge, their assailants had been after Maggie. If they really wanted Lily, why did Raeylan trade her for Drake?

"No they weren't, Sparky. They were after Drake," Kyle stated firmly, glancing between his girlfriend and the road.

Maggie narrated the ugly scene that occurred in the trigonometry room, though every time she mentioned a person called Feralblade, she cringed and stuttered, almost like deciding exactly what to tell him. Kyle deemed that she was purposefully leaving something out.

"I think I saw him," Kyle said when Maggie had finished. "This Feralblade guy: he was wearin' some kinda black armor. I was usin' super speed to get to you guys so I breezed right past him. Plus, I think time wasn't unfrozen yet. I thought he was odd, but I didn't have time to check him out."

Kyle reported his insights about Raeylan's time slowing and teleportation abilities.

"You mean like in *Star Trek*?" inserted Mark, poking his head between the two front seats. "The whole 'beam me up, Scotty' thing?"

"Yeah, like *Star Trek*," Kyle answered curtly, "only we're not in space and not on a starship. Put your seatbelt on and be quiet."

"So the guy Lily saw on the roof," Maggie asked after Mark slunk dolefully back into his chair, "he attacked you and Carter?"

"Knocked me out in one hit, too," Kyle admitted.

He heard a sharp intake of breath beside him and turned in concern. Maggie was looking back at her motionless best friend.

"What about Carter?" her voice was barely a whisper.

"He's dead," Kyle answered flatly.

Maggie's eyes whipped to Kyle. He could see anguish for her childhood friend reflected in her eyes. He felt a swell of pain for the suffering of two people he cared for deeply.

"Dead?" echoed Mark.

A sign designating the direction of the freeway prompted Kyle to check the fuel gauge. Its indicator hovered next to empty. He swore fiercely, cursing the absent owner. *Like we needed anything else to go wrong*, he thought angrily. Maggie's sniffles fed the empty ache in his heart.

"We need gas," Kyle stated.

"I have my wallet in my pocket," Mark offered.

Kyle heard Mark shifting his weight awkwardly, trying to produce the item.

"Do you have cash?" Kyle asked.

"No, only a card."

"We can't use a credit card," Kyle sighed. "It's traceable."

"Then what are we going to do?" Maggie asked jadedly.

Kyle examined the buildings around him, a desperate idea afflicting his ethics. Stealing was not something in his character, yet their survival was at stake. They were going to need gas and, eventually, food and shelter. Without access to money, the four of them wouldn't last long. Kyle knew that they couldn't call for help. Their enemies would be watching their homes for signs of their location. He steered the stolen car into a gas station that was empty of customers. After pulling next to the pump, Kyle steeled his nerves with a slow exhale. Then he turned to Maggie.

"Do you think you can use your powers?" he asked.

"Why?" she asked warily, eyes narrowing shrewdly, already keen to his intentions.

"We need money, Mags," Kyle said.

"What do you need me to do?"

"Distract whoever's workin' in there. Make 'em put 30 bucks on our pump and then take a break or somethin'."

"We're going to rob them?" Mark squeaked. His pallor turned sallow. "Grand theft auto isn't good enough for you guys, we're gonna knock off a convenience store too?"

"Not the store, the ATM," Kyle stated tartly, his own revulsion for the task ahead making him edgy, "and you're gonna help. You get to fill up the tank."

Mark opened his mouth to object, but Kyle darted out the door. He waited while Maggie struggled to exit. She gripped his arm thankfully as she wobbled upright.

"I'm okay," she assured, "I'll wave to you once it's all clear."

Kyle watched with a nervous knot in his throat as Maggie walked into the store and sidled up to the cashier's counter. Moments later, the clerk turned and disappeared into a back room. Maggie waved through the snow-gritted window. The pump's digital readout indicated she'd been successful.

"Fill it up," Kyle ordered Mark, before dashing into the store using his enhanced capabilities.

Once inside, still using his super speed, Kyle noted the surveillance camera and ripped it from its perch over the entrance. Then he compacted it into an unrecognizable wad of plastic.

"Good job, Mags," he said. He took her hand in his and squeezed it gently. "Go back to the car."

He waited until Maggie had crossed the threshold before he smashed his fist into the base of the ATM machine. Whipping behind the counter to pilfer a plastic bag, he returned and filled the sack with over a hundred emancipated twenty dollar bills. He felt a pang of remorse as he crushed the ATM's built in camera, knowing that the money belonged to someone else. Then he zipped back to the car.

"Let's go."

Mark replaced the pump nozzle. In moments, the vehicle was back on the road, the freeway ramp looming ahead. Kyle wondered briefly if he should turn north or south. Then he supposed it didn't matter, since they didn't know where they were or where they wanted to go. The atmosphere in the sedan was heavy with guilty consciences.

"Where are we going?" Maggie finally asked.

"I dunno," Kyle answered. For the first time since he stole the car, Kyle felt useless and unable to fulfill his role as protector.

"Where are we?" Mark wondered.

"Cedar City, Utah," Maggie answered. Kyle looked at her in surprise, but she shrugged. "It was plastered all over the postcards in the store."

"Take the northbound entrance," Mark instructed, suddenly confident, "toward the Denver junction."

"And then what?" Kyle asked as he steered the car into the appropriate lane.

"My grandparents have a cabin in Vermont."

29: One Wing And A Prayer

The first sensation Carter felt as he returned to consciousness was a cold shiver in his injured shoulder. Subsequently, he noticed a gentle pull on his hair, as if someone were stroking it soothingly. His body lay on something soft, its velvet surface enticing him back into slumber. A supple hand compressed his wrist, pleading him to wake.

"Lily?" he assumed quietly.

His tongue felt wooly, like his mouth was full of cotton.

A rich, throaty laugh answered his question. Not the feathery music of Lily's voice, but an opulent sound, more mature and refined—a resonance of experience that had lost its innocence. He felt a shift of the material beneath him and the pressure on his wrist lifted. His eyes fluttered open.

Silvery curtains framed the ornately carved bed on which he lay. Carter sat up suddenly, a rush of remembered alarm quickening his muscles. A muffled moan escaped his lips as the brisk movement jarred his shoulder. Damp air nipped at his bare chest. The new voice spoke, its husky intonation distinctly enunciating each syllable.

"Alas, I regret to report that Esilwen is not present at this time, Lord Kirion. She has slipped through your grasp once again."

Carter's head turned slowly toward the sound, wondering what new foe he faced.

A woman hovered over him. Carter inhaled sharply. She wasn't human.

Her skin glistened with a brassy sheen. Spidery green veins clearly traced the pulse of her blood underneath her skin. She wore a crimson gown, overlaid with a golden breastplate and jeweled gauntlets. Ruby hair spilled around her shoulders, cascading to her waist in a shower the color of blood. The silky waves were held away from her unearthly features by a flaxen headdress. A single wing, shimmering with feathers of scarlet gold, swooped outward from the center of her back.

"What are you?" Carter gasped when he found his voice. "Where's Lily?"

The woman's eyes burned with icy green luminescence, holding him mesmerized. She pushed him purposefully back into the soft pillows, leaning the weight of her body against him. The touch of her hand burned, not unpleasantly, on his bare chest.

"Calm yourself," she instructed with her lush voice, stroking his forehead and running a bronze-tipped fingernail across his jawline. "Raeylan wounded you grievously. It took hours for our healers to stabilize your injuries."

Her leg had slipped from a long slit in the flimsy dress and her naked thigh tightened around his hip.

Carter reevaluated his tactics.

"Who are you?" he demanded. His heart clanged wildly in his chest, despite his effort to suppress it.

"I am Thanati," the winged woman answered, fondling his collarbone with her hand. "General of the Faithful Legion."

"Get off me," Carter ordered, his command reflecting more authority than he felt.

"As you wish, my lord," she answered graciously, immediately removing herself from the bed.

Carter sat up again, slowly this time so as not to aggravate his wound, and scanned the room. A vigorous fire crackled in a stone-carved hearth. Thick rugs covered the slate floor. Heavy wooden double doors opened into a granite hallway, two armored figures standing at attention on either side. If he could somehow distract this woman, he might be able to rush the guards. Escape was a possibility.

"Where am I?" he inquired, flicking his gaze back to Thanati.

"I believe the people of this shard call this land Scotland, my lord," she answered with a graceful bow. Her luminous gaze did not stray from his face. "It took many days to repair this abandoned castle and erect the magical barriers that keep it hidden from the local populace."

"What are you talking about?"

Carter slid off the bed, utterly dumbfounded by her answer. Scotland? Even if he did escape the castle, how would he get home? And what had happened at the school? Had these people hurt Lily? His mind churned, calculating, evaluating, and discarding possible routes of action. Thanati seemed amused by his deliberation.

"Where's Lily?" he insisted again, preparing to launch himself at the door.

"I have told you already, Lord Kirion. Esilwen has fled. But fear not, we will prevail. Commander Feralblade is tracking her location as we speak. The Viridius fool will lead us to her unwittingly."

The name caught Carter's attention, and he hesitated.

"You mean Raeylan," Carter spat with loathing.

Thanati's head tilted with interest and she smiled knowingly.

"Even when you have forgotten him, you speak his name with hatred."

Her blunt declaration surprised him into speaking without thinking. "Of course I hate him. He stabbed me through the shoulder! As for not remembering, I have no idea what you're talking about. I'm sick of these riddles! I want answers! Why did you attack us? What do you want with Lily?"

Thanati nodded deferentially, and swept her arms in front of her body in elegant supplication. Her long skirt twirled about her ankles.

"To save her from herself of course, just as you ordered."

Carter composed his exasperation. Most of Thanati's remarks didn't make sense, but his need for information suddenly overruled his desire to flee. The woman was talking. She seemed willing to provide answers to the supernatural reality that had engulfed Carter and his friends. If he could just discover the truth of their existence, maybe he could save them all. Carter delayed his escape, prolonging the conversation with the general of this so-called Faithful Legion.

"And what do you want from me?" he asked warily.

"With you?" Thanati's eyes glinted brightly inside their bronze sockets. "I want to show you who you really are."

30: Weep What You Woe

Maggie stared forlornly through the frosty glass of the log cabin window. Heavy flakes pattered against the bony limbs of oaks and maples, draping gently across the drooping boughs of prickly evergreens. It numbed the sensation of sound through the thick carpet of trees. The friends' two-week-old footprints lay buried under the tomb of white, all indications of their long hike to the remote location obscured by the massive blanket of frozen flecks. A snow-licked lake reflected the drifting flurry, almost like chipped stars in a grey shroud.

Fourteen days had passed, empty of fantastical altercations. The terror of wolves, swords, and explosions seemed cloaked in a dream, an event that happened on the news, suffered by someone else. Maggie felt as if her life had always been here, in the mountains of Vermont, staring out with quiet melancholy as the snowfall echoed vacantly in her heart.

Everything had changed with Carter's death.

It had taken four days to cross the country, four days of a silent, broken Lily. A few hours after their escape, she had awoken. After hearing Kyle's blunt recount of Carter's fate, she had pleaded with her friends to return home, just to be sure. Kyle's fixed refusal drove her into tearful sobs that lasted as long as their drive to Denver. And that was the last time Lily had spoken to anyone except Mark.

Maggie and Mark both completely agreed with Kyle. To go back would have been too dangerous. Lily stopped arguing. She no longer wept. She ate when given food and obeyed Kyle's orders. But her eyes no longer sparkled. Her lips never smiled. Lily responded to Mark's conversation like someone lost, her will unraveled.

Around the second day of their journey, during a brief stop to eat and fill the car with fuel, they had seen a news broadcast of the tragic details of the "Bonneville High Incident." Just over a third of the student body, nearly 400 students, had been killed during the affair. Several hundred more were reported injured or missing. Aerial footage of the school grounds exhibited the carnage; half of the building had been destroyed, along with most of the parking lot. Several days of suppressed emotion had overflowed inside Maggie as she confronted the visual record of the ordeal and its consequences—it was their fault that so many innocents had met such a ghastly end—and she vomited in the nearest trash bin.

According to the media, the cause of the explosion was still unknown. Authorities were investigating everything from a ruptured gas line to a terrorist bombing. The three of them—Lily having taken no part in the discussion—agreed that the explosion must have had something to do with Carter. It was unlikely that the police would ever discover the truth.

At that point, Maggie felt a surge of empathy for her mother. Kyle had forbidden them—especially Mark, who was still reeling from the abnormality of it all—from contacting family members. Feralblade and the blond warrior would surely be prepared for that. Tara Brooks believed her daughter, and only family, to be crushed under the weight of collapsed steel and concrete. Maggie's lip trembled as she stood next to the window, regretting the pain her mother must be feeling.

At least the friends were safe. The state of Vermont had welcomed them with open, albeit chilly, arms. Their refuge was small, comprised of a kitchen and living area, a short hallway leading to a single bedroom, and a small bathroom behind the main room, a 10 by 10 underground cellar, and a half-loft overlooking the common room. Maggie welcomed the defensibility of the sanctuary. Mark's grandparents had laid away a stock of food, blankets, and warm clothing in the little cabin's basement. According to Mark, there was little chance his grandparents would drop in unannounced. They only visited the site in late spring and early summer. It would be weeks before the four of them would need to vacate and search for another hiding place.

Maggie swept her fingers across burning eyelids. She hardly slept anymore. Her nights were interrupted by the unintentional weeping of her sleeping best friend. Though Lily's waking state was little more than an empty shell, the loss of the person she loved wracked her spirit with agonized sobs during her slumber. The telepath experienced Lily's sorrow through the mind, and there was little Maggie could do to comfort Lily's grief. Maggie felt overwhelmed and useless. How could she promise that everything would be okay when she knew it to be a lie?

Maggie also suffered from nightmarish emergences of Feralblade's unsolicited images. She tried to ignore them, then contradicted them with logic. Their presence had tainted her relationship with Kyle. Every time she looked into her boyfriend's hazel eyes, she felt a stab of guilt. Angrily, she would turn away. Those memories couldn't have been real. She could never have let that vicious man touch her like that.

But even as she denied them, the visions would resurface inside her mind, alight with remembered sensations that she knew Feralblade hadn't planted inside her. His unique smell—something like a blend of jasmine and leather, only more saccharine—or the rhythmic chafing of his sword-calloused fingers against her skin.

Several metallic scrapes and pops clicked behind her, and Maggie turned from the window. Kyle perched on the edge of a weathered stool in the space between kitchen and living room, where he could keep an eye on both the front and rear hallway exits. He finished loading a hunting rifle, a weapon that had been discovered over the mantel, and buffed the barrel with a discolored rag. Maggie briefly considered reading his mind, but decided against it.

Her dismal thoughts had distracted her and she realized too late that she had been staring unintentionally at Kyle for a long time. He stopped fiddling with the shotgun and returned her gaze, his expression unreadable. Maggie felt moisture threaten her tear ducts and turned hastily back to the window. Behind her the stool scraped against the hardwood floor. It creaked with approaching footsteps.

Kyle's strong arms snaked protectively around her waist, pinning her against his broad chest. Her pulse quickened as his breath tickled her hair gently. He didn't speak, but the comfort of his nearness caused the teardrops to defeat her control, and large salty dollops escaped down her cheeks.

"Everything's so messed up," Maggie almost sobbed. Her words were punctuated with breathy pauses as she tried to restrain her sorrow. "Any of us could be next. And if they get Lily—"

"I'm not gonna let that happen, Sparky," Kyle promised, his arms tightening about her.

"They're stronger than we are, Kyle," she argued, turning her cheek against his chest. "Somehow they already know us. What we're capable of. Better than even we do."

"I'm still not gonna let it happen."

"Lily's not okay," she whispered. "I'm not sure she ever will be again."

"I'm not sure any of us will, Blue Eyes."

Maggie battled with her despondency, looking through the window as Kyle held her protectively. Less than 20 minutes ago, Lily and Mark had ventured into the snowy woods for their daily stroll. The routine developed soon after they arrived in the mountains. Lily's first "walk" had occurred the morning after their hike to the cabin. She slipped outside by herself. Maggie, Kyle, and Mark had been busy with securing their new hideaway. No one had noticed her absence until late afternoon. When they did look, a light snowfall had hidden any tracks. Kyle searched for hours, using his super speed to scour the forest. He didn't discover her until the evening stars had sparkled through the clouds. She was curled against a tree, asleep, her cheeks sprinkled with frozen teardrops.

Since then, Mark had accompanied Lily on all her outings to make sure she didn't wander too far. All three of them attended to her continually, afraid she might disappear again. Maggie closed her eyes, listening to the lively crackle of the fire in the hearth.

"There are so many things I don't understand," Maggie offered after a long silence. Her tears had been spent, and she felt somewhat better. "Like why Raeylan let Lily go when Feralblade tried so hard to kidnap her."

Kyle paused in thought. Maggie watched the snow fall in flurry curtains.

"I'm not sure Raeylan's an enemy, Sparky."

Maggie wrenched herself out of Kyle's arms and turned to face him in shock. "But he killed Carter! How could he be anything but an enemy? He was working with those people, wasn't he?"

Kyle stared into the snow. Maggie knew from former conversations that he was analyzing their enemy's battle tactics, testing theories and scenarios in his mind. Over the past two weeks, Kyle had often voiced his frustration over the contradictory events surrounding the school ambush.

"I don't think so, Mags," he replied with deep sincerity, shaking his head from side to side. He turned his gaze on Maggie. "Raeylan could've killed me. He's more powerful than both me and Drake put together. I couldn't 've stopped him from killin' you and takin' Lily. But he let us go."

"So you think Raeylan had a different agenda than Feralblade?"

"Yeah, I do. I think he was only after Drake."

"How can you possibly be sure about that?" Maggie asked.

"'Vengeance.' That's what Raeylan said. Plus, the way he looked at Drake," Kyle answered, his voice growing hard. "I know that look 'cause I've used it myself. Raeylan hates him. But when he talked about you 'n Smiles, he was sad. Like he wanted to save you himself, but couldn't. He had—" Kyle paused, and Maggie could tell he was searching for the right words, "—he had presence. I don't know how else to explain it. From what you said about Feralblade, I can't see this Raeylan guy joinin' up with such a jerk."

Maggie's face squinted in disbelief. Sure Raeylan had let them go—hell, he'd even given them the means to escape—but as Carter's murderer, Maggie would never consider him to be anything other than an adversary.

"But you said he gave you a choice," she argued. "Us or Carter. What kind of person forces you to make a decision like that?"

"It really wasn't a choice, Mags," Kyle returned, folding his arms across his chest. "I'm startin' to think Raeylan knew that before he said it. No matter what I did, he was gonna kill Drake."

"But what does he accomplish by that?" Maggie stated angrily. "If he's not working for the people who've been chasing us, why attack us? Why kill Carter and not the rest of us?"

"Maybe he's workin' for someone else," Kyle said, looking back out the window. "I don't know. But I think Drake was his target. Not us."

Maggie considered Kyle's argument, determining Raeylan's motives to be insignificant. He had killed Carter. He was responsible for Lily's current state of grief. No matter what else he had done, or did in the future, Maggie would never forgive him.

"Do you think he suffered?" Maggie asked in a hushed voice, remembering the physical pain Feralblade had caused her during their encounter. "When Raeylan killed him?"

"No. Drake was unconscious," Kyle said, sliding his arms around her shoulder and pulling her close. "Besides, Raeylan isn't like that Feralblade guy. He didn't strike me as the type to enjoy torturin' people."

As Maggie looked into Kyle's eyes, Feralblade's methods of persecution replayed in her mind, sharper and more poignant than even the actual incident. She shifted away from Kyle, crumpling into a small armchair across from the fireplace. Horrific sobs tore her in half.

When the attack of heartache subsided, she noticed that Kyle had followed her, placing a rickety stool in front of the chair so that he could sit near her. He reached for her hand.

"Sparky, is there somethin' you want to tell me?" he asked.

Maggie heaved with shame and her stomach churned. She couldn't speak as he enclosed her chill fingers with his warm palms. She didn't want him to know the things she had seen. Her eyes locked on the stones decorating the mantel, over Kyle's shoulder so she wouldn't have to look him in the eye. After a few minutes, he licked his lips and shifted uncomfortably.

"Did Feralblade do somethin' to you?" he prompted, forcing himself to steady a quiver in his voice.

Maggie was glad her powers were inactive so she couldn't see the worst imaginings of his mind. Her silence on the subject most likely had him worried that Feralblade had done more to her than a beating.

"Not physically," she confirmed.

Kyle exhaled a sigh of relief.

"I couldn't figure why you kept lookin' away from me," he responded, "like you had somethin' to hide. I thought maybe he'd—"

"No, he didn't touch me. Not like that," Maggie admitted, looking away again.

She needed to tell Kyle about Feralblade's visions, but didn't know how to start. Kyle squeezed her hand, wordlessly encouraging her to share her thoughts. Maggie decided that the easiest way to recount the information was to start with details marked with less embarrassment.

"Do you think maybe we've lived before? Like another life or something?"

"You mean like reincarnation?" He sounded skeptical.

"Or somethin' like that?"

"Yes," Maggie answered. She paused before continuing. "They kept calling us by different names: Margariete, Esilwen, and Kyleren."

"So?"

"Feralblade," Maggie trembled as she spoke his name, "showed me things. Things that I did—I've done."

"Like what?" Kyle asked evenly.

"He showed me—" crimson crept up her features, but she suddenly decided to confront her embarrassment with dignity. She looked unwaveringly into Kyle's face. "I think I spent the night with him."

"Are you sure he wasn't just tryin' to get to you, Mags? Makin' you see stuff to hurt you or somethin'?" Kyle's voice remained calm and nonjudgmental.

"That's what I believed at first," she said, "but these images felt different than when I read other people's minds. I didn't see the pictures from just his perspective—they awoke something inside me. I could remember feelings, sensations—things that surround memory. I don't think what he showed me was a trick. It was something from the past."

Kyle reacted unexpectedly. With one unbroken movement, he swept her into his arms and onto his lap. He kissed her with tender, unconditional affection.

"Maggie," he whispered, rocking her gently as he pulled back. "It doesn't matter."

"How can you even look at me?" she moaned, burrowing her face into his shirt.

He chuckled, his hand nudged under her chin as he turned her face up to his.

"How could I not?"

Maggie hiccupped as light tears consumed her. He brushed them away skillfully with the back of his fingers.

"I don't care what you did in some past life, or even in this one," he said with reassuring cheerfulness. "I will always love you."

Maggie smiled weakly, wrapping her arms around his neck. He kissed her again softly.

"Why?" Maggie asked as he pulled away. "Why me?"

Kyle smiled magnetically. "Because you're the only woman worth havin'. I'd marry you right now if you'd say yes."

"Marry me?" she asked, leaning backward in surprise.

"Yeah, marry you," he verified, touching her face gently.

31: Double Edged Sword

"So what do you think?" Mark asked cheerily, disturbing the echo of Lily's soft tread through the snow.

Lily's attention converged toward Mark's voice, drifting away from the fragments of thought that continually tangled her concentration.

"About what?" Lily inquired, having overlooked the first portion of his conversation entirely.

She wasn't sure how long he had been speaking. His words had blended into the frozen landscape as they walked through the powdery snow.

"I was just pointing out—for the last 20 minutes—how weird it is that Kyle can hotwire cars so fast."

He paused, obviously waiting for Lily to comment. Her focus had already begun to slip somewhere else. Kyle's technological prowess seemed of little interest. Mark seemed of little interest. The falling snowflakes kissed her eyelashes and scraped her cheeks. She marveled at how their crystals matched the state of her spirit—fractured, cold, incapable of generating their own light. Maybe that's why she liked these little outings so much. The flakes reminded her of herself, spiraling downward, lost in a sea of melancholy grey. Mark continued a little tersely as Lily remained silent.

"Where do you think he learned it?" he prompted again.

"Where did he learn what?" Lily asked, Mark's persistence once again treading into her thoughts.

Mark restated his question, this time slinging a concerned glance at his companion.

"You know, all the cars we stole and ditched on our way out here. How do you think Kyle knew how to do it?"

Lily shrugged. Kyle always seemed to be able to coax anything out of machines and equipment. It didn't really matter. The colorless clouds glided morosely across the sky, their hanging tendrils of precipitation at the treetops. Lily thought they looked a lot like stringy claws.

"So I wonder if he was a part of some underground grand theft auto operation," Mark teased.

Lily only heard the last half of his statement. She had been wondering whether those iron grey talons could strangle the life out of the trees.

"Maybe he came to Idaho Falls because he's on the run from the law!"

Lily turned to look numbly at him. Mark interpreted her action as interest.

"It would explain why he didn't mind ripping off all those ATMs. For all we know, he could be a super villain!"

He chuckled at his own humor.

The accusation evoked an odd interaction with the emptiness in Lily's heart. Kyle: a villain. In a way, he had taken that role in her story. By condemning the boy she loved to death, Kyle was directly responsible for the destruction of her future. His restriction on contacting her family had severed her ties with the past. And without past or future, the present was meaningless.

Lily pivoted forward abruptly and trudged through the snow away from Mark. Her sudden motion caught him off guard and he had to scramble to catch her.

Kyle had traded her life for Carter's—for nothing. She hadn't needed help. The black-clothed constructs had been vaporized by her fire vortex. She could have saved Mark and Maggie on her own. A bitter resentment bit her savagely.

He never would have left Maggie like that.

A small part of her yearned to forgive Kyle, but the barrenness of her heart had numbed all emotion. There was only a jagged cavity where her love for Carter had burned itself into hollow ash. She had no forgiveness left to offer.

Mark wheezed next to her, forcing his long legs to keep pace with her quick stride. He laid a restraining hand on her shoulder, and the pair halted in the pattering snowfall.

"Lily, I'm sorry everything got all messed up."

Lily didn't reply. She simply stared through him, as if he weren't there.

"But we can fix this real nice," he said, forcing a merry voice and striving to form a lighthearted smile, "like duct tape on the *Titanic*."

Suddenly Lily felt weighted by his presence. She wanted him to leave.

"C'mon Lily, Carter wouldn't want you to act this way. Cheer up! I am the sidekick after all, if I can't help you feel better, then what good am I?"

His efforts at consolation only managed to splinter the rift already inside her.

"Leave me alone," she stated in a calm, vacant voice, and turned away.

As she stepped forward, a grunt of surprise and a muffled thud sounded behind her. When she looked back to discover the origin of the noise, she met the gaze of twilight, cloudy eyes. Mark lay on the ground, unconscious.

A shudder of fear pierced through Lily's body, the first sensation she had truly felt since the mad flight from her hometown. Raeylan's white overcoat wafted gently in the snow flurry, his rune-gloved hand gripping the sword hilt at his hip. Strands of blond hair licked his face.

Lily took several steps backward off the trail she and Mark had been following. She stumbled as her back collided with the bark of a tree trunk. The visage of her beloved's killer caused the schism in her soul to erupt in a deluge of emotion, a surge of lament and fear so deeply mired in her heart that tears burned her cheeks. She felt drained by the 14 days she had spent devoured by grief. She hadn't the will to fight, even to save herself.

"Are you going to kill me?" she whispered quietly.

As Raeylan stepped forward, his resolute stare softened. The grey eyes glistened with mourning. Lily had the distinct impression that the halo of snowflakes falling around them reflected the sorrow of all the world's unshed tears. His sword arm fell limply to his side.

"Please don't cry, Esilwen," he spoke softly in an unfamiliar accent. "It will steal my strength."

Lily swallowed and brushed the droplets from her face, her distress robbing her of the ability to comprehend Raeylan's intentions. She had expected something sharp and painful, aggressive. But instead she sensed his compassion, a sea of grave regret.

"I am sorry," he continued. "I have failed you again."

"Failed me?"

He knelt in the snow at Lily's feet, head bowed in remorse.

"I was unable to free you from the terror that has hunted you. Lord Kirion has escaped my blade."

Lily didn't understand. She felt pity for the man kneeling in front of her when she should hate him for murdering Carter. This man stirred some part of herself, something she knew she needed to remember. Something she had lost.

"Who are you?" she asked.

Raeylan rose, his eyes regaining their determined fervor. He took a step forward, stroking her cheekbone with his ungloved hand. Lily expected to recoil from his proximity, but his touch felt familiar, tenderly soothing. She knew him. Her soul knew him.

"I hold within me The Guardian of Time," he said. "Let me restore you."

Raeylan's lips caressed Lily's in an embrace that tore open her mind and body alike. Her blood swelled with a fire that was both painful and sweet. Raeylan's power slid into her like a cool spring of water. Thousands of visions washed around her, filling her mind like a whirlpool of stars. She reeled from the flood of images, and her consciousness, fighting a swoon, locked onto a single memory—the most intense recollection.

A face. Carter's face. A visage drenched in blood and death and fear.

When Raeylan pulled away, Lily struggled to retain her sense of self. So many lifetimes. Experience jumbled into experience, threatening to overwhelm her sanity. She didn't know where Lily left and Esilwen began.

"He—Carter," she stuttered, "he's Kirion." Lily shook her pounding head. "What does that mean?"

Raeylan stared at her in agony, silent. Lily drew a breath, trying to sort through the new knowledge. She looked at him suddenly.

"You are here to kill me," she announced.

"I must," Raeylan stated slowly, his steadfast gaze alight with unfathomable pain. "Long ago you forced that pledge from me."

Lily recalled that day, lifetimes past in a forest of crystalline mist. He had refused at first, then pleaded. But in the end he could deny her nothing. He had sworn his vow.

Anguish for his suffering swelled in her breast. Both her hands reached for him, cupping his tortured face.

"Raeylan," she whispered gently, devotedly. "You know he will come for me. You must fulfill your oath. Take my life."

A cold voice jolted through Lily's bones.

"Now that," it said with silky charm, "would be a waste, I think."

Carter stood 20 feet to their left, his lithe body enclosed in silver scaled armor. The emblem of Lord Kirion, a sword encased by a crescent moon, gilded his breastplate. His raven hair glittered with melted snowflakes and his dark eyes flashed with suppressed power.

Raeylan drew his sword and twisted himself into a protective stance, guarding Lily with his body. Dread seeped through her. She had lived this before—died like this before.

"You have something of mine, Raeylan of House Viridius," Carter, now Kirion, accused sardonically, drawing a black blade from a sheath at his side as he approached. The metal's edge gleamed with a sickly violet radiance. "And I am here to claim it."

"She belongs to no one," Raeylan countered with pious wrath, preparing his sword to strike. "Especially not you."

"Oh but she does," Kirion laughed triumphantly, his captivating smile flashing elegantly across his features, "and as you very well know, I will never stop until I have her."

Epilogue

The Phoenix Angel: that is what my hallowed sect called him. God of fire, love, and compassion. It was he who brought the divinities together, he who first proposed war against The Lord of Light in ages past. During the conflict, the five divinities fashioned a mighty spell, intending to strip him of power, restoring peace to the seven worlds.

Instead, it shattered the universe.

The gods destroyed themselves, leaving behind only relics of their divine power, shadows of their former selves. Fohtian's Chalice was one of those holy artifacts. It contained the blood of the fire god himself. We, his attendants, guarded it from those who would use its sacred power for selfish purpose. Any vassal who consumed the emerald liquid would gain a measure of The Phoenix Angel's divine flame, the gift of healing fire, scalding in its compassionate love.

And be damned with eternal life.

Through its curse, The Chalice opened my eyes to the truth. Sacrifice and devotion do not inherently save those you love; sometimes their chosen path will lead them past any hope of redemption. Those corrupted by the pursuit of power, despite another's attempt at unspoiled love, cannot be rescued from the darkness that devours the soul. Even a god.

The Lord of Light is desperate to reclaim his throne. He seeks the artifacts inlaid with the magic of the fallen gods to restore his power.

I am one of those objects.

When Raeylan woke my memories, my past mingled with my present, forming an identity that I only partially understood. The recollections were ancient, disorienting. The woman I was—am—lived, loved, and perished. I have felt the agonies of love, lived the anguish of betrayal. I have found my soul mates, and lost them at the same time. I have suffered death more than once, yet can never truly die.

But perhaps these musings have not been clear enough. I have only shared the end of my story; perhaps I should start at the beginning.

About the Authors

A. Gerry and C. Hall are sisters who share a love of exploring the realms of fantasy and science fiction, together building new worlds of adventure for readers to discover. *Phoenix Angel* is their first novel. They currently live in Southern Utah where they work at a local charter school. Visit their blog for information on their newest releases and new projects.

www.shardwell.com

Also available from A. Gerry and C. Hall:

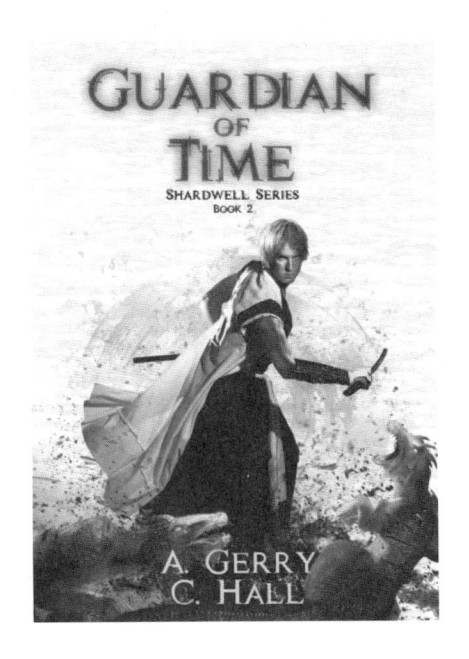